Steadfast

True North #2

By Sarina Bowen

Foreign rights: Patricia Nelson at the Marsal Lyon agency.

For everyone who has battled addiction.
You are my real-life heroes & heroines.

Chapter One

Jude

Cravings Meter: 5

The last time I drove through Colebury, Vermont, I sat behind the wheel of a 1972 Porsche 911 restored to mint condition with a sweet new paint job in Aubergine.

Compare and contrast: three years later, I rattled down Main Street in a tattered 1996 Dodge Avenger I'd just bought for nine hundred bucks. The front fender was held together with duct tape.

The ugly car wouldn't have bothered me if the Avenger and I didn't have so fucking much in common. We'd both ended up in the gutter, broken in body and spirit. The car's muffler was shot. Exposed wires hanging out from under the dashboard were a perfect proxy for my jangled nerves. I was five months out of rehab and I still couldn't sleep more than three hours in a row.

My arrogant teenage self would never have driven this heap, but that punk's opinion didn't matter anymore. I hated that guy. And while I was marking all the changes, I should also add that the last time I drove through Colebury, Vermont, I was high as a kite on opiates.

Today I was stone-cold sober. So at least I had that going

for me.

In the minus column, I was now a convicted felon. I'd served thirty-six months for possession and vehicular manslaughter. I had very little money and even fewer friends. The one lucky thing in my life—a life-saving job at an orchard in the next county—had just ended. In November there were no more apples to pick or sell. So heading home was my only option.

There was, as usual, no traffic in Colebury. The little Vermont town where I grew up didn't have a rush hour. It was more like a rush minute, and that hadn't started yet. I made one last turn and the houses got smaller and the sidewalks became uneven. Three years later, the place was still as familiar as the back of my hand.

I would have never come home if I could have avoided it.

Pulling onto my father's property, I shut off that loud-ass engine. Nickel Auto Body had the corner lot. On the left was our little old house with the sagging porch. On the right was a two-bay mechanic's garage.

When I was a teenager, I'd thought the sign over the garage doors should read *Nickel and Son.* The year after high school I'd worked at least as many hours here as he did. But I'd never asked my father to make the change, because that would require conversation. My father did not converse. He also did not praise or even scold.

Instead, he drank.

I'd pulled the jalopy into the driveway between the house and the garage. My arrival brought my father out of the garage's shadows. I saw him mosey out the door, eyeing the unfamiliar car. He was probably hoping I wasn't a bill collector.

I climbed out, watching for some reaction on my father's face.

He blinked twice. That's all I got.

"Hey," I said, reaching into the backseat for the two duffel bags holding everything I currently owned.

"You're out," he said.

Thank you, Captain Obvious. "Been out for six months," I said. "I've been picking apples in Orange County."

"Oh." My whole life, he'd spoken in one- and two-word sentences. I used to think he was just a man of few words. Now that I'd spent a lot of time in addiction meetings, I'd decided that his silence was a way to avoid slurring his words. It was almost two o'clock, which meant that he'd probably drunk half his flask already.

"So..." I cleared my throat, wondering what would happen next. "There's no more farm work until the spring. I was hoping to stay in my old room, if it's available." Tipping my chin back, I looked up at the narrow windows above the garage. The same faded yellow curtains still hung up there.

I saw him squint then, looking me up and down. "Yeah," he said after a pause. "Okay."

"I'm clean," I added, in case he was trying to figure that out. Unlike so many of the addicts I'd met, I'd never had a fight with my father about my drug habit. He'd ignored it. He'd ignored *me*. The last time I'd seen my father was during the first month of my sentence. He came to visit me in prison exactly once. It was a long, stilted twenty minutes while we looked at each other from opposite sides of a beat-up table, trying to think of things to say. He'd been my only visitor for the entire three years I'd served.

To be fair, one other person had *tried* to visit me. But I wouldn't see her.

"Actually..." I dug in my duffel bag for my keys. There were only a few of them: the Dodge, the garage, my room, and a fourth one, which I extracted from the metal ring by digging my fingernail between the coils. When the key was free, I offered it to my father.

Slowly, he removed it from my hand. "Why?" he asked simply.

I glanced toward the house where I grew up. "You probably keep some liquor in the house. I don't drink anymore. It's easier for me if I stay out of there."

He gave me the squint again, but this conversation wasn't going so badly. "I can work, too," I offered. I *needed* to work, of course. After buying the Dodge and factoring in the parts I needed to keep it running, my savings would take a serious hit.

I'd saved most of the money I made at the orchard, since room and board were included. But I didn't have enough to start a new life elsewhere. Yet.

I would have stayed on that farm forever, regardless. Living here above the garage, with ghosts all around me, in a town where I knew *exactly* where to score drugs? It was going to be the hardest thing I'd ever done.

"Not much work these days," my father said. "Got nothin' but a scratch repair today."

This did not surprise me. In the bad old days, even at the height of my drug addiction I'd gotten a lot of car repair done while my father "managed" the place. He must have lost customers when I'd gone to prison. There was no way he'd stepped up to keep pace with the work after my arrest.

I kept my voice neutral, because I didn't want to piss him off. "I was thinking I could put out a sign saying I'd put on snow tires for forty bucks."

"Might work," he muttered.

"I'll try it," I said quickly.

We stared at each other for a second. I'd expected him to look a whole lot older. I don't know why. Maybe because I felt about a hundred years old myself.

Finished with the conversation, my dad pointed toward the garage. "Gotta get back," he said.

"Right."

Walking away, he pointed at the Dodge. "That's a piece of shit."

"I noticed."

And that was that. The weirdest father/son reunion in the world was over. Letting out a big, relieved breath, I watched his coveralls disappear into the garage. They probably hadn't seen the inside of a washing machine since I got sent to prison.

But he hadn't turned me away. So I had that going for me.

With my duffel on my shoulder, I walked down the driveway between the house and the repair garage. Nothing here had changed, either. The paint was still peeling, and there was dead grass poking through cracks in the asphalt.

In Vermont, we called November "stick season." It was a

dark month after all the fall color had faded from the trees. The sun went down every day at 4:30, and we didn't yet have the clean white snow to hide all our sins.

The driveway dead-ended into an alley, where the weathered exterior stairs up to my room were found. But I didn't quite make it that far. When I turned the corner, I nearly stumbled into a small, low-slung car parked tightly against the garage's rear wall. It was covered from bumper to bumper by a heavy black tarp.

At the sight of it, my heart climbed into my throat. My physical reaction was the same as if I'd just spotted a dead body.

In so many ways, I had.

Bending forward, I grabbed a corner of the black tarp, lifting it just a few inches. Underneath, I saw exactly what I feared—a splash of Aubergine paint. It was a factory color at Porsche in 1972.

Dropping the tarp, I took a step back, as if caught doing something illegal. I didn't have a clue why this monument to my stupidity would be sitting here. In my mind, it had vanished along with the life it took three years ago. If I'd stopped to actually consider its whereabouts, I would have assumed that my father sold it whole for junk. He always took the lazy way out.

But here it was, right in the spot where I'd have to pass it several times a day, trying not to notice how the front passenger side was crushed from striking the tree.

At least the tarp hid the missing windshield, through which a two-hundred-pound college lacrosse player had flown to his death, his neck snapping on impact.

Just standing there, looking at the broken shell of my former life, I began to feel itchy. Not *literally* itchy. But "itchy" was the closest word I had for a drug craving. I felt a sort of restless tremble in my limbs and a hollowness in my chest. Some people described it as a hunger or thirst. But that wasn't quite right, either.

Whatever you call it, there was an ache inside me that I longed to soothe. And I moved through each day a little lost, trying to fill an empty spot in my soul. But it never went away. Five months out of rehab, I still felt it all the time. It showed up when I was stressed or bored. It showed up when I was tired or underfed. Sometimes it showed up even when everything was going well.

It was never, ever going to stop. There was no cure. You just *lived* with it. The end.

The edges of the tarp shifted in the breeze, as if taunting me.

At rehab they always said: "Move a muscle, change a thought." So that's what I did. I hiked the straps of my duffel bags a little higher on my shoulder. Then I skirted the Porsche without touching it again, and took the shaky wooden stairs two at a time up to my room.

I hadn't been here for more than three years, but it felt oddly familiar to slide my key into the lock and push the door open.

Musty. That was my first reaction. And then, *messy*. I didn't own much, but all my possessions were strewn around the room, as if an earthquake had struck in only this spot.

My room had been searched and not by careful hands. Dresser drawers were open, their contents thrown about. The mattress was askew, the result of someone searching underneath. The items on my bookshelves were topsy-turvy.

I dropped my bags on the disorderly bed and walked straight through to the bathroom. My eye snagged on a pink bottle of salon shampoo which had waited these three years in my shower.

It was *hers*. Sophie's.

Reaching out, I plucked the bottle off the shower shelf and flipped open the cap. And the scent overtook me right away— green apples. Standing there, remembering how Sophie smelled, it was like a sock to the gut. Of all the things I'd lost— my good name, the chance to get a decent job, my carefully restored car—none of them mattered as much as Sophie. She was gone from my life, and it was a permanent condition. No way to fix it.

I realized a minute later that I was still standing there in my wreck of a room, holding my nose over a plastic shampoo bottle like a moron. But there's no shame in missing someone. Trust me—I am well versed in shame. The pile of things I was ashamed of doing was as tall as Mount Mansfield. Missing her wasn't a crime, though. Anybody would.

Capping the bottle, I set it down again. Then I turned my attention to the toilet, which was the real challenge here. First I flushed it, just to make sure it still worked, because I might have something I needed to flush down in a moment.

Now came the hard part.

I eyed the tank cover, wondering what I'd find inside. Probably nothing. It hadn't been a very original hiding place. But when I'd squirreled away my pills, I wasn't trying to conceal them from the cops, who would know exactly where to look. I was only hiding them from Sophie.

I used to be *so* proud of the way I kept my two loves separate from one another—the drugs and the girlfriend. Even when I was snorting an unsustainable quantity of oxy, I was still functional in the garage and still a good lover. What an achiever!

Until the night it all went wrong.

Since then, I'd played the *what if* game many, many times. What if she'd known? What if I'd been forced to admit my problem sooner? What if I'd slipped up in a small way, which prevented the ultimate disaster?

What if was a pointless exercise. Ask any addict.

Slowly, I lifted the dusty tank cover, peering over the edge as if there might be a serpent inside to bite me. And really, the pills I'd kept out of my life these past months were worse than any snake.

But there was nothing there. My old hiding place had been discovered, and whatever stash had been here on the worst night of my life was long gone—discovered by the police and parked in an evidence locker wherever they kept the contraband found on losers like me.

And thank God. Today I would not be truly tested.

Sure, I'd probably have flushed the pills right down. But you don't know until you've got them in your hand. There was a chance that I would have pocketed one, just in case of emergency. But to an addict like me, that emergency would inevitably have come within the hour.

In rehab, I'd learned that the relapse rate for opiate addicts was over fifty percent. Lately that depressing little statistic rattled through my mind all day long. "But that means almost half of us *don't* relapse," some cheerful soul had pointed out in group therapy. "You can choose to be in *that* half."

Easier said than done.

Feeling the first hit of relief since I'd rolled into town, I set the tank cover back in place. Then I got to work straightening up. When I stripped the bed, a cloud of dust rose up, making me cough. So I opened the window in spite of the November chill. I needed to air out my room. Air out my lungs. Air out my whole goddamned life.

* * *

It took me several hours to get the place halfway to inhabitable. I dragged the shop vac up the stairs to attack the dust. I made a trip to the laundromat, going to a fast-food drive-through while my sheets and towels dried and eating in my awful car. It was nothing like the home cooking I'd been eating on the Shipley farm, but it got the job done.

By nightfall, I was able to put clean sheets on the bed and then collapse onto it. I shut off the lamp and let my eyes adjust to the shadows of my old room. These days, falling asleep was always tricky and staying asleep was impossible. On the Shipley Farm, I'd roomed in a bunkhouse with three other guys. I used to lie awake listening to them snore.

My room here at home was going to be much quieter—just quiet enough to make room for all the demons in my head. Lying here made me think of *her*, too.

Sophie.

I wondered where she was right now. New York City, probably. She'd have a small place somewhere, because singers who were just starting out didn't make any money. She'd have roommates.

Or a boyfriend.

I forced myself to imagine who she might choose as a

partner. He'd have to be my opposite, since Sophie wouldn't want to be reminded of her unfortunate choices. That made him a dark-haired guy, maybe with olive skin, and wearing an Italian suit. Hopefully he had a high-paying job—in finance or real estate. He'd earn enough to live in a safe neighborhood and take Sophie out for expensive dinners.

Of course, the Sophie I knew wouldn't want to date a banker. That smacked of her father's choices for her. But maybe she'd met this guy during intermission at the Metropolitan Opera. Her banker had an artsy side and season tickets in a private box. He probably invited her to watch from his excellent seats. And since Sophie had a standing-room ticket, she accepted...

My brain snagged on one detail. Were private boxes even real, or were those just in old movies?

In prison I'd had to entertain myself like this for hours. When there was nobody to talk to, I went on journeys inside my head. Before prison, I was a talker. Too much of a talker, probably. But these past three years I hadn't had a lot of conversation. Even at the Shipley Farm, where there were always people to talk to, I didn't say a whole lot. They were such a nice, normal family. I preferred to listen. Who wanted to hear a lot of sentences that began, "In prison, we..."

Nobody, that's who.

A single set of headlights illuminated an angled section of my ceiling from left to right. Then it was dark again. The nighttime sounds were different here. I was used to the call of the barred owls on the Shipley Farm, punctuated on some nights by coyotes howling nearby.

I missed the bunkhouse. Privacy was not a luxury for me. If I got out of this bed and went to find a fix, there was nobody who'd notice or care. I'd needed those six AM milkings to keep me on the straight and narrow. I needed the watchful eyes of Griff Shipley on me while we worked the farmers' market stall.

This was going to be so hard—every minute. In Colebury, a fix was always in reach. Some of my druggie friends were probably within a mile of me right now. Still getting high. Still dealing. Colebury reeked of all my old mistakes and desires.

Sarina Bowen

The itchy void in my chest gave a throb, and I rolled over to try to quash it. But that only reminded me of another absence. I stuck my nose in the pillow and took a deep breath, wondering if any essence of Sophie might remain.

But she was long gone.

Chapter Two

Sophie

Internal DJ Tuned to: "You Keep Me Hangin' On" by The Supremes

"Mom?" I called from the kitchen. "Did you make a shopping list?" After stuffing my wallet into my pocketbook, I threw on my trench coat. I was running a little late for work, as usual. "Mom?"

Silence.

Holding in my sigh, I walked through the house to the living room, where my mother sat in her chair, staring out the window. The cup of tea I'd brought her a half hour ago sat untouched beside her.

"Mom? The shopping list?" I said one more time.

Her head turned toward me, but her eyes were still flat. "I didn't get around to it," she said.

Of course you didn't. She never got around to anything at all. During the hours when my father was at home, at least she appeared for meals and responded to simple questions.

But he'd left for work a half hour ago, and so she'd curled in on herself already, settling in for a long day of staring out the window, as useful as a paperweight.

"We probably need coffee," she offered. "Your father is so

15

unpleasant when we run out."

Thanks for that insight. "Sure. I'll just wing the rest," I promised. "Bye."

Without waiting for a response, I trotted back through the kitchen, grabbed my pocketbook and ran out to the garage. I climbed into my Rav4 and started the engine. Then I counted to sixty, because Jude had always said that an engine needed a minute to warm up.

I didn't appreciate the fact that I thought about Jude three or four times a day when I started my car. Or every night when I lay down alone in bed.

There was a lot about my current situation that I did not like. I never thought I'd be living in my parents' house at twenty-two. But halfway through college, I'd moved home. My mother became a zombie after Gavin's death, and I'd wanted to help out. But I'd thought it was temporary. Who knew she would still be barely functional three years later?

Before the accident, my mother was like a forcefully orchestrated performance of Beethoven's Fifth—a wave of ambition and pure will in every breath. She raised two children while working full time for the Vermont Department of Libraries. She directed our church's Christmas pageant for fifteen years straight. She raised money for breast cancer, literacy and clean water in Africa.

Now? She did none of those things. These days she was a funereal dirge, played one-handed on an out-of-tune organ.

When my sixty seconds were up, I reversed out of our driveway and headed for work.

I had no clue how to help my mother heal. I'd made appointments for her with a therapist, but she refused to go. So I took over the grocery shopping. And the cooking. So long as a meal appeared on our family table each night, my father could pretend that we weren't an entirely dysfunctional family. And since my mother was never going to rise to the occasion, the shopping and dinner making had become my problem.

Nobody wanted my dad in a snit, that was for damned sure. That would solve nothing. He was a bully and didn't seem to care that my mother never improved. The situation at home was bad, but I had a job that I liked, and I was six weeks away from finishing my college degree.

On autopilot, I headed through our neighborhood, toward the state highway linking my smaller town with Montpelier. Since I was a bit late for work already, I didn't have time to stop at the new bakery for a latte.

Driving over the speed limit was out of the question. When your father was the police chief, it was bad form to violate any traffic laws. Not that I minded a little rule breaking, it's just that it caused me too much grief later. The deputies enjoyed ratting me out to Daddy.

These were my thoughts as I put on my brakes for the stop sign at Harvey and Grove streets. Out of the corner of my eye, I saw movement just inside the open bay doors at the Nickel Auto Body Shop.

I looked. (Of course I looked. Anyone would.) But I didn't really expect to see him there, standing beside a beat-up Dodge that was up on the lift. And even when my throat seized up around the single, shocking word that flew to my lips—*Jude*—I still didn't truly believe it.

Because he couldn't possibly be standing there, right inside the garage, running a calm hand along the tattered bumper of an ugly car. But that arm stretching up to the car—I *knew* that arm. There was a bramble of roses tattooed on the bicep. And that hand had touched my body *everywhere*.

Forgetting myself, I just sat there, one foot planted squarely on the brake, staring at what could only be a Jude mirage. A few of the details weren't right. Jude's hair would never be that lightened, sun-kissed color. And he wouldn't be caught dead in that flannel shirt. We used to *mock* the standard Vermont uniform. Mirage-Jude was too big, too, with a broad chest and visible muscles on his back when he moved his arm. My Jude had always been lean, and when he'd left my life he'd been downright skinny.

At the time, I hadn't wanted to understand why.

Most crucially, Jude couldn't *possibly* be standing twenty feet away from me on an ordinary November morning, right in the center of Colebury, inspecting a heap of a car. If he were actually here, I'd *know* it. I'd feel it deep inside, the way the bass line of a good song vibrates through your chest.

Behind me, a car tapped its horn, and I barely registered the sound. I was still taking in the shine of his too-light hair and the muscled line of his forearm. The horn tap turned into a full-blown blast, which finally brought me out of my dream state. Vermonters never honked, which could only mean that I'd been staring at Jude for quite some time. With a hasty glance in either direction, I let up on the brake and gunned the accelerator.

Somehow, I arrived at work ten minutes later, which was miraculous since I didn't remember any of the drive. But there I was, shutting off the engine in a parking space behind the hospital. I jerked the keys from the ignition and tossed them into my bag, but I didn't get out of the car yet.

Deep breaths, I coached myself. Gripping the steering wheel, I put the side of my face against its cool center. My heart shimmied along at a disco rhythm while I tried to get over my shock. I knew Jude was out of prison. We'd been notified when he was released. But that was six months ago. I'd been on edge for a few weeks last spring, but he never turned up. After that, I forgot to worry about seeing him here in Colebury. My heart believed he had left Vermont just as thoroughly as he'd left my life.

My heart was a goddamned idiot, obviously.

A tap on the window startled me so badly that I spasmed upright.

"Sorry," mouthed the man outside my car.

"Jesus and Mary, mother of God." I fumbled for the door handle. "Denny, you nearly gave me a heart attack."

"I'm sorry," he said again. "But you were slumped over, like someone having an aneurism. Like someone who needed the hug of life."

"That's for *choking*." My tone was a little harsher than I meant it to be. Denny was a good guy, if awkward, and it wasn't his fault that I was freaking out. I got out of my car and followed my coworker toward the building on shaky knees.

"Seriously, are you okay?" He held the hospital door open

for me, and I took my first lungful of the institutional air that we breathed all day.

"I'm fine," I lied. "Just having a moment."

"Is it your mom?"

Denny was nothing if not attentive. He knew something of my frustrations at home. And everyone knew of my family's tragedy. After it happened, my brother's death was in the paper for two weeks straight. First there were the sad stories— *Police Chief Loses Firstborn*. Then came the gritty details of the crash investigation, and the revelation that the poor police chief's son had been thrown from a car driven by a junkie who was jacked up on painkillers.

The newspapers didn't tell the whole story, though. They didn't reveal that the junkie in question was the boyfriend of the chief's daughter, who had been repeatedly forbidden to date him. That bit of scandal didn't make the papers, out of respect for the grieving family.

We'd been in the news for weeks, and yet some of the really important questions went unasked. Such as: where on earth were the golden boy and the junkie going together that awful night?

"Sophie?"

I realized I was standing in front of my desk like a sleepwalker. And I'd never answered Denny's question. "Yes?"

"Can I hang up your coat?"

I scrambled out of my trench. "Sure. Thank you!" I was losing my manners as well as my mind.

When he walked away, I rounded my desk and sagged into the chair. *Get a grip, Soph*, I ordered myself. But it wouldn't be easy. When I was seventeen, I thought Jude was sent to me from heaven. When I was eighteen, I let him take me there. When I was nineteen, he broke both my heart and my family.

He'd been gone for three and a half years now. I'd shed an ocean of tears for him. The first year had been the roughest. My family was a grief maelstrom, and since Jude was the cause of it, I hid my broken heart. Nobody had wanted to hear me say that Jude had never meant to hurt anyone. Nobody cared that he'd obviously been in need of help. They didn't want to hear that he'd been (mostly) wonderful to me.

That he'd been the only one who listened when I spoke.

My father couldn't tolerate Jude even *before* he killed my brother. When I'd begun my teenage obsession with Jude, it had taken my parents by surprise that good girl Sophie could become a rebellious teen. I'd dyed my hair black and got a tattoo on my ass. It was ordinary kid stuff, but my father raged and threatened.

He'd also snooped in my room. When he'd found a receipt for condoms, my father had forbidden me to even talk to my boyfriend anymore. He'd ranted that Jude was trouble, but my heart didn't listen. Instead, I just lied more often and snuck out at night.

Things got a little less tense when I'd moved into the dorms at University of Vermont for my freshman year of college. My father assumed that the forty-five miles from Colebury to Burlington would lessen Jude's influence in my life. But we only carried on more freely. Jude's Porsche wore a groove into highway 89, and I spent every weekend with him.

Then, one ugly spring evening just after freshman year ended, state troopers showed up at our door, hats in hand. That night Jude proved all my father's points in one fell swoop. As our front door opened to reveal the officers' hats in their hands, my father won every fight we'd ever had.

That night will always be a blur to me. I remember my mother screaming, then fainting in the living room.

"But what happened to Jude?" I'd asked in those terrible moments of confusion. Nobody answered me. It was twelve hours before I'd even learn that he was alive. As the awful story began to unspool, I ached for him. To know you've killed someone, even in such an awful, careless way, would be terrible. It was all so horribly sad.

I kept my empathetic thoughts to myself, of course. Nobody would even say Jude's name in my home. The only name on anyone's lips was Gavin. Poor Gavin. Gavin the great. Lacrosse hero. Beloved son.

On the outside, I did all the right things. I stumbled through my brother's wake and then his funeral.

But secretly, my heart tore open for Jude. After he made his plea-bargain and went quietly off to prison, I'd tried writing him. I wrote several letters in quick succession. They were all variations on "why?" and "what happened?" I'm not proud, but they also contained plenty of "I love you" and "why won't you talk to me?"

It wasn't until weeks after Jude's conviction that I received a large envelope from the Northern Vermont State Prison, containing all of my letters. Unopened. A single sheet of paper inside read, "Letters refused."

By then, I'd understood that Jude was sick, addicted and in pain. And I knew he'd done a terrible thing. But I never expected him to turn his back on me. I'd cried a brand new river of tears over those returned letters. I was just so angry that he'd reject me on top of all his other crimes. How *dare* he.

Hell, I was *still* angry. Sitting there at my tidy desk in the hospital's Office of Social Work, my hands were tightened into fists. I wasn't at all prepared for his reappearance. Tonight when I went to the grocery store after work, I knew I'd look for him in every aisle. I'd look over my shoulder at the gas pump and standing in line at the bakery. In our town of nine thousand, it was inevitable that I would eventually run into him.

I was *never* going to be ready.

Something landed on my desk with a thunk. It was a covered coffee cup from the hospital cafe. "Thank you so much," I said immediately, looking up into Denny's serious brown eyes.

"My pleasure. You just looked like you needed a little lift this morning."

You have no idea. "Thanks," I repeated, pulling the cup toward me. Even without lifting the lid, I knew I'd find a skim milk latte inside with a sprinkle of cinnamon. Denny knew me. Denny *studied* me. And once a month or so, he asked me out. I always worded my refusals gently but firmly. I hoped he'd stop asking. He was so *nice*, though. Turning him down made me feel like a diva.

"You know it's time for the staff meeting, right?" He tipped his head toward the conference room.

When I looked, there were people gathering around the table already. *Shit!* I leaped out of my chair and grabbed the latte.

I was two steps away before I realized that Denny hadn't followed me. Looking over my shoulder, I saw him smile. "It's your turn to report the case load, isn't it?"

With yet another muttered thanks to Denny, I snatched the folder off my desk and headed for the meeting.

Pull it together, Haines, I ordered myself. Denny shouldn't be saving my ass. He and I were in competition for the same job. We were both graduating at the end of the semester, and the hospital had only one full-time position available. He would probably get it, since his degree was a master's and mine was a bachelor's. Come January, I'd probably be begging them to extend my internship while I scrambled to find a real job.

Given mornings like this one, it would be hard to begrudge Denny the victory.

The two of us were the last to sit down. Our department was small and fairly informal, but since I was gunning for a permanent job here, appearing ditzy was a bad idea. There were five full-time social workers, with Denny and I as part-time help while we both finished degrees. Mr. Norse, our boss, a friendly, rumpled man in his sixties, opened the meeting with a discussion of next year's budget forecast.

Naturally, my mind wandered right back to Jude. Those budget forecasts didn't stand a chance against my troubled ex, with his piercing gray eyes and tight jeans.

We became a couple during my junior year of high school. But even before we'd ever had a conversation, I'd been aware of Jude. He was the boy who'd always slunk into class late if he felt like it. The teachers didn't even give him a hard time, because there would be no point. He gave off an aura of "I don't care what you think."

I'd found him ridiculously attractive. It wasn't just his too-long eyelashes, either. I'd had it bad for his attitude. I was a cautious good girl, always too fearful of authority to say the things inside my head.

Watching him became my hobby. But the idea that Jude

Nickel would ever look my way had been pretty ridiculous.

One afternoon at school I was in a tizzy trying to set up for a school band concert. The copy machine had jammed while I printed the programs, and folding them had taken longer than I'd thought it would.

So I was well behind schedule when I reached the gym. Someone had already set up a couple hundred folding chairs in rows, and I'd been asked to drop a program onto each one of them. There I was, slapping programs onto the chairs, when the fire door opened and a cool breeze flew through the room, sending those programs airborne before they went skating to the floor.

Frantic, I'd grabbed them up again, setting everything back the way it should be. And then it happened a second time! My blood pressure rose as I chased another set of programs off the floor. Stomping over to the emergency exit, I kicked the doorstop, and the door began to swing closed.

A tattooed arm shot out at the last second and held it open. "Do you mind?" asked a gravel-toned voice. "I'm having a quick smoke here." A zing of nervous energy shot through my gut as Jude Nickel peered through the door at me.

"Seriously?" I snipped. "That's against about ten rules."

He raised a single eyebrow, as if questioning *my* sanity. That casual, wordless statement made me feel hot everywhere. Jude always had. Whenever he glanced at me, I never knew where to put my eyes. And now he was actually studying me for the first time.

"I need the door shut," I said, gathering my wits. "I have to get this done in the next ten minutes."

Still blocking the door, he held up a hand as if to silence me. Then he took a last puff and let it out. Finally, he crushed the cigarette under his boot.

I waved my hand frantically in front of my face, trying to keep the smoke away from me. Cigarette smoke would not be good for my vocal chords.

That's when Jude had *grinned*, and I became even more addled. That hundred-watt smile of his made all the girls stupid. I was so astonished to find it pointed my way that I

23

frowned back at him like an idiot.

Slowly, as if he had all the time in the world, he slid past me and into the auditorium. I closed the door, all huffy, and the new breeze chased another ten programs off their metal chairs.

He surveyed the mess with a frown. "You need a hand?"

Did I? Probably. But I wasn't going to ask. Jude made me feel jumpy. "I got it," I said, diving toward the nearest row of chairs, plopping programs onto the empty ones as if my final grade depended on it.

Where I was frantic, Jude moved like a cat—all confidence and no hurry. That sleek body slid into the row where I'd begun. He bent over, showing off a very fine ass, plucking programs off the floor and putting them back onto the seats.

I watched him out of the corner of my eye, trying not to be obvious about it.

He paused to glance at the front of a program. "A band concert? I didn't know you were in the band."

"I'm not." My brain snagged on the notion that Jude had noticed me. Sort of. Well, noticed the band and my absence in it. I filed that away to worry about later.

"Then why is this your problem?" he asked, holding up the program.

"Good question," I grumbled. "If you want something done by someone who never complains, I guess you ask a goody-goody choir girl."

"Huh," Jude said, slowly placing another program on a seat. "Thing is, I'm not convinced you're as good a girl as everyone thinks."

"That's ridiculous," I said immediately. Because I was *exactly* as good as everyone thought. And I was really freaking sick of it.

He wasn't looking at me, so I almost missed his next words. "Naw. I saw you throw away that note on Mr. H's desk."

My hand froze on the next folding chair. I didn't think anyone had seen me do that. "Mr. H is a dick," I said quickly. It was true, too. The teacher had snatched that note from a girl in our geometry class who he always picked on. She'd turned red when he'd dropped it on his desk, so I knew the contents would embarrass her.

When I'd gotten up to sharpen my pencil, Mr. H had been at the other end of the room, helping a basketball player with his homework. With a single flick of my finger I'd sent the note into Mr. H's garbage bin as I passed by.

Jude gave me the hundred-watt smile *again*. "See? Not such a good girl."

The idea that he thought so made me feel prickly hot. And not in a bad way.

For two months after that odd little exchange, we had no more interaction. But whenever he entered a room, my face felt hot and the back of my neck tingled with awareness.

Jude ignored me until one afternoon when I was alone in one of the little practice rooms off the music wing. I was working on a vocal piece for the Vermont All State Competition, and I *really* wanted to win. I'd had the foolish idea that my father would take my musical ambition more seriously if I could demonstrate that I had potential. I was preparing "Green Finch and Linnet Bird" from Sweeney Todd, because it showed off my soprano range.

I'd sung it a million times already, and I knew the piece well. But my delivery was unsatisfying, and I couldn't figure out why. A change of key hadn't helped, either. I was hitting the creative wall and frustrated as hell over it. I remember slapping my finger down on the iPod wheel to stop the music, then yelling "FUUUUCCCCCCKKKK" at the top of my lungs.

It wasn't like me. I didn't even know where that obscenity came from. It was probably the first f-bomb I'd ever said out loud.

From the other side of the practice room door came laughter. I jerked the door open, wondering who had heard.

When I popped my head outside, I saw Jude leaning against the hallway wall, grinning at me. "Problem?" he asked in that smoky voice.

I looked both ways down the hall before answering him. "Just frustrated."

"Reeeeeally," he said, his tone full of suggestion. "Maybe I can help with that."

I flushed immediately because he'd *almost* made a sexual reference. And Jude exuded sex, which was a subject I knew nothing about. "I doubt it, unless you're a vocal performance expert."

He toyed with an unlit cigarette between two fingers. "That's an awfully frilly song you're singing in there. Anyone might be *frustrated*." He gave me a slow, distracting smile.

Jude's quick diagnosis of the problem was annoying, yet it *was* a frilly song. It required a ton of control and a tight vibrato. But it came out sounding... constricted.

He was right, damn it.

"Maybe," he said, tucking the cigarette into a case in his hand, "the stakes aren't high enough? The birds are trapped in their little cages. So what? They have brains no bigger than your fingernails. It's a good-girl song. There's nowhere to go with it."

It stunned me that he'd listened so closely to the lyrics. Because Jude never appeared to listen to anyone. It was part of his too-cool-for-school vibe. I didn't know what to think about that.

So I argued with him. "It's a metaphor, okay? The singer is trapped in her lecherous guardian's home, pining for freedom. And he wants her body. How are those stakes not enough?"

Jude rolled his eyes. "See, it *is* a good-girl song. The frightened virgin singing to the birdies. Nobody could rock that song. Now, if she *wanted* her guardian, that's a song I'd like to hear."

Whoa. I needed to end this conversation, stat, because I was having trouble holding Jude's storm-colored gaze. My eyes kept wandering over to check out the smooth curve of his biceps where they emerged from his black T-shirt. I could only see partial tattoos, and I wanted to see the whole picture. "Well." I cleared my throat. "I don't think the judges would like your version."

He just grinned, training those dark gray eyes on me. And I was staring. Again! "Fine. But what *does* a bad girl sing at this thing? Whatever it is, you should sing that."

I was still staring when he winked and walked away.

A week later I'd received a "picket fence" score (a line of perfect 1 ratings) singing the very naughty "Defying Gravity" from *Wicked*. It was a bad-girl song to its very core. I'd taken Jude's advice, and it had made all the difference.

Under the conference room table, someone kicked my foot.

Yanking myself back into the present, I found every face turned in my direction. Beside me, Denny looked pointedly down at the caseload folder in front of me.

With my face burning, I flipped the cover open. "Sorry," I stammered. "Last week we closed four cases and got seven new ones for a caseload gain of three. One of those is a re-admit, which falls to Lisa. Two are brand new. One of the new cases is pediatric."

Our director nodded from the end of the table. "Tell me about the pediatric case."

Luckily, I knew the details without looking. "Eighteen-month-old girl recently diagnosed with profound hearing loss."

"How does it take parents so long to figure that out?" Denny wondered aloud.

I'd met this family, and I had a theory. "This is a single mother who lives with her parents. She seems like an awesome mom, honestly." Even though she was only nineteen, I'd been impressed with her devotion. "She's young, and this is her first child. So she didn't have a lot of basis for comparison. Also, she spends so much time with her baby, I think she's just really used to nonverbal communication. After the baby missed some speech milestones, the pediatrician started asking questions."

"Sophie, would you like to be the primary?" my director asked.

"I'd *love* to," I said quickly. It was a good sign that he'd asked me to take the file. And what a great case! Nobody was dead or dying. There was only a cute, happy toddler who happened to be deaf. My role would be to help the family find therapy and services that they could afford.

He nodded at me. "Very well. Come to me with any snags. And you'll give us an update at next week's meeting."

"Yes, sir." Even after my years with Jude, my old good-girl habits were still there, shimmering just below the surface. And sometimes they were really fucking useful.

We adjourned, and I went back to my desk determined not to slide back into a Jude-induced panic. But I was still unsettled. I *must* have been, or else I wouldn't have made the mistake I made next.

"Sophie, are you really okay?" Denny stood over my desk, concern in his eyes.

I avoided his chocolate gaze. "Yep. Promise." If I told him who I'd seen this morning, he'd guess where my head was right now. But I didn't want sympathy, and I most certainly did not want to talk about it. The only way to survive living in a small town with Jude was to keep my own counsel.

"How about you prove it by going bowling with me tomorrow night."

"Bowling? Are you a good bowler?" I looked up then and saw all the usual signs—nervous eyes and a shy, hopeful smile.

Fuck.

"I'm a terrible bowler," he said quietly. "But that just makes it more fun."

Aw. I didn't want to give him the wrong idea. But we were friends. And it was just bowling. "Sure," I said, knowing it was a bad idea.

The way his face lit up when I said yes made me feel guilty already. "Awesome. I'll pick you up at seven." Then he ran off before I could change my mind. Smart man.

I tossed my empty latte cup in the trash and leaned back in my office chair. *Damn you, Jude Nickel. See what you made me do?*

Chapter Three

Sophie

Internal DJ Tuned to: "Crazy" by Aerosmith

Thursday, I rushed home to make lasagna for dinner. That way there'd be leftovers, and I'd enjoy the fruits of my labors even though I wasn't dining with my parents tonight. Denny had texted me earlier asking if we couldn't make it 6:30 instead, so we could have dinner at Max's Tavern before bowling.

That made it more like a date than I would have wished. But I said yes, because haggling over a half hour only made me more of a bitch.

I'd removed the lasagna from the oven already, but it was still a volcanic temperature. So I dashed into the dining room to set the table. Earlier I'd asked my mother to handle that, but she hadn't bothered. *Big surprise.*

Mom wandered into the dining room just as I counted the napkins out of the hutch. I had to stop myself at three. Even three years later, I was regularly tempted to add one for Gavin. I used to mention things like this to my mom, hoping that talking openly would make it easier for her to move past her grief.

29

It didn't. And tonight I didn't need to start her on a weeping jag right before it was time for me to run out of the house. "Here," I said, handing her the napkins. "What shall I pour you to drink?"

She took the napkins, but ignored the question.

Holding in my millionth sigh, I went into the kitchen to pour her a glass of iced tea and my father a glass of wine. I poured an inch of wine for myself, too, before setting everything on the table.

My father came downstairs just as I began cutting the lasagna into squares. How do men do that, anyway? It takes a special kind of skill to show up precisely when all the work is finished.

"Evening, Sophie," he said, taking his place at the head of the table. Although he hadn't been in the military for twenty years, he still had the haircut and the bearing. And a stiff greeting was the only kind I ever got from my father. Three years later, I was still being punished for my role in Gavin's demise.

"Evening," I murmured, sitting down to only a nip of wine.

"You're not eating?" he set a piece of lasagna on mom's plate and then eyed the empty space in front of me.

"I have a date."

My father's body went rigid. "With who?"

Wow. *Watch Daddy panic.* Apparently I wasn't the only one who'd noticed that Jude was back in town. Just to fuck with him, I waited a beat too long to answer, while his eyes bored into mine. "Denny from the hospital," I said casually. Honestly, it was hard not to crack a smile. Because the look on his face was priceless.

"That had better be true," he said, setting down the serving spoon.

"Why would I lie?" I asked softly.

"Why did you used to?" he returned.

Well, touché. Score a point for Dad. In high school I'd done a lot of sneaking around with Jude, and more than once I'd been caught in my lies.

Jude and I had started up shortly after our discussion

about music outside the practice rooms. One rainy October day he offered me a ride in his car. Instead of driving me home, he'd brought me to a coffee house in the next town. For three hours, my hands sweat with nerves while he told me funny stories about learning to fix cars. I laughed too loudly about the time he'd left a tire iron on the roof of somebody's car and had to cruise around the neighborhood until he found the car in question so he could get it back.

Staring into his silver eyes, I attempted to hold up my end of the conversation. His attention was like a laser beam— bright and impossible to ignore.

When it was time to go, we'd had to run across the rainy parking lot to his car. When the doors were shut, Jude cranked the engine. "The car needs a minute to warm up," he'd said. "How shall we spend the time?"

"Thumb wars?" I suggested. I held out a hand to him. (I remember feeling *impossibly* bold for suggesting this.) I had no experience with boys, because nobody wanted to try anything with the uptight police chief's daughter.

So I didn't see it coming. He grabbed my outstretched hand, then leaned across the gearshift and brushed his lips over mine. "You're so fucking cute," he whispered. And then he slanted his mouth right down onto mine and kissed me.

Still shocked, I let out the least sexy noise in the world— something like "errrf!"

Apparently, all engines *did* need a warmup. My first reaction was shock. I could barely believe that Jude Nickel's mouth was teasing mine. On the first kiss, I could taste the peppermint tea he'd been drinking and feel the scrape of whiskers against my face. But his lips were soft, and when he pressed closer to me, I melted into him. And when he coaxed me into opening up for him, I was just *gone*. Our first kiss lasted half an hour.

By the time Jude drove me home, my lips were swollen and bruised. I'd *never* been kissed like that before. When he pulled up in front of my house, I practically stumbled up the drive. I was late for dinner, with my father peering out the window as I slammed Jude's car door.

31

I was glad of the rain, because my panties were so wet that I'd feared it would show through my jeans. But the rest of me got drenched just from running into the house.

"Where were you?" my father bellowed when I stepped into the kitchen.

"Choir practice ran late," I said.

It had been my first Jude lie. But not my last.

"Sophie," my father brought me into the present and out of my reverie again. I was having a lot of those this week. "Did you know that punk was back in town? Has he tried to contact you?"

I shook my head. "I only learned it by accident. If you're so worried, why didn't you warn me? Seriously. I could have used a heads up."

My father grunted. "Because I hoped he wouldn't stay."

"I won't be seeing him," I promised. Not that I owed my father anything. But he was easier to live with when he thought you were on board with his wishes. And Jude's silence had made it perfectly clear that we didn't know each other anymore.

"He's slick," my father said, serving a portion of lasagna onto his own plate. "He'll tempt you."

My inner seventeen-year-old wanted to roll her eyes. Dad had cast Jude as the serpent in the garden from minute one. After it became obvious that Jude and I were dating, he'd warned me away. My brother had been his ally in this war, ratting me out when he saw Jude and I together.

"What do you want with that loser?" my brother had asked. "Skinny asshole thinks he's God's gift. I could drop him with a single punch."

I'd never listened to either of them. Because even though Jude coaxed me into doing a whole lot of things that would have turned Dad's hair white, he was a devoted boyfriend. And Jude *listened* to me, the way my parents never did.

My senior year had been rocky at home, with my father on a tear all the time. It was the first time in my life when I hadn't cared what my father thought, and that drove him crazy. Even though I knew that listening to my own heart was important,

Dad's disapproval was still hard on me. It bothered me that he'd always loved Gavin best, because Gavin was the lacrosse jock. My brother wasn't a nice person, but still our father saw him as the perfect son.

And that was *before* Gavin's death. Now? My father could barely stand to be in the same room with me. Forking lasagna into his mouth, he gave me a familiar warning glare.

There was a knock on the front door. *Denny to the rescue!* "Got to go!" I said. My father actually followed me to the door. "Jesus, Dad. I'm almost twenty-three."

Ignoring my objections, he swung the door open to reveal Denny standing there in khakis and a turtleneck sweater. He looked like the very model of an acceptable date.

I pushed past my father, which probably made me look rude. But when your father treats you like a teenager forever, these things happen. "Bye, Dad!" I said at the same moment that Denny opened his mouth to greet my father. Grabbing Denny's hand, I tugged him off the porch.

"In a hurry?" Denny muttered, jogging ahead of me to open the car door.

"Yep. Thanks." I got in and pulled the door shut.

He climbed into the driver's seat. "Did your father just give me the once over?" he laughed. "That's kind of cute."

"No, it really isn't."

"Well at least he cares," Denny said.

I didn't want to argue with Denny. "I guess."

He flicked his eyes over to me. "You think he doesn't?"

I held in my sigh. "I think he likes reminding me that I have shitty judgment. It was me who brought the Evil One into our midst," I explained. "He's never going to forgive me. Every morning I ask myself why I'm still living here. And then my mother does something dotty and I feel guilty enough to make it through another day."

Denny's voice dropped. "I'm sorry." He was easy to talk to, and I was glad to have a friend at work. I wasn't attracted to him, though. Not even a little. I really shouldn't have agreed to see him tonight.

We rode in silence for a minute, and I stared out the

window. I looked for Jude, of course. It wasn't rational, but a broken heart never is. Maybe this would be the shove I needed to leave town. When the hospital gave Denny the full-time spot, there would be nothing left for me here except the knowledge that the only man I'd ever loved was walking around out there somewhere. I'd be on edge every day of my life.

Inevitably, one of those eventual sightings of Jude would be him in a parked car, lip-locked to some other girl. That was going to sting.

I didn't want to live like this—full of confusion and guilt all the time, and heartbroken in a hundred ways at once. I didn't *mean* to hold a torch for someone who had broken my family, gone to jail and then refused all my letters.

But even a glimpse of him had given me palpitations. As if my subconscious had recognized a piece of my soul before my brain got a chance to speak up.

Last night I'd lain awake just knowing that he was less than a mile away. He was probably in his old bed, where we used to steal away to make love. My freshman year of college, he'd drive to Burlington every Friday to fetch me for the weekend. We'd spend Saturday in his bed, exhausting ourselves. I *ached* remembering those times. The way he'd smile at me, hovering over me in bed. We were so hot and heavy he could just cast a gaze in my direction and I'd feel desire.

Those were the good times. If I wanted to stay sane, I'd have to remember the bad times, too. The times when he showed up late. Or when he'd take me to a party and disappear, only to reappear with jumpy eyes.

The night he didn't show up at all.

I'd let him get away with that behavior because I hadn't wanted to acknowledge that side of Jude. And I'd been so thrilled that someone as exciting as him could love me that I looked the other way. I hadn't wanted my father to be right, either. My father hated my boyfriend because my father was good at hating.

My convictions had been firm and unwavering.

Then, one clear night in May, Jude offered my brother a ride somewhere. The newspaper reporter was unable to discover where. Apparently Jude was so high that night he couldn't remember the crash. A tox screen found enough opiates in his bloodstream to stop an ox.

Jude's car hit a tree on the side of the two-lane road where they traveled. My brother flew from the car and snapped his neck. He wasn't wearing a seatbelt, but we're not supposed to dwell on that. Instead, my parents focused only on the fact that Jude had a drug problem. Everyone wanted to know how I could have been so stupid as to date a man who'd drive while intoxicated.

Three years later and I was still trying to figure that out.

"You look like you could use a burger and a beer," Denny said. He'd pulled into a spot in the town lot, and now was watching me from the driver's seat.

"I really could. This has been a hell of a week."

His face got soft. "I'm sorry. Maybe this was a bad idea."

"No," I said a little too forcefully. "You are a force of good in the world, Den. Seriously."

I'd never seen Denny's face light up quite so brightly as it did then. He hopped out of the car and ran around to my side, and I let him open the door for me. "Hey, Denny?" I asked, climbing out.

"Yeah?"

He was standing right in front of me, which made it easier to say what I needed to say. "I want to thank you for herding me in the right direction yesterday." When I said this, his face took on a strange, intense expression. (Later I would kick myself for misinterpreting this.) "When I needed your help yesterday, you—"

My apology was cut off by an unexpected kiss. Unexpected and very wet. Wet the way a *car wash* is wet.

Holy...!

My instinct to flee kicked in just a wee bit too hard. Instead of gently pushing Denny back, I jerked away from him, slipping between his body and the side of the car. Only when I'd put some distance between us did my manners reemerge. "Sorry," I gasped. "I..."

"Jesus Christ," he said, putting his head in his hands. "*I'm* sorry. I thought you were saying..." He took a deep breath. "I'm such an idiot."

What *had* he thought I meant?

"You were thanking me for herding you to the *meeting*," he said, his voice strained. "Not herding you to go out with me."

"Yes of course..." And wasn't *this* embarrassing?

"Wow," he said, staring at his shoes. "I've screwed up dates before. But it usually takes me a couple of hours."

I was too embarrassed for him to agree. I'd been worried that I'd have to give him the brush-off after tonight, but I thought it would wait at least until the weekend. Now a long silence hung between us. I had no idea what to do.

"I'll take you home," he said, pulling his keys out of his pocket. He still hadn't looked at me again.

As much as I wished I could zap myself home to my bedroom with a book and a cup of tea, it would only make tomorrow more awkward. I saw Denny every day at work. I even saw him on Wednesday nights at church. "Bowling," I said.

"You don't have to do that," he said. "Really. I get it. I'm sorry."

"Come on," I said, ducking around him and heading down the sidewalk. "We're going to skip the tavern, but that means we can have some of those greasy wings at the bowling alley."

"You like greasy wings?" he asked, with something like relief in his voice.

"Sometimes they hit the spot." I kept going, heading toward the bowling alley.

A moment later, I heard him following me.

Sophie and Jude are both 17

Sophie and Jude never go to each other's houses.

She knows her father too well to bring Jude around. Her father is a bully, and he'll try to intimidate Jude. And when that doesn't work (because Jude didn't seem intimidated by anyone) he'll try to make Jude feel like a loser somehow. He'll say something about tattoos being trashy or ask Jude where his mother is.

And they never go to Jude's house, either. Whenever Jude speaks of his father, he refers to him as "that mess." Sophie is pretty sure he doesn't want her to witness the mess in person. So she never presses him on the issue.

"I got my father to promise me something," Jude says one day out of the blue. "Next year after graduation, I can move into the room over the garage. It will take some work to fix it up, but I'll like having my own place. You can come over, too."

Now there's a thrilling idea. She gets shivers just thinking about being truly alone with him.

For now, they spend a lot of time in his car, listening to music on the radio and talking. Tonight they're parked outside the Colebury Diner, where she and Jude have planned to indulge in ice cream sundaes after a little time alone.

It's December and awfully cold, so they hug each other to get warm.

Their making out has progressed from reaching over the gearbox to her sitting in his lap. Sophie's lips glide up the side of his face. She takes a gentle taste of his temple before kissing his forehead, dropping kisses at his hairline.

Her cleavage is almost at the level of his face. She wishes he would touch her already. Her breasts are so full and achy whenever they're together.

Sophie is tired of waiting. She's wearing a V-neck T-shirt, too, damn it. Doesn't he notice? She tips her head backward a little way, arching her back.

A low, guttural sound escapes his lips. Jude leans forward, his lips finding the base of her throat. Desire floods her as his lips tease this new, sensitive place. He raises a hand, caressing her ribcage. She wishes he would just stick his hand up her shirt and touch her, damn it.

What's the use of having the sort of tattooed boyfriend who keeps fathers up at night if he won't even get rid of her damned virginity for her?

Jude groans then tugs her chin down for a proper kiss. His tongue slides against hers, his tongue piercing torturing her. She forgets her frustrations, because Jude is perfect. His eyes are open as they kiss, taking her in, not missing a thing. He makes her feel cherished. If she said that word out loud it would sound silly. But his touch is reverent...

There's a loud bang on the door of the car and Sophie jumps half a foot in surprise.

Jude just tips his head back and grits his teeth. "If your asshole brother dented my car, I'm going to fucking punch him."

Sophie grabs the lever and opens the car door. She jumps out and faces her brother, who's laughing with his idiot lacrosse friends. Usually Gavin is busy doing keg stands at his frat house, but the asshole is on a month-long Christmas vacation at the moment. "What is your fricking problem?" she demands. Is there no place on God's green earth where she and Jude can be alone?

"Thought you needed an interruption. Don't do anything stupid with your trailer-park boyfriend."

Even without looking at him, she can feel tension rising off Jude. He's too smart to start something with the police chief's son and his loyal posse of heavies.

Gavin leans in to take a look at the interior of the Porsche. "Have you thought about selling me this car yet?"

Jude shakes his head slowly. "I told you already. Too many hours of my labor in this baby. I could never do it."

"Maybe if you'd quote a price, I won't tell my father what it is you two do in this car."

"There is nothing to tell," Jude says easily. "We're on our way inside for ice cream." He pats Sophie on the hip. "You can pick the flavor."

Sophie gives her brother a glare. Not that he notices.

Jude nudges her gently out of the way so that he can stand up, too. He doesn't look Gavin in the eye, but he makes a careful show out of locking the door and pocketing the key. Mine, his actions say as he closes the car door with a click.

Mine, his hand says when he palms her lower back.

They go inside and find a booth, but his face is stony now.

Sophie finds his feet with hers under the

table and finally gets a smile. But it's only fifty or sixty watts.

Chapter Four

Jude

Cravings Level: 7 and rising

Ninety-six hours in Colebury. And every one of 'em hard.

As I'd feared, business at my father's garage was dead. Not a lot of people wanted to hire an auto body repairman who sways while he gives you your estimate.

Yesterday I'd put my plan into action. It cost me seventy dollars to buy a shiny new A-frame sign for outside the shop. When I was done sliding the new lettering into rows, it read: SNOW IS COMING! SNOW TIRES SWITCHED $40.

"Might work," my father had mumbled from behind the little TV he kept in the garage.

But I'd heard on the shop radio that snow was forecast for next week. This was *totally* going to work.

I got my first customer one hour after I put out my sign. An old woman pulled up outside and gave her horn a quick tap. I ran out to see what she needed.

"I do need to put my snow tires on," she said, blinking watery eyes at me from her lowered window. "But I'm afraid I can't lift them into my trunk. They're stacked in my garage."

"Where's that?"

"Main and Alder," she said, naming an intersection on the opposite end of town.

Beggars can't be choosers. "I'll follow you in my car."

She would prove to be the first of a steady stream of customers.

Yesterday I changed the tires on four cars. Then this morning I'd put the sign outside first thing. By the time I closed up shop at five thirty, I'd had a dozen takers. I'd been so busy that my father came out to help me and to make sure that all the money went into his till.

He probably planned to pay me the same twelve dollars an hour that he'd paid me when I was eighteen. That was some bullshit right there, but I wasn't going to argue right away. For a couple weeks I'd keep my mouth shut while I built up the garage's revenue. I needed to make myself indispensable for longer than a day before I began making demands.

Besides, I was happy to let my father handle the cash. I didn't want to walk around with a pocket full of twenties. A guy with a recent drug habit was better off using his debit card for everything. I kept barely ten bucks in my wallet these days, because dealers didn't accept plastic. Any barrier I could put between myself and a quick fix was a good idea.

And physical labor was good for what ailed me. The only trick I knew for staying clean was to stay busy. Today that was easy enough. Exhausted, dirty, and reeking of tire rubber, I went upstairs for a quick shower. I used Sophie's shampoo, and the green-apple scent rose around me in a mist. So now I would smell like a girl, but that was okay with me, because it was as close to a girl as I was likely to get anytime soon.

Without a kitchen of any sort, I had to leave home every time I was hungry. So I got into my wreck of a car and puttered into the center of town. I couldn't eat fast food for every meal, so I went into Max's Tavern and ordered a Chicken Caesar wrap to go. The place was abuzz with guys enjoying happy hour, and all the tables were full of happy, sociable people.

I envied them.

Once upon a time I'd had friends, but they were all off limits now. The friends I'd made in high school were the type who showed me how to crush oxies and snort them.

That's why the rate of relapse was so high among druggies like me. It's easy to be a champ in the controlled environment of rehab. You can promise yourself anything. Then you come out again, and the world is the same fucked-up place it was when you went in.

When my sandwich was ready, I paid and left. I would have

loved to plunk down on a bar stool and order a beer like a normal person. But I wasn't a normal person. I'd given up that title when I'd learned how to dull my pain with drugs.

So I got back into the Avenger, carefully stretching the sandwich wrapper across my lap to catch any crumbs.

When I had the Porsche, I didn't like to have food in it. Sophie used to roll her eyes when I suggested that we eat elsewhere. "We have sex in your car all the time," she'd point out. "But dear God—don't eat a granola bar."

Another fun part of being in recovery is rehashing all your ironies. I'd always kept my *car* clean. Meanwhile, I was dumping toxic substances into my body just as often as I could afford to.

Good times.

I'd only eaten one bite when a shiny sedan pulled into a parking spot on the other side of the divider, a few rows down from me. A dorky-looking guy in a turtleneck jumped out and hurried around to open the passenger door, making me grin. A first date, probably.

When the girl stood up, I stopped grinning.

Sophie. My heart gave a squeeze. What the *hell* was she doing in Vermont?

I tossed the sandwich onto the passenger seat and leaned over the steering wheel to peer out into the night.

It didn't matter that her hair was longer than it used to be or that she was wearing an unfamiliar coat. The confident set of her shoulders was all Sophie. And the streetlight caught the classically beautiful curve of her cheek as she turned toward the guy.

Even before I finished this thought, Mr. Turtleneck stepped into her space and grabbed her chin. Then he planted a kiss on her mouth.

My blood stopped circulating.

But then it started right up again when Sophie's hands flew out to either side in a panic. Her body jerked to the side as she tried to get away from him.

With my heart in my throat, I fumbled blindly for the door handle in what was still an unfamiliar car.

By the time I'd managed to step out of my car, Sophie and her attacker were talking again. She'd crossed her arms in front of her chest, and he'd taken a heathy step back. His head was bowed in what looked like contrition.

Jesus fuck. There was nobody on earth in whose life I was less welcome to interfere. Sophie would be better off if she didn't set eyes on me until the end of her days. But I wouldn't stand by while someone *manhandled* her.

I took a hot breath and tried to get a grip on myself.

I wasn't near enough to hear what Sophie was saying to this dickwad. But she looked calm as she began to walk away. Then she seemed to pause, as if waiting for him to follow.

After a moment and another exchange of conversation, he trailed after her.

A second later, I was back in my seat and starting the engine. I backed out in a hurry, but then eased around the row of parked cars. They were walking side by side now, though Sophie still held her arms folded in that protective stance. When they'd gotten twenty-five yards down the sidewalk, I turned out of the parking lot and followed them.

It wasn't a long chase. A minute later they crossed the parking lot toward the bowling alley, of all places. I'd been there once with Sophie for a high school friend's birthday party.

Sweater guy held the door open for her, and seconds later they disappeared inside. I stopped my car. *Don't get out*, I begged myself.

And I didn't. But my pulse was elevated, and my nerves were raw. Really raw. Everything was just so wrong. Sophie wasn't supposed to be in Vermont at all. She was supposed to be living a brand new life in New York. And she sure as *hell* wasn't supposed to be with some asshole who couldn't control himself.

As I gripped the steering wheel with white knuckles, the itch came for me. And I heard a panicked echo of my own voice in my head. *I can't handle this right now. I just need it to ease up for a minute. Just a little.*

Even before I knew what I was doing, I'd swung the car onto the road again. Three turns later, I was cruising down a dark street at the edge of town.

Yesterday I'd spotted the dealer on the way to pick up that old lady's tires—a guy in a hoodie, sitting out on his front porch in spite of the chill. When I'd driven slowly by, he'd followed my car with his eyes.

A dealer on the clock. They were everywhere if you knew what you were looking for. And I knew.

My heart was still banging away in my chest, my breath coming in gasps. I needed *relief,* and I didn't care what it cost me. Just a little hit would be enough. Just one. Ten dollars wouldn't buy me much, so it couldn't get too ugly. *Just this once*, the echo in my head assured me.

My brain locked onto the search, and I cruised slowly down the street, looking for the porch with the dude in the hoodie. *Where'd you go? Where'd you go?* my gut chanted.

Nothing.

I stopped the car at the end of the street and turned around. Slowly, I cruised back. I *thought* I knew which house it had been, and there were lights on inside. If I cruised around the block, he'd probably reappear.

But now another car turned down the street, moving slowly. I didn't like the look of it. It was a feeble act of self-preservation, but I stepped on the gas. If there were cops watching this house, and I made a buy, that would be it for me. A bust for buying drugs would send me back to prison faster than you can say "loser."

These tiny coincidences—the missing dealer (probably on a pee break) and the other car—they were just enough to get me off that street. But it wasn't enough to make my craving stop. Nothing was.

Still feeling shaky, I drove through town. When the highway entrance ramp appeared, I got onto it. The steering wheel was sweaty in my hands, but I kept going. Fifteen miles later, I exited again, my beat-up car turning down a country road, and then another.

Maybe it was just the reflex of five recent months spent here, but I found myself turning at the Shipley Farms sign and pulling up their lengthy gravel drive. The farmhouse was all lit up inside, and I recognized two extra trucks in the driveway.

It was Thursday night. Which meant Thursday Dinner, a weekly social event the Shipleys did, alternating weeks with the neighbor down the road. A dozen or more people would be gathering inside for supper and board games.

I was in no way fit for company. So after I killed my growling engine, I just stayed behind the wheel, listening to the engine cool. I wouldn't go inside. But just sitting here wasn't a terrible idea. I was safe from myself right here. There weren't any drugs on the premises. And I'd been clean every single day that I'd stayed here. This little spot on the map was proof that I could do it.

Maybe only a crazy man drives twenty miles to sit in someone's driveway. But at that moment, it made all the sense in the world to me. Tipping my head back against the headrest, I tried to calm down.

After a couple minutes, the kitchen door opened. I thought I'd escaped detection, but apparently not.

May Shipley's shoes crunched across the driveway toward my car. She opened the passenger door and sat down, shifting my uneaten sandwich into her lap. "Hi Eeyore."

"Hi, Pooh Bear," I said, relieving her of the sandwich. I shoved it into the bag and tossed it onto the back seat.

I could feel her eyes on me. We were just about the same age. Of all the Shipleys, she was the one I'd felt closest to during my months here. May and I had worked a lot of farmers' markets together. Back in July, when I'd mentioned that I was supposed to be attending Narcotics Anonymous meetings, she found one for me and drove me there once or twice a week, knitting her way through the hour in the back row.

"You okay?" she asked now.

I shrugged, because I didn't want to lie to May. But a shrug wasn't a lie. And I really had no clue how this night would end.

"Forget your toothbrush?" she teased.

My voice was flat. "Forgot how to get through the day without heroin."

Her eyes were deep pools of empathy. "Did you use?" she asked me calmly.

46

I shook my head. "Nope. Came close, though. Swear to God, if the neighborhood pusher hadn't been on a piss break, I'd be off the wagon right now."

She reached over and squeezed my shoulder. What she *didn't* do was spout any wisdom. May was as solid as they came.

Another door on my shithole car opened, and May's brother Griffin Shipley climbed into the back seat. "This where the party is?" he asked, closing the door against the chill.

I grunted.

"Is there a reason you're not coming into the house?" he asked, bumping the back of the driver's seat with his big knees. Griffin was built like a Mack truck. Farming gave you muscle, but he'd be a huge guy even if he sat at a desk all day.

"I just drove out of town because I needed an hour away from my place," I said. "Didn't realize it was Thursday Dinner."

"You just have naturally good timing," May said, nudging my elbow with hers.

"Yeah." I chuckled. "I excel at timing." You have to have impeccable timing to kill your girlfriend's brother the only time the two of you ever got into a car together.

"Is this a sandwich?" Griffin asked. I heard a rustle, and then he said, "Mmm. Chicken Caesar."

"Don't eat Jude's food!" May yelped, spinning around to glare at her brother.

"Why not? Mom and Audrey are slicing up a giant ham right now. This is just a warm-up. Bite?" He offered the wrap to the front seat.

"You keep it, man," I said. Food didn't appeal to me when I was feeling twitchy.

"We'd better go inside," May said, reaching for the door. "Heads will roll if dinner doesn't start on time."

"I should go home," I muttered.

She turned to pinch me on the arm. "No freaking way. You're here already."

"Didn't mean to invite myself to dinner."

"Get out of the car, Jude. There's apple-cranberry pie." She knew it was my favorite.

My empty stomach picked that moment to growl, which made her laugh. "Come on. *Out.*" She gave me a shove.

Caving, I got out and followed the two of them through the kitchen door, because I really could not go back to Colebury right now. Mrs. Shipley stood at her worktable, slicing ham into slabs. "Good evening, Jude," she said. "It's lovely to see you."

Lovely of you to show up empty-handed for dinner. I was such an asshole. "I'm sorry to just drive up without calling."

She lifted an eyebrow. "I specifically invited you back for Thursday Dinner. *This* is Thursday Dinner. You are only allowed to apologize for arriving late. Now wash your hands and find yourself a beverage." Then, having no more time for discussion, she set down her knife and hefted the platter of ham.

The Shipleys were good at dealing with strays, that was for sure. I found a water glass in one of Mrs. Shipley's cabinets, and filled it. Then I carried my drink of choice through the double doors and into the crowded dining room.

Candles lit the enormous table, where most everyone was already seated. At the far end sat Isaac and Leah Abraham, the hippie neighbors from a few miles down the road, their toddler on Isaac's knee. The Abrahams were an odd pair in their late twenties. They'd run away from an honest-to-God cult somewhere out west. Then there were the other Shipley kids, Daphne and Dylan—a set of seventeen-year-old twins, Grandpa Shipley, and a cousin, Kyle, who'd picked apples with us over the summer.

Everyone turned to look when I came in. "Hey," I said stupidly. But as full as the room looked, there was an empty seat on the bench next to Zachariah, so I moved around the table and snagged it. Zach wasn't much of a talker. He was a stray, too. A couple of years ago, he'd been booted out of the same cult that the neighbors had escaped. So Zach hitchhiked his way across country to find them. He'd turned up on their doorstep without shoes and without having eaten in days.

Here he sat now, two hundred pounds of blond, solid muscle. If you Googled the word "healthy" you'd probably find a picture of Zachariah. He knew more about farming than I ever would, and he was an excellent mechanic to boot.

Mrs. Shipley, Griffin, Audrey and May brought the rest of the food out of the kitchen and set in on the table. While they took their seats, I bowed my head for what I knew came next.

"Dear Lord," Mrs. Shipley began, "thank you for these gifts we are about to receive. Thank you for bringing friends to our table..."

The prayer went on, and my eyes made a covert trip across the candlelit faces around the table. I'd pointed my car in this direction for a reason, even if I hadn't realized it in my freaked-out haze.

Well done, subconscious.

The months I'd spent on this farm were pretty much the most perilous ones that an addict can have. You're out on your own again, and you need to rebuild all your habits from scratch, since the old ones practically killed you already.

This farm had functioned like an accidental halfway-house for me. There weren't any locks on the doors like they had at rehab. But the farm was in the middle of nowhere, and I'd had no car. So there had been no way for me to get drugs without really working for it. I would have had to borrow a vehicle and wander around Orange County asking questions.

But I hadn't done that. I'd stayed clean.

And the Shipleys were just so fucking nice to me, even though I was that loser who'd just come from jail and then rehab. I have no idea why they'd hired me, except that farm labor was really pretty tight in the summertime, and my parole officer was a friend of theirs.

From July through October, I'd slept in their bunkhouse out back. There had been four of us in there, including Griffin. At first I'd assumed that he slept in the bunkhouse to keep an eye on the help. But that wasn't the reason at all. He'd given his bedroom to his aging grandfather, and the farmhouse was crowded. Last month he'd moved in with Audrey a half mile down the road.

This family had been nothing but good to me. I'd done hard labor all day long and fell into bed at night. And when I'd inevitably woke (because recovering addicts sleep like shit), I would just lie in my bunk and listen to the others breathe. They'd sounded calm, and it had made me feel calmer, too. Eventually, my tired body would drift to sleep again until it was time to get up at dawn and work my ass off.

I would have stayed forever.

"Amen," Mrs. Shipley finally said. There was a smattering of "Amens" to follow hers, and then busy hands began lifting and passing plates around the table.

"No muffler yet?" Zachariah asked, passing me a platter of ham after hefting two fat slices onto his own plate.

"I ordered it. Should come in on Monday."

He nodded. Zach had driven me to look at the car in Montpelier when I was trying to find something cheap. He didn't have a car, either. But Griffin had let us use his truck to go check out the vehicle.

I'd wanted company, too. Because if Zachariah was beside me, I knew I wouldn't even be tempted to look around the back streets of Montpelier for a dealer.

That had been three weeks ago, but it felt longer. At that point, I'd suspected that moving back to Colebury would be hard.

But I'd had no idea that I was about to be sucker-punched by the knowledge that Sophie was still in town. And getting harassed by some asshole in a turtleneck. Sitting there in the comfort of the Shipleys' dining room, I fought off a shudder.

Zachariah passed me the roasted potatoes. I found myself taking less food for myself than I did when I was a rightful employee of this place and not just a hanger-on like I was tonight. But Zach filled his plate with the righteous determination of a man who knows he'll be shoveling cow shit before six AM. Life had knocked Zach around twice as hard as it ever had me. His people had taped his hands behind his back and rolled him off a flatbed truck when he wouldn't fall in line with their bullshit. Yet the guy sitting beside me had never touched a drug in his life. (Or a woman. But that's a whole different story.)

It was hard not to compare my shitty solutions with all the

ways he'd managed to cope. Treatment meetings had taught me that addiction was a disease, one that I had and Zachariah didn't. According to them, I wasn't supposed to compare myself to Zachariah, because he didn't walk around all day with a body that craved smack.

It sounded nice on paper. The problem was that I remembered the exact moment my friends offered me a line of painkillers to snort. I'd said yes instead of no, even though I'd known it was a dumbass thing to do. The rest is (ugly) history.

My name is Jude Nickel, and I am an addict. Also, I'm a big fucking idiot.

* * *

After dinner I helped clear the table. And while May did the dishes, I dried.

"What's it like being back at home?" May asked me, handing over a dripping-wet mixing bowl.

"It's... awful," I answered.

May laughed. "That is uncharacteristically candid of you."

"Isn't it?" We worked in silence for a couple of minutes. "The problem is that it's hard to behave differently in the same old environment. Every time I step inside my old room, I *feel* like the junkie I used to be. Like the air in there is fucking toxic."

She gave me a quick glance that was brimming with empathy. "Isn't there somewhere else you can be?"

"I do the math, like, hourly. But I can't get a decent job until I've been clean and out of prison for a while. And without a real job, I can't move away. Besides, even if I had some kind of roommate situation for cheap, there's no telling what the roommates might be into."

And who wants a felon for a roommate, anyway? *Shit.*

She shook her head. "Look, if you ever just need to get away for a night, the bunkhouse is always there. Zach is the only one sleeping out there right now."

I seriously did not want to have to take her up on that offer. But, hell. It was better than relapsing. "I appreciate it," I said.

"Anytime, honey," she said. "Now let's have dessert."

Chapter Five

Jude

Cravings Level: 4

I felt saner after my evening with the Shipleys. When I drove home to Colebury afterward, I was full of food and not so itchy. And, as I said my goodnights, the family made it clear that I was expected for dinner again next week.

This made a huge difference to my outlook on life. If I didn't show up next week, they would wonder why. And if I relapsed, I wouldn't be able face them.

Somehow, their expectations were just enough to get me through the weekend, which I spent changing out snow tires.

My father's appearances in the garage could be measured in minutes these days. Apparently, my reappearance had made a good excuse for him to go on a bender. I saw him carry a case of malt liquor into the house on Saturday night while I worked late in the garage, my fingers freezing numb. I worked with the garage door open so that passers by would see activity inside.

At least I had my anger to keep me warm.

Sunday's last customer paid by cash, which meant that when his car pulled away, leaving me tired and completely alone in the darkened garage, I had two twenties in my hand.

My first thought was: I wonder how much smack I can get

for this?

Thank you, rewired neurons. For how long would my opiate-addled brain reach for that idea first? One year? Two? Ten?

I shoved the money into the pocket of my coat and went right to the grocery store, where I put $38.29 worth of food into my cart. It was loser food, of course, because my cooking resources were limited to things I could nuke in the crappy little microwave I'd bought at Goodwill on Friday afternoon.

I chose a frozen meal to have as my dinner. I only bought one, though, because I didn't have a freezer. So the rest of the stuff in my cart was mostly canned soups and stews. For a treat, I bought a package of cookies and a carton of milk, which I could keep cool by putting it outside my door on the staircase up to my room.

While I paid for this feast, the checkout girl kept sneaking looks at me from underneath her too-long bangs. Either she was someone who'd known me in high school, and was therefore sneaking looks at the druggie felon who'd killed his girlfriend's brother, or else she was admiring my tats.

It could really go either way.

On my way out of KwikShop, I saw a guy standing under the awning, hoodie up over his head, hands in his pocket. "You need anything, I got it," he mumbled as I passed by.

My gait quickened as I headed for my beater of a car. *Great.* As if I needed to know one more place in the world where drugs could be found.

I dropped my grocery bags on the passenger seat and went home to my quiet little cave of a room.

At rehab, they say, "Be kind to yourself." I was trying to do just that. In less than a half hour, I'd be eating a (microwaved) meal. I had enough food, and some cookies. And I wasn't in prison or coming down off a high.

Progress, I chanted in my head.

Progress.

* * *

One minute at a time, one hour at a time, one day at a time, I kept going.

The new muffler arrived and I put it in. My car no longer sounded like a Harley. And I made it to another Thursday Dinner. This one was at the Abrahams' house, and this time I brought a bottle of red wine, even though I wouldn't be drinking any. With something in my hands when I arrived, I didn't feel like a total sponge.

I sat next to May at their table and soaked up the good vibes of the people around me. May got tipsy and told me a funny story about accidentally locking herself in the chicken coop.

For another week I'd persevered.

In the minus column, I still couldn't sleep. The worst hours of the night were from about four to about five-thirty in the morning. Inevitably, I'd fall asleep a half-hour before my alarm was set to go off and then wake up insanely groggy. To combat this problem (and to avoid harming myself in a sleep haze during the first hour of my workday) I mainlined Pepsi before, during and after each tire change.

Business was decent, but I was dealt another blow. On Monday, a cop pulled into the garage's driveway and wrote me a seventy-dollar ticket for obstructing the sidewalk with my new sign.

By far my biggest accomplishment of the week was staying silent while he wrote it out. I wanted to rage at him and argue that his own vehicle was presently obstructing far more of the sidewalk than my freaking sign.

I didn't say a word, though. Anyone with a felony record *cannot* talk back to a cop. It's just a fact of life, and one that I'd be living with forever. And the seventy bucks? *Just the cost of doing business*, I told myself. The police chief had probably noticed I'd come back to town and declared it open season to harass me.

After he left, I dragged my sign inside the garage. That meant more days working with the doors open, in the hopes that people could even see the damn sign. My hands were red and numb by noon every day.

Also in the minus column—my cravings were pretty fierce. I hadn't been to a NA meeting since coming back to Colebury.

Before I left the Shipley Farm May had printed out a list of nearby meetings. The only one in Colebury was on Wednesday afternoons at four o'clock.

That was a working hour for me. And when Wednesday rolled around, I was doing actual bodywork—fixing a dent in somebody's Highlander. But I made myself close the garage down at three thirty. My father hadn't made an appearance for several hours. I locked up, then knocked on the front door of my childhood home, which was always weird. He came to the door looking glassy-eyed.

"I shut 'er down," I said. "Got somewhere I have to be."

"What if somebody comes?" he asked.

I just stared at him for a second, waiting for the logic of the question to kick in for him. In other words—*what the fuck would you do without your slave boy?* But no light shone in my old man's eyes. "Guess you'll have to deal with them," I said, finally.

Then I turned and left him there, puzzling over it.

After a quick shower, I walked to the church instead of driving. It was only about four blocks, and I told myself that I needed the exercise. But really, I just wanted to walk through the first snowflakes of the year. They were thick and wet, landing on my face and in my hair. The sidewalk began to turn white, and my feet made tracks on the pavement.

Up ahead, the stone church fit in with this pretty picture, too. It was the same Catholic church that Sophie's parents had dragged her to every Sunday during high school. She wasn't a big churchgoer, my Sophie. She hated sitting through the service, and she avoided it every chance she got.

I knew I shouldn't be thinking of her as *my Sophie*. But at the time it had been true.

The door handle was wrought iron—the kind they don't make anymore. I gave it a yank. Inside, a hand-lettered sign on the wall read "NA Meetin Downstairs." The missing G could have been a mistake, or it could have been ironic. Either way, I found myself descending into a far less picturesque part of the building. There were fluorescent lights and dinged-up old plastered walls.

I knew I was in the right place when I saw the carafe of coffee and the cheap paper cups sitting beside a powdered creamer. (There must be a law on the books somewhere that you couldn't bring a bunch of addicts together into a room without offering them some really bad coffee.) They also had the regulation metal folding chairs, just three rows of them.

A small meeting for a small town.

There were half a dozen people in attendance already. I took a seat on the end of the second row and waited. Addicts came in all shapes and sizes. The guy who sat down next to me looked like he'd stepped out of an ad for Harley-Davidson. But the woman who seemed to be hosting the meeting looked like a librarian.

When the room was full(ish), the librarian opened the meeting. "Hi, I'm Linda, and I'm an addict. Thank you for coming to the Colebury Narcotics Anonymous meeting. This is meant to be a safe place for all, so I must insist that no drugs be on your person at our meetings. If you are carrying anything please remove it from the room at this time. Although drugs are not welcome in this room, users are. Membership to this fellowship is free, and you are a member when you say you are."

She paused to take a breath, and then she asked someone to read the Why We Are Here passage from the handbook.

The Harley dude volunteered. He took the dog-eared book, flipped to the text and began reading.

The words were soothing in their familiarity. The message was a simple one, but there was power in hearing it as a group. We were all here because we couldn't manage ourselves on drugs. We put our habits ahead of all else. Because we did harm to ourselves and others, and because we needed to change our ways in order to survive.

Sitting in a meeting always reminded me that the problem was bigger than a few bad decisions or shitty willpower. It wasn't just me.

"We have a speaker today," Librarian Linda said. "Robby has brought his mother to celebrate three years clean."

There was polite applause, which I joined. Three *years*. I

didn't know Robby's story, not yet. But even if he'd only given up pot and Doritos, I was still jealous.

Robby himself looked to be about my age or maybe a few years older. It was hard to say. But he had a nice tight haircut and healthy glow.

He began to tell his story, and it was one I'd heard many times. Boy steals his father's prescription painkillers. Boy's friends teach him to snort them. Boy can't give up the habit and begins to steal from his parents.

Change a detail here and there, and you'd have my story, too. I'd stolen petty cash from my father's till. I'd started with oxys, too. When my habit got too expensive, I took to stealing parts from a junkyard owner who'd trusted me. I sold them on eBay and snorted the proceeds.

Robby hit bottom by ODing. He was lucky to be alive. I hit bottom by killing someone and was also lucky to be alive.

"I know I'm always going to be fighting this disease," he said. "But I know that I can win, and that my family is here to help me."

Ah, and that was where our stories parted. Robby's mom sat there beaming, tears in her eyes. My mom ran off with another man when I was eight. My father got drunk the night she left and never really sobered up.

Sometimes these stories really buoyed me. But today wasn't one of those times. Robby's beaming mother just grated on me. She reminded me of the stage mothers that Sophie used to have to deal with. *Isn't my kid great? Listen to the way she hits those high notes in Ave Maria!*

I didn't begrudge Robby his success, though. I really didn't. I'd give my left nut to have three years clean.

Before the meeting ended, we went around the circle. Most people gave a little update about how their week had been.

"Would you like to say anything?" the librarian lady asked.

I just shook my head.

When it was over, I sprinted into a bathroom I'd seen on my way into the room, mostly because I didn't want to chat with anyone. I didn't want to be greeted, hugged or asked whether I would come back next week.

My tactic worked. The meeting room was empty when I passed through again. I made it all the way up and onto the darkened sidewalk before I saw another human. He was seventy-five years old if he was a day, and slowly shoveling an inch of slippery snow off of the sidewalk. But he had on the wrong kicks for the job—black dress shoes. And I could tell that he was trying hard not to slip.

"Let me get that," I said. My voice was rough from underuse.

He looked up, and I noticed that he had a priest's collar on under his coat. "Am I doing that poor of a job at it?" His eyes twinkled with the question.

"No, um, father. But I think I have better traction." I pointed at my work boots.

With a smile, he handed over the shovel. "I'd appreciate that, son." He stood there, watching as I began to strip the slush off the walk in long sweeps of the shovel. "Of course the snow held off until our facilities person went home for the day," he said, conversationally.

"That's usually how life works," I said.

"True. And we have many people coming to dine this evening, so I can't have them sliding around everywhere."

This wasn't going to be a big job. It would only take a couple of minutes. "You don't have to freeze," I said. "Just tell me where the shovel goes, and I'll put it away when I'm done." Or maybe he wanted to make sure I wouldn't steal the shovel. It was easy to guess that I'd just come from the NA meeting.

"Bring it inside when you're through," he said. "One of my parishioners has gifted me with an apple pie. It's only fair that I should cut you a slice as payment for your labors. Do you like apple pie?"

I grinned down at the sidewalk. "There are very few things that I like better." The first three that came to mind were heroin, sex and punk rock. But I kept that to myself.

"I'm glad to hear you say that. Because if you didn't like apple pie, I'm not sure we could be friends."

I barked out a laugh. "That's not a very Christian attitude, father. What would Jesus say?"

"He'd say, 'more for me.' My office is at the end of the hallway. Will I see you inside?"

"Five minutes," I agreed.

The main level of the church building was much nicer than the basement. After shoveling the sidewalk, I leaned the shovel just inside the door and walked down a brick-lined hallway to an elaborate wooden door that stood ajar. The office had a thick oriental rug on the floor and a giant walnut desk.

But nobody was inside.

"There you are," the priest said, coming up behind me. In his hands he held a wooden tray. I moved into the room, where he set it down on the desk. There were two thick slices of pie and two cups. "Coffee?" he asked me.

I shook my head. "Smells good, but I wouldn't be able to sleep."

"Ah," he said wanly. "I'm familiar with the problem. But on Wednesdays my day is long, so I indulge. How about milk, then?" He lifted the generously sized creamer and held it over one empty teacup, waiting for my answer.

Was I really sitting down with a priest for pie and milk? It seemed that I was. "Yes, please."

"Have a seat," he said, pouring.

I took one of the cushioned chairs and sat, folding my hands in my lap. The old man was nice enough, but it was still a bit like getting called to the principal's office. He passed me a plate and a fork and set the cup on the desk close enough for me to reach. "Thank you," I said. "I didn't know there would be pie in my day."

He picked up his coffee cup. "To pie. May we have it every day."

I reached forward until our cups touched. "Amen."

Chuckling, he picked up his fork. "This is a very special apple pie, I'll have you know."

"I can see that." It had cranberries, and a crumb topping. I broke off a chunk with my fork and took a bite. A very *familiar* bite.

Across from me, the priest did the same, and then groaned in what I'd describe as a very non-priestly way. "Exquisite," he

60

said.

I stifled my smile. "Can I ask you a crazy question?"

"Yes. And whatever it is, I can guarantee you that this office has heard a crazier one."

"Okay, it's not *that* crazy. I was wondering if Ruthie Shipley made this pie."

He looked up in astonishment. "A boy of exceptional talent! He names the piemaker in just one bite! There should be a game show for your talent."

Now he had me laughing. "She's the only piemaker I could identify. I just spent several months working on the Shipley farm. We had pie most nights after dinner. I probably picked these apples."

"You are a very lucky man." He beamed at me. "A priest would never compare his parishioner's baking talents aloud, but I will say that whenever Ruthie Shipley or one of her daughters approaches with a box, I am careful to carry it directly to my office."

"You'd be crazy not to."

"What did you say your name was, son?"

For a moment, I actually considered lying. To a priest, no less. "It's, um, Jude Nickel." *I just did three years for killing one of your former parishioners.*

Either he didn't recognize the name from the news, or he was a very even-keeled host. "Nice to meet you, Jude. You can call me Father Peters."

"Thank you for the pie, Father Peters. I really miss Mrs. Shipley's cooking. The canned soup I've been eating the past couple weeks just isn't the same."

He peered at me thoughtfully. "Like I said, Wednesdays are busy around here. Perhaps you should stay for dinner..."

I opened my mouth to make an excuse. This was just about the nicest five minutes I'd had all week, but I didn't want to overstay my welcome.

He held up a hand, as if to preempt my argument. "Before you refuse, let me finish. We usually have about a hundred and twenty-five guests, and they come for all different reasons. Some are elderly, and just need a reason to leave the house.

Many are food insecure. Not only do I think you should dine with us tonight, my friends in the kitchen could use your help."

"You mean, like, I could volunteer?"

"That is precisely what I mean. Do you peel potatoes?"

"Sure."

"Is there somewhere else you need to be right now?"

I pictured my empty, darkened room over the garage. The evenings I spent there were torture. "No, sir."

He beamed again. "Finish your pie. The volunteers need you."

The milk in my cup was sweet and cold. I drank it down, then chased the last crumbs of Mrs. Shipley's pie around on my plate. It wasn't like me to volunteer at a church dinner. I wasn't a joiner. But food was an excellent motivating factor. And every hour I spent away from my old life, the better.

I was sitting there thinking unusually positive thoughts when someone knocked on the doorframe. "Father Peters?"

"Come in, my dear."

Looking up, I received the surprise of a lifetime. There in the doorway—wearing an apron, her hair in two pigtails—stood Sophie Haines. My ex-girlfriend, and the only person who'd ever loved me.

The silence that followed was deafening. Looking down at me, Sophie's mouth fell open. She put one hand on the doorjamb to steady herself.

I'm sorry was my only thought. I had no idea she'd be here on a random Wednesday, working in the kitchen of the church that she'd never wanted to attend when we were together.

"Sophie," Father Peters said into the vacuum of our silence. "Do you need me in the kitchen?"

She spoke to him without taking her eyes off me. "You, um, told me to tell you if Mrs. Walters came to take her shift. She's here."

"Excellent!" The priest clapped his hands. "Mrs. Walters is ninety years old, and the only one brave enough to operate our old dishwashing machine," he explained to me. "Thank you, Sophie."

After another pause, Sophie seemed to gather herself. She

backed out of the doorway, then turned and walked quickly away.

"I should go home," I said.

But Father Peters shook his head. "I don't think that's for the best." His blue-eyed gaze pierced through me. I had a feeling that this man didn't miss much. "My hungry parishioners will be needing their dinner no matter what once transpired between you and Miss Haines."

Yeah. He didn't miss a damn thing.

I was still formulating my argument when he stood up suddenly. "Follow me, young sir. I hear a sack of vegetables calling your name."

Chapter Six

Sophie

Internal DJ tuned to: a primal scream

On my best night, managing the Community Dinner was like conducting Beethoven's Fifth with a kazoo band. It was mayhem. But tonight? My mind was a speed-metal tune—all noise and no order.

It was shocking enough to spot Jude in Father Peters's office. But when the priest led my ex-boyfriend to the prep table in the back corner of the kitchen, my ability to concentrate was officially shattered.

Jude was given a large stack of carrots to peel. While I stared, he took up the peeler and began shaving off their orange skins in authoritative stripes.

For the next hour, my eyes wouldn't go where I wanted them to go. There was a ton of work to be done, yet I kept sneaking looks at Jude in the corner prepping vegetables like he was born to it. Before tonight, I'd never seen Jude touch a vegetable or even wash a dish.

It was the weirdest damned thing I ever saw. He kept his head down and plowed through a mountain of carrots and potatoes. When they were peeled, old Mrs. Perkins brought him a cutting board and a chef's knife, and he began quartering the potatoes like a man on a mission.

"Sophie," Denny said after he arrived and began to pitch in. "How many serving stations do you need? I count four dishes on the menu, but you only set up three stations."

"Oh."

"So which is it?"

"Um..." I looked around at all the work getting done in the kitchen. "Four stations," I said slowly.

"Are you okay?"

"Uh-huh," I lied, my eyes flicking back over to Jude. I kept noticing strange details about him. He'd rolled the sleeves of his flannel shirt up, exposing muscular forearms that I did not want to notice. But they flexed with each strike of the cleaver.

"Who is that, anyway?" Denny demanded.

I dragged my eyes back to Denny. "It's Jude." Even as I said the words, I knew it was a mistake, because I really couldn't let myself talk about it now. "Did Father Peters open the doors yet?"

But Denny wasn't going to let it go. "Whoa. That's *him?* Seriously?" Denny stared at Jude in open fascination. "Why here?"

My thoughts exactly. "Denny, could you set up another serving station?" *Because I'm busy having a breakdown.*

He gave me a long, appraising look. "Sure."

Things got a little better when the diners began to show up. I put myself on the serving line, where it was more difficult to stare at the bulky, uncharacteristically helpful ghost of Jude. I was still trying to resolve all the strange little inconsistencies between my memory and the man at the prep table. His piercings were gone—the barbell from his eyebrow and the studs from his upper ear. And when Father Peters passed by saying something I couldn't quite catch, Jude answered "Yessir," in a quiet voice that lacked the edge I was so familiar with.

I was like Dorothy in Oz, seeing the familiar transformed into something odd. But in this musical, I was clearly cast in the role of the scarecrow. If I only had a brain, I might be able to stop staring and start serving chicken.

"Denny," I said, dragging my attention back to the matter at hand. "Would you take charge of the biscuits? Don't let the kids take a handful." I put him at the opposite end of the table from me, so he wouldn't be able to ask me questions.

I served chicken all through the early rush. Father Peters flitted around the dining room, greeting everyone. Then he joined the line, and when he reached me he asked for two plates. "One is for our newest helper."

My flinch was involuntary, and Father Peters saw it. "Sophie, I'm sorry he gave you a surprise today. But the church belongs to all God's children. And it's a small town, sweetheart."

"I know." *But really?* When had Jude ever been to church? And there was one problem. "My dad would freak if he knew."

The priest sighed. "Perhaps. Though your father is quite welcome to volunteer on Wednesday nights if he wishes."

I looked up into Father Peters's sharp blue eyes and knew that he had a point. After my brother died, the church allegiances in my family had all flipped like coins. These days, my mother sat through Sunday service in a trance and never volunteered for anything anymore. My father never set foot in the place.

And me? I'd become the family churchgoer. It wasn't because I'd found religion. It was because Father Peters was one of the few people in town who understood what had happened to my family after our tragedy. Three years later, he still visited my mother once a week at home.

So when he'd asked me to help out on Wednesday nights, I'd said yes immediately. And I'd recruited Denny to help, too.

Father Peters heaped two plates with chicken and vegetables. At the end of the line, Denny added biscuits. Then the priest disappeared into the back to serve dinner to my ex-con ex-boyfriend.

If the night got any trippier, I'd probably start clicking my heels together and singing Judy Garland tunes.

"Would you like a breast or a leg?" I asked the next person in line.

To Jude I said nothing at all that night. By the time the

last food had been served, he'd cleaned up his prep station and disappeared into the night.

* * *

I didn't tell my parents that Jude had showed up at church that night. I decided that it was a fluke, and there was no chance that Jude Nickel had gotten religion. Furthermore, there was no chance that he'd turned up because of *me*. My brain turned this thought over and over like a hamster running on a wheel.

The following Wednesday, I got to church around four-thirty, and he was nowhere in sight. I put the earliest arriving volunteers to work prepping chili with all the fixings, cornbread and salad.

Sneaking up on Father Peters's office, I heard no voices inside. And when he waved me in, I found that he was alone this time. The twinge I felt was relief, right? It couldn't possibly be disappointment.

"Evening, dear. Did you find the beans and spices? Mrs. Perkins dropped them off but could not stay."

"So we're down a man?" I asked. That left Denny and me and Father Peters. And Mrs. Walters on the dishwashing machine.

Father Peters stood up. "It will be fine. We'll dish out the chili, but the rest can be self-serve."

I led the way back through the hall. Just before we turned into the kitchen, I saw a stream of people climbing the stairs from the basement and exiting onto the street. The paper sign that pointed toward the basement was one that I'd seen before, yet never paid much attention to. "NA Meetin."

Jude appeared at the end of this trail of people, and that's when it clicked. Now I knew *exactly* how Jude had come to appear in this building on Wednesday nights. Narcotics Anonymous.

Oh shit.

Backing up hastily, I ducked into the kitchen and made a beeline for the walk-in refrigerator for a moment alone. Maybe I was an idiot, but there was something shocking about Jude sitting in a room full of people and saying, *I have a problem*. It wasn't something my Jude would ever have done.

It was a good thing that Jude was getting help, right? I should feel nothing but happy for him. Standing there in the chill of the fridge, a shameful wave of anger pulsed through me. Because...*now* he was getting help?

When we'd been together, I ached to hear him say, "I've got to kick this little habit that I try to hide from you. I'm going to do something about it."

But those words never came. And then suddenly it was too late.

I stood there, my hands on a tray of ground beef, wishing Jude had chosen to get healthy somewhere other than Colebury. But he was here in this building whether I could handle it or not. So I put on my game face and headed back to the kitchen. When I passed Jude, he was already dicing onions with the finesse of a cooking-show host.

Without a word, Denny got to work browning ground beef in two giant commercial-sized pots, whistling to himself. Two weeks ago I'd assumed that our friendship had been permanently damaged by our worst date ever. But somehow that hadn't happened. Instead, he'd asked out a girl from the accounting department. And she'd said yes. They were going out for a second time tomorrow.

I was happy for Denny. At least one of us had a plan to move forward.

"Incoming," I said, tipping a quarter cup of chili powder into the pot. I'd given myself the task of measuring the spices. It was a simple job, perfect for someone whose brain fled the building every time Jude walked into it.

Not simple enough, evidently.

I'd neglected to remove the white butcher's paper from the counter. It sat there while I finished up with the cumin and coriander. And when I walked away to return the spices to the closet, I didn't pay much attention to a slightly acrid smell in the air.

Ten seconds later I heard Denny gasp. When I turned to look, I saw him leap back from the stove. Orange flames licked the butcher's paper. Old Mrs. Walters gave a shriek from the dishwashing station.

Before I could even work out what to do, Jude slid from behind the prep table, moving across the room with the easy grace of a cat. He grabbed the narrow, unburnt end of the paper, and with a flick of his wrist, he dropped the burning mess onto the tile floor. Then he lunged for a sodden dishrag on the counter and tossed it onto the flames.

I heard the sizzle of steam and saw more gray smoke. But I was still glued in place.

Jude grabbed another damp cloth off the dishwashing station and dropped that, too. Then he stepped on it several times.

Before I'd even processed that the fire was out, he'd slipped back behind the prep station, picked up his knife and resumed cutting onions.

Over my head, the smoke detector began to shriek, its piercing sound giving voice to the panic I'd felt since Jude appeared.

Father Peters ran into the room. "What's happening?" When he saw the remnants of the former blaze on the floor, he didn't say anything. He simply walked to the side door and propped it open, allowing the smoke to escape.

If only my troubles could be vented so easily.

Chapter Seven

Jude

Cravings Meter: a solid 6

Coming back here tonight was a bad idea.

Sophie was rattled, and I didn't like knowing that I was the cause. Maybe that sounded vain, but I knew my girl. She was the kind of person who could get up on stage in front of hundreds and rock a complicated vocal solo without a single quavering note. She was a rock.

But both times I'd worked in this kitchen, she'd come unglued. And a kitchen fire? I didn't want to be the cause of loss of life or property. Me, who'd already done damage enough.

But they were shorthanded tonight, so I wasn't about to just walk off the job. And, if I were being honest, I wanted to get another look at the guy who seemed to be stuck to her side. He was the same guy I'd seen plant one on her in the parking lot two weeks ago. Tonight he'd traded his turtleneck for a button-down.

God, it was none of my business. But if Sophie wasn't living the life she'd always planned, I wanted to know why. And if there were people in it that didn't treat her right, I wanted to know that, too.

So I prepped vegetables and I watched the two of them, even though it was clear that my presence made everyone nervous. Mr. Buttondown kept sizing me up from the corner of his eye. So when he came over to fetch all the onions I'd chopped, I couldn't help myself. The moment he approached, I raised the knife and brought it down with unexpected vehemence.

The top of an onion was severed from the body with the force of a guillotine removing someone's head.

Mr. Buttondown startled, and I had to hold in my chuckle. He nearly turned tail to run for it. But he recovered, shoving his hands in his pockets, dropping his chin and asking for the onions.

I stared him down for a second. After all, what was the use of being a convicted killer if you couldn't scare people once in a while? There weren't any other perks, that was for damned sure.

Using the big chef's knife blade, I scraped a heap of onions in his direction. "Here."

Without a word, he scooped the pile off the cutting board and into a bowl. Then he hurried away.

I moved on to the garlic and then the avocados. Tomorrow was Thanksgiving, so I'd imagined the church supper would be dead tonight. But that wasn't the case at all. When they opened up the doors, I had a partial view of the serving line where Sophie stood dishing up bowls of chili. It smelled amazing, too. My stomach grumbled as I worked.

The next time Mr. Buttondown came by, I made sure I was sharpening the knife. Christ, I was about as subtle as a Saturday morning cartoon, but he practically quivered anyway. Maybe I'm an asshole, but I still couldn't figure out what had happened that night in the parking lot. And if this dude thought nobody was paying attention to his actions, I wanted him to know that somebody was.

But the joke was on me. Apparently I wasn't as attentive as I thought, because while washing my knives, I looked up to find Sophie standing right beside me, her green eyes burning a hole into me.

Startled, I dropped the knife with a clatter into the sink.

"Jude," she said. My chest ached just hearing that word on her lips. "Thank you for putting out that fire earlier."

I swear it took me an awkwardly long time to answer. The fact that she was speaking to me at all was an unexpected gift. "You're welcome," I said eventually. "No big deal." I grabbed the knife, shut off the water and reached for a towel.

She sighed, and I heard the weight of a hundred unanswered questions in it. "Where did you learn to cook?"

"Prison kitchen." Her eyes got so huge that I had to chuckle.

Sophie swallowed. "Ask a stupid question…"

"Yeah." I grabbed the sponge off the back of the sink and began washing the sink itself, just to keep busy. It was either that or stare at her.

"Jude, there's something I need you to do for me."

My heart tripped over itself, and I couldn't look her in the eye. *Don't come back here.* Those were the words I thought she'd say next.

"Lay off of Denny, okay?"

"What?" I looked up in surprise. Then I realized that Denny must be Mr. Buttondown.

"Denny. My coworker."

"Your coworker," I repeated, trying to do the math.

Her lips pursed with frustration. "You heard me. Be nice."

Nice. "When have I ever been nice?" *Except to you.* That went without saying. I was always nice to Sophie, because she'd treated me like I mattered. There were precious few people who did, and that was *before* I went to prison.

She gave me a tiny Sophie eye roll, the one I'd always received when she was trying to show me that my bullshit didn't fly. I missed being schooled by Sophie. She was a straight shooter, and twice as smart as I'd ever be. Ignore her at your peril. "Jude, go get some chili."

"Yes, ma'am."

She gave her pretty head a shake. Then she walked away whispering something under her breath that I didn't quite catch. But it sounded like "Wizard of Oz."

Chapter Eight

Sophie

Internal DJ tuned to: "Satisfaction" by the Rolling Stones

Thanksgiving at the Haines household was not a cheery affair.

Before noon I put a small turkey in the oven. My mother was nowhere in sight, of course, so I settled in to cook an entire Thanksgiving meal by myself.

As I set the cutting board on the counter, I realized that I had no idea why I even bothered. It was a pointless charade. My mother didn't care about Thanksgiving dinner. My father didn't care about anyone.

Before Gavin died, we'd had a real family holiday. In the morning, I'd watch the Macy's Thanksgiving Day Parade to see which Broadway actresses would sing solos. But my father and brother would eventually win the remote control away from me so that they could watch football. It wasn't exciting, but it was normal.

These days I lived in a tomb.

As I pulled the vegetables out of their drawer in the refrigerator, I heard the strains of an announcer's voice coming from my father's den. He still watched football. But his son—a promising athlete—wasn't sitting beside him anymore. And he was never getting over it.

Dad still blamed me. My penance was pretending to enjoy cooking a turkey dinner. And my father would pretend to enjoy eating it.

I chopped celery for the stuffing. Then I opened a bag of potatoes and began to peel them. The task sent my traitorous mind straight to Jude and the scene in the kitchen last night. Goddamn him. I couldn't believe that I'd been foolish enough to ask him where he'd learned to cook. *In prison*, he'd answered. Then the corners of his mouth had quirked up, as if I were an amusing child who couldn't help asking stupid questions.

Standing there in the kitchen, I groaned aloud. Nobody was listening to me, though. Nobody ever did.

* * *

By five o'clock I'd done it all.

Sure, I took a few shortcuts. Cranberry sauce from a can. A pie from the bakery. But a real Thanksgiving dinner was on the table. I fetched my mother from her spot staring into space in the living room. I fetched my father from the football game. Taking my seat, I stifled a sigh.

My father stood at the head of the table, carving pieces of turkey onto our plates.

For a few minutes, we passed dishes around, and conversation was unnecessary. But after the silence became heavy, I thought of something to say. "I have a new case at work. The cutest toddler who's deaf. She can't hear a thing, but she likes it when her mother sings. She puts her hand right here." I covered my chin and my lower lip with my hand. "It's like she knows her mother is making noise." I'd had them in my office on Tuesday, and it was fascinating to watch.

"Poor kid," my father said.

"Not for long. The doctors think cochlear implants might restore her hearing. And she's only eighteen months old."

"Can they do that for a child so young?" my father asked, heaping stuffing onto his plate.

"It's *better* to do it young. Older patients sometimes can't get used to them. We just have to figure out how this family can afford it. They have health insurance, but the deductible is five thousand dollars."

My father nodded slowly. "That's good work you're doing."

A rare compliment from my father. Who knew? "What's new with you at work?"

He gave a chuckle and shook his head. "Just keeping the peace, trying to improve the neighborhood. Can't believe the Nickel kid is getting any business at his father's garage. I had one of my boys write him a ticket for putting his new sign on the public sidewalk."

Just like that, the food in my stomach turned to wet concrete.

"Gave him a ticket," my father said, stabbing a piece of turkey with his fork. "But I plan to shut that place down."

"How?" I asked, hating the sound of the question. If I sounded interested at all, my father would fly into a rage.

"That lot is in a residential neighborhood. He shouldn't have a garage there."

I swirled mashed potatoes around on my plate. This was dangerous ground for me. But the legality of Jude's father's business had been challenged before. "Wasn't that tried before? They won, though," I pointed out.

My father only chuckled. "They won *before* a murderer and a drug addict lived there. I can get them off that property. One of my officers wants to buy that lot and build a duplex there. That will take a bite out of them."

I set down my fork. "That won't bring Gavin back."

My father set his wineglass down slowly. He liked to make me wait and squirm before the outburst that we both knew was coming. "Really, Sophie? You'd take his side? You disloyal little *bitch*."

As the word hung there over my homemade meal, my mother got up from her chair and drifted out of the room. Hanging onto my own calm by a thread, I watched her go. "Daddy, I wish Jude hadn't come back to town. But that doesn't mean I'd cheat an old man out of his home."

There was a silence while my father stared me down. I

knew I shouldn't have said anything. Old Man Nickel had barely said three words to me during the years when Jude and I dated. I knew he wasn't exactly a pillar of the community. But I'd defended him out of anger at my father.

God, I was such a hypocrite. But that was the effect my father had on me.

"You are to have no contact with that man or his son," my father said.

"I don't think you have a thing to worry about," I lied. "I wrote Jude in prison and he never answered."

Daddy's face reddened. "I told you *never* to do that—"

"You told me never to do a lot of things! But I wanted to know what Gavin was doing in his car that night. And nobody will ever *talk* about what happened!"

His face was the color of raw meat. "Keep your nose out of it! You never fucking listen!"

Somehow I kept my voice level. "You haven't *ever* listened to me. We're even."

"There is no *EVEN!*" he screamed. "You live in my house, you do as I say!"

I knew he wasn't going to like what I said next, but I couldn't stop myself. "I don't live here for the free rent. I'm here for Mom. She's a wreck, and you don't seem to care."

My father pushed back from the table with violence in his eyes, and I tensed all of my muscles. He picked up the gravy boat and hurled it against the wall, where it shattered into pieces, splashing gravy everywhere.

Holy. Crap.

I leapt up on shaky knees and high-tailed it out of the dining room, walking blindly toward the kitchen. I had no destination in mind other than *away*. My purse and car keys were upstairs, damn it. But my coat and shoes were beside the kitchen door. With shaking hands I put them on.

From the dining room I heard the sound of a chair being kicked into the wall.

Shit.

I opened the kitchen door and stepped outside to find rain. My heart sank again. Even a walk around the block would be a trial. Awesome. But I did it anyway, exiting our garage and taking off down the wet sidewalk. It was breezy, too. I hugged my coat around me to keep the wind from whipping it around and tried to think where to go. On Thanksgiving everything was closed. I could try to fetch my car keys without crossing my father, and then drive... where? Some truck stop with sludgy coffee?

The rain on my face was really the least of my problems.

As I proceeded through Colebury, there were few signs of life. The houses were lit up, but traffic was nil. Until I hit Main Street, where an unfamiliar car slowed to a stop beside me. The window lowered. "Hey. You okay?"

Jesus H. It was Jude. It was as if I'd summoned him like a genie by invoking him to my father. "I'm fine," I grumbled. I kept walking.

He inched along beside me. "Get in the car, Sophie."

I stopped walking and approached the car. "Why?"

"What do you mean, why? Because it's pouring."

"Where are you going to take me?" It's not like I had a destination in mind.

Clear eyes blinked up at me. "That's really up to you."

I stepped closer, still unsure what to do. On the passenger's seat sat a white bag. "What's that?"

His expression turned weary. "I can only guess where your mind goes when you're asking me that." He picked up the bag so I could see that it was from the grocery store. "A chocolate pumpkin cake. Can't you smell it?"

I could, actually. I put my hand on the door lever, but I was still feeling weird about this. "You're the very last thing I need today."

He didn't even look offended. Not one iota. "That is true about ninety-nine percent of the time. But it's Thursday, so it's not true right now."

I opened the door. "What? You're, like, a better man on Thursdays?

"That's right." He placed the cake on the backseat. As he twisted his body to set it down, I got a glimpse of his sixpack beneath the hemline of his T-shirt. There was a flash of golden skin, and a peek at the trim strip of light brown hair descending into his jeans.

This was probably why I slid onto the passenger's seat. My ex-con ex-boyfriend—a drug addict and convicted man-slaughterer—flashed me his happy trail and I got into his car.

One wondered why my father didn't trust me.

"Where to?" Jude asked, pulling away from the curb. "You're welcome to come to dinner with me, but I won't get back until late, probably."

Once more I went over my options. And... wow. That was a depressing three-second calculation. I didn't have any of the kind of friends that you could just drop in on at Thanksgiving. There was Denny, who would always take my call. But he'd want to know my troubles, and I didn't feel like talking about it. I had terrific friends from college, but they'd all moved away after graduation six months ago.

"You can come with me," Jude said quietly.

"Where?" I asked, still using a crisp tone. I hadn't sounded like such a brat since my teenage days. But my attitude was my only weapon against the sea of memories that choked me every time I looked at Jude.

"Some friends' house. But it's in the boonies, off exit three."

"Nice friends?" I asked. And that wasn't belligerence, it was just self-preservation. Jude had been a drug addict when we were together. There was a lot that I'd chosen not to see. I'd never make that mistake again.

Beside me, he sighed. "I wouldn't take you anywhere that wasn't nice."

"Okay," I whispered as the rain beat down on the windshield. "Thank you," I added a little too late.

He drove through the rain, and for a while neither of us said anything. With the windshield wipers working furiously, he took us onto the highway heading south, driving slower than I'd ever seen him drive. I would have made a joke about it, except it wouldn't have been funny. The last time he'd had a member of my family in my car, there'd been a funeral three days later.

Eventually the rain slackened, becoming only a mist. He

relaxed back in his seat, one muscular arm braced forward on the wheel. I sat in the passenger seat, trapped in a time warp. Watching Jude drive was something I'd done too many times to count. Once I'd given him road head on this very stretch of highway. We'd been heading to an outdoor concert in Norwich. It had been a warm summer night, and I'd been feeling every kind of frisky. So I'd bent over and unzipped his jeans.

When I'd gone down on him, he'd pulled off at the next exit, parking the car behind a shuttered gas station. He didn't let me finish him. Instead, we ended up fucking in the passenger seat.

God. Now my face was *flaming* just remembering it. How on earth did people move on? The times I'd had with Jude were just too hot to fade from my memory. When I was a hundred and five, I'd still be able to recall losing my virginity to him. I could be blind and deaf and shriveled up like a raisin, and get wet and horny just remembering the way he whispered in my ear after sliding into me for the first time. *"Now you're really mine."*

I should never have gotten in this car.

"You always take walks in the pouring rain?" he asked suddenly.

"No."

"Just... felt the urge?"

I sighed. "No, Jude. I just didn't want to be at home tonight. So I left."

To his credit, he didn't ask again. But I'd squashed the conversation, and now he was probably regretting ever picking me up. "How are you doing, anyway?" I managed to ask.

He gave the steering wheel a funny smile. "It's Thursday night."

"You mentioned that."

"So I'm doing really well."

"You're not making a whole lot of sense."

He rolled his shoulders. "Well, you know that cliché that says to take life one day at a time? I can't even do that. It's more like a one-minute-at-a-time kind of thing. So I don't have the luxury of making a lot of sense. Sorry."

I didn't know what to say to that, so I said nothing.

After a while, he turned on the old car's radio, and we listened to a story on Vermont Public Radio about a Windsor County farmer who'd just won an award for her sheep's milk cheese.

It ended and the weather report came on, so I shut the radio off. "Never once have I heard you listen to public radio."

"Well, it's pretty useful in prison," he said. "Radios are allowed but not computers. It was the only way to keep up with the outside world. And also it reminded me that I was still in Vermont. Otherwise, that place was like being on the moon."

That shut me up fast. I'd never doubted that Jude deserved punishment for what he did. But three years in prison wasn't something that I ever wanted to experience. Public radio seemed like a pretty healthy coping mechanism.

"What was it like?" I whispered, before I could think better of it.

"Gross," he said right away. "Everything was dirty all the time. The toilet. The beds. The people. Nobody there had any hope."

"Except for you?" I asked, making myself sound even more naive than I'd already proven to be.

"Not even me," he said firmly. "Especially not me."

He left the highway in Randolph and then began to steer the car up a hill. "My friends have a dairy farm and an orchard. You might know them from church. The Shipleys?"

"Sure I know the Shipleys. I went to Sunday school with May and Griffin. But how do *you* know them?"

"I worked here until about three weeks ago. Lived in the bunkhouse."

"Oh." So that's where Jude had gone after he was released from prison. He'd been in Vermont all this time? How odd to think that I'd seen Mrs. Shipley at church on Sundays, usually with one of her daughters. "Mr. Shipley died a couple of years ago. Right around the time..." I didn't finish the sentence. *Right around the time Gavin died.*

"Yeah," Jude said. "I never met him. Must have been a good guy, though. All the rest of 'em are."

"He was. Who runs the dairy farm now?"

"Griffin. He's expanding, actually. More cider, less dairy. His cider just won some kind of award."

"Wow. Griffin's only... twenty six?"

"Something like that."

I wanted to ask more. I was dying to know how Jude had gotten that job in the first place. But now the car was bumping along a dirt road, and we were turning onto a long driveway. Ahead of us I could see a big old farmhouse with lights burning in every window.

Jude pulled up behind a beat-up old truck and killed his engine. Then he reached into the back seat for the pumpkin cake (flashing his abs again!) and got out of the car.

I climbed out too, feeling a bit like Alice when she's gone down the rabbit hole. The Jude I knew didn't bring cake to somebody's family supper. He didn't do farm work, either. Wordlessly, I followed him up a couple of steps and into the Shipleys' kitchen door. There were an improbable number of people in the steamy kitchen, and several of them greeted him the moment he entered.

"Jude's here!" one of the Shipley sisters called. It was the teenaged one—Daphne. "Oh, hey. Sophie, right?" There was curiosity in her eyes.

"Right," I said, feeling like an intruder.

"Hey, what's in the box?" her brother Dylan asked. He darted across the room and took the cake from Jude's hands. "Sure smells good!"

"It's..." he got out. But then something small crashed into his knees, and he looked down.

"Ow!" came from the floor.

Jude bent over and picked up what turned out to be a toddler. "Easy, Maeve," he said, holding the little person up to his face. "You okay? Do you remember me?"

"Yood," the little girl said affirmatively.

"Close enough," he smiled then, and I could only stare. I hadn't seen a full-wattage Jude smile in what felt like forever. And I'd never seen him hold a child. She looked small against his broad chest. The sight of her there made my own chest shimmy.

There had been a time when I thought that someday I'd have Jude's babies. I'd never described this fantasy to him, because we were so young it was laughable. And even in my wildest daydream, I wasn't bearing this hypothetical child until my career on Broadway was well established.

But I'd wanted to. I'd wanted to be the girl who tamed the wild boy. I pictured his tattooed arm rubbing my pregnant belly, and then holding my child against his bare chest.

My adolescent heart had some pretty crazy flights of fancy.

"Where's your mama?" he asked the tiny human politely. She pointed one stubby finger in the direction of what could only be the dining room.

Jude beckoned to me and I followed him. We almost made it across the busy kitchen when Mrs. Shipley caught up to us.

"Jude!" She ducked in to kiss him on the cheek. "Happy Thanksgiving. And Sophie Haines! It's good to see both of you." She patted me on the arm.

"Ruth," Jude said. "Sophie was at loose ends tonight, so..."

Ruth held up a hand. "Don't you start apologizing, sir. We've had this conversation before."

"Yes, ma'am."

She gave my elbow a friendly squeeze. "Lovely to see you, honey. We have the year's new cider in the dining room. Griffin will pour you a glass, and dinner's almost ready."

"Is there anything I can do?" I asked. I felt pretty sheepish, walking into their kitchen on Thanksgiving.

"We've got it down to a science," she said, waving a hand at her daughters. "Have a drink, or if that's not your style, there are sodas on the porch keeping cold."

"Thank you," I said.

"It's honestly better if we get out of the way," Jude said, reaching back to catch my hand in his. The sensation of his fingers closing over mine made me feel even more muddled than I already was.

Jude led me through a doorway and into a spacious dining room. Even before I stepped over the threshold I was surprised by the number of voices rising up in conversation. This was quite the party, and that was a good thing—it made me less of an interloper.

The moment Jude went through the door, more voices called his name. I followed just in time to see May Shipley hug-tackle him. "You're even on time..." Her gaze slid to me. And then her eyes widened.

The room grew quieter, and I felt eyes on me. Jude put an arm around my shoulder. "I think you know Sophie from church?"

May blinked, and then seemed to recover from her surprise. "Of course. Good to see you, Sophie. It's been a while since we had to wear those angel wings and a halo in the Christmas pageant."

"I'm pretty sure they wouldn't let me near the angel's wings anymore," I said. "And forget the halo."

More than a few people laughed. "Let's find her a chair," May suggested.

Jude handed the toddler off to a young couple, and I was introduced in quick succession to the parts of the Shipley family that I didn't know by name. Griffin Shipley introduced me to his girlfriend, Audrey, two cousins, an aunt and an uncle and an elderly grandfather. There was also a hunky blond farmhand named Zach and two more neighbors.

"Got that?" Jude joked after the introductions were made.

"No," I said, and everyone laughed.

"Let me get her a glass of cider," Griffin said. "Actually, grab *two* glasses, Audrey. I want her to taste the Dooryard and our prizewinner."

"Yes, captain!" his girlfriend quipped, opening a cabinet full of stemware.

"You know they win awards for these?" Jude asked. "The price of all that success is that he has to talk like a French wine snob. You should hear how they go on about the *terroire* and the fruity overtones and the mushroomy lowlights."

"Mushroomy lowlights?" I laughed.

Griffin snorted. "That sounds like something in the laundry hamper after we muck out the dairy barn."

Jude smiled at me as I took the first glass from Griffin. To say that this evening had become much more interesting than I'd expected was a massive understatement. I tasted the cider. Truly, it was wonderful—just the right balance of sweet and tart. "Wow," I blurted. "This is great."

"Tell him the flavor is 'round.' That's snobspeak for 'good.' He pops a boner if you say it's 'round.'"

"Stop." I gave Jude a slight elbow jab. "It's really good. No mushroomy lowlights. Here." I offered Jude the glass.

Jude gave his chin a tiny shake. "No thanks. Not my thing."

"Really? It's awesome." I held the glass out still, because it was unlike him to refuse to try something.

Jude didn't say anything, but Griffin's wince made me realize the stupid mistake that I'd just made. Jude didn't taste the award-winning cider because it was *alcoholic*. "Shit, I'm sorry," I whispered.

"No big deal," he said, and he meant it. His eyes were amused. "You and Griff can drink my share. I'm just gonna say hello to Zach for a minute, and find myself a soda." He slipped away.

Griffin and Audrey explained what made the two ciders different, and I tried to listen. But I couldn't stop tracking Jude as he moved around the room greeting people. He looked comfortable and happy. My heart splintered every time he smiled.

Jude found us seats side by side. Two full-sized dining tables had been lined up, end-to-end, and I counted sixteen people around the table. Yellow candlelight flickered on faces and brought out the sun-bleached highlights in Jude's hair.

"Let's say grace," Mrs. Shipley said. "Dad? Will you do the honors?"

Everyone at the table began to clasp hands. I took the tiny hand of the toddler beside me with my left hand. And then Jude's palm slid onto my right. I closed my eyes against the feel of it. His big hand was roughened from work, as it had always been. The familiarity is what really killed me. It was hard to be here with this oddly sanitized version of Jude. The wearer of flannel. Diet Coke in his glass. This was a Jude from an alternate universe. But I knew if I slid into his arms he'd feel so achingly familiar—broad and warm and strong and so very *mine*.

"Amen," mumbled Grandpa Shipley.

Jude dropped my hand again.

Chapter Nine

Jude

Cravings Meter: 2

Thanksgiving at the Shipley's was a lot like the other Thursday Dinners, only with fancier side dishes and more guests. And Grandpa Shipley wore a bow tie.

But it was special to me, because I'd never been to a traditional Thanksgiving dinner before. Not since grade school, anyway. When I was a kid, my dad and I got take-out and watched football on TV. He'd buy himself a bottle of whatever and end the night passed out in his chair. Happy holidays.

Sophie would have loved to invite me over, but her father gave her so much grief about me that I always begged off.

So this was nice. Though bringing Sophie with me was probably stupid. Getting her out of the downpour wasn't wrong. She'd been wet and ornery looking, and now she looked happy and relaxed with the Shipley clan doing its thing, drawing her into their center.

But it was still a dick move, because I know I'd done it to show off. *Look at me, I have friends who aren't druggies. I'm such a winner.* But of course it was a goddamned lie. Just because the people in this room hadn't seen me at my worst didn't mean that they were really mine.

Christ. I was such a user. Of drugs, and now of people, too.

On this grim thought, I did something weird and reflexive, something only an addict would do. I looked down into the glass I was holding, wondering *how come I can't feel a buzz yet?*

Because it was a glass of soda. *Right.*

Sigh.

Dinner was delicious, as always. I helped wash dishes afterward.

"What can I do?" Sophie asked as I scraped odds and ends off a cutting board into the compost bin.

The kitchen was pretty crowded. "Have another cider. Or ask the twins if they need help setting up dessert? They're probably making homemade whipped cream. And they're usually looking for someone to take a turn with the whisk."

Sophie gave me a curious smile. "Okay. I'm on it."

I watched her walk away. She was wearing a pretty plum-colored top that was just a little bit see-through. But I didn't need sheer fabric to picture the smoothness of her skin. I wore the memory of Sophie like an imprint on my soul.

May caught me looking. "It's good that you and Sophie are patching things up," she said quietly.

I turned to look her in the eye. Addicts get really fucking good at eye contact. It's a great cover up. *I'm staring you down, so I couldn't possibly be lying right now.* "Not really," I said. "Tonight is just a fluke."

She squeezed my wrist and plucked a dishtowel off its hook. "You never know. Maybe you two need each other."

"Don't say that," I muttered. "Nobody needs *this.*" What Sophie needed was a train ticket to New York. I still hadn't asked her yet why she wasn't already there. I was afraid to hear the answer—that somehow I'd fucked that up for her, too.

May snapped the towel at my ass. "That's my Eeyore. Always looking on the bright side."

"It's my specialty."

"Wash faster," she said. "They're going to cut the pies soon."

* * *

We stayed through a single round of Who Am I—the game where someone tapes a little slip of paper to your forehead with a famous person's name on it, and you have to ask questions of the other partygoers to figure out who you're supposed to be.

It was just the sort of game that I'd usually begged off from when I'd lived here. But May and Sophie ganged up on me.

"Fine," I caved. "But I get to pick both of yours." So I put "Miley Cyrus" on Sophie's forehead and "President Obama" on May's.

May wrote mine, but Sophie taped it on. When she leaned over me, I got a whiff of green apple shampoo.

"Am I Eeyore?" I asked immediately.

May rolled her eyes. "Too obvious. Try again."

"I need another piece of pie to play this game," I said. "Anyone else?"

They both claimed they couldn't eat another thing, so I helped myself. Zach stood at the dessert table, a scrap of paper taped to his head. It read: *Zac Efron.*

"Let me guess. The twins did yours?"

Zach grinned. He was a man of few words.

"At least yours is flattering. Mine is some asshole, right?"

He shrugged. "Don't ask the former cult member for help with cultural trivia. But I'm pretty sure yours isn't cool."

It took me a single lap around the room to figure out that I was supposed to be Donald Trump. And when Sophie figured hers out, she came over and threw the scrap of paper at me. "*Miley Cyrus?* You made me the worst singer to ever sell a million records? You are *such* a shit, Jude Nickel." She slapped my arm.

"Never said I wasn't."

At that, May gave me an ornery eye roll. "Coffee before you go?"

I shook my head. "We'd better head out."

May hugged me. "I'll find Sophie's coat. Come back next week. Bring Sophie," she added quickly.

My answer was noncommittal. "Thanks, Pooh Bear."

After a fast round of goodbyes, we were headed toward Colebury again. Sophie was quiet in the passenger seat. Rain spattered against the windshield, and I drove slowly again. Once again I was full of food and warmed by company. If I ever described this moment to a treatment counselor, I knew they'd tell me not to forget it. "Even the grimmest lives have moments of beauty," I'd heard an addict say once. "Don't miss 'em."

"That was nice," Sophie said eventually, echoing my thoughts.

"They're good people." I slowed down to exit the highway.

"True." Another beat of silence went by. "Why does May call you Eeyore?"

I snorted. "I don't know. It's just our shtick."

"Are you guys a thing?"

The question made me sit back in surprise. "No way."

"How come?"

Because we're both in love with other people. I couldn't say that, though. "She's a good friend." One of the only ones I had. "She used to drive me to meetings after we worked the farmers' market together."

Sophie's next words were so quiet that I almost didn't hear them. "I'm glad you're getting the help you need."

The streets of Colebury were deserted tonight. I pulled to a stop around the corner from Sophie's house. There was no way I could be seen dropping her off. I killed the engine. The sudden silence closed around us. There was only the gentle tap of raindrops on the car and the knowledge that we were truly alone together for the first time in years.

Sophie sat very still. Her eyes cut to mine, and my heart gave an unwelcome squeeze. Whether it was wise or not, I was sorry the night was over. "How about you?" I asked softly. "Are you getting what you need?"

With a tiny tilt of her head, she looked out the passenger window. "Sometimes," she whispered.

"How come you're still in Vermont?" I asked. "I thought you'd be giving Miley Cyrus a run for her money by now."

"I..." She sighed. "That's not a short conversation."

"You don't have to tell me," I quickly backtracked.

Sophie turned her chin to me one more time. "Thank you for rescuing me tonight."

There was so much vulnerability in her sweet face that I found it difficult to form a reply. I cleared my throat. "I know I screwed up badly, Soph. But if you ever needed my help, there's really nothing I wouldn't do for you." Even at a whisper, my voice cracked on the last word.

Sophie's eyes welled. She put her hand on the door lever. "Goodnight, Jude."

I didn't think I could answer her. So I only raised a hand to push a lock of hair out of her face.

That was my fatal mistake. Because everything changed when I touched her. Sophie's cheek landed in my palm, her skin silky and cool. I shivered at the contact, and Sophie felt it. Her eyes locked onto mine. Pink lips parted, and she bit her bottom lip.

Kissing her wasn't a decision I made. It was just inevitable, the way a clap of thunder follows lightning. We leaned in at the same time. I closed my eyes so that I didn't have to see the little spark of shock on her face. But my blindness changed nothing. *Sophie.* Our lips brushed together on a sigh. And then my mouth melted onto hers. I kissed her so slowly. Once. Then twice. Even in my haze of yearning I knew I should memorize every second.

"Mmm," she whispered. Gentle fingers wove into my hair.

I knew this wasn't allowed, but that only made it sweeter. I touched my tongue to the seam of her lips, asking permission, and she opened for me on a sigh. When our tongues slid together, it only confirmed what I already knew—she tasted like the sweetest gift I'd ever been given.

The first time I ever kissed Sophie was in a car in the rain. That kiss had made my blood surge with lust and hope. But this one made me ache with impossible longing.

Sophie pressed even closer, and I felt my pulse kick up a notch. But this wasn't supposed to happen anymore. *We* weren't supposed to happen.

It killed me, but I gentled the kiss. I wasn't ready to pull away just yet, so we ended up forehead to forehead, our sorrowful gazes mirroring each other. "Goodnight, sweet girl," I whispered. "Be well."

She only blinked at me for a second before slowly straightening up. Without another word, Sophie opened the car door and got out.

The sound of the door closing again reminded me of a jail cell slamming shut.

Chapter Ten

Sophie

Internal DJ tuned to: "Pompeii" by Bastille

I ran through the rain, welcoming the drops that fell on my face. I needed the shock of their chill to slow down my thumping heart. My mind was a dance tune, loud and pulsing with energy. But when I ran up the walk toward our house, its brooding silence began to choke me before I even reached the door.

The porch light glowed the same warm yellow as the neighbors'. Appearances lie, though. There was nothing warm and cozy at our house. Just three people swimming through their own pain. When I closed the door behind me, I flicked off the porch light. I hung up my rain-spattered coat and kicked off my shoes.

I ran through the darkened kitchen and upstairs. In my room, I got ready for bed. Wearing an old T-shirt and flannel shorts, I climbed into my bed in the dark. The T-shirt I'd grabbed was Jude's, of course. I'd stolen his Phish shirt a long time ago when we were still in high school. But it still reminded me of him. *Everything* reminded me of him. I lay there, heart thumping, the taste of him still fresh in my memory.

It was just like high school. I used to come home from our dates all stirred up, my panties damp with unfulfilled desire.

Kissing Jude had been a terrible idea. It was bad enough that I missed having him in my life. I already had the guilt of pining for the guy who killed my brother. But now I found myself thinking about the feel of his rough hand around mine, and the scrape of his stubble against my chin while we kissed.

I rolled over, dropping my face into the pillow. The mattress was firm beneath my hips, and I wished it were Jude underneath me instead of foam and fabric.

Sophie is 17, Jude is 18

Sophie's junior year of high school is all about kissing. They kiss in his car, as punk rock blares from Jude's speakers. They make out until she's gasping with need, her thighs clenching, her fingers stretching out his T-shirt as she clings to him.

This is the year when she realizes how sick she is of being a good girl. She would do anything Jude asks. The only thing that prevents her from stripping him down and fucking him is her own inexperience. She isn't afraid of sex, but she's afraid of doing it wrong.

It's really a miracle that anyone survives her teenage years.

After a frustrating winter of making out in the car, spring arrives. They relocate their make-out sessions to the top of Tapps Hill. A gravel road winds to the top, where a "scenic area" is marked by a sign and a lonely picnic table. On the other side of the road is a clearing secluded by an unruly row of lilac bushes. Jude keeps a picnic blanket in his trunk, and now their make-out sessions go horizontal.

It's glorious.

Sophie loves the press of his hips on hers when he rolls on top of her. She can feel the hard length of his erection through his jeans, and it's both thrilling and terrifying.

They stay there for hours, kissing until their lips are bruised, listening to the peeper frogs singing their chorus in the vernal pools.

Still, things stay pretty civilized until the night she happens to wear a skirt instead of jeans. The costume change isn't premeditated, but if she'd known that Jude would finally put his hands on her, she would have started dressing like the cheerleading team weeks *earlier.*

His hand starts on her knee, then winds slowly up her thigh as they kiss. It seems to take a lifetime until his fingers slip beneath her panties and cup her bottom, rubbing softly.

Sophie whimpers in encouragement. His fingers circle and tease. Then—praise Jesus—they dip between her ass cheeks and slide forward into the slickness that's waiting there. She's ridiculously, embarrassingly wet for him, and Jude makes a sound she's never heard before— a moan so deep and low that her whole body shivers in tune with it.

Jude growls, pulling her body closer to his, rearranging his grip so he can touch her more easily. She's trembling in his arms as his fingers begin to explore all her softest places. She grips his shoulders and pants into his mouth, too turned on to be embarrassed.

His fingertip circles lower and she thrusts her tongue into his mouth to show him how much she likes it. Her entire existence is reduced to bottomless kisses and his questing hand. It's exquisite. With shaking hands she reaches for the button on his jeans and pops it open. Mr. Restraint seems to lose his tight grip on the situation for a moment. His kisses grow wild and clumsy as she lowers his zipper and slides her fingers down the hard length in his underwear.

The wildness of the moment makes her feel crazy. She whimpers into his mouth then breaks their kiss, bringing her lips to Jude's ear and whispering, because some things are easier to say quietly. "Just do it," she begs. "I want to feel you inside me."

Jude groans, biting his lip until she's sure he tastes blood. "We can't yet. You know I want to."

"Nobody has to know."

"Doesn't matter," he rasps. "The chief already assumes the worst. I need to be able to look that fucker in the eye and know I didn't have sex with his baby girl before she turned eighteen." He pushes her hands away

from his erection and sighs.

Sophie is disappointed, and more than a little embarrassed to be turned down. She's never asked for it before, not in words, anyway. "I'm counting the days until my birthday," she grumbles.

"I know." He kisses her then sweeps his thumb between her legs in a slow, torturous circle. She forgets to be embarrassed. "I'm giving you my dick for a present. Gonna tie a bow around it."

She's too turned on to laugh. "Tell me what else you're going to do."

Thinking it over, he rubs his lips over hers until she stops him with a nip to his lower lip. "I'm gonna start by laying you out in the moonlight and kissing you everywhere."

She gasps because she's imagined this very thing too many times to count.

The naughty whisper continues. "I'm going to get you all heated up with my tongue. Then I'm going to slide slowly inside..." Now he pushes a fingertip right where she wants him. "Then I'm going to tell you over and over again how much I love you until you come." Jude's mouth crashes down over hers, and she moans into his mouth.

His kisses are wild and hungry, and his fingers are shameless. She loses herself in his touch, moving her hips in time with his heartbeat until she's shuddering and sobbing his name.

Chapter Eleven

Sophie

Internal DJ stuck on: "Helpless" from Hamilton

After tossing and turning for hours, I finally fell asleep and stayed that way until almost eleven.

When I went downstairs, I was dismayed to find that nobody had put away any of the food. So the day began with me throwing away a dried-out turkey and all the fixings. Fun times for someone who ran a community dinner once a week where every resource was precious.

It took me hours to clean the kitchen after that. I could hear my mother's TV shows in the other room, but I was too angry to go in and make nice with her. As I scrubbed hardened mashed potatoes off the serving bowl, I felt as hopeless as I'd been since the first ugly days after Gavin's death.

Three years later, and my family was still a disaster. No— three and a *half*. Jude's sudden reappearance had made me stop and calculate just how bad things really were.

With the kitchen cleaned, I went into the dining room to consider the gravy splatters on the wall and the rug and the broken crockery by the baseboard. My blood boiled as I knelt on the carpet, picking greasy shards of my mother's gravy boat out of the muck. I threw them away in the kitchen trash.

Then I rested on my knees, wondering how to get gravy out of the rug and off the painted wall. When a voice behind me fired off a question, I was so startled that I jumped.

"Where were you last night?" my father demanded.

"Jesus." I whirled on him. He was leaning against the doorframe, a tumbler of whiskey in his hand. My father almost never drank. But now he looked trashed. His eyes were unfocused, and his shoulders swayed.

"Asked you a question," he slurred. "Where were you?"

"Out. With a friend."

"Who?"

I got to my feet, wary. "My friend Denny," I lied.

"You seeing him?"

"None of your business." One lie, one truth. That was fifty percent more honesty than I used to give my father. I was so tired of ducking his wrath. My father's rage seemed really pathetic all of a sudden. Broken dishes and whiskey. "Why don't you clean this up?" I heard myself ask. Both my mother and I avoided making demands of him. Right at this second, I couldn't remember why.

His face screwed itself into an ugly expression. "Don't change the fucking subject."

"This *is* the fucking subject," I snapped. "I'm not some junior deputy you can order around. And I'm not Cinderella. You want to throw a temper tantrum in your dining room? Fine. But don't expect me to get the stains out."

"Bitch." He moved so fast I didn't see it coming. A loud slap rang out as the side of my face combusted in pain.

Reflexively I grabbed my cheek and lurched backward, colliding with the very wall I'd asked him to clean. The carpet was cold and swampy under my bare feet and I almost slipped as I pivoted to change direction and exit the room. I pushed past him and raced up the stairs, then slammed the door to my bedroom.

Jesus fuck. I hadn't slammed my bedroom door since I was a teenager. The teenaged fights were all about Jude, of course. Now he was back in town, and I was back to fighting with my father.

Rinse, repeat.

That depressing realization sent me to my messy bed, where I curled up, pressing a hand to my stinging cheek.

I have to get out of here. That was abundantly clear. I was three weeks away from graduation, at which time I would probably have no job. When the hospital chose Denny over me for the full-time slot, I'd need a backup plan and a new place to live. I'd stayed in this house too long.

After a while there was a gentle tap on the door. "Sophie?"

For a moment I didn't answer. What would my mother do if I moved out? Would she even remember to feed herself? "What?"

She opened the door and took two steps inside. Then she closed the door behind her. "Don't do that," she whispered.

"What?" I sat up on the bed.

She shook her head, the bags under her eyes standing out like purple moons on her face. "Don't rile up your father. I can't take the noise."

And here I'd thought I couldn't get more upset. "Don't *even*," I sputtered. "I don't have to take his bullshit." *Or yours.*

"He's your father."

Oh, please. "He's my *jailer.*" Hell. "Mom, do you know what an enabler is?"

She just looked at me with dull eyes.

"No? Well, look it up. Because I think I'm yours." I got off the bed. "I'm going to shower. Kindly step aside."

She didn't move, and my blood pressure spiked once more. I was just *done*. Putting two hands on her shoulders, I nudged her aside. Then I opened my bedroom door and slipped out.

In the shower, my anger burned hotter than the water. Something had to give. But the something was always me.

Chapter Twelve

Jude

Cravings Meter: 4

During the night, all that rain turned to snow. And when it fell onto a surface that wasn't quite frozen, the roadway would become slick as hell and all the car accidents would happen. Today the cops and tow trucks would be busy with fender benders and irate drivers who didn't take the weather into consideration when they stepped on the accelerator.

I should talk, though. I'd managed to drive my Porsche into a tree at fifty miles per hour on a clear May evening.

The snow brought business into our garage in spite of the holiday weekend. It wasn't even ten thirty when some poor woman wearing hair curlers pulled a late-model Volvo into the drive. There was a big dent in the fender and scratches, too.

"I slid into the stone wall that rings our property," she said. "Can you fix it?"

I ran my hand over the dent. It wasn't all that bad. "Sure. I can pop it out and fix the paint. But if you want like-new perfection, you'd need to replace the fender. That means ordering parts."

She wrung her hands. "My husband gets home from visiting his mother tomorrow," she said. "Is there any way you could do it today?" Her blue eyes begged me to say yes. Either her husband was an evil troll, or she'd made a habit of running expensive cars into stationary objects.

"I'll do my best," I hedged. At least the paint was black. I should be able to match it with what we had on hand.

I called her a taxi and then went happily to work on her dent. Someone else's misfortune was a boon for me. Busy hands were the only thing keeping me sane today. I turned the garage radio up loud and slipped a rod up under the wheel well of the Volvo. The hours rolled by as I tinkered with my repair job.

My father didn't come into the garage all day. Not once. I took one break for nuked food, but otherwise I worked on that dent until late afternoon. I did a kickass job. When the woman returned for her car, she didn't even blink at the price for five hours of my labor.

"It looks great," she gushed. "Thank you so much."

I put her check in the till then drove through a fast-food place for dinner. Back in my room, the usual itch came back. It wasn't too bad—maybe a three out of ten. But the holiday weekend stretched out before me, long and empty. And the memory of kissing Sophie last night in my car tortured me.

A bottle of whiskey would take care of that, my asshole brain suggested.

I stretched out on my bed with an old copy of Joseph Conrad's *The Heart of Darkness*. It wasn't exactly a light read, but I didn't mind. I was just getting to the creepiest part when I heard the creak of someone's footsteps climbing the stairs to my room.

The hair stood up on the back of my neck, and I set the book down. I couldn't think of a soul who would visit me here. If it happened to be an old friend from my past, chances were that I wouldn't want to see him.

When the knock came, it wasn't gentle. "Jude?" The voice was female.

Sophie.

I jumped off the bed and pulled open the door. And there she stood in the dark, arms crossed, looking up at me with big, angry eyes.

"Hi?" I said, confused.

Before I knew what was happening, she stepped over the threshold. Sophie kicked the door shut and then leaned against it. "Are you staying in Colebury?" she demanded. "I have to know."

"Uh." *Shit.* "I don't have much choice. No other garage will hire me."

My brain was playing catch-up. But my body was clueing in to the fact that Sophie and I were barely two feet apart and standing within spitting distance of the bed where we'd had more sex than sleep. Her chest rose and fell with quick breaths, and her cheeks were flushed.

Wait—one cheek was redder than the other. Was that a handprint? I pushed the hair away from her face for a closer look. "What the fuck?" I whispered. "Who did that?"

"Who do you think?" Her words were like little chips of ice.

Jesus. "Your father?" With a gentle thumb, I traced the outline of what must have been a horrible slap. "Did you tell him you were with...?"

"No! I'm not an *idiot.*" She grabbed my wrist and flung my hand away from her face. Then she grabbed my flannel shirt in two hands and looked up into my eyes. Her gaze was fiery and fierce. "Can you be the *one* person who doesn't make me feel stupid today?"

Time paused like a held breath as Sophie's hands pressed against my body, their warmth searing my pecs. We stared at each other while confusion rippled through me. And then everything got even more complicated. Sophie rose to her toes and yanked me into a kiss.

I'd never been so stunned. The feel of her soft mouth on mine was so unexpected and yet so familiar it was too much to bear. As our lips did a slow slide together, my breath hitched. But I couldn't pull back. *One more taste*, my asshole brain suggested. Bracing both of my palms against the door, I leaned into her sweet mouth.

She opened for me immediately. When our tongues touched, I had the sensation of falling or running too fast downhill. She tasted like Sophie. She tasted like the best thing that had ever happened to me.

Warm hands curled around my biceps. When I nipped her lip, she whimpered, and my dick perked up like a lonely stray who suddenly smelled a feast. I thrust my tongue against hers, and she moaned into my mouth. Her hands went to the buttons on my shirt.

That's when I remembered who I was, and just how bad an idea this was.

Although it hurt me, I dragged my mouth off Sophie's. Angling to the side, I leaned my forehead against the cool metal door. Our bodies were still pressed together, but as long as I didn't kiss her, I could probably have a lucid thought or two.

Her hands went still on my ribcage, their warmth burning through my shirt. "Jude," she whispered. "What happened to saying you'd do anything for me?"

To the surface of the door I said, "That's still true."

Her fingers wandered up the centerline of my chest and then down again. She was trying to kill me, and surely I deserved it. "Then why did you stop?"

Wasn't it obvious? There was no way in hell that Sophie and I could be together. It didn't matter that I was still in love with her. And it didn't matter that we had always had the sort of combustible attraction for one another that was immortalized in rock songs. "Why are you here? Serious question."

She made an angry sound. "Why was I *ever* here? Because we want each other."

"Not all the things we want are good for us."

"No kidding. But who does it hurt?"

Me, I thought immediately. Just having her here in my room hurt so bad. I was bleeding out memories. The taste of her cherry lip gloss on my tongue. The scent of her hair enveloping me. We'd spent so many hours in this room burning up the sheets.

"Who does it hurt?" she repeated. "Not my brother. He's gone. And not my family. They don't give a fuck about me anymore."

My heart broke at the sound of that. But I'd given up my

right to weigh in on her family drama the day her brother died. I stood up tall and looked her square in the eye. "Soph, I'd give you anything. But I don't have a lot to give." That was the God's honest truth.

We were so close together—pancaked together—that she was able to state her purpose in the softest whisper ever heard. "I haven't been properly fucked in three years, Jude. After all that's happened, are you going to make me beg?"

I swear I practically burst into flames at the sound of her sweet mouth whispering *fuck*. It took all my effort to keep my hands on that door. I wanted to yank the clothes off her body instead. "You haven't been fucked in three years?" I repeated on a whisper. I pressed my forehead to hers and stared down into those eyes at close range.

She blinked up at me. "I said *properly*."

Jesus Christ. She'd issued a fucking *challenge*. She'd always pushed my buttons effortlessly. I'd do anything for my girl.

A small voice in my head corrected that notion. *Anything except for the one thing she needed most from you. Sobriety.*

But it was easy to push that thought aside, because Sophie had just made me picture someone else's hands on her skin. God, how I loathed that idea. My fingers itched to reclaim what was mine. I wanted to cover her with my body. Touch her everywhere.

My self-control was perilously close to breaking. How utterly familiar.

"Jude," she whispered, and those naughty hands coasted down the center of my belly until her hand skimmed over the waistband of my jeans, then lower, finally covering my rock-hard cock. "It's just sex."

My heart broke again when she said that. There was no such thing as "just sex" with her. Not for me.

She popped the button on my jeans, and I squeezed my eyes shut. If she thought a good fuck was the best I had to offer her, it was hard to argue that point.

And who said I didn't know my place in the world?

Sophie unzipped me, and I let her. But then I caught her

questing hands in mine and kissed her again. She whimpered at the first slide of our lips together. As our tongues tangled, I put my hands on her hips and backed into my room, towing her with me. She tried to push me toward the bed, but I wasn't having that. Too much like the old days. I caught her jaw in my hand and dove into her mouth for our deepest kiss. *One* more taste. That was all I allowed myself. If she wanted to do this, we were going to do it my way.

I grabbed her jacket and shucked it to the floor. Seizing her hips, I turned her around to face my dresser. There were two clean shirts on top but I swept them to the floor. Sophie caught on right away. She dropped her elbows to the surface for me.

"Good girl," I murmured, tracing a hand down her ass. Her response was a moan. She was wearing a sweater dress that felt soft under my fingers. "Gonna fuck you just like this," I growled, lifting the dress. There was a pair of tights underneath, so I grabbed the waistband and shoved them down. No panties. There was only soft, smooth skin and her perfect, round ass in my hands. I wrapped one hand around her hip and slid my palm down her belly, into the trimmed V of soft hair. She whimpered when my fingers met wet pussy. And I groaned like the horny beast I was.

That was it. My conscious mind gave up the fight and let my desperate body take over. My mouth found the back of Sophie's neck, my lips worshipping her soft skin. She dropped her head, moaning, as I teased her sweet body with my fingers. I circled through her slickness, desire pounding in my ears.

Mine, mine, mine, chanted my asshole brain.

With my free hand I yanked my jeans and briefs down just far enough to release my aching cock. Sophie pushed her ass into my crotch, trying to get closer. We were a tangle of half-shed clothes and raging need. But there was still one detail to manage.

Until now I'd avoided looking into the tarnished, old mirror over the dresser, because I knew that staring into her eyes would only make this tougher on me. But now I met Sophie's reflection. "Do you still have…" When we were together, she'd gotten an IUD.

"Yeah, go on," she panted. In the hazy mirror, her eyes begged, trapping mine in their tractor beam of desire. So I was staring right at her as I bent my knees, lined up and teased her clit with the head of my dick.

Her eyes went half-mast with pleasure, and her lips slackened. It was the sexiest fucking thing I'd ever seen. My heart beat so hard that I could feel it in my ears. Sophie pushed back against me, so full of wanting that I couldn't stop myself from doing it.

For the first time in years I pushed inside a girl. *My* girl. The clutch of her wet, velvet pussy was everything I'd ever wanted. This moment was never supposed to happen again, and I didn't have any idea why it was happening now. But I broke out in a sweat as a new wave of lust washed over me.

I had to brace, tightening every muscle in my abdomen, barely staving off climax. And I had to break Sophie's gaze, tipping my head back. I took a few seconds to inspect the old plaster ceiling overhead.

With a couple of deep breaths I held myself together.

Sophie went still. And when I dropped my chin, I found her staring at me. "Okay?" she mouthed.

"Sure," I lied, snapping my hips forward, taking myself deep.

The sudden force meant that Sophie had to grab the dresser to brace herself. I liked that, so I did it again. This is what she wanted, after all. *It's just sex*, she'd said.

It's just sex. It's just sex.

Repeating that would be the only way to keep my eyes dry. "This what you wanted?" I grunted.

"*Yes*," she gasped. Her knuckles were white where she held the dresser, and her eyes were shut. "More."

"I got more." With every thrust I heard myself give a breathy grunt.

"Jude," she moaned, and I gritted my teeth.

See? I could have raw, angry sex with the love of my life. Slowing things down, I held onto her hips, my wet cock gliding slowly in and out. *It's just sex*. But it was so sweet I knew I couldn't last much longer. "You want my hands on you?" I murmured.

"Yessss," she whispered, her heavy-lidded eyes finding me in the mirror again.

"Yeah? Where." Sophie whimpered, pushing her ass back to meet me. "I can't hear you, pretty girl. Where do you want me to touch you?" I dug my fingers into the flesh of her hips. "Here?"

She shook her head clumsily.

I'd had enough of her sweater dress. I tugged and she lifted her arms off the dresser so I could yank that sucker over her head. There was only a little black bra underneath, and I had it off and flung away a few seconds later. There was something nice and dirty about getting her so naked while I was still dressed. In the mirror her tits bounced with every one of my thrusts, and I groaned at the sight of it.

"Touch me." Her voice was a throaty gasp, and I had to grit my teeth against the urge to come.

"Where?" I grunted. My body was on fire. With one hand I yanked my shirt over my head just so I wouldn't burn to the ground. But that was a mistake, because now so much of Sophie's skin touched mine. In the mirror, I could see my body straining against hers.

Fuck.

Sophie grabbed one of my hands and yanked it down her body until my fingers grazed her wet clit. I began to touch her, swirling my fingertips over that swollen bud, dipping down to coat myself in her wetness before teasing her again.

"Harder," she begged.

"Yes, ma'am." This sex slave was glad to oblige. I was so hard it hurt. My balls ached for release. I braced one hand on the dresser beside hers and pumped hard into her. The other hand I curved around her sex, my fingers sliding against all that was left of our once golden connection. I could feel the force of my dick hammering home. She had once been all mine, and I'd squandered it.

Bearing down, I reached for the end of my pain. I was approaching the point of no return, and I no longer cared about anything but release.

"Oh," Sophie sobbed. I felt her shudder beneath me. She sagged against the dresser, moaning.

Someone bellowed, and it must have been me. *Jesus fuck.* Release roared through me and the room swam with the force of it.

Then we were both bent over the dresser, half ruined and breathing hard. With the last bit of my energy I wrapped an arm around Sophie's waist and dragged her backward three steps until we both toppled onto the bed. I kicked off my jeans because I was too hot and too sensitive to have anything touching my body.

With a sigh, Sophie rolled onto what used to be her side of the bed, her body curled so that she faced the door. We'd ended up exactly where I hadn't wanted us to land, slotting ourselves right into position in both my bed and my memory.

But I was too spent to mind very much. I was still coming down from a powerful orgasm—the body's best natural drug. Endorphins smoothed out my ragged edges, leaving me limp and peaceful. Sophie's legs were tangled with mine, and without thinking I stroked the arch of her foot with my own. A silent minute passed and then another. Sleep was about to become a real possibility when I saw Sophie's back contract sharply. I put my hand on it and felt her move again. A jerk. A *sob.*

She was crying absolutely silently.

Acting on instinct, I hiked my body closer to hers, tucked her hips into my groin and dropped an arm over her waist. It was the classic position for offering comfort. Too bad I'd fucked up both our lives so completely three and a half years ago that I had no meaningful comfort to offer.

Her next sob was not at all silent. It was a raw, primal sound.

And it tore me right in half.

"Shh," I said, kissing her shoulder. That was all I had for her. A "shh." Useless.

"I'm sorry," she gasped. "I shouldn't have come."

I couldn't really disagree. She shouldn't be here in my room or in my life. Crying was a pretty sane reaction. "I know it's hard. Some shit is just sad, and there's nothing you can do." I felt my own failure in my chest like a knife.

"I'm so *angry* at you," she sobbed.

"I know, baby. I deserve it."

"You refused my *letters.*"

Shit. I pressed my hand against her back. "Soph, I didn't throw them out of my cage like an angry monkey, okay? I was detoxing. Cold turkey. And there were all these things I was supposed to take care of—a visitors' list and forms." I swept her silky hair off her neck and squeezed the muscles in her shoulder. God, the view of her body lying here was so familiar it ached. But the ache was like a sore muscle after a workout—necessary and not altogether bad. "See, I was busy throwing up for three weeks. I couldn't take care of business like I was supposed to."

Sophie seemed to calm down enough to listen to me. She sniffed quietly, and her breathing slowed.

"Nobody really explains anything in there, either," I said, whispering. "I hadn't signed for your letters yet, and I wasn't sure if I should. I didn't think I deserved anything from you. And when I finally got well enough to ask somebody about them, they said it was too late. And I figured it was just as well. I wasn't any good for you, anyway."

I could hear her trying to calm down. She took a deep, slow breath. "But nobody *else* was good for me either. I spent weeks wondering where you'd gone and what had really happened. Nobody ever answered my questions. And nobody wanted to hear that I was sad. No one will say your name at my house."

Who could blame them?

"And you wouldn't speak to me. That was just *cruel.*"

The knife in the center of my chest gave a twist. All I could do was hold her a little closer and apologize again. "I'm sorry I left you all alone. But I chose that shit I was putting up my nose over everything else. I didn't know how to stop."

Her voice was raw when she spoke. "You could have told me you needed help."

As if. Now I told her a big lie. "If I'd been able to admit it, you would have been the one I'd told." But the truth was exactly the opposite. Sophie was always going to be the *last* person in my life to know. I'd have let everyone else down first. She'd always put me on a pedestal I knew I didn't deserve. But it had been my plan to stay there. I would have never let her see my ugly side if I could help it.

Turns out I couldn't.

"I loved you so much," she said.

Loved. The word made my eyes sting. Her use of the past tense wasn't a shock. But it hurt all the same.

Maybe she was waiting for a response from me, but I didn't have one to give. And now I was just *spent*—drained both in body and soul. I lay there just holding her, struggling to keep my eyes open.

"I need to go home," she said eventually. "My father will freak out again if he comes home from second shift and I'm not there." She sighed.

That woke me up again. "Are you safe there?"

She sighed. "Yeah. It was just a slap when I got in his face."

Damn it. Wasn't that how it always began? "Why do you live there, anyway?"

Her voice was flat. "My mother is not doing well. After sophomore year, I moved home to help her out. It's a long story."

That was the only kind we had anymore.

Sophie extracted herself from my embrace, sat up and flung her legs over the side of the bed. Then she grabbed her tangled tights off the floor and began pulling them on.

I stumbled to a standing position and shook out her dress. She took it without meeting my eyes. I pulled on my jeans over nothing and zipped myself up. *The aftermath.* Sophie and I used to curl up together in my bed and fall asleep. This felt tawdry.

After slipping on her bra and dropping the dress over her head, she sat there on the edge of my bed a minute longer, biting her lip.

I sat down beside her.

"Sorry I brought my bag of crazy to your door," she said softly, her sad eyes finding me again.

"My bag of crazy barely sneezes at yours," I whispered. "And I hadn't had sex in over three years, so..."

She let out a strangled laugh, but her eyes got wet again. She jumped to her feet. "I'm going to go now. Maybe I'll see you at the church." Stuffing her feet into her shoes, she grabbed her coat off the floor. "Goodbye, Jude."

I stood up as she put her hand on the door. She hesitated for just a second, so I stepped into her space and I kissed her on the forehead. "Take care of yourself."

Her sigh weighed a ton and a half. "You too."

Then she was gone. And I was left with a bed that smelled like her and no reason to hope that she'd ever be back.

Chapter Thirteen

Jude

Cravings Meter: 5-6

"Who had a good week?"

Very few hands went up in the basement of the church.

"Who had a tough week?"

I found myself raising my hand, participating for the first time ever. But how could I not raise my hand? This had been one of the longest weeks of my life.

The discussion leader nodded. "That's how it is the first week of December, my friends. The holiday season is hard. Every single year. The expectations. The family togetherness."

"The drunk uncles. The eggnog," a guy in the front row put in. He received a quiet chuckle for his efforts.

"Who wants to share how their week was difficult?" Ms. Librarian's eyes locked onto mine. "Would you like to say something?" she asked me.

That's what I got for raising my hand for the first time. "My name is Jude, and I'm an addict. Started with opiates. In prison I switched to heroin." I cleared my throat. "The cravings were bad this week..." That wasn't a good explanation for the problem, though. "I mean... they're always bad. It's just that this week I felt like I forgot why it matters so much. It was harder to remember why I fight them at all." *Fuck*. That was a little more honesty than I needed to spew. That was the trouble with participating. I could never figure out where to stop.

"Okay," she said. "Why *do* you fight the cravings? Tell us your goal. Saying it out loud helps me sometimes."

"I don't want to go back to jail," I said. That was a good enough reason for anyone.

"Sure, but what do you want instead?"

"Uh." I regretted raising my hand. "I want the cravings to stop. I want a better job and a nicer place to live. *Fuck*, I might as well ask for a purple pony."

Several people laughed, but not Linda Librarian. "There are so many people in this town that have all those things. Why not you?"

"Because I have a felony conviction?" Now I was scowling at a nice older lady. *Nice*. Note to self: do not engage. That way lies the abyss.

"Be kind to yourself," she said. "Especially this month. I've made a list for myself." She pulled a piece of paper from her back pocket and read from it. "Watch an old movie. Eat a good meal. Get outside. Stay away from toxic substances and toxic *people*."

"Amen," muttered someone else.

I stopped listening. Some days I was able to get on the bandwagon and take some hope with me when I left this room. But today wasn't going to be one of those days. The week had been a string of long hours in the garage, each one of them tainted by the itch. It was like a fly buzzing in my ear. I'd swat at it, occasionally thinking I'd won. But a few minutes later it would be back, the sound of its tiny wings like torture.

Sophie's visit wasn't exactly to blame. Her brief, explosive presence couldn't make my body want drugs any more than it already did. But it had depressed me. Hearing her cry wrecked me. It forced me to see for myself how badly I'd hurt her. I couldn't fantasize about her happy life in the big city anymore.

I'd always thought that *one* of us could end up getting what we wanted. But even that was too much to ask.

At the front of the room, someone prattled on about finding

his purpose in life. I looked at the clock on the wall, counting the minutes until the hour was over. The week may have been grueling, but Wednesday night was almost here.

Before she'd left my room on Friday night, Sophie had said, "Maybe I'll see you at the church."

I'd thought she'd say *please don't come to the church.* But she didn't.

And now the hour of power here in the basement was almost done. I sat up straighter in my chair and waited to be dismissed. Whether it was a good idea or not, I was heading up to the kitchen after this. I told myself that I needed to see her face and to know that she was okay.

But, fuck. I really just wanted to see her.

"Let's not let this month undo all our good work," the leader was saying. "We can handle this. It's December second. We've got thirty days of the holiday season to survive. Next week I'm bringing cookies to rally us. But not *holiday* cookies! Fuck that."

She got a chuckle for dropping an f-bomb. But there was something else she'd just said that suddenly had me paying attention. It was December second.

Sophie's birthday.

I sat there in my folding chair wondering how Sophie celebrated her birthday these days. The first time I ever watched her blow out a candle she was turning seventeen. That was six years ago, but it felt like a lifetime. We'd just started seeing each other, and she'd made sure I knew it was her birthday. I'd brought a fancy bakery cupcake to school in a plastic box so it wouldn't get crushed. At lunch we sat in my car so I could light a candle for her and taste the frosting on her lips after she ate it.

We'd been impossibly young.

Twice more after that we celebrated her birthday together, each one involving greater amounts of nudity.

While I was busy getting a little lost in my head, the meeting broke up. I stacked my folding chair with the others and followed everyone up the stairs. Maybe Sophie wouldn't even be in the kitchen tonight if she had birthday plans.

At the top of the stairs I headed down the hall toward the kitchen door. I peeked through the oblong window and saw her in there, spatula in hand, standing over the stove.

The sight of her flooded me with inappropriate relief. It was stupid of me to care where Sophie spent her birthday. In fact, I ought to be rooting for her to have a night out somewhere with friends. But the sight of her made me happy. I lived for Wednesdays and Thursdays. Pathetic as that was, a weekly glimpse of Sophie (along with some quality time with the Shipleys) kept me sane.

Instead of pushing open the kitchen door, I turned around and walked out of the church. It was five minutes after five. Where could a guy find a birthday cake at this hour?

I didn't have my car with me, so a trip to Foodway wasn't going to work. And since Colebury, Vermont was postage-stamp sized, there was really only one option.

Trotting the two blocks toward Main Street, I found the storefront I was looking for. Crumbs looked like an expensive little bakery. It hadn't been here before I went to prison. And I was pretty sure I was on a fool's errand. Indeed, when I reached the door, the little front seating area was dark. The sign in the window indicated they'd closed at five. But I still saw lights on in back. So I knocked on the front door. When nobody came, I knocked again. Harder.

Finally, a harried-looking woman in an apron emerged, squinting at the front to try to figure out who was pounding. She walked over to the glass door but did not open it. "We're closed," she mouthed.

"I really need a birthday cake," I yelled. "Please?" I gave her my best harmless smile, but that wasn't easy for me. I've never looked harmless.

The woman wavered. I saw the indecision flicker in her eyes. "Come around back," she said finally.

She didn't have to ask me twice. I jogged around the building, finding a metal door in the alleyway. She opened it, still looking worried.

"I'm sorry," I said immediately. "I forgot someone's birthday, and she's really important to me."

The woman rolled her eyes. "If this is some kind of trick, it's pretty much the lowest thing I've ever heard. And karma is my middle name."

"Karma and I are well acquainted," I assured her.

She smiled. "When I said karma was my middle name, I meant it literally."

"What?"

She tapped the nametag on her apron, which read *K.K.* "This stands for Katy Karma. Look." She grabbed her pocketbook from under the counter and flipped it open.

I peered at her driver's license. Sure enough, it read Kathryn Karma White. "Shut the front door," I teased.

"Weird right? So which cake do you want?" She beckoned me over to a refrigerator with a glass door. "There's a Black Forest cake—that has cherries in the middle. Or German chocolate. Both are twenty-five dollars. You got cash?"

Shit. "I have ten bucks cash and a credit card."

She sighed. "Cash register is shut down already."

This was never going to work. *Sophie, I failed you again. Story of my life.* "Okay—I'll leave my card here, and you can charge it tomorrow. And I'll leave my ten bucks too."

She heaved a big sigh. "If you get me fired..."

"I know. Karma."

"Which one do you want?"

"Black Forest," I said quickly. "She likes cherries."

"Lemme get a box."

Ten minutes later I was walking back into the church, feeling kind of stupid. Sophie probably had an entire birthday party planned. But hey, nobody could have too much cake. The other people in the kitchen would probably like it.

"Please tell me that's a pie and that Ruthie Shipley made it." Father Peters came toward me in the hallway, his grin wide.

"Sorry to disappoint." His smile was contagious. "This is second best." I glanced toward the kitchen. "It's Sophie's birthday. During cleanup, would you mind..." I held out the box. "It should be, um, from all of us."

Father Peters took the box from me, looking thoughtful. "I didn't know it was Sophie's birthday. I was with her mother a couple of hours ago, and she didn't mention it."

"December second," I said. "I'm positive."

The old man nodded slowly. "All right. I'll dig up a candle."

Candles? Fuck! "Thank you, sir."

I washed my hands in the men's room and then ducked into the kitchen. Sophie didn't even notice. And that's as it should be.

Chapter Fourteen

Sophie

Internal DJ tuned to: Ingrid Michaelson's "Be OK"

It hadn't been easy for me to walk into the church kitchen tonight. My face was burning before I even preheated the oven.

I'd gone to Jude's place and begged him for sex. Then I'd burst into tears.

Who does that?

So much for showing him what he'd given up. The only thing I'd showed him was that I was *nuts*.

To make matters worse, I'd had to arrive early to start the lasagna. It was a Community Dinner favorite, but it took a lot longer to make than our other dishes. So I had that much more time to let my embarrassment marinate. When five o'clock arrived, I browned sausage meat while watching the door.

As always, I both dreaded and craved the moment that Jude would fill the doorway. Lately I was even worse than I'd been in high school, when I used to live for the day's first glimpse of him. Later—my first year of college in Burlington— I used to wish away the week's worth of classes so that I could duck into his car on Friday nights and spend the weekend in his bed.

Those were the days when I felt invincible. It had been Jude who finally convinced me to talk to my father about music school. "You can either keep doing what your parents want, or you can be a singer. At some point you have to choose," he'd pointed out.

He wasn't wrong. So I'd screwed up my courage and brought up Juilliard to my father. To my surprise, he'd made a deal with me: if I completed two years at the University of Vermont with excellent grades, he'd pay for Juilliard, as long as I saved up to help with my New York City rent.

And I was *ecstatic*. Suddenly, a life onstage seemed possible. The next few months were so thrilling that it took me a while to notice that Jude wasn't doing so well. He'd seemed to retreat into himself. And eventually I'd figured out that the time he spent with his sketchy friends involved substances other than cheap beer and the occasional bong.

Once I even asked him point blank if his friends were into pills. I'd seen things passed from hand to hand. But I was still trying to give Jude the benefit of the doubt. He'd brushed aside my question. "There's some recreational stuff. Nothing to worry about."

So I didn't.

My bag of crazy sneezes at yours, he'd said the other night. But my training in social work had taught me that anyone can be tested by life. Nobody is invincible. Jude hadn't handled his pain in a very productive way, but he also hadn't had any help.

Not even from me, who'd loved him best.

Jude was a convict now. That was never going away. It killed me to know his criminal record was a permanent mark against his character, because there was a lot of good in Jude.

He might tell you to your face that he wasn't a nice guy, but I knew that was just a front. And here I was, making lasagna, thinking about Jude. *Again*. Gah.

At least now I was thinking about his *character*. I'd spent much of the last four days thinking about his naked body. Monday I'd caught myself staring into space at work, distracted by the memory of his strong arms bracing me against the dresser. When he'd taken off his shirt, I'd been stunned to see all that muscle. He looked like Super Jude. And in the mirror, I'd watched his expression as he'd teased me. He'd closed his eyes and turned his face to the side, the way you turn your eyes from a harsh light. But his beautiful mouth had fallen open with pleasure, and his chest rose and fell with each labored breath.

He was beautiful. And as much as I regretted acting like a crazy woman, I'd be savoring that image for a long time.

Denny showed up to help with the cooking, and that got me out of my head a little. He had taken most of the day off at the hospital to do school work. "How's the thesis-writing going?"

"Good. How are you, anyway? You've been quiet this week."

"I'm fine. Just busy." *Busy thinking about the sex I had with the man I'm not supposed to want. And busy feeling grumpy that my family forgot my birthday.*

If I told Denny it was my birthday, he'd whip up some kind of impromptu celebration, probably involving a marching band and a piñata. But I didn't want to be that girl, and a twenty-third birthday wasn't all that important.

Still, the people who are supposed to love you ought to remember.

I'd spent the morning grinning at my phone, since my college friends all sent me funny pictures and jokes. My besties asked me when I was going to come and visit them in Philadelphia, Boston and L.A.

"Maybe after my graduation is official," I'd replied. If I were jobless, I'd have the time for a trip, if not the cash.

My graduation would be another thing my parents would ignore. Since my brother never got his, it would be too painful for them to acknowledge mine.

Denny helped me with the cooking. He boiled the noodles while I finished browning the meat. Then we began opening giant cans of sauce.

"That's a good look for you," I teased Denny, pointing at the frilly apron he'd put on over his clothes.

"Sauce stains," he complained. "It's the only apron I could find." Gamely, he layered the noodles into one giant pan while I did the same in another.

"What are we serving on the side?" he asked.

"There's spinach. A farmer donated the last of his crop. But it needs to be washed and chopped."

"Should I ask...?" His eyes flicked toward the back corner.

Jude had not appeared the first ten times I'd looked for

him. But now I turned my head and there he was. Jude stood behind the prep counter, tying a bandanna over his hair. He wore a tight-fitting T-shirt reading "Norwich Farmers' Market, Est. 1977." His biceps flexed as he fiddled with the knot behind his head.

A fine sweat broke out on my back.

Fuck.

"Soph?"

"Right," I said a little too quickly. "Yeah. He should, um, take care of the veggies. The spinach is in the, uh, walk-in." I gave Denny a little shove in Jude's direction.

For the next hour, I tried to steer clear of Jude. But it didn't work out so well. The eggs I needed to stir into the ricotta cheese were stacked up on the prep table. When I headed back there my traitorous eyes locked on his big hands as they piled cut spinach into a kitchen bin. Those hands had been *all* over my body in the very recent past.

Yikes.

"Evening," Jude said, his voice low and steady.

"Evening," I repeated as casually as possible. *Nope! I'm not thinking about you bending me over any furniture right now. No sir.* I picked up the carton of eggs.

"You have any garlic?"

"What?" I raised my eyes.

His gorgeous eyes blinked down at me. "Fresh garlic. For the spinach. It will taste bland otherwise."

"Um, I'll check." Setting the eggs back down, I spun around and headed into the supply closet. Alone inside, I took a deep breath and scanned the shelves for garlic. There was garlic *powder*, but that wouldn't taste nearly as good. It took me far too long to notice a cardboard box at my feet filled with—wait for it—about two dozen bulbs of garlic.

I grabbed a few of them and trotted back out to the kitchen, proud of myself. They landed with a thunk on the prep table.

It wasn't until I returned to the ricotta cheese that I realized I didn't have any eggs. They were back on the prep table.

"Forget something?" Jude asked when I returned for them.

"Uh-huh." I watched as he raised the flat side of the knife, then brought it down with a smack onto a big clove of garlic. I was just about to ask why he'd do that when he picked up the clove and casually flicked the skin off of it. That was a neat trick. Removing the skin from a clove of garlic usually took me ten minutes and at least as many curses.

And now I was staring.

With my eggs in hand, I ran off to go back to work. I broke eight eggs into a mixing bowl. But the Gods of awkwardness weren't done with me yet. I needed a whisk, and those were kept in one of the drawers under the prep table. Probably.

Once again, I circled the prep table, where Jude was mincing salt and garlic together into a fine paste. I tapped one of the drawers. "If you could take a half step to the right..." My face was burning up again—just the side effect of my stupidity.

Jude moved and I opened the drawer only to find it full of chopsticks.

"Um," I said, closing it. I walked around behind him to the other side. "Sorry..."

He shifted his body out of my way for a second time, his hands still busy with the knife and cutting board.

There wasn't quite enough space for me to get the whisk. "Jude, I really just need another inch."

His response came in a voice so low that I almost couldn't hear him. "That's not what you said the other night, baby."

I grabbed the whisk from the drawer as his words sank in. But when my feeble brain took in the ridiculous joke he'd made, I positively *erupted* with laughter. First, a gasp. Then a choked-out snort.

Then? Unrestrained giggling.

Jude kept on mincing garlic, but I saw the sides of his mouth twitch.

The problem was that I couldn't stop. All the stress I'd held in these past couple of weeks came pouring out. Howling now, my stomach contracted against my will, and I had to put a hand on the counter to steady myself. Trust Jude to make that joke in a *church*.

For a minute there, I couldn't even breathe. Trying to calm

down, I watched Jude scrape the garlic into a ramekin. "You gonna be okay?" he muttered.

Was I? It was probably too soon to tell. I flicked tears off my face and forced myself to quiet down. But even as I took a deep breath, shudders of follow-up hysteria threatened. Clutching the whisk, I pushed off the counter. In a tiny show of solidarity, I touched his arm on my way past him.

I felt a tingle of warmth in my body from even that ridiculously brief contact. God, I was such a wreck.

Back at my own workstation, I whisked the eggs and tried to breathe slowly. But I still felt the twitch of raucous laughter threatening me. And when I turned around, I caught Jude watching me, his eyes twinkling. And a new burble of laughter escaped from my belly.

"What on earth is so funny?" Denny asked, the ruffled apron askew on his waist. That too made me want to laugh.

"Nothing," I gasped. "Just... let's not forget to make one of these pans vegetarian. I think there's some zucchini."

That only made me wonder what rude joke Jude might make about zucchini. I held in another bout of laughter while Denny stirred ricotta cheese into beaten eggs. I felt lightheaded from all the laughter and more than a little crazy. But alive. That was the effect Jude had always had on me. He made the world a weirder, rowdier, more unpredictable place.

"Let's cheese up these babies," Denny said, holding a spatula like a sword, pointing it into the lasagna pan.

"Lead on."

* * *

If you'd asked me five years ago where I'd spend my twenty-third birthday, I would have guessed I'd be out clubbing in the Big Apple or performing on Broadway. That's where I'd always thought my life would go. There were a whole lot of complicated reasons why it hadn't.

Instead, I served at least two hundred rectangles of lasagna. As it happens, handing a plate of hot food to someone who needs one is really a lot of fun. Maybe working at a Community Dinner isn't very glam, but I'd recommend it as a birthday activity to anyone who's borderline depressed. There were two hundred happy people at my birthday party, even if none of them knew we were celebrating.

By the time Mrs. Walters and I were nearly through scrubbing baked-on cheese from the lasagna pans, I was tired but not unhappy.

"Don't anyone leave just yet," Father Peters said as he passed by. "There's something I need to show all of you. Give me five minutes."

I was just wiping down the serving station's glass sneeze guard when I smelled a whiff of something like matches or fire. Given last week's disaster, that had me turning around in a hurry. But the only thing on fire was a candle. And it was sitting on top of a gorgeous chocolate cake decorated with cherries.

In a big baritone, Father Peters began to sing. "Happy birthday to you!"

Well, crap. My eyes started watering immediately. Denny's face broke open in surprise, and then, singing along, he darted over to the sink to get me a tissue.

There were quite a few voices singing now and, goddamn it, a tear rolled down my cheek. "Happy birthday to you!"

Father Peters slid the cake onto the countertop. "Make a wish, my dear."

A wish? What a fraught concept. If you strung together all the things I'd ever wished for over a birthday cake, it would be a pretty funny list. Toys. A Pony. (Didn't happen.) The starring role in the high school musical. (That one came true.) And *Jude*. (Also a win. And then a loss.)

The old birthday wish was a tricky proposition. I closed my eyes and wished my twenty-fourth year would be *just* a little less complicated than the few that came just before it.

But really, what were the odds?

I blew out the candle, and my handful of well-wishers cheered. "This is beautiful," I said, truthfully. "Let's eat it."

Denny got out some plates, and old Mrs. Walters muttered something about the extra dishes. So I served her a fat slice, which she ate. I cut slices for everyone except Jude, who had disappeared just after I blew out my candle.

I was stuffed by the time we got around to hand washing the plates and forks, but a quarter of the cake still remained. "I'll grab the box from my office," Father Peters said. "You have to take that home."

When he returned, I thanked him profusely for the cake. "You just kill me sometimes," I added. "This week has been rough, and..."

He held up a hand. "My dear, I would happily take credit. But I'm not the one who remembered your birthday, and I'm not the one who brought you a cake. But I do hope you have a happy birthday and a wonderful year."

For a second I could only blink at his watery blue eyes. "It wasn't you?"

He shook his head. "I can't be trusted to remember everyone's dates. It's Mrs. Charles who sends out the parish birthday cards."

"So... who did this?" I looked down at the bakery box in my hands.

Father Peters smiled. "It seems that he prefers to remain anonymous."

He. It wasn't Denny—he'd given me a "why didn't you tell me it was your birthday?" speech. And Denny just wasn't that good of an actor.

That only left Jude.

"Good night, Father Peters," I said slowly.

"Good night, love. And happy birthday."

I left my car behind the church, and I walked to Nickel's Auto Body. For the second time in a week, I climbed the wooden stairs behind the building. I knocked on the door and then held my breath.

A few beats later I heard a ragged voice say, "Yeah?"

After a moment's hesitation I tried the knob, and the door gave way. Except for a single lamp burning in the corner, it was dark inside. I heard the low pulse of a song by Citizen Cope. But I didn't see the man I was looking for. "Jude?"

"Right here." I looked down and found him on the floor, shirtless, his feet tucked under the rail of the bed, his hands behind his head. My eyes got a little stuck on the unfamiliar six-pack he was sporting these days. Jude tightened his abs and sat up, and I realized that a set of sit-ups was responsible for this mouthwatering moment. "Something wrong?" he said, tilting his head and considering me.

It took another second until I could drag my gaze away from him and back to the box in my arms. "Um, did you get me a birthday cake?"

He let out half a chuckle and got to his feet. "I plead the fifth."

"Why? I mean... you didn't even stay for a piece of cake?" I stepped all the way in and closed the door behind me.

Jude sat on the edge of his bed, his chest still expanding rapidly from the workout I'd interrupted. "I don't know. I wanted you to have something nice, but I didn't need the credit."

"Why?" I asked again. I put the box on the dresser. (*The* dresser. I was never going to look at that piece of furniture the same way again.) Then, uninvited, I went to sit beside him on the edge of his bed.

A pair of serious eyes studied me. "It was just a little thing, Sophie. If I got you a cake every day for the next thirty years, I still couldn't make it right between us."

"I really liked it, though."

His eyes softened. "I'm glad."

"Do you want a piece? There's plenty."

For a second his face remained unchanged, and I panicked. *I shouldn't have come here. He's going to ask me to leave. I am a fool.* But his chin tilted upward and he smiled. I felt it like sunshine on my face. A full-on Jude smile, just for me. "Sure, baby. I'd love a piece."

Sure, baby. He used to say that all the time in the same voice—rough and smooth all at once, like whiskey. I got up to get the cake box so that he couldn't see my face. *Dying here*, I thought, flipping open the top. To be in this room with Jude was to have memories crash over my head at intervals like waves. And just when I managed to push one out of my mind, a new one would sneak up and clobber me.

There was a pile of plastic forks and napkins on the

bookshelf in the corner of his room, so I swiped one of each before I brought the cake back to his bed and set it down. He looked in the box. "That's too big to be just one piece," he said.

I handed him the fork. "Just do your best. I don't really feel like taking it home to my parents' house."

Jude stuck the fork into the end of the piece, a naughty glint in his eye. He took a bite. A second later he let his eyes roll back in his head.

"I know," I said. "It's awesome."

"They called it Black Forest," he said, licking his lips.

"Let's call it Awesome Forest."

He took a second bite. Then he forked up a third and offered it to me.

Heat rose on my cheeks as I opened my mouth to receive it. Jude fed me the bite gently, and our eyes locked. I felt goosebumps break out on my arms. At the last second, Jude angled the fork to smear my lip with frosting on the dismount.

"You ass," I complained, and he laughed. The sound of his laughter—low and naughty—cranked my heartstrings a little tighter. It used to be this easy between us. When Jude and I were alone together, the rest of the world didn't exist.

That's what I'd thought, anyway. Until our little world cracked in two.

Jude sat back, as if putting a little distance between us. Maybe he felt it, too—the tightening of the invisible cord between us. "So. What did you get for your birthday?"

I wasn't quite ready for that question. "Well," I whispered, feeling my sadness rise to the surface again. "For my birthday I received one Awesome Forest cake."

He set the fork down inside the cake box and set the box on the bed, waiting for me to go on. When I didn't, his brow creased with concern. And then my stupid eyes watered.

I swear to God, the entire time that Jude and I were a couple, I only cried for sad movies. But now I could not be in the same zip code with him without springing a leak.

Jude reached for me. He lifted me by the hips into his lap as if I were a little girl. And I hid my face in his neck as if I were one. He smelled of clean flannel and laundry detergent.

"My girl is having a rough time," he whispered. "I'm sorry."

"It's not a big deal," I mumbled, trying to backtrack. "Birthdays don't really matter when you're twenty-three. But it just *wears* on me sometimes—all the petty, dysfunctional bullshit." *And I don't have anyone to talk to about it, because you left me all alone.*

I was still angry at Jude, and I probably always would be. But the strong arms holding me close took the edge off my anger. With one big palm Jude began to rub my back. His hand slid up to scoop the hair off my neck, and when his fingertips grazed my nape, I shivered.

I didn't want to think about my birthday anymore. I just wanted to bask in Jude's arms. The stubbled skin of his neck tickled my nose, and it was all too easy for me to place a kiss there. So I did. And then I kissed him again.

Jude's body went completely still.

As my lips worshiped his neck, he made a sound of surrender—half sigh, half groan. His arms tightened around me. But still he did not make a move.

I wanted him too, though. *One more birthday present, please.* With soft lips, I kissed a line down into the hollow of Jude's throat. Then I parted my lips and sucked gently on his skin. Beneath me, his breath hitched.

That's when I knew I'd won.

Shifting my weight, I spun around to straddle him. Lust-darkened eyes met mine, and there was a question in them.

Leaning in, I pressed my lips against his, hoping to kiss that question away.

Jude gave a groan against my mouth. He kissed me once. Twice. "Sophie," he grunted. *Kiss.* "You shouldn't be here." *Kiss.*

"Thank you, Captain Obvious." *Kiss, kiss. Kiss.* I rubbed my hands up and down his inked biceps. Jesus, he had bulked up.

"Where's your car?" he asked between kisses. But then he pushed me down on the bed, stretching out over my body.

The weight of his hips on mine made me crazy. "Church parking lot," I breathed.

He flexed his body against me. "But what if somebody...?"

"What if you just shut up?" I reached for his shoulders, but he did a pushup, levering himself up and off of me.

Something like worry crossed his features. "You make me crazy, Sophie."

I ran a hand up and down his bare chest, and his eyes closed. "Yeah? Well back at you, babe. We both have first-class tickets on the crazy train. But it's my birthday, and you're the only one who remembered." My logic was thin at best. But Jude shivered at my touch and lowered himself onto my body again. His mouth found mine, hot and determined. I opened for him right away.

And then we were just *gone.* Deep kisses and hands everywhere. I couldn't get enough of his beautiful chest. I traced every new ridge of muscle with my fingertips. Jude's hand slid into the crease between my legs, and I squeezed my thighs together to show him how much I wanted him.

We struggled out of our clothes in a ridiculous way due to our inability to stop kissing. My T-shirt got stuck because I wouldn't let go of Jude's mouth. So he turned his attention to the zipper on my jeans instead. He unzipped me, and I hiked up my hips to let him yank the fabric away from my body.

The feel of his fingertips sliding into my panties made us gasp together. "So slick and sweet," he growled. "You feel like *mine.*"

I couldn't answer him because I was too busy yanking him in for another kiss. An addiction is when you can't keep away from something that's bad for you. Maybe Jude was a drug addict, but I was a Jude addict.

He got the rest of my clothes off finally. Then we were skin to skin, Jude lying on top of me. We were staring into each other's eyes, and I wanted to die of happiness. I let my hands wander up his thickly muscled arms to his big shoulders. "You got so big in prison," I gasped.

His next kiss had him chuckling into my mouth. "That sounds really badass, Soph. But I got big lifting bushel crates of apples at the Shipleys'."

I tightened my legs around his waist. "Do me, farm boy."

"As you wish." He reached back, his palm landing at my ankle. He skimmed my shin with his big hand, making me shiver. Then he claimed my mouth in a blistering kiss. I was practically quivering with anticipation when he gave a purposeful thrust and filled me.

"Ah!" we both gasped, and the sexy grimace on his face was beautiful.

We melted together in another kiss, and Jude began to rock. He set a slow, aching pace that would have been torture if I didn't have his mouth on mine. I threaded my fingers through his thick, wavy hair and sighed.

And then he *smiled* at me between kisses. I saw a flash of the old Jude—naughty but sweet. That smile affected me even more than the slide of hot skin against skin. My pulse kicked up a notch, and I tugged him closer. I crossed my ankles behind his ass and squeezed.

Jude groaned as he picked up the pace. "Fuck, Sophie. I can't go slow with you. Never could."

He wasn't the only one. My breath came in short, happy puffs as he rode me hard. I felt my joy crest. Kicking my legs out to the side, I arched up to meet him.

Crying out his name, I bucked one more time. Jude growled into my mouth and then planted himself deeply. We pulsed together, gripping one another as if certain something would try to tear us apart.

Because something always did.

* * *

I floated back down to earth slowly. Last time I'd entered Jude's room, I'd told him, "It's just sex." What a crock of crap. He was everything to me. It's just that I was only allowed to have everything for an hour before it disappeared again.

But today was my birthday, and tonight I was a glass-half-full kind of girl.

Jude shifted his weight off me and rolled to his side. But then he pulled me close, and I snuggled into his shoulder.

Maybe he expected me to burst into tears again, but I wasn't going to. There would almost surely be more tears over Jude. But I'd save them for later. Tonight was too sweet for tears.

We lay there quietly for a few minutes, holding each other. Eventually my busy brain came back online, and I asked Jude a question that burned brightly in my mind. "How did you get hooked on drugs?"

He gave a snort. "Really? You want to go there right now?"

I gave his bulky chest a single kiss. "I want to understand."

He grumbled. "Remember when I sprained my ankle at the end of junior year?"

"Sure."

"They gave me painkillers at the E.R."

I tried to rewind my memory that far. "But that healed up quickly. I thought you didn't need those pills."

"I didn't. But I had them on my desk. And Gibby and Dex were like, 'Let me show you what those are really for.'" Jude sighed again. "They taught me how to crush and snort prescription painkillers."

Jesus. "That was it? Boom? Just like that?"

His voice was low and quiet. "Yes and no. When you first start, it's just fun. That shit made me feel invincible. And one pill lasted a couple of days. But pretty soon your body adjusts, so I needed more. I started buying them. I told myself that it was no big deal."

I gave him another little kiss to thank him for telling me. But he wasn't done.

"That's how it always goes. I've sat through a lot of meetings by now, and everybody's story is pretty much the same. You think you have it under control. You're still showing up all the places you're supposed to show up. And nobody's really noticed that you have to duck into the bathroom periodically to blow a line. And it's easier to get through the day, because the things you're afraid of don't seem so bad when you're high."

"What were you afraid of?" I asked immediately.

But Jude just shook his head.

I'd already pressed my luck tonight, so I let it go. "And how about now? I know you're going to that meeting in the church basement."

"Mmm," he said, kissing my shoulder. "In a week they'll give me a six-month tag. It's a plastic keychain. Pretty anticlimactic, really."

"Six months is nothing to sneeze at."

"Thanks." He sounded weary. "Feels like six years, though."

"Why?"

He lifted my hair and kissed my neck. "You don't want to hear this crap."

I pushed up on an elbow, giving up a kiss from Jude for the first time that I could remember. "Actually, I do."

Jude licked his lips. "My body won't let me forget the shit I used to put in it."

"So you have cravings?" I knew the right terminology. You can't work in a social work office without learning these things.

"Every damn day."

"What does it feel like?"

"Nagging. Like a twitch. Or an irritating tag in the back of your sweater. And you *know* just a little hit would make it go away. Some days I can't remember why it's so important not to. That's why I sit in that church basement. It's not for the shitty coffee. It's so they can remind me why I stopped."

I curled up beside him again. "Did you ever try Suboxone? People say it's a game-changer."

Jude poked me in the hip. "What do you know from Suboxone?"

"I work in the hospital—the social work office."

"Really?"

"Really."

"Sounds like a depressing job."

"It's not. Well, it can be. But mostly it's great. The people who come in there are in crisis, and we get to sort 'em out. I never go home at night wondering why I bother."

"That makes one of us."

I rubbed his back. "I could find you someone who writes prescriptions for Suboxone."

He was really quiet for a second, which probably meant that I'd overstepped. "I don't want it," he said eventually. "I

137

don't want to treat a drug addiction with another drug."

"That's fair," I said quickly. I sure hadn't come here to get all up in Jude's business.

"It's not just the principle of the thing," he said quietly. "I don't want to have to think about dosing myself. Like—is it time to take my pill? What if I took it early just this once? I don't want to tangle myself up like that."

I ran a hand up and down the ridges of his perfect chest. "That makes sense. I'm sure you know what you're doing."

He laughed. "Not hardly. But it's not all bad. I just had some really good... chocolate cake."

I pinched him again, and he rolled onto my body for a kiss.

And we were both smiling.

Chapter Fifteen

Jude

Cravings Meter: 3

When I opened my eyes the next morning, sunlight was streaming through the windows.

That never happened. Somehow I'd slept the whole night through. While grinning at my ceiling, I had a private chuckle. Sex had thrown a switch and put me right to sleep.

I sat up, rubbing my eyes. The Sophie Cure would be temporary, though. If there was anything I understood about my body it was that the cravings always returned. At least for now, I felt better than I had in a long time. If I'd learned one thing in recovery, it was to appreciate the easy minutes. Because you might not get more of them for a while.

Even better—today was Thursday. I had an evening with the Shipleys to look forward to. Tonight I'd bring something from the bakery where I'd bought Sophie's cake. I had to go there anyway to get my credit card back.

After a quick shower I threw on my work clothes and headed downstairs. In the alley I paused, because that fucking wreck of a car was still there. I'd taught myself to walk past it without looking. But it was twice now that Sophie had come through this alley. She'd had to walk past the car that killed her brother. On the outside chance that she might come back some time, I knew I had to finally deal with the fucker.

I circled the Porsche the way you circle an enemy. With one phone call I could have the whole car towed away as junk. But as a vintage car nut, I just couldn't do that. What a waste. So I started at the back of the vehicle, because that section had not been damaged. Lifting the tarp, I saw two taillights, still perfect.

After heading into the garage, I fired up my father's ancient computer and looked at listings for vintage Porsche taillights on eBay. Looked like the lenses alone were worth fifty bucks each. I put up an auction listing for them, then shut down the computer.

Baby steps.

If they sold, I'd have to figure out what to do with the money. I no longer wanted anything to do with that car, but I could give the money to Sophie. She could dust off her music school fund.

Meanwhile, I was confronted with another long day of being underemployed. My tire-changing business had all but dried up. After a couple of snowfalls, most of the people who were planning to suit up for winter had already done it. And the ones who still believed that "all season" tires were good enough hadn't dented their fenders yet.

My father had deigned to work yesterday, completing a dent repair. And since two days of work in a row would clearly be too much effort for him, I doubted that he would turn up this morning.

That was just as well, because I didn't want to hear his opinion on my next project.

Yesterday I'd bought some exterior paint at Home Depot, along with a scraper, a decent brush and some rollers. The garage hadn't seen a paint job in years. If I wanted people to bring us their bodywork, I knew I had to make the place look alive.

First, I took our power sander outside and fired it up. Even with safety goggles and a face mask on, removing the old, peeling paint was nasty work. But I covered a lot of territory in an hour and a half. And then Mrs. Walters—the old lady who ran the clanking dishwashing machine at the church—pulled in with her set of snow tires to swap out.

"This will take about forty-five minutes," I said, burying my surprise.

She waved a gnarled hand. "I'm going to lunch with my girls. We'll be two hours at least. Longer if the gossip is any good."

"See you in a couple hours," I said.

Whistling to myself, I put her car on the lift and got to work. Sometimes I tried to guess what sort of car a person drove, and I never would have guessed this one. It amused me to know that Mrs. Walters drove a Subaru Baja, which was an odd miniature pickup that I'd always admired. Subaru didn't make 'em anymore, and that was a shame.

The Baja was the sort of car that teenagers buzzed through town with their snowboards in back.

I was tightening a lug nut when someone walked into the garage. "You're early, Mrs. Walters."

"Not early. Late." The voice was male, and made of gravel.

I forced myself to stand up very slowly. No point in showing fear when you don't yet know if there's a reason. "Can I help you?" I asked a dark-eyed stranger in a denim jacket and a beanie. The only thing distinguishing him from a thousand other guys in Vermont was the angry-looking scar across his cheek.

"There's something I'm missing, and I think you know where it is."

Turning my head, I made a show of checking the space behind me for someone else. "You can't mean me. I don't even know you. And I've been in prison for three years."

"Yeah? Well just before that your new dealer gave you some product. We're looking for his stash."

Shit. I held my hands loosely as a show of indifference. But I was boiling inside. "In the first place, I didn't have a new dealer."

The guy all but rolled his mean little eyes. "Gavin Haines, asshole. Don't talk to me like I'm stupid."

"I didn't. Gavin wasn't my dealer. He hated my guts. The night he died was the only time I ever hung out with him. He gave me a free sample, because he wanted me to introduce him to some of my junkie friends. And you must know how that ended. If I'd had his stash in my car, the cops would have found it. I would have been sent down for intent to distribute."

"He had more shit than they found," my ugly visitor said. "Where is it?"

I gave him an exaggerated shrug. "I wouldn't know. Why would you even ask about this three years later? If it hasn't turned up, I don't think it's turning up."

This creep lifted his ugly chin and stared at me. "Where did he hang?"

Jesus Christ. This was not a conversation I wanted to have. "I'd be the last to know. He had a place in Burlington with his frat buddies, but I never got closer than the front yard. You want me to guess? He could have had a storage unit somewhere. Or maybe he put it in a gym locker—that's where they always look on TV."

The asshole stared me down again, and I felt the seconds tick by. I'd done well so far at keeping my irritation to myself. But everyone had a breaking point, and I was reaching mine.

"Maybe he kept it at home."

I laughed, but it was a bitter sound. "In the police chief's house? No chance."

"Maybe the chief was in on it?"

I shook my head. "You'll never convince me of that. The man is an ass, but he's not dirty. The stick up his butt is made of rebar."

My interrogator raised an eyebrow. "So the son was going off in his own direction, and he knows his daddy didn't like you, so you're a good pick to help him."

"You are full of theories, aren't you? And maybe if his association with me lasted longer than two hours, you'd be onto something." I would repeat this story until my dying day. And it was easy to do because I was telling the truth.

But if he didn't get the fuck out of my garage soon, I didn't know what I would do.

"Maybe the daughter knows something," he said slowly.

My blood stopped circulating. "No chance. They weren't

close."

"But you were."

My heart spasmed in my chest. "Sure I was. But I lied to her all damn day back then. That's what an addict does."

The next fifteen seconds probably took fifteen years off my life. He watched me, his eyes burning with irritation. I measured the distance between myself and the lug wrench and waited to find out if I was going to need to lunge for it.

"You find it, you call me," he said finally. He took a card out of his pocket and set it on Mrs. Walters' rear tire.

My heart thumped with relief. Slowly, as if it didn't matter to me at all, I turned back to my lug nut. "I'm not finding a thing. I don't leave this place except to get food and go to meetings in a church basement."

"Yeah? Don't let me find out that ain't true. It would be really damn easy to plant some shit in your garage, and then tell the cops where to find it. I hear they want your ass gone from this town, anyway."

"Don't waste your stash," I grumbled. "I *never* bought from that guy. Like I said—he wanted me to introduce him to some friends, but we barely made it that far. Wish he hadn't given me a sample. I'm never going near that shit again."

"That's what they all say." He laughed.

I grasped the wrench, my grip tightening on the metal. I wanted to lash out, and the grip I had on my self-control was flimsy. Shit. If I were smart, I'd ask this asshole to come around every day to remind me why I stay sober. Bad decisions looked like this—like a dealer in your face over a stash of drugs from three years ago. I'd brought this on myself.

I dropped my eyes, praying he'd just go already. His stare burned me a few moments longer. Finally he walked out without a word.

I flicked his card in the trash and went back to work.

After I finished with Mrs. Walters' tires, I went back to painting. But this time with gritted teeth and the first drug cravings of the day. And it was only eleven o'clock.

By the time five o'clock rolled around, I was sweaty, shaky

and coated in a gritty layer of paint dust. I put my tools away, looking forward to a shower and a trip to the Shipleys'.

"Waste of time," my father said suddenly.

I spun around, almost dropping the paint scraper I was holding. I hadn't heard him walk in, and I was a little jumpy after my visit from the goon squad earlier in the day. Taking a deep breath, I tried to calm down. "Place needs a coat of paint."

"Not if it'll be knocked down."

"What?"

My father held out a hand, offering me a piece of paper.

I took it and read. It was a Cease and Desist order from the planning board of the Town of Colebury. "The automotive business operating at 2371 Granite Road is out of compliance with the property's zoning designation as LDR-2, Low Density Residential."

My father's face was slack when I looked up again. Maybe he'd dulled the pain with some whiskey before showing this to me. Or maybe he'd been a drinker for so long that I could no longer find the new expressions on his face.

I held the letter out to him. "This happened before, right? When I was in junior high? That time, you got them to agree to an exception for 'mixed use,' right?"

He shrugged. "Sure. But here they come again. Takes money and brains to fight 'em off. Don't have much of neither one."

That was the most self-aware thing my father had said in years. How depressing. "Do you know anyone you could ask for advice?" But I already knew the likely answer. It wasn't that my father had burned all his bridges. It's just that he'd allowed them to wash downstream, board by board. Numbness and neglect were his habits.

After a bunch of talk therapy at rehab I was excellent at diagnosing other people's problems.

"Maybe," he said. Then he shuffled over to close the register. I wondered if he'd even respond to the letter or just turn up the volume on the TV and wait for the city to show up with a bulldozer.

Tomorrow I was supposed to paint this place, and now I

couldn't even remember why. My shoulders were as tight as boards, and my dirty fingers clenched into fists. At that moment, I would have smoked, drank, inhaled or injected any substance anyone might hand me.

Instead I went upstairs to my room to shower, because it was time to go to the Shipleys' dinner.

Thank fuck.

Jude and Sophie are 18

Sophie's birthday has come and gone, and Jude is leaning over the engine of his car, tinkering with the connections. But all he can think about is sex.

When he started up with Sophie a year ago, he gave up other girls. And therefore sex.

He knew what he was getting into. (Or not into, as the case had been.) He knew Sophie hadn't had a boyfriend before, and he'd never rush her. And the wait would be totally worth it.

The rule he'd made about her eighteenth birthday was meant to help him stay strong—to make the moment less arbitrary. Without that line in the sand, they would have gotten carried away on any of the hundred occasions they got hot and heavy in his car or under a tree in the woods.

But now the deadline has passed, and every minute of the last ten days has felt heavy with yearning.

His phone buzzes in his back pocket.

Jude releases a breath of air, and it's actually shaky. He's vibrating with anticipation as he pulls out the phone to read the text. We're at Tracy's now. Come over.

He washes his hands carefully, making sure to get any motor oil off of them. He pats his other pocket to make sure his wallet is there. Inside that wallet are two condoms, brand new.

Hell. He's actually a little nervous, which is

ridiculous. He isn't the virgin in this situation.

Later, he won't remember the walk to Tracy's house. Her parents are gone for the weekend, but Sophie's dad doesn't know that, and Sophie has arranged to stay over.

When he arrives at the pretty farmhouse on the edge of town, Sophie is alone in the living room. "Hi," she says, looking shy, closing the door behind him.

"Hi yourself. Where's...?" He doesn't finish the question, because a loud, rhythmic thumping starts up just overhead. It's the sound of a headboard hitting the wall. "Oh."

"Yeah," Sophie says, her cheekbones pinking up.

"Uh...uh...uh...unnngh. TRACE!" a male voice shouts.

Jude and Sophie stare at each other for a second before they both burst out laughing. Jude wraps her into a hug and their bellies shake against one another. "Let's go into the den," Sophie gasps between laughs.

He follows her through the kitchen and into a low, cozy room with sectional sofas and a TV. It's the sort of room that happy families live in. Tracy's younger brothers' video games are arranged into denim-lined baskets, and the TV remotes are lined up like soldiers on the coffee table. A Christmas tree glows in the corner, beside a brick fireplace.

"You've got to see this," Sophie says, grabbing one of the remotes off the table. She points it at the fireplace. With an airy whoosh, a gas fire jumps to life behind the fire screen. "Isn't that silly?"

"Yeah." Though the warm, flickering firelight is both beautiful and effortless. A high-functioning family home is like a foreign country that Jude stumbles on from time to time. He's mostly learned the language but everything still seems a little unfamiliar.

Sophie sits in the corner of the sectional and he flops down beside her. "Should we watch a movie?" he asks. They haven't been alone together like this in a week or so. But he isn't about to jump on her like an animal.

"Do you want to?" Sophie asks carefully.

Everything is suddenly so awkward. And they're never awkward with each other. "Baby we can do whatever you want. Seriously. Just because Tracy and her guy are bonin' doesn't mean we have to…"

She stops him with a hand on his chest. "Jude." Her voice is low and serious. She turns to him, eyes flashing. "I listened to my friends moaning for twenty minutes before you got here, because I was afraid to leave the living room in case I missed your knock. And I have been waiting a long time for you to have sex with me. If you don't whip it out right now, I may not be responsible for my actions."

Jude nearly swallows his tongue. "Well, honey." It's a miracle that his voice is nearly steady. "Guess you'd better close the door."

Sophie leaps up to shut the door to the den.

Jude's heart bangs away inside his chest as he repositions himself on his side, his back to the cushions. When she returns, he waves her down for a kiss.

Tentatively, Sophie spreads herself out

against his body, her hand on the waistband of his jeans. They've been horizontal before, but opportunity and privacy make it seem brand new. "Hi," *she whispers.*

Jude leans forward, finding her soft lips with his. He can't think too hard about this or he'll be intimidated. He's never been anyone's first time before. It's downright nerve-wracking. But when he cups her head, instinct kicks in.

Sophie moans into the kiss. The sound unhooks his self-consciousness. Both his arms wrap around her and he dives in. Love you, his tongue says against hers.

Need you, her hips say against his.

They make out until she's panting, and his dick is harder than the lug wrenches hanging in the garage. Sophie's fingers shove at his T-shirt. She's trying to undress him while they kiss. It will never work.

"Sit up a second," *he begs.*

When she rights herself, her face is flushed, and her lips look slick and bee-stung. Gawd. So beautiful. He lifts her T-shirt over her head and drops it on the floor.

She reaches around behind herself and unhooks her bra. When she casts it aside, he can't even breathe. Sophie is always so put-together, in cardigan sweaters and with her hair tied back in a shining ponytail. He's touched her so many times, but this is the first time he's seen her truly topless. Her breasts are lush and full, with generous pink nipples.

"What?" *she asks, self-conscious. Her hands come up to cover her breasts, and the sight of her touching herself tightens his balls. There aren't* even words for how she looks right now—all sweet and innocent and turned on at the same time.

"You are so fucking beautiful," he grunts out. "Take off your jeans."

She lifts her chin. "You first."

Jude doesn't need to be asked twice. He peels off his shirt then pops the button on his jeans while Sophie stares. He shimmies out of them, kicking off his socks.

"Keep going," she says, her voice trembling.

It's fun to disarm her this way, the same way she disarms him. So he drops a hand to his aching dick, giving it one slow stroke through his black boxer briefs. When he meets her eyes, Sophie swallows roughly, looking a little nervous now. "Hey," he says, laying a hand on her head. "It doesn't have to be all or nothing. We could just fool around a little."

She shakes her head. "Now is our chance." She stands up and sheds her jeans and a little pair of white panties, while Jude quietly dies five times over. Just a glimpse of the curve of her hips makes him want to ejaculate immediately. He shucks off his briefs, kicking them away. Then he lays on his back. "Come here."

"Wait," she says. "I have condoms."

Jude, you dumbass. He didn't mean to make her worry about that. "Me too." He fishes around on the floor for his jeans and pulls one out. "But we don't need this just yet. We're going slow. Now come here and kiss me."

She kneels over him, her breasts right in his face. If he died right now he would still consider this a perfect life. "Fuck." He pulls her down clumsily so he can lick those pink nipples. They're larger than he expected, and somehow that seems scandalous. He closes his lips around her breast and sucks.

Sophie grips his shoulders, her gasp helpless. He lets his hands wander up her naked hips while he tongues her nipple. She presses into his mouth and groans. He slides a hand between her legs and feels how wet she is already, and his dick leaks in sympathy.

They've waited so long and now he isn't even sure if he can get inside her without blowing his load just from the foreplay.

He releases her nipple with a wet pop and reaches for the condom. Sophie tries to catch her breath. She's braced above him, her arm on the back of the sofa, her very naked body visible everywhere.

Jude closes his eyes as he tears open the packet, taking a short break from the most erotic sight he's ever seen in his life. Calm down, he orders himself. He rolls the latex down and the condom's tight grip steadies him.

"Lie down, baby," he says, shifting out of the way.

"Okay," she whispers, taking his place on the sofa.

Jude kneels between her legs, nudging her knees apart. Then he drops his mouth to her beautiful pussy and kisses her.

"Oh!" she gasps.

He gets down on his elbows, drags his lips against her softness. She's ridiculously sweet. He's never done this for a girl before, and it's even better than he'd imagined. The musky scent of desire envelops him, and he tries his first lick.

The result is a vise-grip on his hair and the most beautiful whimper from Sophie's lips. "Oh God," she cries when he does it again. "Jude!"

He's immediately hooked. The more he tastes, the more he wants. Her legs splay open for him. The look of uncertainty is gone from her blissed-out face. So he goes to town with kisses big and small, licks and a couple of gentle sucks. Sophie curses and moans, gripping his head and then his hair.

Then she starts begging. "Please, Jude. P-please."

She's so close. He's made her come many times with his fingers, and he knows all the signs. He'd planned to get her all riled up before doing the deed, so it's now or never. Sitting up a little, he wipes his face with one hand. Then he grips the base of his cock and lines up against her. He closes his eyes.

One sweet push and he's home. Her warmth grips him like a fist, and he braces himself to stave off the orgasm that's been waiting since the moment she took off her bra.

Her gasp opens his eyes. She's staring up at him in shock. "Are you okay?" he asks immediately.

"Yeah," she breathes. "Just..."

"Hurts?" His libido dials back several notches in a hurry.

"It did," she admits. "But now it's already less."

"Do you want to stop?" He leans down to kiss her nose.

She shakes her head. "Never."

His heart spasms with happiness. He gives his hips a gentle roll, and her eyes widen. He stops again. "Hey." He strokes her cheek with his hand. "Tell me how to help you relax."

"Just kiss me."

Yes, ma'am. Their mouths melt together. He slants his head to make each kiss more perfect than the one before. She sighs beneath him, relaxing into the beautiful rhythm of their making out. They're champions at this part already. They kiss and kiss, and Jude's hips can't resist getting in on the action. Her mouth is so sweet and she's firmly underneath him, just like in every one of his dirty dreams.

Sophie's knees squeeze his hips, and she begins to meet him for every slow thrust. Her breathing hastens. She strains against him as if stretching for something that's just out of reach.

He's not going to last much longer. Hell, it's a miracle he's held it together for this long. So he sits up a little bit to make enough space between them. Then he slips his fingertips down to tease her clit, just the way she likes.

"Oh," she pants. "Ahh..."

Sweating now, Jude pumps his hips and bites his lip. But the sight of her lush, naked body writhing beneath him is almost too much. He closes his eyes, hopefully buying himself five more seconds of patience. He'd wanted to make her first time perfect.

Then he hears it—the high-pitched gasp of victory. She sobs his name as her body clenches around his cock.

Sweet Jesus. He drops back down for one last

kiss and lets go completely, thrusting with abandon. His balls hitch tight and his muscles clench and he gives a happy shout against her lips. He comes so hard that he sees spots in front of his eyes.

High on victory and satisfaction, he drops his face into her neck and whispers all the sweet, lovesick things he can think of.

And every one of them is true.

Chapter Sixteen

Sophie

Internal DJ tuned to: Billy Joel's "Pressure"

It was hard to believe that my last set of final exams was upon me.

This—my final semester—I'd only taken two courses. My senior seminar on public health required only a take-home exam, but it was a bear. And my statistics course was no picnic, either.

Two classes didn't sound like a lot, but I'd been working twenty-five hours a week at the hospital. That left the weekends for homework and housework. No wonder I had no life.

That would have to change in the New Year. Many things would change—I'd need to get a full-time job and move out of my parents' house somehow. Staying there another year would never work.

But first: exams.

To get through the next few days, I employed two tactics. The first was record-breaking coffee consumption. The second was forbidding myself to think of Jude.

Whenever a particularly tricky statistics concept bedeviled

me, it was tempting to close my eyes and remember the feel of his scruff against my face and the press of his hips against mine. A girl could get lost in a memory like that.

But there was work to be done, and I chose to do most of it in places I didn't associate with him, like the student center, the university library and—closer to home—Crumbs. Jude and I had never been there together because it had opened while he was in prison.

Time marches on whether you notice it or not. It was hard to believe that my diploma was in reach. After Gavin's death, there had been moments during college when I thought I wouldn't make it to the finish line. Friends and roommates had come and gone, most of them focused on parties and schoolwork, blissfully ignorant of the fact that your family and then your life can fall to pieces when you're only nineteen.

Those difficult years were behind me now, and I would soon have a degree to prove it.

I'd arranged to take the next Wednesday off from the hospital in order to study and attend a statistics study session with the course's TA. But I'd never bail on the Community Dinner. When evening came I put my books aside and headed over to the church.

Once again I walked into the church kitchen with fear in my heart. But this time I wasn't afraid that Jude would be there. Instead, I was afraid he *wouldn't* be. There weren't any promises between us. We could never have a real relationship again. For all I knew, Jude could get a better job and vanish into the wind.

Somehow I'd already begun measuring my time in terms of Wednesdays. That couldn't be a good thing. But there it was.

"How are the exams going?" Denny asked me when I walked in the room.

"Okay, thanks. One down and one to go." My gaze traveled over Denny's shoulder to the place where it longed to rest. And there he was in all his tight-T-shirt glory, strong forearms flexing over the prep table as he chopped up something leafy and green.

"Sophie?"

"Yeah?" My gaze snapped back to Denny. I'd been staring at Jude like a lovesick fangirl. "What's um, the green stuff? My head is so full of, um, statistics that I can't remember the menu."

Denny's face implied that he didn't believe me. But he answered the question anyway. "It's taco night." His thumb jerked back toward Jude. "Cilantro for the pico de gallo. I asked him to do the garlic next."

"Right," I said brightly. "I'll fetch the ground beef."

I marched my overheated self into the pantry and opened the door to the walk-in cooler. The refrigerated air felt good against my flushed skin. Carrying fifty pounds of ground beef at once was above my pay grade, so I hefted only the top carton and backed out of the walk-in.

My ass ran straight into Jude.

"Hey," he said, catching me and then my box of meat. "Careful."

Careful. I was so far past careful that it wasn't even funny. The woodsy scent of his aftershave enveloped me. I took a deep breath of Jude.

"Hey there," he whispered.

"Hey." My voice was breathy. *Get a grip, Sophie.* I turned to face him. "How was your week?"

"Shitty." He grinned.

"Why?"

He shook his head. "Nothing for you to worry about. Things are looking up, now. Wednesday and Thursday are the best days of the week."

"Yeah?"

Jude set the box down on a stepstool. And before I knew what was happening, he'd pushed me up against the door to the walk-in. Those silver eyes came in at close range. "Yeah." Then he kissed me.

Oh, sweet Jesus. His mouth slanted over mine, the pressure bossy and delicious. An angel choir sang a chorus of hallelujahs as his hips pressed against mine. When I parted my lips, he deepened the kiss. Then his tongue made a long, sweet pull against mine. I forgot where we were. I forgot my own name. My hands gripped Jude's waist, and I gave myself over to him completely.

It was useless pretending otherwise; I was gone for him. Always had been. He thrust his tongue into my mouth one more time and then eased up, smiling at me. The whole episode lasted maybe thirty seconds before he pulled away.

I stood there panting. The angel choir in my head had switched over to a dirty, groovy channel. I wanted more, and I was probably doing a bad job of hiding it.

Jude kissed me on the nose. "I'm leaving my door open tonight in case you feel like swinging by."

"Okay." My knees felt wobbly. But I knew they'd be wobbling right over to Jude's place after the dinner service was over.

Jude leaned over and snagged a couple of bulbs of garlic out of their bin. "You need me to carry some meat?"

"What?" I was busy admiring the muscles in his forearm when he closed his hand around the garlic.

With an amused glance in my direction, he pointed at the ground beef in the box I'd brought out. "Meat. Do you need me to carry some of it?"

"Yes, please," I said. "Thank you."

Jude grabbed the box and walked out of the room.

I went back into the walk-in for another case of ground beef and to cool off my overheated body.

* * *

We served a lot of tacos. Hundreds of them. By eight o'clock I was ragged from constant trips between the serving line and the prep stations.

"What are we doing with the leftover refried beans?" Denny asked. "Is this enough to take over to the food pantry tomorrow?"

"No," I said. "Compost it, or take them home with you."

"Woo-hoo!" Denny said. "Nachos for me tomorrow."

My eyes tracked across the room, where Jude was slipping on his coat. I watched him leave. And then I cleaned up for another thirty minutes. By that time, I decided it was safe to follow him home. I put the last of the clean dishes in the storage cabinets and closed them for the night.

In the kitchen, I found Denny waiting for me, my coat in his hands.

Crap, I thought immediately. And just as quickly I felt guilty for it. Sometimes Denny walked me out to my car, just to be nice. I supposed I could always drive my car around the block and re-park.

This reminded me of high school, and not in a good way. Hooking up with Jude forced me to sneak around like a teenager.

Denny held up my coat.

"Thanks," I said, slipping my arms into the sleeves one after the other.

He lifted it onto my shoulders, then gave me a pat. When he spoke, his voice was so low that I almost couldn't hear it. "Please be careful, Sophie."

"What? Why?" When I turned around to check his face, he wore a sober expression. That's when I realized that he was onto me. "How did you...?"

He lifted his chin toward the pantry, and I felt my face heat. He must have seen us going at it against the walk-in door. *Smooth, Sophie.*

"I'm just worried about you," he said, fishing a pair of gloves out of his pockets. "Do you know the rate of relapse among opiate addicts?"

I shook my head, because I was suddenly too upset to speak. How *dare* he imply that Jude would start using again? *None* of this was any of Denny's business. And not only was it rude to Jude, it also implied that I was an idiot. I knew Jude's road was a tough one. But when a man was working so hard to stay clean, it seemed impossibly cruel to say out loud that he wouldn't make it.

"Over fifty percent," he said.

Stepping backward, I yanked my gloves out of my pockets. "If I ever have a problem with addiction, remind me not to come to you for encouragement."

Denny's mouth fell open, and he wore the startled expression of someone who had just been slapped.

"Goodnight," I said through clenched teeth. Then I turned and ran out of there. My shoes clicked on the tiles as I pushed the church's pretty wooden door open.

Moving quickly, I headed down the sidewalk toward Jude's street. The cold air on my face was a relief, and it helped to cool my anger. I knew Denny was a good guy *usually*. And he had always been a loyal friend. *And he's jealous*, my conscience put in. But the real reason that I would be able to put this awful moment aside was that Denny didn't know Jude. He'd never seen the way that Jude took care of me. He'd calmed me down a million times when I was stressed out over school or mad at my father for belittling me.

Jude had shored me up in so many ways. The least I could do was show a little faith.

And what's more, he'd always told *me* that I could beat the odds. When I wanted to make music my career, he'd never said, "Do you know the rate of failure for singers is over fifty percent?"

Life was risky. All of it. And I wasn't about to give up on Jude just because some medical researcher didn't like the odds of kicking his habit.

My feet took me closer to him.

The streets of Colebury were silent at night. Decorative candle-style lights lit the windows of many of the old wooden houses I passed. That was a thing in Vermont. We left them up all winter, too, not just at Christmas. These days there were solar-powered light-sensitive models—you didn't even have to remember to turn them on. I'd bought a set at the grocery store last year so that the police chief's house would look as though somebody cared enough to turn on the holiday lights.

When I turned onto Jude's street, the houses got smaller and the porches saggier. But there were candles in many of the windows.

Not his, though.

I climbed the stairs as quietly as I could. After a light tap on the door, I tried the knob. It released in my hand. "Jude?"

The only sound came from the shower.

Ten seconds later I'd tossed my coat and all my clothes onto his desk chair. Stark naked, I went into the bathroom. Without a word of warning, I pulled the curtain open.

Jude gave a startled grunt, but then quickly got over his surprise. Big hands pulled me under the spray. Then I was pancaked against a hard, wet man while his hands cupped my ass. "Baby," he rumbled.

I raised myself up on tiptoes to press my mouth over his, and received a happy growl for my efforts. Then there was nothing but wet lips and wet tongues. Steam and skin sliding against skin. The world was a small place where it rained warm water and kisses.

The very hard cock pressing against my belly begged to be touched. I dropped a hand down to stroke him. Jude moaned. "Want you so bad."

"What are you waiting for?" I gasped.

"Hold on to me," he ordered.

When I reached up to grasp his shoulders, Jude lifted me. Pressing my upper back against the shower wall, he lined himself up and slid inside. And once again I was full of Jude. Tipping my head back against the tiles, I sighed. For a moment nothing more happened, and that was fine with me. In music, the silence in between the songs can be as affecting as the most powerful crescendo. This moment was just the same. I opened my eyes to find Jude watching me.

Then his hips pulsed—the opening bass line of our song. I throbbed against him—adding to our melody. He rocked. I rolled my hips. We were complete right then. There were no naysayers. There was no past, and there certainly was no future.

Listening to the rhythm of Jude's increasingly ragged breaths, I gave myself over to this moment. Our song rose to a fevered pitch, and I listened hard to every note while it lasted.

* * *

Afterward, we were two damp and sated people lying on the bed together. His hand wandered mindlessly up and down my back.

"Jude?"

"Mmm?"

"Why did you give my brother a ride that night?"

I expected him to protest at the question, but he didn't. "I don't remember. Guess he needed a ride, that's all."

"Really? You two weren't friends."

"Nope."

"Then why did he ask you?"

"Don't know," he said quickly. *Too* quickly. "And I guess we can't ask him."

There was something tight about his voice that put me on edge. "After the accident, I asked a lot of questions that nobody answered."

"I'm sorry." Jude rolled onto his stomach, propping his chin into the crook of his elbow. "I'm sorry for everything that happened to you after I fucked up."

"I know you are. But it bothers me that I don't really understand what happened that night."

Jude sighed. "The problem is that I don't either. I don't remember the accident at all. I don't remember getting into the car, and I don't remember getting cut out of it. First thing I remember is getting smacked around in an interrogation room."

Wait. "They *hit* you?"

He made an unhappy sound in the back of his throat. "I killed the chief's *son*. There wasn't a cop in the state who could get in trouble for roughing me up. Of course they hit me."

"Why did they interrogate you at all?"

His gray eyes softened. "Same reason you are, baby. You have questions with no answers."

Still. I'd always assumed that Jude was taken to a hospital after the accident, because that's where people who'd been in accidents went. Didn't they? "Who hit you?"

Jude pinched the bridge of his nose. I'd officially killed the mood, that was for sure. "I don't know his name. The same guy who busted us that time for making out in my car at Pigeon Pond. Younger guy with the receding hairline?"

"Newcombe. I remember him. He moved to Arizona, or somewhere."

"Good riddance." Jude rolled onto his side and hauled me into his arms. "Why do you get to ask all the questions, anyway? I got one for you."

"Hit me."

"Why aren't you at Juilliard?"

Ah. "I changed my mind. That's all."

"What? *Challenge.* You used to practice every day for two hours, Soph. I may be the dumbest guy you know, but you're going to have to do a little better than 'I changed my mind.'"

I craned my neck to look at him. "You're not the dumbest guy I know. Not by a long mile."

"That's nice of you to say, baby. But you didn't answer my question. Do you still sing?"

"In the car on the way to work." I put my head on Jude's bare chest. "And in college I started learning to play the guitar and accompanying myself. But there hasn't been time for that lately."

Jude grunted, and I felt the vibration under my ear. "What a waste."

Maybe. But it wasn't the tragedy that he thought it was. "Do you remember how I used to make you listen to the original-cast recording of *Flying For You?*"

Jude's chest rose and fell as he chuckled. "Even after three years, I'm pretty sure I could sing the whole thing from start to finish right now."

"The soprano's name was Penny Lovejoy, and I worshipped her."

"I remember."

"Do you know what she does now? She's a realtor of fine homes in New Jersey."

A big, warm palm landed on the back of my neck. "Okay. And that's why you didn't go to Juilliard?"

"Partly. There were a lot of reasons. But I didn't change my plans on a whim. I did a lot of recon. My voice teacher hooked me up with some of her old students in New York, and I went down to visit them. It was kind of horrifying."

"Why?"

"These girls were successful by any measure—they had

small parts on Broadway or on tour. They were working singers, which is amazing. But none of them felt even a little bit secure. And they auditioned like crazy. One of these girls said to me, 'A professional singer is a professional auditioner. If that doesn't appeal to you, do something else with your life.'"

Jude was silent for a minute. "You hate auditioning."

"Yep. I really do."

"But what if she was wrong?"

I shook my head. "She wasn't. I tagged along with her to an open call for an off-Broadway musical, and there were girls in line around the fucking block. They were singing scales to stay warm, and every one of them had amazing pipes. And I just saw that and started to wonder whether I wanted it badly enough. I love music. But I didn't want to show up for cattle calls and get excited just because the director tugged on his ear or scribbled on his pad while I was singing."

"Juilliard would have been fun, though."

"Yeah." I sighed. "Sure. But now I'm getting a degree in a field that has actual jobs. Also, it allowed me to stay here in Vermont when my mother needed me."

"What are you going to do when she doesn't anymore?"

As if. "I'll figure something out."

Jude and I cuddled and kissed until I had to go. It was torture climbing out of his warm arms and putting on my clothes. "I count down the days until Wednesday," he whispered. "Keeps me sane, knowing that if I stay strong all week I get to see you."

I leaned over the bed and kissed him one more time so that I didn't have to answer. For the next six days I'd look for Jude on every street corner, just hoping for a glimpse. He didn't keep me sane—he made me crazy. Until he'd showed up again I hadn't realized how lonely I was.

My life seemed more impossible now than it had at any other point these three years.

His strong fingers stroked my back as I leaned down to put on my socks. "Have a good week. I'll be thinking about you."

"I'll be thinking about you, too. Every day," I confessed. *Every hour, when I'm supposed to be writing my last exam and trying to figure out how to fund treatments for a deaf toddler.*

One more kiss. One more sweet hug against his firm chest.

Then I got the heck out of there, hurrying down the steps outside his room. Running off into the lonely night.

Chapter Seventeen

Sophie

Internal DJ tuned to: "Blue Christmas" Elvis version

"Come on in, the kitchen is this way," I said to the caterer, holding open our back door.

"I got it," the woman said, her arms wrapped around a tray. "I remember from last year."

Of course she did. My father's annual holiday party was just another reminder that my life had been in the same rut for a while now. *Next year*, I vowed to myself. *This won't be my life.*

I had to get out of here.

But tonight I was trapped. I held the door three more times for the caterer and her assistants, and then for my father. "Evening," he grunted as he passed me. We were barely speaking these days. "Food's here, huh? What did your mother order this time?"

Ouch. I'd done the ordering, of course. Because calling in the menu would require ten minutes of focus, which was ten more than she could spare us. "Pigs in blankets, of course, because there would be a riot if we cut those off the menu. Pulled-pork sliders. Potato salad. Cheese quiche for anyone who doesn't eat meat." Hopefully no vegans had joined my father's police force since last Christmas. Because they were going to go hungry.

My father made no comment. He just kept right on going through the house, past the rooms I'd spent all day cleaning. Every year he threw this shindig for the cops who worked for him and their wives. Departmental money was tight, so we hosted the party. Which meant that I spent hours cleaning our house and trying to make the place look festive.

Today, instead of hitting the books, I'd picked out a Christmas tree and decorated it myself. I put a wreath on the front door and candles and pine boughs on the mantel. By five o'clock I'd been tired, dusty and covered in pine sap.

And all the while I asked myself *why*. My life-long good-girl streak was partly to blame. But if I blew off the party, my father would scream at my mother and possibly at me. And there were guests coming. Our dysfunction wasn't their fault or their problem.

Leaving the caterers to their work, I climbed the stairs.

"Mom?" I found her in the bedroom, staring at the television mounted on the wall. She was watching a cooking show. Oh, the irony. This woman used to be so busy cooking that she didn't watch TV. "Mom? Let's go. You have to get dressed for the party."

She clicked mute. "What shall I wear?"

I didn't bother withholding my sigh. My mother remained *just* functional enough to fake it. If she drooled on herself or spoke in tongues, it would be easier to force her to get some professional help. "The green Christmas sweater and black slacks?" I went over to her closet and found the sweater in question. "You have thirty minutes." After thrusting the sweater into her hands, I left her alone.

Showering left me with just fifteen minutes until the guests would arrive. So my big act of rebellion was to don my favorite pair of jeans. Usually I'd put on tights and a dress, but tonight I just didn't fucking feel like it. As a compromise, I pulled on a pretty sweater and shimmery earrings. And then I slicked on some red lip gloss and a generous coat of black mascara.

Good enough.

Downstairs in the dining room, caterers did laps to and from the kitchen. My father stood drinking a glass of scotch in their midst, oblivious to the frantic pace around him. He looked me up and down when I walked into the room. "That's what you're wearing?"

My mouth gaped open. "Seriously? Why do you care?"

He stirred his ice cubes with a finger. "Don't think you've met Nelligan yet, right?"

I shook my head. But I knew the name—he was my father's youngest officer.

"I think you'd like him," he said. "He's single."

"Um, that's nice?"

The doorbell rang, ending our conversation. I snagged a glass of wine off one table and a miniature pig-in-a-blanket off another. My father wanted to set me up with a cop? That was new. And now I couldn't wait to meet this guy. If my father thought he was suitable, I was betting on some pasty dude with tape on his glasses and a stutter.

* * *

Officer Nelligan wasn't all that bad. Sure, he was wearing a sweater vest. I didn't know anyone still wore those. And he kept calling me "Miss Sophie," which made me feel as though I were trapped in an old movie. But he was friendly and unassuming. He was like Denny with a southern accent and a gun on his hip.

"May I get you another drink, Miss Sophie?" he asked, his blue eyes wide over his freckled nose.

"That would be lovely. Thank you." I'd already made the rounds, greeting everyone once. I'd eaten my weight in little hors d'oeuvres. Now the final hours of the evening needed only to be endured.

While Nelligan trotted off to refresh my cabernet, I decided there was a question I should ask him. So far we'd stuck to the safest of topics. I'd assured him that even a southern boy could

Sarina Bowen

learn to snowboard. And he'd assured me that even a northerner could get to like grits.

"So," I said when he brought me a fresh glass of the inexpensive hooch that my father served his officers' wives. (The cops were all drinking beer, because no cop would be caught dead drinking cabernet.) "I suppose you've heard all the gossip about me."

The guy's eyes widened only slightly. "I don't listen much to gossip."

"I'm sure you're a good boy," I said, tilting my head in a way that could only be described as seductive. "But you can't live in this county and work for my father and *not* hear all the shit that went down here before."

"I heard y'all went through a bad time," he said diplomatically.

"Truth," I said, touching my wine glass to his beer bottle. "And I'd really like to move on, but it's not easy." I held his eyes while I said it. They absolutely warmed. If I wasn't mistaken, Nelligan liked the idea of me moving on.

"Well." He gave me a shy smile. "If there's any way I can help, maybe you'll let me know."

"Actually—" I smiled back at him, feeling like the most evil troll in the world. "—there is something I've been meaning to ask for. And I think you could help."

"Name it," he said.

"I would like to read the police report from the night of my brother's accident. Nobody ever showed it to me." I understood why, I really did. We were all so raw and devastated at the time. But I'd assumed we'd pull together enough at some point to have an honest discussion of what happened that night. Even now, the questions I asked were shot down immediately.

Clearly my new pal Nelligan was not expecting this request. "Um..." he fumbled. "I shouldn't really do that without your father's permission."

"Really?" I said, tossing my hair in a way that was less than subtle. "It's a public document. If I file a request, I can get it anyway. Do you really want to make me do that?"

His expression turned sheepish. "I guess not."

172

"This way I could read it without upsetting him."

He scratched his head, still looking uncomfortable. "How would that work, exactly?"

"We could meet for coffee. You'll bring the file. How is that difficult?"

He smiled. "All right, Miss Sophie."

Chapter Eighteen

Jude

Cravings Meter: 4 and Escalating

Winter was beautiful in Vermont. I'd forgotten how nice our town looked with a little snow on the porches and Christmas lights in the trees. I put wreaths over both garage doors—real ones, with red bows. It was all part of my plan to perk up the garage and attract more business.

I finished painting an interior wall of the garage. Somehow another sober week was strung together—all seven days.

On eBay, I sold several Porsche parts. Packing and shipping them kept me busy for at *least* a whole hour. My PayPal account was accumulating blood money, and I needed to mention it to Sophie. I kept putting it off, though. My time with her was precious and reserved for better things.

The following Wednesday went down much like the last one. After working the church supper, I went home and showered, leaving the door open. This time when Sophie arrived I was already on my back in bed. When I heard her footsteps on the stairs, I lifted my arms overhead, tucking them behind the pillow.

She opened the door and spotted me there, stretched out, my chest on display, the sheet tented over my erection. She gave it a pointed frown. "You started without me?"

"Maybe." I dropped a hand down to my dick, stroking my fingers up the underside through the sheet. "Didn't know for sure if you were coming over." That was teasing talk, of course. We'd exchanged several hot glances over various food preparations.

I don't think we were subtle, either. We must not have been, because her boy Denny had looked grouchy as hell tonight.

Sophie stripped out of her jacket and hung it on my doorknob. She kicked off her shoes and then stood there a second just watching me. "Pull the sheet down," she demanded.

As I tugged it off, she knelt on the bed. One second later her lips closed around my dick. I threaded my fingers through her hair and forgot all about car parts on eBay.

* * *

After another very satisfying hour together, she lay in my arms and drowsed for a while. "Tired tonight?" I asked her, kissing her forehead to help her stay awake.

"So tired."

"I wish I could just tuck you in and let you sleep."

She'd sighed. "Me too."

But we couldn't do that, and we both knew it.

"Wednesday is the best day of the week," she whispered, trailing the backs of her fingers over my face.

"They don't call it 'hump day' for nothing."

She laughed and gave me one more smile. "Maybe we could see each other over the weekend."

"How?" We had to be so, so careful. Her father would freak if he knew we spent time together, and I didn't want to make Sophie's life any more difficult than it already was. Even our Wednesday trysts made me feel guilty.

"Stowe is ninety percent open already. Want to go snowboarding?"

I did. Lift tickets were probably almost a hundred bucks, though. And there was another problem. "I can't. No board or boots."

"Where are they?"

I pulled Sophie closer, and it killed me to answer honestly. I did it, though. "I sold them for almost nothing because I needed a hit."

Sophie inhaled too sharply. It was the gasp of someone who understood more than they wanted to. But this conversation was absolutely necessary. Part of recovery is learning to get this shit off your chest and admitting to the people you love all the ways you've hurt them. "I did a lot of shit I'm not proud of. Hate telling you about it. But you should know."

"What else?" she asked, her voice an uncomfortable scrape. She might not want to hear these things, but Sophie was wise to learn exactly what I was capable of.

Just in case she dabbled in the same kind of improbable, romantic thoughts that occasionally got the better of me, she needed to know who she was really dealing with.

At yesterday's NA meeting we'd talked about all our "nevers." As in—the shit an addict says he'll never do and then does anyway. We all have them.

"Before I went to prison, I did painkillers, right? I snorted them. But in prison that shit was too expensive for me. The only thing I could afford was heroin."

She stiffened in my arms. "Like, with needles?"

"Just like that. I shot it in between my fingers to avoid track marks and in between my toes. Anywhere I thought it wouldn't show. It was the last thing I thought I'd ever do. And then I was still trying to hide it."

Sophie was silent for a minute. "You can just buy heroin in prison?"

"Yup. I bought cigarettes and food with my paycheck and traded them for heroin. The prison doctor gave out clean needles. It's a very efficient little economy they have working in there."

"Ugh. I hate thinking about you doing that," she said to my chest.

"Me, too," I said quickly. *And yet if you handed me a needle right now I might do it again.*

The first time I shot heroin it took me to a sweet, forgetful place. But then it just left me wanting more, and afterward the high was never as good. I hated that shit with all my heart, and I loved it, too.

How fucked was I?

Sophie didn't ask any more questions. The truth was that I'd been more honest with her these last few weeks than ever before. Weirdly, this was as healthy as our relationship had ever been.

It's not a relationship, I reminded myself. Just two people relieving some sexual tension on Wednesday nights. That's all we could ever be. And even while I wanted more, this arrangement prevented me from relying too much on Sophie's company.

One of these days it would end for good. Sophie was almost done with school. She'd hinted at having to look for a new job. And I had to leave Colebury eventually. As long as her father was chief of police, this town would always be my enemy. I'd been stopped—and my car searched—twice this month. Once the cop said I didn't signal a turn. But he let me go with just "a friendly warning," because we both knew it was bullshit.

The second time the cop didn't even give a reason. "Step out of the car, sir," was all he said. I complied, of course. But these days the only place I drove was to the Shipleys' and the grocery store. I walked everywhere else I needed to go. The police had made me into the most eco-friendly resident of Colebury. Griff Shipley would be so proud.

"You could rent a snowboard," Sophie suggested suddenly, interrupting my morose thoughts.

"Sure. But what if one of your dad's deputies goes to the mountain on his day off? You know it's a bad idea if we're seen together. I don't want to make your life more difficult."

"Fuck," she grumbled in frustration. "There has to be somewhere we could go."

I stroked my fingers through her hair and didn't argue. She needed to realize it for herself—there were no cheery options for us. We were stuck, and there was no unsticking us.

Before Sophie left, I tugged her down for one more lingering kiss. I held the back of her head, making sure I got a good one before she went. It had to last me a long time. "Bye,"

I said, instead of *I love you*. Saying it out loud would only be more depressing. Because I couldn't have her. Not for keeps.

"Bye," she'd said instead of *I love you, too*.

The sound of the door closing behind her had made me flinch. I went to sleep feeling sad and woke up feeling worse.

Thank God it was Thursday, though, and I could spend the day looking forward to an evening with the Shipleys. I showered and headed down to the garage at eight AM. When I touched the doorknob, the door creaked open under my hand.

Weird.

A chill climbed up my spine, and instead of going inside I just stood there for a moment. I hadn't left the garage open last night. I'd never do that. We had too many expensive tools in here. As a recovering addict, I knew all too well that anything of value might be stolen by somebody who thought he could get a few bucks for it.

"Hello?" I said into the darkness. I supposed there was an infinitesimally small chance that Dad had come in here already.

Silence.

I reached inside and flicked on the lights. Everything looked just as I'd left it. And there was nobody here. So I shook off my wary feeling and made some coffee in the drip pot I kept in here. Then I got to work organizing our collection of paints and finishes.

My efforts were rewarded in the late afternoon, when someone rolled in to ask about a custom paint job. That never happened.

The young man had driven up in a Prius. While he got out, I circled the car, looking for the dent. But there wasn't one. He wanted a perky paint job in lime green. "I own a solar-panel installation business," he explained. "The car is going to be, like, an advertisement on wheels. I'm going to add decals."

"Gotcha," I said, inviting him inside to look at our paint catalog. I wanted this work. Paint jobs weren't cheap. "Show me your logo. Let's see what would make a good color choice."

The logo was black, and he picked out the craziest, brightest green paint on the page. "Nobody's going to miss you in that color," I said.

"I know it's a little much, but I want to be visible."

Not a problem. "You know, if you angled a white stripe down the door right here, your logo would pop even more." I pointed.

The guy rubbed his beard. "That is not a bad idea. I want it legible."

"Exactly."

He clapped his hands. "Okay. Let's make this happen. What do I do?"

"Make a deposit, and I'll order the paint. I can fit you in next week." *Or anytime.*

"Good deal," he said, and we shook on it.

My father came in after that, probably because he smelled money. "You quote it right?" he asked when I told him about the paint job.

"Of course." *You dick.* "Don't forget—tomorrow's payday," I prompted him.

His answer was a grunt, but my reminder would probably do the trick. Sometimes he just plain forgot to pay me until I asked. When I was behind bars I'd bet he didn't even keep track of the books. He probably just spent whatever landed in the till. But I wasn't going to bust my ass for free. Every transfer from his bank account to mine put me one step closer to freedom.

At last it was quittin' time. "I'm out of here," I said. "Got dinner with friends." I'd started showing up to the Shipleys' early on Thursdays. It allowed me to help out in the kitchen and also spend a few minutes gossiping with May.

But first, some preparations. I got cleaned up and then took a walk to Crumbs. I'd become quite the regular customer. Their cakes were far from cheap, but they were quality. And K.K. was my new bff. She usually gave me a free cookie for the road.

The bell on the door jingled when I walked inside. Even though it was almost closing time, there were people seated inside, nursing the last espresso of the day, I supposed. I was distracted by the Christmas lights that K.K. had hung over the counter. I almost didn't notice Sophie sitting at one of the little tables. But she lifted her pretty face, and even that small movement had my gaze zeroing in on her.

When our eyes met, hers went wide. And then they dropped down to her coffee cup, which she studied as if the secret to life was written there.

Across the table from her sat a guy.

Shit. As my stomach bottomed out, I hastily looked the other way.

I knew Sophie and I weren't supposed to be a couple. Nobody could know about our Wednesday nights. But we hadn't run into each other like this before, and to watch her actually ignore me gave me heartburn. It really drove the reality of the situation home—all I would ever get were a few stolen moments. No more than that.

"Hey, hottie," K.K. teased. "What are you in the mood for this week?"

"What's good?"

"Well, if you like your cake to look like wood"—she wiggled her eyes suggestively—"I recommend the Buche du Noel. It's a French-Canadian thing."

The cake did, indeed, look like a yule log, complete with some lichen piped onto the side for realism. The damn thing was forty bucks, though. "Those crazy French Canadians. I think I'll take a cheesecake tonight," I said, pointing. Then I put my credit card on the counter.

"Always a solid choice." She moved away to box up my purchase

I stood there with my back to Sophie, feeling like shit. And eavesdropping. "Thank you again," Sophie was saying. "You've been so helpful."

"It's my pleasure, Miss Sophie. Let's do this again sometime."

"Absolutely."

If I could have stabbed myself with the ballpoint pen on the counter, I would've.

"Well, Officer Nelligan, I'd better be on my way in a few minutes."

Shit. The base of my spine tingled. No wonder she'd looked freaked out when I walked in. That was a *cop* she was sitting with. The guy worked for her father.

"I thought you were going to call me Rob."

I took my cheesecake and got the hell out of there.

When I went into the alley to get into the Avenger for the trip to the Shipleys', I could hear the garage phone ringing away inside.

Crap. The garage phone was the only way anyone could reach me, since I was too cheap to buy a cell phone. I heard the ringing stop. But then it started right up again immediately.

Fine. I unlocked the garage and ran for the phone, answering it before it went to the machine again. "Hello?"

"I'm so sorry," Sophie said right away. "That sucked. I feel shitty. But that guy I was sitting with works for—"

"I get it." My voice sounded tight, even though I really did get it.

"If one of my dad's deputies had a hunch that we were..." She cleared her throat. "They'd harass you."

This was true. They were harassing me already, but I wasn't going to worry her about it.

"Anyway, he's helping me with a question. It wasn't a date or anything."

It sure looked like one. Somehow I managed not to say that out loud. It would sound jealous as fuck. I took a deep breath. "Soph, you should go on as many dates as you want. With people you don't have to pretend not to recognize."

There was a deep silence on her end of the line. "I don't want to date anybody, Jude."

"You don't want to be with somebody nice and normal? That can't be true."

"Fuck normal! Normal is dull. That's what you told me when we were seventeen."

"Yeah? I was a bonehead when I was seventeen." *Still am.* "Don't try to sugarcoat this, okay? I can't be that guy sitting at the bakery with you. We can't go out for coffee and go to the movies. So we're just torturing each other right now. We fuck on Wednesdays and pretend that it isn't going to end badly."

"Jude!"

"What? Tell me how this ends."

"I don't want it to end at all."

"Really? You want to spend the rest of your life meeting me for ninety minutes on Wednesday nights? That's not living."

"Things could get better."

"How, Soph? How is that possible?"

"I haven't figured it out yet."

I snorted. "We are so fucked, and nothing you can say will convince me otherwise."

There was dead air between us, and I knew I'd been an ass. But it was for her own good. The silence stretched on. Later I would realize that the silence between us was the only reason I caught on to what was happening upstairs.

Over my head, I heard a creak. Which meant that there was somebody *in my room*. "Sophie," I whispered. "Where are you right now?"

"Sitting in my car behind the bakery. Why?"

"I gotta go," I said quickly. "We'll talk tomorrow, okay?"

"We will? How?"

Another creak sounded above me. "Gotta go for now, babe." I hung up the phone. Then I yanked a lug wrench off the wall.

Standing still, I listened again. I heard another creak. And a thump. Then the sound of feet running down shoddy wooden steps.

That got me moving. I exited the garage and crept toward the back just in time to see someone in a black hoodie running down the alley away from me. My chin snapped upward to look at the door to my room. It was standing open. But nobody else emerged.

With my heart in my mouth, I climbed the steps and flipped on the lights. My room was trashed. Again. It had been searched in a hurry. My drawers were empty, the contents strewn everywhere.

Rage pulsed from my chest and through my limbs. I mean—what the fuck? Did the cops do this? Or those fuckers who came into the garage to ask me about some stash of Gavin's?

My fingertips twitched, and then I had a drug craving so powerful that I had to just stand there clenching my fists, my eyes screwed shut.

Fuck. When I was released from prison, people told me to "stay out of trouble." But what the fuck do you do if trouble comes looking for you?

I didn't straighten up my room. I closed the door and locked it again. Whoever searched the place seemed to be able to come and go at will. I walked down the stairs and got into the Avenger. Then I drove straight out of town toward the Shipley Farm.

Do not pass Go, do not score a hit.

Chapter Nineteen

Sophie

Internal DJ tuned to: "Breakdown More" by Eric Hutchinson

After that horrible conversation with Jude, it was hard to put my game face on and walk into my house again. The police report that Officer Nelligan had lent me was zipped into my book bag. And even though neither of my parents had searched my things since high school, I was careful to carry the bag upstairs and deposit it on the floor of my room before starting a homemade noodle soup for dinner.

Chopping onions at the kitchen counter made me think of Jude. Hell, everything made me think of him. He'd sounded so angry on the phone. And so discouraged.

The covert nature of our affair didn't bother me very much, because the people in my life weren't honest with either me or themselves. My father buried his grief in anger and misplaced blame. My mother crumbled under the weight of hers and refused to talk about it even with someone trained to help.

My honesty was a gift that I chose to bestow on the people who deserved it. And lately, Jude was the one who best fit that description.

But I'd seen that hurt look on his face when he'd spotted

me in the bakery. Until today, I don't think I understood how hard it was to be Jude. Sometimes I chafed against the label of That Girl Who Dated the Druggie. But the judgment on him was so much worse. He walked around every day under the weight of having killed a man.

At the bakery, he was stung when I couldn't acknowledge him. But if I hadn't been sitting with a cop, I would have.

Probably. If my father suspected that Jude and I were in contact, he'd freak. I needed a little more time to figure how to get out of my father's orbit without abandoning Mom.

My diced onion chunks weren't nearly as precise and uniform as Jude's, damn it. I wanted to stand next to him in a kitchen somewhere and watch him work, without having to disguise my interest. Hell, I wanted to stand together in *our* kitchen. Wherever that mythical place might be.

Jude didn't think it would ever happen. I wanted us to be more optimistic than that. I wanted him to *try*.

Feeling blue, I sautéed the onions with carrots and celery. Then I added chicken stock, broccoli, noodles and water. I left it simmering for a bit, then I added leftover chicken, because my father bitched whenever I didn't put meat in a meal.

Feeling like Cinderella, I brought my father his portion in the den. It's not that I enjoyed waiting on him. It's just that I didn't want to have a sit-down family meal.

He looked up in surprise when I carried in the tray.

"I have a headache and an exam to study for," I explained. "I'll be in my room."

"Your mother?" he asked, taking the tray.

"I set her up in the kitchen. She's reading a magazine." *She never speaks to us, anyway.*

Having satisfied everyone to the best of my abilities, I went upstairs with my own bowl of soup. I cleaned all the schoolwork off my desk and closed the door. After pulling out the police file, I ate my supper while examining the file's exterior. The tab listed a date from three-and-a-half years ago and simply, *Haines, Gavin.*

Pushing my empty bowl aside, I took a deep breath and then flipped open the cover. I was afraid there would be photographs. But I didn't see any yet. The top page was a neatly executed summary. *Report: Fatal Accident Investigation.*

I'd never been told exactly how it all went down. But now the order of events was spread out in front of me, as tidy as the outlines my high school teachers used to demand for research papers. At 7:53 a motorist had made a 9-1-1 call from the two-lane highway heading north out of town. At 7:55 two of my father's deputies were dispatched, along with an emergency vehicle (The Lifeline Highliner) from the fire department.

The first responders arrived all around the same time. They found one Gavin Haines in a prone position in the ditch. He'd been thrown from the vehicle and was not breathing.

One Jude Nickel was trapped inside the vehicle. He was non-responsive.

At 8:10, seventeen minutes after the first 9-1-1 call, a second ambulance was dispatched.

Ten minutes later the LifeLiner departed the scene for the trauma unit at Montpelier Medical with Gavin Haines onboard. He would be pronounced dead on arrival.

The report didn't have much to say about the next hour. The door of a Porsche 911 was "forcibly removed," and Jude Nickel was extracted. He was taken into police custody when officers left the scene at 9:12. There were no notes about Jude's condition or about any medical treatment he received.

I turned the page.

Interview Record: Jude Nickel. At 9:14 Mr. Nickel was read his Miranda rights and verbally waved his right to both silence and an attorney.

I shivered when I read that statement. Jude had told me that he came to in an interrogation room with Newcombe hitting him. So on page two, I was already reading lies. Jude had also said that no cop in Vermont would take it easy on the guy who killed the police chief's son.

If Jude read this spotty account of that awful night, would he even be surprised?

I kept reading. There was a medical report for a blood test "done at the scene." The result was consistent with "prescription opioids." There was an affidavit by the county's DRE (Drug Recognition Expert) swearing that he had evaluated Jude at the station house and found him to display symptoms of "profound intoxication."

And yet he'd waved his Miranda rights. How were those two things compatible?

I got up and walked away from the file, as if the distance from the pages would help me think. I'd noticed there was no mention of my father anywhere in those notes. But he'd been there that night—he'd gone into the station a while after the terrible knock had come at our door. He'd waited for Father Peters to arrive. And then he'd strapped on his gun and left the house. I didn't see him until the next day.

Just thinking about that night made me tremble. I'd dialed Jude's phone over and over. I probably tried a hundred times. The officer who came to tell us that Gavin was dead hadn't said a word about Jude. So I'd called the station house, but my father hung up on me when I asked him.

I'd spent the night crying and shaking in this very room. Alone.

Now I found myself staring out the window at our darkened street. But that wasn't going to get any of my questions answered. I went back to the police report and examined every last page. There weren't any photographs at all, which was weird. Maybe Nelligan had left them out intentionally to save my feelings. That was something I needed to know, so I fired up my laptop and wrote him an email. But before I hit "send," it occurred to me that I didn't want my questions hitting a station email account. And I didn't know Nelligan's private email address.

But I did have his phone number.

I sat down on the floor between my bed and the exterior wall. This is where I'd always parked my ass when I needed to have a private conversation with Jude.

Nelligan answered on the second ring. "Hi there," I said.

"Hi, Miss Sophie. How are you on this fine evening?"

I chuckled at his cheesy greeting. "Fine, thank you. And I called to tell you again how much I appreciate that you brought me this file."

"I hope it's not too tough to read," he said.

"It's not easy, honestly." I had to tread carefully. "I mean, I know that Gavin is gone. And now I know a little more about that awful night, and that's important to me."

"Good."

"I was wondering if you edited out the photos to take it easy on me, though."

"Well, I would have considered it, except there weren't any."

My neck tingled. "None?"

"My guess is that they're stored somewhere else, in deference to the chief."

That didn't sound right to me, though. The file said that my brother was rushed to the hospital, where he was pronounced dead on arrival. So photos taken at the scene would not have shown anything graphic or bloody. "Maybe," I said. Asking Nelligan to snoop wasn't a good idea. He was a stranger, and I couldn't push him to sneak around behind my father's back. "Thanks again, Nelligan."

"You're welcome, Miss Sophie."

After we hung up, I went back to the file. I read every scrawled note in the margins and every line of the copy. I found two more odd things that didn't sit well with me. Someone had scrawled "tox screens for Haines and Nickel" into the margin of the file's index page at the back. But there was only one blood test in the file—Jude's. And who would test a dead passenger? Maybe that was an error.

The other odd thing was that it said "door forcibly removed to evacuate passenger." That should have read *driver*. My brother was thrown from the car through the windshield, and Jude was stuck inside. But one line of the report had it backward.

Feeling like Encyclopedia Brown, on a fresh sheet of notebook paper I began to list every detail that bothered me.

1. Jude waives rights, but Jude is wasted.
2. Where were they going that night?

3. No photos of the car. Why?

4. No mention of drugs found? Yet Jude was charged with possession.

5. Two tox screens?

6. Wrong door/side in notes

I read over the list again, certain that this report was fishy. Maybe it was only shoddy work. But seriously? Which employee of my father's would want to do a lousy job on the most important police report of the year?

Using my phone and a faxing app, I took pictures of every page then emailed them to myself.

Then I tucked the forbidden file away in my bag again, zipping it shut tightly.

Chapter Twenty

Jude

Cravings meter: 4 and holding steady

On the following Wednesday afternoon—after polishing off a sandwich I'd bought for myself—I went back to work on my new customer's Prius.

His bright green paint had arrived, so I'd had the customer drop the car off yesterday for prep work.

"Can I get you to put the decal on when the paint job is done?" he'd asked.

"Probably," I said. "I don't have any experience with those, but if I can get enough information about the process I'll do it for you."

The guy nodded. "The nearest dealer of these custom decals is fifty miles away. I couldn't find anything closer, so I'll probably need your help."

"Okay, man."

That was something I should look into. It wouldn't hurt to have another line of business to offer. Another skill. Another way out of Dodge.

The first morning with his car I'd primed the panels. Now, with a block of 600-grit sandpaper, I smoothed everything out.

Body work was a strange corner of the auto repair market.

Instead of making the car perform better, you're only making it look nicer on the outside. When I was a teenager it seemed so pointless. Fix the dent in a little roller skate of a car? You're still stuck with a little roller skate of a car. I would have rather rebuilt engines until they roared like beasts.

These days I was more patient with bodywork. I liked the idea that rough patches could be sanded out and that bumps could be smoothed again. If not in my life, than on a car. I'd set myself up near the window, with a lamp over my other shoulder. The two sources of light helped me to suss out any tiny imperfections in the surface.

The Green Day CD I'd been playing in our old stereo box ended, leaving me in silence. I heard only the sweep of the sanding block and my own breathing.

And a bump against the back wall.

I froze, the sanding block hovering over my work. A bump could be nothing. But I was feeling paranoid these days. Not only were the cops on my ass, but I was worried about the drug dealer who'd stopped by to pay me a visit. My gut told me I wasn't rid of him yet.

Silently I set the sanding block onto the panel and slid out from behind my workspace. Yanking my goggles off, I set them down.

There was another bump, softer this time. It was possible I was about to bust an alley cat or a kid with his soccer ball. But better safe than sorry.

I slipped out of the front door and walked quickly up the driveway between my father's house and the garage. When I peered carefully around the corner toward the back, the first thing I saw was the tenting of the tarp over the Porsche.

Someone was fucking with my wreck of a car.

"Hey!" I said loudly, stepping into the alley.

A startled gasp accompanied the perpetrator's leap away from the car.

It was...*Sophie*?

With my pulse racing, I cursed under my breath. "What are you *doing* back here?"

"Jesus." She put a hand over her heart. "Do you always leap

out from between the buildings?"

"I'm sorry," I said quietly. "Thought you were…" *A drug dealer still looking for his stash.* "A vandal."

Sophie crossed her arms, looking guilty.

"What *are* you doing?"

"Just looking," she said quickly. "At the car."

"God, why? I've been trying to get that thing out of here so you wouldn't *have* to look at it." Shit. The last time we spoke it had not been a good conversation. And now I was practically yelling at her. "Do you want to come inside?"

She gave the car a sideways glance and then smoothed the tarp down on its crumpled front. "Sure." She followed me into the garage. "Happy Christmas Eve Eve," she said with a little smile.

It was true—I had almost survived the holiday season. "Back atcha, babe."

"You're not going to get rid of the car right away, are you?"

"Uh…" I didn't understand why she'd care. "It's taking me a while. I've been selling some parts on eBay. There will be some money coming your way from it."

"Money?"

"Sure. Maybe two thousand bucks if we're lucky. Could be less, though. Depends on how much I can salvage. You can put it in your music school fund."

"I don't have a music school fund."

"You should."

Sophie sighed. "You're getting me off topic."

"What *is* the topic?"

"You don't mind if I look at the car, right? I have questions. There's something I don't understand about what happened that night."

Fuck. "I don't see what good could come of thinking about it." There were too many people in my life asking all the wrong questions. Some shit should just stay buried.

"Jude." She crossed her arms and cocked a hip against the grungy counter.

"What?"

"Have you been honest with me?"

I snorted. "No, Sophie. When we were together, I got high behind your back every damn day. That's pretty dishonest, don't you think?"

"That is *not* what I mean, and you know it! When I asked you about where you and Gavin were going together, you told me you didn't remember. But there must be *something* that stands out. Gavin was a complete shit to you every chance he got. Why would he ask you for a ride when there was a whole house full of frat boys to do it?"

Oh, Jesus. "You know what?" I pointed at the dismembered Prius. "I'm in the middle of a job. It's not a good time."

"Will it ever be a good time? Because I feel like you're ducking me. That makes you just another person in my life who won't tell me the truth. You're supposed to be the one who does, Jude. *You.*"

Now my hands were sweating, and I felt a familiar itch in my limbs. "Sophie, I'll see you at the church tonight, okay? Let me get through this." I meant the drug craving that was suddenly making my T-shirt stick to my back and not the custom paint job on the table behind me. Hopefully she couldn't tell.

She peered up at me, and I saw judgment in her eyes. I'm sure I deserved it, too. "Okay. Later." She sighed.

"Later," I echoed. But then I couldn't resist closing the distance between us and kissing her forehead. With a sigh, she put a hand to my shoulder and squeezed. I never wanted any trouble between us. But life was just so fucking complicated.

Shit.

She left, and I paced the garage for a couple of minutes, feeling twitchy. I went over to a chin-up bar I'd installed when I was fourteen and banged out a quick set of ten. A little muscle fatigue was just what I needed to soothe the tension knotting my insides.

I bent over for a hamstring stretch and counted slowly to ten. In my mind, I pictured the warming hut at the top of Mount Mansfield, where I used to like to snowboard. Back in tenth grade, the top of that ski hill was my favorite place. Nothing bad ever happened up there, and you could see all the way to New York on one side and New Hampshire on the other.

Deep breaths, I ordered myself. *This too shall pass.*

At rehab, they'd taught us some meditation techniques. I was pretty shitty at meditating, but one thing the psychologist said had stuck with me. "The goal of meditation is not to make you all into superhumans. The goal is to remind your brain that focus is a *choice*. That a place of calm is always waiting for you if you seek it."

I hoped she was right.

After putting in a half-hour more work, I began cleaning up. I shut off the work lamp over my table and swept sanding dust off the Prius's panel.

The cravings were still going strong. Maybe that's why I sensed the intruders before I saw them.

The bulk of someone's form cast a shadow in the window light. Then it disappeared again.

Cops, my subconscious offered up. Unease coiled low in my belly. I hoped Sophie hadn't been spotted here by her father.

Whoever was outside my door was trying to be stealthy. I tensed, wondering what was coming. Slowly, I set the sanding block down. I wanted something heavier in my hand. Unfortunately I only had time to take one step before the door burst open.

Leaping toward the tools hanging on the far wall, I almost made it.

Almost.

I was reaching for the lug wrench when someone kicked my feet out from under me. I barely got my arms up to cushion my head by the time I hit the concrete floor. Instinctively I curled into a ball, and so the first kick landed at my back. The boot hit so hard that I saw stars. When I tried to inhale, I couldn't do it.

"You think that's bad? Tell us where the shit is or I will finish you."

Not cops.

Fuck.

The pain from the drug dealer's kick was so fierce that it took a moment before I could even force the words out. "Don't know. Never did."

The next blow landed at my kidney, and then the next one made me shout in pain.

"WHERE!" shouted the goon. "Check his pockets," he said to someone. "And the cash register. The shit has to be here somewhere."

It's just pain, I told myself. I gave myself a count of three to recover, then I rolled away from my attackers. I made it about three feet before someone came at me from the opposite side. Fuck, there were three of them. But I could see a tire iron just out of my reach...

That's when I took a boot to the head. And everything went black.

Chapter Twenty-One

Sophie

Internal DJ is set to: "Blue Christmas," Jewel Version

Community Dinner Night was the usual chaos. Everyone was in a Christmassy mood except for me. Even Mrs. Walters was singing Jingle Bells in time with the clanking of the dishwashing machine.

Jude wasn't at the prep station.

I put two-dozen chicken legs into a baking dish and sprinkled my signature spice mixture over them. And I tried not to fret. He was just pissed at me, probably. Or maybe there was some rush job at the shop that needed his attention.

There was no way to text him to confirm any of these theories. I hated how tricky it was to reach him, so I'd bought Jude a pre-paid phone for Christmas. I'd planned to give it to him tonight, after a round or two of sweaty make-up sex.

But where was he now?

"Exams all done?" Denny asked, grabbing the pan of chicken and sliding it into the oven.

"Yeah. Turned in the take-home on Monday." I snuck another glimpse of the prep station. Still empty.

"How's your pediatric case coming?" he asked, breaking

open another package of chicken.

I put an empty pan in front of him. "Well, the child is getting her cochlear implant soon, but they haven't figured out the financial piece yet. I'm helping them apply to three foundations for assistance," I said, reaching for the spices. "I think we have a good shot of finding a donation to cover the deductible for the little girl's treatment. I want her to have it before she turns two."

"Cool," Denny said.

"Mmm," I replied, distracted again. I couldn't help replaying my conversation with Jude. I'd basically called him a liar. Could he really be angry enough to blow off the dinner?

"Everything okay?" Denny asked.

"Sure, why?"

"Because you've been staring at that oven door for a long time."

I turned around on a sigh. "Sorry. What's next?"

"Are we mashing the potatoes? Or are they going to be just boiled, and tossed with butter?"

"Um, boiled I guess. The mixer has been on the fritz, I think."

"We could smash 'em," Denny suggested.

"Okay?" My eyes made another involuntary trip over to the prep table. It was still empty.

"Is something the matter with Jude?" Denny asked quietly.

The question made me grumpy. "If I said there was, would you give me another lecture?"

"Oh." He sighed. "Look, I'm sorry about what I said—"

I held up a hand. "Let's just forget it. We have potatoes to smash."

Stepping around Denny, I went back to my work area, cleaning all the chicken wrappers off of it. Worrying about Jude made me feel disloyal, because I kept wondering if he'd gotten into trouble. My mind spun a scenario wherein he had a really stressful week...and then did something stupid to ease himself.

The truth was that I'd never be able to look at Jude with the same naive eyes as my teenage self. Even if he and I were able to be a normal couple, I might always worry about him turning to drugs. If he were late to come home, or missing for a couple of hours, I'd wonder why. It would be a lot like dating someone with a history of unfaithfulness.

And now I hated myself for thinking these disloyal thoughts. Even worse? We'd argued. If Jude fell off the wagon right this second, I'd feel responsible.

"We're down a man?" Father Peters asked, surveying the kitchen with his fists on his hips.

"Seems so," Denny said.

"Funny how we come to depend on every volunteer," the priest said, frowning. "What should I do? Doors open in forty-five minutes."

"Peel some potatoes?" Denny suggested. "I'll help."

"Let's go."

I looked over the serving station, which was already set up. And then the oven timer buzzed, so I donned an oven mitt to check the first batch of chicken legs. That first night when Jude had appeared, we were serving this same meal. I'd been comically distracted by his presence. And now I was distracted by his absence. I had the sinking feeling that it would always be this way between us. Tortured.

Damn you, Jude.

Chapter Twenty-Two

Jude

Cravings Meter: 0

Beeping. That was the first thing I heard. I didn't have anything in my room that made that beeping noise. So where was I?

For a few minutes, I forgot to worry about it. I was just so groggy, and drifting felt good. Although I felt some pain in my side, the ache lacked sharp edges. And *I* lacked sharp edges. Everything was liquid.

Except for that beeping sound. And the voices in the background.

Voices?

I opened my eyes and saw a grid of unfamiliar ceiling tiles. The walls in my peripheral vision were white. I tried to place the voices in the background, but they were indistinct. And then I heard an amplified voice over some kind of loudspeaker. "Paging Doctor Weaver. Doctor Weaver to the fourth-floor data center, please."

A *hospital.* I was at a fucking hospital.

That woke me up enough to remember some of what had happened. Those goons at the garage had kicked the shit out of me, and now I was in the emergency room.

Shit.

I closed my eyes again and tried to take inventory. My head was foggy. Things hurt. My right arm, for one. It was bound up somehow, so that I couldn't move it. I also had pain in my left side. I wasn't wearing my clothes anymore. My legs felt bare beneath the sheet they'd put over me. And something was stuck to my left hand.

Opening my eyes, I turned my head gingerly to the left. Indeed, there was tape on my hand. I spied a thin tube running from the taped part of my wrist and upward. By craning my neck, I could see that the tube ran to an IV bag hanging from a pole. Inside the IV bag was a clear liquid. Fluids.

Something bothered me about this, but it was hard to say what. My focus on these problems was pleasantly blurry. I let my eyes fall closed again, floating on my own drowsiness. I felt peaceful.

I felt *drugged*.

My eyes flew open again. Wrenching my head to the side, I peered up at the IV bag again. There was a tag on it, but I couldn't read it from here. Didn't matter, though. I already knew what was in the bag.

"Fuck!" My voice was hoarse from disuse. I tried to move my right arm to grasp for the tube in my left arm. But my right arm was held tightly against my body with a sling. And even trying to move it caused a shooting pain in my forearm. "*Ah*," I gasped, surprised by its intensity.

My heart began to pound, and I tasted bile in my throat. Fucking *painkillers*. I'd had six months! Six whole fucking months. And some asshole doctor just fucked me over. The back of my throat began to burn.

Turning my attention to my left wrist, I gave it a good tug. But the tape held. I gave it another yank, and the result was not what I'd hoped for. The IV tower tipped toward me, hitting the bed and then slowly sliding to the floor with a crash.

A woman in nursing scrubs came running at the sound. She looked at me and frowned. "Mr. Nickel. You're awake. What happened here?"

I lifted my left wrist. "Take it out. I can't have painkillers."

She leaned over for the IV stand, righting it quickly. "You had surgery, Mr. Nickel. The doctor had to remove your spleen, because it was ruptured." She put a hand over the IV tape at my wrist. "I know it's a lot to take in."

I yanked my wrist away. "You don't understand. I can't have narcotics. I'm an addict." I could feel that shit swimming through my veins, too.

"What's the problem here?" A clean-cut young man came into the room wearing a white coat with *Dr. Flemming* stitched onto the pocket. Really? The teen doctor was going to help?

Fuck me. "I had six months clean," my voice wobbled as I tried to explain. "Now there's smack in my arm."

Teen doctor's eyebrows shot up. "What?"

My eyes were hot now, from anger or frustration or what-the-fuck-ever. "Get it out," I said, lifting my head. If I sat up, maybe they'd hear me. "No narcotics for me. I'm an addict." How many times did I have to say it? I struggled upward.

But the nurse lunged, pushing my shoulder back down to the mattress. "Don't do that. You have stitches."

Boy did I ever. Pain bloomed in my side, and I blinked back tears. "Please take it out," I begged. *"Please."* And even if she did, I knew exactly what would happen anyway. Whether I got rid of the drug in my arm now or tomorrow or whenever, I was going to have withdrawal symptoms. First I would get the shakes and feel panicky. The panic was almost the worst part. Then the nausea would come. My stomach would rebel, and I wouldn't be able to sleep. And even if I withstood the hours of shaking and puking, I'd be left with cravings far worse than anything I'd felt in months.

Again. I'd done this to myself by taking drugs in the first place. I'd taught my body to want it. And for the rest of my life, I was shackled to this problem.

"Uh," Teen Doctor said, his hand behind his neck. "You need something to control the pain."

"I can have ibuprofen," I said, trying to stay calm. But I wasn't calm. I was *doomed.*

"Let me look into it," Teen Doctor said, scribbling something on my chart. Translation: *I don't have a clue what to do for you.* "I'm going to evaluate our options."

"Good," I said. "Take this shit out of my arm while you evaluate."

Nobody moved.

That's when I figured out how to solve the problem myself. Raising the IV hand to my mouth, I secured the little tube in my teeth and—

"Hey!" the nurse said, grabbing my hand. "I'll take it out."

And, God bless her, she did, while my twelve-year-old doctor slipped out of the room.

The nurse put a Band-Aid over the IV wound and then gave me an appraising look. "How is your pain for now? Is it manageable?"

"Yeah." The pain was the least of my problems.

"I'm going to bring you a drink of water."

"Uh, thanks."

"Who can we call for you?" she asked. "You were brought in alone."

"How did I get here?" I asked suddenly.

"Ambulance. I believe they said your father called 9-1-1."

"Did he, now. *Impressive.*"

"Should we call him?" the nurse asked.

"No," I said quickly. "He doesn't really drive because he's drunk all the time."

She frowned. "Who then?"

"Nobody."

"A friend?" she pressed. "Unless there are complications from your surgery, you'll be out of here in a couple of days. Your arm is broken and you're recovering from major surgery. You'll need somewhere to go."

I closed my eyes and fought off a shudder. "And I'll be detoxing. Don't forget that."

She squeezed my good hand. "There's got to be someone."

Sure, lady. Because addicts have so many friends. I couldn't even ask Sophie, who would probably want to help me. But she couldn't. And there was nobody whose job it was to look after assholes like me...

My eyes snapped open. Actually, there was someone who did that job on purpose. "Father Peters," I said. "At the Catholic church."

"Okay, honey. You mean St. Augustine?"

No, that didn't sound right. "The church in Colebury." Fuck, I didn't even know where I was. The hospital outside of Montpelier, probably.

"All right," she said soothingly. "First water, then I'll call Father Peters."

She walked away, and I closed my eyes again. When would I stop being surprised at the shit that happened to me? In the back of my loopy, angry brain, I knew that the IV and the broken arm weren't even the worst of my problems. The assholes who'd beat me up were still out there, still looking for their missing stash. And I would probably get a visit from a police officer, too.

Fuck my life.

Chapter Twenty-Three

Jude

Cravings Meter: Just Kill Me Already

It took Sophie a day to find me.

Too bad it didn't take her longer. By the time I heard her gasp at the doorway of my hospital room, I was sweating and shaking and cursing God for my existence. Against Teen Doctor's advice, I'd refused to continue with the IV painkillers. My big plan was to detox before they kicked me out of the hospital. I knew it was going to be bad, and I had this perverse idea that the people who did this to me should see that.

Also, there were nurses here ready to bring me ice chips and to tell me to stop shouting "FUCK" at the top of my lungs. More than once already they'd threatened to sedate me against my wishes. They said that if my withdrawal symptoms didn't fade soon, it would fuck up my healing and put a strain on my heart.

But Father Peters had turned up to calmly demand that Teen Doctor listen to me. "He says he doesn't need the narcotics. Why don't you give him more over-the-counter painkillers?"

"We'll let you try it your way," the doctor said. "But if your vital signs don't improve soon, we'll have to use something stronger."

Fuck that. Nobody who ever detoxed would do it *twice* in a week.

Yet with each new wave of nausea, my determination splintered. *I really do need a little something for the pain*, my idiot brain suggested. Never mind that they'd given me industrial strength ibuprofen. My body was craving that floaty feeling I'd woken up with. I wanted to drift on sweet numbness again.

And I couldn't.

So when Sophie burst into my room, I was right in the middle of the worst of it. At least I hoped so. I was lying on my back in a pool of my own sweat, my broken arm throbbing, the wound in my side burning. I was trying to stay quiet, but it wasn't easy. Sometimes my teeth chattered, and sometimes I could swear there were bugs crawling over my skin.

"Oh my God," she whimpered, her slender hand landing on my good elbow.

Instinctively I turned my head away from her. "Not now," I said through a clenched jaw.

"Who did this?" she gasped.

Me.

"Please. Tell me what I can do?" She put a hand in my nasty, sweaty hair.

God. I reached up and pushed it off. "Please go," I said, my voice like gravel. I knew I was being an asshole. But I did *not* want her to see me this way. This right here—this was the reason I'd hid my problem in the first place. She was the one person in my life who thought I was somebody worth knowing. I never wanted to show her the truth.

And now a new wave of nausea threatened me. Bile rose hot and bitter in my throat. I choked it back, and Sophie touched my face. "Jude?"

My stomach lurched. "GET OUT," I hollered. Then I used my good hand to push her away from the bed. I grabbed the shallow little plastic tub the nurse had left beside me and I gagged over the edge of it.

"Oh," Sophie gasped. "Poor baby."

The nurse—Angela was her name—ran into the room, and stepped on the button that elevated my bed a little bit. "Are you choking?" she asked me, and I shook my head. We'd done this a few times already. She turned her head over her shoulder. "Wait in the hallway, sweetie," she said to Sophie.

I spit into the little tub. "Don't let her in here," I bit out.

Angela looked me over with worried eyes. Then she offered me my cup of water. "Rinse." After I spit again, she carried the tub away and washed it. When she came back, she sponged off my face with a cool cloth until I shivered. "This can't go on," she whispered. "I'm worried for your stitches."

"They're fine," I mumbled.

She moved my sheet down and pushed the fabric of my gown aside to see my bandage dressing. "Okay. How's your pain?"

"Who knows?"

Angela sighed. "I don't like this. You're in too much distress."

"Not your problem," I said, flopping my head back on the pillow.

"Actually, it is. Try to sleep?" she suggested. "Can I pull the blinds?"

"Why not?" I didn't know if it mattered. Nothing mattered. I was surly to Angela because I was pissed off at the hospital. Which made no sense.

But nothing did.

I closed my eyes to try to nap a little. Even if I only got fifteen minutes, it would be a blessing.

* * *

As always, my sleep was fitful. The crawling sensation kept returning, which meant I did a certain amount of thrashing around. But I locked my eyelids down tightly and tried to sleep. What I wanted to do was curl up in a ball, but I couldn't roll onto my right because of my broken arm. And I couldn't roll left because of my surgical incision.

I was in hell, pure and simple.

When I next opened my eyes, there was someone sitting in my darkened room. *Sophie?* I lifted my head to try to see.

My visitor cleared his throat, and it was definitely not Sophie. It was, of all people, Denny from the church. Sophie's coworker.

I flopped my head back again. I'd told Sophie to leave, and I'd meant it. But I was still disappointed. The heart wants what it wants. And mine wanted both Sophie and opiates. An impossible combination.

Denny got up and came to stand beside me. "Hi. I know I'm not the person you were hoping to see."

"There's nobody I'm hoping to see," I said, my mouth dry. I didn't want him to give Sophie the all clear. Because I was never going to be all clear.

He grabbed the styrofoam cup off the table beside me and angled the straw toward my mouth. I needed water, so I took a sip even though I had no idea why he was here.

"Sophie cares about you," he said.

"Really?" I rasped. "You're here to chew me out for refusing to talk to her before?"

He shook his head. "No, although that would be fun." He set the cup down again. "I'm here because it's my job."

"Oh." Now I felt stupid. He was a social worker in this hospital, and so was Sophie. And now I knew how she'd figured out I was here.

"Yeah. You're my case."

"Lucky you."

He shook his head. "I told Sophie that you'd relapse."

"I think I just did."

"No, you didn't." His tone was sharp. "I understand why you feel sorry for yourself right now. But I think you're the toughest person I've met. A hopeless case lets the hospital medicate him. Because the doctor ordered it, right?"

"It was a doctor who gave me my first pills. "

Denny shrugged. "Still. There are more opiates in this building than you can shake a bedpan at. And you turned them down. You're a B.A."

"A what?"

"A—" He dropped his voice. "—a badass."

I snorted, but when I did, it tugged on my surgical wound.

And I felt cold all of a sudden. A chill usually preceded a new bout of nausea. I eyed the plastic tub on the table, measuring its distance from me. "I'm glad we had this chat. But what do you want?"

He shifted his weight. "Two things. Sophie has been calling around, trying to figure out your next move."

I grunted in surprise. I hated the idea of Sophie having to bail me out. And I couldn't imagine what my "next move" was. Moving made me ache or it made me puke.

"Ruth Shipley wants you to stay at her place when you're released from here."

Closing my eyes, I tried to picture it. When I'd landed on their farm last July, I was fresh from a thirty-day inpatient drug treatment program. I was finished detoxing, and I'd buried my cravings under ten or twelve hours of hard physical labor a day.

This time I'd be sweating on a bed in the bunkhouse, trying not to claw through the walls. And the hole in my gut meant I'd be nearly helpless. "I can't go there," I said.

"You don't have a lot of options," he said quietly. "You don't carry health insurance, which is illegal by the way."

"Thanks for the update."

"You could go to a nursing home that charges on a sliding scale. But some of them aren't so nice."

"I don't want to puke on Ruthie Shipley," I said honestly. And just saying the word made me feel green. My feet were hot and my hands were cold. I was disgusting even to myself. So I'd rather be alone.

"Well, that's why I need you to listen to my second idea," Denny said. "I came up here to suggest that you try some Suboxone," he said, surprising me. "Sophie said you didn't love the idea, but she's been calling around. She found a doctor who will prescribe for you after you leave the hospital. And that doctor will consult for you right now. You could have your first dose today."

"Nobody here said anything to me about Suboxone." And they'd all had their prescription pads handy. I'd assumed that I couldn't have it because of the surgery, or something.

Denny shook his head. "The hospitalist is young, and it's a controversial drug. But Sophie and the doctor she reached think you could really be helped."

"Okay," I said.

Denny blinked at me. "Okay? You mean you'll try it?"

"I wanted to do this without another drug. But I can't take it anymore." Even now I was fighting off another wave of nausea. I needed to stop puking and start healing.

"You *have* done it, fool. This setback is not your fault. Sophie warned me that you were a stubborn a-hole."

"I am."

"Let the doctor help the stubborn asshole, okay? I'm going to make a call," Denny said, edging for the door. "Don't go anywhere."

As if.

* * *

A while later, Teen Doctor and Nurse Angela brought me this strange little strip which I was supposed to dissolve in my mouth. It made my throat feel disgusting, and I nearly yarfed up the medicine.

Nothing happened. I was still cursing life.

So after fifteen minutes they gave me another one. "It's not working," I mumbled. And didn't it just figure?

"Just wait," Nurse Angela said while I made grumpy faces at her.

And then, at around the thirty-minute mark, all my symptoms suddenly just…leveled off. It was as if the roar of a jet engine had been powered down, leaving me in a peaceful silence. My stomach still felt empty, but the waves of nausea subsided. My hands weren't shaking anymore, and the crawling skin was *gone*.

I was *not* high, though. Not at all.

The Suboxone was some serious juju.

And it was totally fucking odd to be suddenly transported to a state of sobriety even though I knew all too well the sensation of quickly getting high.

I took several deep breaths in a row, because breathing had just gotten easier.

"It's working, isn't it?" Angela had snuck up on me. "You look calmer." She fastened the blood pressure cuff around my arm and shifted the stethoscope to her ears. After a minute of silence, she ripped the velcro off. "That's impressive."

I thought so, too. "You know what's weird? I'm kind of hungry."

She smiled. "They might green-light you for some food. Let me check."

It wasn't mealtime, though. I'd lost all track of the hour, but apparently lunch was over and dinner wasn't happening soon. But Angela brought me something resembling Gatorade. And when Denny turned up again, he brought me a small bag of pretzels—the kind you could buy out of a vending machine.

"Thanks," I said, eyeing them. Not only did I still feel like a heel, I couldn't open the bag one-handed.

Denny watched me for a second. Then he picked up the bag and pulled it open, setting it down on the table beside me. "Sophie needs to speak to you."

Shit. "I was such a dick to her this morning. Or last night. Whenever that was."

Denny perched on the doctor's stool. "She understands. And she's not coming up here again until you tell her that it's okay."

It wasn't okay. I was still a disgusting mess. And I didn't even know whether this moment of relative comfort would last. For all I knew I'd be sweating and hurling again in a half hour. That was the whole problem with me. It was never over. Sophie needed to understand that. She was a smart girl. She should get the hell away from me.

I grabbed a pretzel and tossed it in my mouth. When I chewed, it tasted like the best goddamn thing I'd ever eaten. Seriously. Like ambrosia. Could a guy get high on a pretzel? "Thank you for this."

"It's nothing. Is there anything else you need?"

Unfortunately there was. Now that I was able to think straight, I was going to have to deal with the police. "I need to report my attack to the police."

Denny nodded. "All right, that's something I can help with.

Do you want me to call them?"

"I do," I said slowly. "If you make that call, they're more likely to respond." Sophie's father would probably throw a parade if someone managed to kill me. It was no surprise that they hadn't shown up to ask me what happened. And it's not like I expected them to bring me justice.

But the drug dealers who'd tried to shake me down might get the crazy notion that Sophie knew something. And I couldn't let that happen.

"Okay. I'll do it before I leave tonight. Do you need a lawyer?"

"What for?"

Denny studied me. "I don't know. If you were mixed up in something..."

My head gave a throb. I almost opened my mouth and told him that I'd never been mixed up in anything illegal. But the truth was that I used to steal car parts from an old man and sell them on eBay. My righteous anger shriveled pretty fast when I remembered that. "All I'm involved with these days is car repair," I said instead. "But I do have to tell the police that the assholes who beat me mentioned Sophie's name."

Denny paled right before my eyes. "Really? Why?"

"To get under my skin," I said. "They want something from me that I don't have. They were trying to motivate me, which won't work. So they mentioned her name. And that's why her father needs to hear about it, even though he doesn't care if I hang."

"Jesus. You're going to get Sophie in trouble," he said.

"Not if I'm careful. Nobody has to know that we..." I sighed.

Denny looked miserable. "Will you please call her? Once I tell her the Suboxone helped you, she'll be waiting to hear from you."

That was probably true. But I'd just proven myself to be not worth the wait. "I'll call her eventually," I said. I'd done her wrong *again*—and not just by yelling at her to get out of my hospital room. My real crime had been carrying on with her these past few weeks. *It's just sex*, she'd said. But that wasn't true. If I kept her in my life, she wouldn't go off and find someone better. Someone who wasn't one bad day away from repeating detox.

Denny stood quietly, appraising me. "She has some things to tell you."

"But I thought *you* were my social worker?" And now I was being a dick again.

Denny rolled his eyes at me. "I am. But what Sophie wants to tell you is personal."

Great. "In a couple of days, then."

He gave me an unhappy look. "Just do it." He reached into his shirt pocket and pulled out a business card. "That's our office number. Call her. Or call her cell. She said you'd know the number." He tossed the card onto the table and walked out.

After he was gone I finished the pretzels. But I did not call Sophie. She'd be better off if I never ever called her.

Chapter Twenty-Four

Sophie

Internal DJ: A manic version of Jingle Bells

Denny came back down to our office at about six o'clock, where I was still at my desk pretending to work. On Christmas Eve. I'm sure I was very convincing.

He stood in front of my desk, his arms crossed, a thoughtful look on his face.

And I sat there holding my breath, hoping he'd tell me Jude was okay. I'd been a wreck all day. First thing in the morning I'd come into work as a favor for our boss, who was traveling. The whole point of showing up today was just to check the roster of new admissions, to make sure there weren't any new patients who needed help from the social work department.

When I'd seen Jude's name on the list, I'd stopped breathing.

Denny was here today because I'd called him in. A social worker can't take a case if the patient has a personal connection to her. After I found Jude and realized that he'd been given narcotics against his will, I'd called Denny in a panic.

"Suboxone works," Denny said now. "It's pretty cool, actually."

"Yeah?" I felt my shoulders begin to unclench. "He looks

better?"

He nodded, his face grave. "He looks like himself again."

"That's amazing." I felt the sudden urge to cry. When I saw what the hospital had done to him—giving him the very substance he'd spent six months avoiding—I'd just wanted to break something.

"He knows all the things you're doing for him." Denny frowned, chewing his lip. He seemed to be biting back some sort of criticism. *Quelle surprise.* There was no planet on which Denny and Jude would understand each other.

"...but he was an asshole to you?" I guessed. "You can tell me. I won't even be surprised."

Denny shook his head. "He was polite to me."

"Then why do you look like you just ate a vomit-flavored jellybean?"

A disgusted grimace crossed his face. "Is that a thing?"

"It's a thing. Now what are you trying not to say?"

He shrugged. "I asked him to call you and he said he would 'eventually.'"

Well, ouch. "Jude is probably in a lot of pain," I said to cover my reaction.

"I'm sure he is," Denny quickly agreed.

"He doesn't want me to see him that way."

His face softened. "Truthfully, if I spent the day puking, I wouldn't really want you to witness it, either."

Aw. I was just going to put my disappointment out of my mind for one more night. So I changed the subject. "Did he tell you who beat him up?"

Denny flinched. "Let's go get some dinner somewhere and we'll talk about it. It's late and I'm starved."

It was Christmas Eve. No doubt my parents were at home wondering when I would turn up to make dinner. To keep the charade alive for one more day. But tonight I just didn't have it in me. "Sure," I agreed. "Let's do it.

* * *

We drove back to Colebury for dinner, parking our separate cars on the street by the church, then convening on the cold sidewalk to decide where to eat.

Neither Denny nor I was willing to suggest Pete's Tavern, because that was where we'd been headed on the night of our disaster date. So we ended up at our town's burrito joint. Nobody called it a Mexican restaurant, because everyone knows you can't get real Mexican food in Vermont. Case in point: Denny ordered the Thai wrap.

When we were finished, Denny tried to pay but I'd already handed my credit card to the waitress.

"How did you do that?" he asked. "She hadn't even brought the check."

I wiggled my fingers in the air. "Fast hands. Now tell me already—who beat up Jude?"

Denny wiped his mouth carefully and sighed. "It's not clear. But the men were looking for some kind of drug stash that's been missing for three years. Jude doesn't have a clue who they are, but he told them once already that he didn't know a thing about it."

"And they beat him up anyway?"

"I guess they thought he was lying." He cleared his throat. "Jude is going to report his assault to the police. Whoever put him in the hospital is looking for something that he doesn't have. But here's the thing—he thinks they know who you are, too."

Well *that* gave me a new shiver. "That's crazy. I don't have anything that Jude's old friends would want."

"A smart person would understand that. But apparently these aren't smart people. So you need to be a little paranoid right now, okay?"

"Okay."

"Just keep your head up, and if I feel the need to walk you to your car, just let me."

"All right. You're a good man, Denny. Santa won't put any coal in your stocking tonight."

He gave me a sad little smile.

Chapter Twenty-Five

Jude

Cravings meter: 1

"How's your pain?" the nurse asked me. It wasn't Angela today. This nurse was older with a dour look on her face. But she used gentle hands to check the dressing on my surgical wound.

"It's...still there," I grumbled. "Whenever it's time for the next dose of ibuprofen, I'll be ready."

"I bet you will. For now, it's time for this." She removed a little piece of what looked like tape from an envelope with my name on it. "Under your tongue," she said.

I placed the strip of Suboxone in my mouth and it began to dissolve right away. The stuff didn't taste good, but that was the least of my problems. Almost twenty-four hours after those first doses I had no cravings at all. I didn't have the shakes, and I didn't want to puke.

If I were a religious type, I'd be down on my knees thanking God for a miracle right now. "Can I ask you something?"

"Sure."

"When can I have a shower?"

The older woman smiled at me. "You must be feeling better. But we don't want to get your wound wet."

"Can't I, like, tape a plastic bag over it or something? I'm desperate here." The smell of detox lingered on me—sweat and worse.

"I'll make a deal with you. Eat everything they bring you for lunch, and then afterward I'll see what I can do."

"Thank you."

She walked out, and I looked up at the muted TV, wishing for something to distract me from all the things I couldn't fix. Now that my cravings were gone, all my other troubles came into sharper focus. Mostly I was worried about Sophie. Next on the list came work—I was probably going to lose the paint job for the guy who ran the solar business. My right arm wasn't going to be functional enough to hold a paint gun for who knew how long. And yet I'd have a whopping hospital bill by the time I was ready to work again.

Everything was fucked up, but I felt better than I had in months because I didn't have any drug cravings.

Weird.

* * *

I'd never stayed in a hospital before now. Overall, I found the experience only slightly less humiliating than prison.

To shower, I had to strip down in front of my nurse. She stuck a big watertight bandage on me. Then I took a quick shower while holding my right arm out of the curtain. Luckily the shampoo was in a dispenser on the wall. I was able to clumsily squirt some onto the edge of my hand and then slop it onto my head.

The hot water felt divine, and I would have liked to stay there a good long time. But the nurse was waiting for me, and my knees felt shaky. So I shampooed and swiped more of their liquid soap all over my body. Then I rinsed and got the heck out of there.

A one-armed guy can't easily wrap a towel around his body, so she left me alone to dry off, and then she slipped a clean hospital gown over my shoulders. When I emerged from the bathroom, someone had already changed the sheets on my bed.

Things were looking up.

I did the splenectomy-patient shuffle over to the bed and

sat down on it. The nurse was just tucking me back in when a uniformed police officer stepped into the doorway. I recognized him from the bakery—he was the same cop that Sophie had sat with over coffee.

Don't hold it against him, asshole, I coached myself. I'd jump at the chance to linger over coffee with Sophie, too. Who wouldn't?

"Jude Nickel? I'm Officer Nelligan."

"Hello, sir." I was going to be polite if it killed me. "Sorry to drag you over here on Christmas."

"Yeah? I'm the low man on the totem pole, so I was already workin'. The social worker said you needed to make a report?" He looked down at me as if he smelled something really bad.

No love for the town junkie. Color me surprised. "Yeah, I got jumped. The first time I'd ever seen these guys was a few weeks ago."

Officer Nelligan could barely contain his derision. "Don't know the guys, huh? We hear that a lot."

"I'll bet you do." I sighed. "Look. As I'm sure you know, I went to prison for three years, and then I was out of town for six months. About a month after I came back to town, this guy shows up at my garage looking for some drugs that went missing three years ago. But they weren't my drugs. And I told them that."

"You know their names?"

"No, but I can describe the guy in charge. Big scar on his cheek." I drew an imaginary line on my face to demonstrate.

He didn't reach for his pad of paper. "Okay."

The dude was not getting the message. "I know you don't give a rat's ass if someone kicked the shit out of me. And I really don't blame you. But I need you to go to your boss and tell him that two dudes are asking a lot of questions about that night three and a half years ago. And they're not afraid to mention Sophie Haines as someone who they might want to visit next."

That got his attention. Officer Nelligan pulled the visitors' chair around to face me and sat down heavily. "You're not shitting me, are you? You wouldn't use the chief's daughter to get us interested in some thugs who beat you up?"

"Fuck no." *Jesus.* "I know I'm just another dumbass convict to you, Officer, but I'm not actually so stupid that I'd lie to a police officer just for shits and giggles."

He frowned. "You're just worried about Miss Sophie."

"Of course I am. These guys want whatever they're looking for, and they're willing to break some bones to get it."

He flipped open his pad of paper. "Are you and Miss Sophie back in touch these days?"

Fuuuuuck. The cop's blue eyes lifted to mine, and I'm sure he saw me hesitate. "I'm going to tell you something, but try not to get Sophie in trouble."

He made a little grunt of acknowledgement.

"I attend a Narcotics Anonymous meeting on Wednesdays at the Catholic church. And Sophie runs the Community Dinner that happens afterward. I have seen her a couple of times at the church."

He raised one eyebrow. "That's it?"

"Yeah. You can tell that to Chief Haines or not. It's your call. But if the chief flips, Father Peters might lose his best volunteer, or I might lose my drug treatment meeting."

Nelligan reached up to pinch the top of his nose between two thick fingers. "Fine. Now tell me exactly what these punks looked like."

* * *

Denny showed up later, just as I was switching off the TV. Daytime television was just about the most depressing thing in the world. "Hey," he said as a greeting.

"Hey. Happy Christmas."

He plunked himself down where Officer Nelligan had sat before. "You're getting out of here tomorrow."

"Tomorrow?" *Shit.* It wasn't that I loved this place. But I couldn't even shower without help.

Denny nodded. "I think you should go to the Shipley family."

"I didn't call them," I admitted. I knew if I asked them to let me stay there a little while, they'd say yes. But I didn't want to be their problem.

"Sophie called for you. And Griffin Shipley is going to pick you up tomorrow when you're discharged."

"Oh." *Shit.* I didn't want that. But what was the alternative? My own father hadn't turned up to see if I was alive. Sophie would probably take care of me if I asked her to, but I didn't want her father to find out. "All right. Tell Sophie thank you."

He rolled his eyes. "You tell her. Jesus."

"Fine, I will. Today." I'd kept her as far away as possible while I was puking and sweating. But now that I'd stopped, facing her again was still going to kill me. This recent bit of shitty luck only made me more of a liability to her. Thugs knew her name because of me. A trip to the hospital flattened me. I had money troubles again.

We couldn't carry on like we had been. And telling her that was going to suck.

Denny turned to go.

"Hey, man—" I stopped him.

He looked over his shoulder.

"Thanks for all your help. I really appreciate it."

Denny scowled. "Just doing my job."

Then he disappeared. But not two minutes later Father Peters walked through my door. "Merry Christmas," he said with the usual happy smile.

"Shouldn't you be leading mass?" I asked.

He sat down in the visitors' chair. "Already done. Twice. And last night at midnight. It's my busy season. I look forward to December 26th. Nothing left to do but eat leftovers."

"Sounds good." My appetite was definitely coming back.

"I hear the Shipleys are springing you from this place tomorrow."

"Yeah." I wanted to protest this arrangement. But then I tried to picture myself opening up a can of soup and heating it in the microwave. One handed, without straining my surgical wound. "I'm such a disaster."

Father Peters shook his head. "A disaster is someone who doesn't *try* to take care of himself. Your father springs to mind."

Oh boy. "You went to see my father?"

The priest nodded. "At first he wasn't handling this setback very well."

I laughed. "What a surprise."

"I'm sorry, but I don't find it funny. When I look at your father I see someone who's afraid to live. Losses terrify him."

"He's not scared. He's just lazy." It came out sounding angrier than I meant it to.

The priest rubbed his fingertips together. "I know it looks that way. But it takes courage to want things, and to pursue them. Staying numb means you can never be disappointed."

Unfortunately I knew a little too much about that.

"But I told your father how we'll you're doing. That you go to meetings and help out on Wednesday nights. I get the feeling you haven't kept him up to date on your progress."

"I guess I haven't." But why would I? He never cared before.

"He was impressed, Jude."

"But not impressed enough to show up here and drive me home. So I guess I'll go to the Shipley's. For a couple days, at least."

"Good man. You can use this to arrange the details." He pulled a small box from his pocket.

"A phone?" I couldn't tell because there was Christmas paper on it. "Is that from Sophie?"

"She said to tell you it's a gift," the priest said, handing it over. "She's worried about you."

I flinched. "Yeah. I wish she wouldn't, though. I'll be all right. And if I'm not, well..." There were so many ways my life could blow up. I didn't want her to witness any of them.

"You don't think you're good for her."

"Of *course* I'm not good for her." Who would argue that point?

The priest smiled at me. "Maybe you weren't *always* good for her. But it's not a fatal condition. St. Augustine said it best—'It was pride that changed angels into devils; it is humility that makes men as angels.'"

I didn't know what he was trying to tell me, so I said nothing.

"If you love Sophie, let her make up her own mind about it."

Of course I loved Sophie. It's just that I didn't trust myself.

Father Peters stood up and squeezed my good elbow. "Once you're on your feet, I'll expect you on Wednesday nights again. Merry Christmas, Jude."

If only.

Chapter Twenty Six

Jude

Cravings meter: unconscious

The trip to the Shipleys' was harder than I thought it would be.

I sat in the passenger seat of Griffin's truck, clenching my jaw every time the gravel road became uneven.

"Sorry, man." Griff gave me a sidelong glance, his hands clutching the steering wheel.

"S' okay," I said through gritted teeth. My surgical wound was healing up nicely according to the doctor who discharged me from the hospital. But I had all the bone-deep aches of someone who'd been beaten to unconsciousness three days ago.

Griff parked the truck closer to the farmhouse than he usually did, as if transporting someone's grandma. "If you can get yourself inside, there's a piece of pie in it for you."

"That's some serious motivation." I turned to Griff, "I really can't thank you enough for this. I hate that you have to take me in."

Griffin frowned. "Let me ask you a question—if I showed up on your doorstep after someone beat the shit out of me, would you let me in?"

"Of course I would."

"Right." He shrugged. "So don't sweat it. Let's go eat pie."

I couldn't use my right arm to open the truck's door. So I slowly turned my torso in order to reach across my aching body with my left hand.

Griff got there first, though. The door opened before I could get to it. But at least Griff stood back and let me figure out how to use my left hand to exit the truck without killing myself.

He wasn't wrong when he pointed out that I'd help him in a heartbeat. It's just that I was always the one needing the help. I was sick of it. I was sick of me. Everyone else must be, too.

* * *

I'd assumed that the Shipleys would put me in the bunkhouse for a couple of nights. That's where I'd stayed this summer. But Ruth Shipley had other plans. After I spent half of an achy hour at their dining room table over pie and coffee, she patted my hand.

"You look exhausted honey. Come with me."

When I followed her into the Shipleys' TV room, I saw that she'd already made up the couch for me with sheets, blankets and two pillows. Just the sight of it made me tired.

"Why don't you see if you can nap?"

I think I fell asleep the second my head hit that pillow. And then I slept most of the next three days. It was the weirdest thing. I hadn't slept so much in years. I woke up once in a while. Audrey handed me a mug of a delicious, spicy soup, once. Another time, May fed me a cookie. I woke up a couple of times to find Ruth Shipley standing over me with my doses of Suboxone and aspirin.

Sometimes Griff would sit down and declare that we were going to watch a movie, but invariably I'd drift off after the first hour. My dreams were tangled, incoherent things. I was wandering the edges of town on foot. Sometimes I was following Sophie and sometimes I was trying to evade her.

Then her brother stepped out from behind a tree, bleeding down his head and neck. "No you don't," he said. Gavin swung, and I ducked. Then I tried to make a fist and it didn't quite work...

I woke with a gasp to find May Shipley's worried face leaning over me. "Fuck," I swore.

"Sorry!" She took a step backward. "Bad dream?"

"Yeah." I was sweating like crazy. "Jesus." I pushed the covers off and took a minute to get control of my rapid breathing.

"You okay?" May asked. "You've been asleep for so long we're starting to worry."

I scrambled to sit up, and my surgical wound didn't hurt as much as it had a couple of days before. "I think I needed it. Haven't slept much for three and a half years."

"Aw." She gave me a sweet smile, and I marveled at how easy I felt with this family.

"Would it be a pain in the ass if I took a shower?" I asked May suddenly. God knew I needed one.

"Nope. I was going to offer you that anyway. You'll need the waterproof bandage. They sent three of them with you from the hospital. Hang on."

I sat there another minute, trying to figure out how a shower would work. I couldn't put the bandage on my chest myself because my broken arm gave me shitty dexterity.

But May just walked into the room and sat down on the narrow strip of couch beside me. "Lift up your shirt," she said. One-handed, I managed to raise my tee over the bandage.

She picked at the tape and gauze on my torso. There were two new battle scars on my body—one on the left side a few inches under my heart, and one down the middle. "The incision is looking so much better," she said, wadding up the old bandage and setting it on the floor.

I peered down, agreeing with her. The weird thing was that I didn't remember her seeing it before. The past couple of days were a blur.

May put the waterproof bandage on me and then stood up. "I'll start the downstairs shower."

"Where is everyone?" I asked, following her. The house was so quiet.

"They went to the movies in Montpelier. It's half-price ticket day."

"It's Tuesday? Jesus."

May laughed. "True story."

She started the shower for me then left the room. I got undressed clumsily then stepped under the spray, holding my arm outside of the curtain. My shoulder began to ache immediately from the awkward angle.

"Doing okay?" she called.

"Yeah. Except..."

"What?" her voice came closer.

"Can I hand you the shampoo to pour in my hand?"

"Sure. Give it here, clumsy."

"Isn't this more fun than the movies?" I asked while she squeezed shampoo into my left palm.

"They were seeing *The Revenant*," she said. "I don't want to watch anyone get mauled by a bear."

"No spoilers," I complained, rubbing the shampoo everywhere I could reach.

May laughed. "Wash your hair. I'm going to make some coffee. Just leave the water running when you're done and call me. Towels are waiting out here."

"Thanks," I said for the hundredth time.

"De nada." She disappeared.

I did my thing, my broken arm drooping more and more as I got tired. But the water felt so fucking good.

The bathroom door opened again. Then a gentle hand cupped my elbow, supporting my arm. That felt better. "Thanks," I mumbled, trying to rinse off. "I'll just be another second." In spite of May's instructions, I fumbled the faucet off with my left hand.

Since I was dripping wet and naked, it startled me to hear the shower curtain begin to slide open. But then I was even more startled to find Sophie was the one who'd opened it. "Hi," she said shyly.

"Hi." I just stared at her pretty face, drinking her in.

"You didn't call me," she said, picking up a towel. But her eyes twinkled.

"Uh, I've been..."

"Asleep for three days," she said, breaking into a smile. "I know. I'm just teasing you. May told me you've practically been Rip Van Winkle. How do you feel?"

"Better," I said, realizing it was true.

Sophie pressed the towel against one side of my face and then the other. "I missed you." She put one hand on my naked hip and then kissed my chin.

Damn. Her soft lips on my skin felt amazing. She wrapped the towel around my wet body and then pulled me into a hug. "Mmm." I pulled her closer and took a deep breath of her apple-scented hair. Sophie. We stood there for a while, just holding each other.

Then, with a sigh, Sophie began to dry me off. And I let her. She ran the towel over my chest, and then I turned around so she could reach my back. Her hands lingered on my ass, and she pressed a kiss to my back. "Come out of there so I can dry your hair."

I stepped carefully out of the bathtub and wrapped the towel around my waist. I couldn't tie it one-handed, so I just held it closed. Sophie grabbed another and toweled off my hair, then finger-combed it. I stood there and let her fuss over me. There were big problems between us and too many things that still had to be said. But for those ten minutes I refused to worry about it.

"I brought you some clothes," she said.

"You did? From where?"

"From your room. Your father gave me the key. They're in the TV room." She jerked a thumb over her shoulder.

"Seriously?" I was trying to picture Sophie and my father having a conversation.

"Yeah. I mean—he had all the paint protection garb on, so he couldn't hand it to me himself. But he told me exactly where to find it on the hook in his kitchen."

"He was painting...a car?"

She gave me a quizzical look. "Of course a car. A Prius. Lime green with a white section on the door. Looked great."

Wow. I never would have believed my father would have the resolve to step in and finish that job.

Back in the TV room, I found that May had changed the

sheets on the couch. There was also a note on the pillow. *I'm doing some reading up in my room. Holler if you need anything.*

Seemed like May had made herself scarce.

Sophie plucked my Farm-Way T-shirt out of a shopping bag and carefully pulled it over my head.

"Thank you," I said quietly as her soft hands smoothed the clean cotton over my chest. She was only a few inches away, and her nearness overwhelmed me. I just wanted to pull her down on the sofa, curl my body around her and never let go.

She blinked up at me, her wide eyes solemn. "There isn't anything I wouldn't do for you," she whispered.

It was a perfect echo of the words I'd said to her on Thanksgiving. But I really wasn't ready to hear it. It wasn't that I didn't want Sophie in my life. I wanted her very badly. I just wanted there to be a better me to give her in return. Not some guy who got beat up by drug dealers, who was currently couch-surfing at his only friends' house.

Right.

I took a couple of steps away to regain my composure, closing the TV room door so I wouldn't flash May while I changed. A pair of my boxers was visible in the bag Sophie had brought, so I plucked them out.

Sophie tugged the towel out of my grip. "Sit down," she said.

"I can handle this part," I said, sitting on the edge of the freshly made-up couch.

To my surprise, she dropped to her knees, put her elbows on my thighs and began dropping kisses at the juncture of my groin and thigh.

"Fuck," I whispered as goosebumps rose up on my skin. "Sophie," I warned.

"The door is closed. Since when are you a prude?"

I groaned as she began dropping open-mouthed kisses across my lower belly. It quickly became clear that my dick had been uninjured by this latest bout of bad luck. As Sophie leaned in, blood flowed south, and quickly. She wrapped her arms around my body, resting her cheek against my thickening cock. Her sigh was deep and soft against my skin. She turned her head a few degrees and kissed the tip of my cockhead sweetly. "Sit back," she commanded. "Let me make you feel good."

And just like that, I was getting blown on the Shipleys' couch on a chilly Tuesday evening. Wind rattled the windows as she stroked her wicked tongue from my root to my tip. "Oh, damn," I stammered. Her lips parted and she took me deep. My body began to crackle everywhere, like fresh logs catching in the fireplace.

Whoosh. I was just gone.

"Mmm," Sophie moaned around my dick. She gave a good, hard suck that had my eyes practically crossed. "Love the taste of you," she whispered, her eyes flicking up to look at me. Then she ducked back down and took me into her mouth again.

The sight of her head bobbing over my cock was crazy-making. With my good hand I gathered her hair in my fingers. "Fuck," I gasped as her own hand slipped between my legs to stroke my balls. Rolling my hips forward, I bit back a moan. "You kill me," I bit out. "Come here. Want your mouth." I tugged her upward.

Sophie rose and our lips crashed together. Right away I pushed my tongue into my mouth, tasting her. Claiming her. No matter how many hours I'd spent trying to convince my heart that Sophie was off limits, my body always fought back. *Mine* said my good arm, pulling her in close. *Mine* said my mouth as I welcomed her in.

Mine said Sophie's hand as she palmed my dick, stroking me like a champ.

I was already close. Too close. "Ride me," I invited, knowing my injuries would prevent me from doing my best work in bed.

But she just smiled against my lips, swirling her thumb over my slit. Sophie played me like one of the pianos in the practice rooms where she used to sing after school, her sweet voice rising up to slay me every time I heard it. I rolled my hips, fucking her hand, because I couldn't resist.

"Look out," I gasped as my pleasure began to crest.

Instead of getting out of the way, Sophie slid quickly down, taking me into her mouth once again. The exquisite shock of it broke me, and I groaned so loudly that the cows out in the barn probably heard me. Then I was coming and cursing and stroking her hair one-handed.

When the dust settled, I was leaning against the back of the sofa, breathing hard. Sophie kissed my belly softly, relaxing against my hip. "You spoil me," I said quietly.

"Someone should." She got up and found my boxers and the clean pair of sweats she'd brought me. Dropping those in my lap, she picked up a glass of apple cider that May had brought me earlier and drained it.

I pulled on my clothes and then lay down on the sofa. "Come here," I demanded. "I want to hold you."

She looked down at me and frowned. "I don't want to hurt you."

"Oh, *please.* I'm too mean to die. Get down here."

Carefully, she curled up with her back to my chest. I kissed the back of her head and hugged her with my knees. "All we've ever had were stolen moments," I said, even though it was too sad of an idea for this moment. "I wish I could hold you all night."

"You will," she said quickly.

"Not likely."

Sophie peered at me over her shoulder. "Why do you do that? If I looked at the world that way, I'd lose my mind."

"And you shouldn't be a pessimist. You have lots of choices."

"I have the same number that you do."

I shook my head and started to argue. But she rolled over and grabbed my chin. "When you're back on your feet, you'll see. I know you've had a bad run, but it's going to get better."

Arguing the point would only make me sound stubborn. So I kissed her on the nose and just settled into the moment. She nestled against my chest and everything was right with the world, if only for a short time.

"Is there anything I can do for you?"

I almost said no, but then I remembered something. "Actually, can you check my eBay account for me? I might have sold a couple of Porsche parts."

"Sure. If you tell me your password."

Oh, man. *Busted.* "It's Sophie2010."
She looked up, a question in her eyes.
"The year I first kissed you. I'm a sap, I know."
"I like saps."
"Good thing." I squeezed her a little tighter.

Chapter Twenty-Seven

Sophie

Internal DJ set to: "Auld Lang Syne," the Barenaked Ladies version

Jude napped for a little while, and I lay there, just happy to be with him. Maybe he was still too sick and achy to see it, but things were about to turn around for us. After a while I heard May in the kitchen, so I got up and went to talk to her.

"How's he doing?" she asked, stirring a pot of beef stew on the stove.

"Okay I guess. He doesn't complain to me, though."

"That's good?" May guessed, peeking at me from beneath her bangs.

"Yes and no. I think he's worried, but he won't admit it. He'll *never* admit it." Even as the words left my mouth, I knew how much they bothered me. "Before, he preferred to get high than to tell me he was afraid."

"Men, right? They don't think they can speak their feelings."

"Right. Although in Jude's case, he grew up without anyone to tell them to. His mother split when he was young, and his father drank his feelings away."

May winced. "Hello, role models."

"Yeah."

"Stay for dinner?" May asked. "The rest of my family has obviously abandoned us. I think they said something about going out for pizza."

"Sure, thanks! What can I do to help you?"

"Not a thing. Audrey made this stew yesterday, so it's incredible. Do you want to wake up Jude? We could get him to sit at the table like a human."

"Good plan."

"The rolls I'm warming in the oven will take ten minutes, though. So no rush."

I went back into the TV room and perched on the edge of the couch. When I put a hand on Jude's chest, he raised his good hand to cover mine without opening his eyes. "Hi," he said, and the sound of his husky voice strummed right through me like a guitar chord. I missed him. I *craved* him.

"May heated up some stew for dinner. If you get up in ten minutes you can dine in a vertical position."

He opened his eyes and smiled at me. "Sounds exciting."

"I know, right?"

His fingers stroked mine. "So what have I missed in the past few days while I did my Rip Van Winkle imitation?"

"Ah, well..." I had no idea how Jude would react to the questions I was about to ask him. "I've been doing some digging."

"What for?"

Clasping his hand in mine, I confessed. "I've been reading the police file from your accident three years ago."

"What?" Jude removed his hand from mine and pushed himself upright with his good arm. "Why?"

"Because I still have some questions. I think we should hire an investigator, Jude. I'm not kidding."

He blew out a frustrated breath. "That is a very bad idea, Soph. All that will happen is that your father gets pissed off."

"Fuck him," she whispered.

"No thanks," he said through clenched teeth.

"He doesn't get to decide what questions I ask anymore, though. I've given him way too much power over me."

"Yeah? Well, let's review," Jude said sternly. "The last time my name came up in conversation he slapped your *face*. He's threatening to condemn my garage, which is the only place I can earn a living. And his guys pull me over whenever they fucking feel like it. And you want to poke that bear?"

"Yes! I think there's something fishy about the way your case was handled. Get this. Yesterday I learned that your trial lawyer—the public defender? He was disbarred last year. For *negligence.*"

Jude made a face. "That doesn't shock me. But I still don't know why it matters. Gavin is dead, baby. Even if my lawyer slept through the trial, that will never change. I already did my time, I got out. The only way life gets easier is if I make enough money to get out of that town so I don't have to let them hassle me."

My blood pressure spiked. "Jude Thomas Nickel," I demanded. "That's not how it works with you and me. We never let the bastards win."

After I said those words, I wished I could take them back. Because they assumed too much. I was back to thinking of Jude and me as two people against the world. But as I watched him turn his perfect face away from mine, my confidence wavered.

"Look," I whispered. "What if there's a slim chance that a judge agrees with me? They could reopen your case if it was mishandled. What if you don't have to be a felon?"

His eyes squeezed shut. "Funny. I just spent three years trying to come to grips with being one."

That was the point when I should have taken a goddamn hint and dropped it. But I didn't back off, because I had a gut feeling that there was finally something hopeful on the Jude and Sophie horizon, and I would not be denied. "If your conviction was overturned, you could get a job anywhere."

He actually snorted. "I'd no longer be a felon. But I'd still be a drug addict with hospital bills and a three-year hole in his employment record. How many convictions are actually overturned each year? One? Two?"

"Jude," I begged quietly. "Don't do that."

"Don't do what?"

"I'm saying that I want to believe in our future, and you're telling me not to bother."

His beautiful eyes looked up at me in the same measuring way they always did, only this time I felt like maybe I fell short. "I care a great deal," he said eventually. "That's why I don't *see* a future for us."

"I…" My words got stuck in my throat because Jude had just hurt me worse than my father's slap. "I'm trying to tell you how much I love you, and you just say I'm crazy."

"I'm just saying that even if your father framed me, which sounds ridiculous, I'm still an addict who's one bad day away from a relapse. There's no way we can blame your dad for everything. I pull all my own worst stunts." He put a hand on my belly. "You were a good girl when I met you. But I wanted you to be a bad girl. And look where it got us?"

Now my eyes were stinging and my face was hot. "I'm not my parents' good girl, and I'm not your bad girl," I said, my voice shaking. "Those are just bullshit labels. And since when are you interested in other people's opinions?"

"I'm sorry." He swallowed hard. "You're right. That was a stupid thing to say. You've always been your own girl." His eyes shone with great kindness, and his thumb stroked over my rib cage. But it didn't help even a little bit, because he hadn't taken back the part that really bothered me.

I don't see a future for us.

"You think you're being smart about this," I said, my eyes beginning to sting. "I know you hate it that other people are taking care of you right now. I know that is hard to swallow and that you'd rather take care of yourself. But I'm begging you not to be so short-sighted. Because someday I might need help from *you.* Did you think of that? When things go wrong for me, who's going to be there to pick me up?"

He drew a slow breath. "Someone stronger than I am, I hope. Someone who doesn't have a history of solving his problems with a syringe."

Somehow I'd let this conversation go too far down an awful path. I wanted to backpedal—to have this talk another time. But Jude took his hand off my belly and laid it on his own chest.

Then he took another deep breath as if steadying himself to do something hard. "I don't want you to think about the accident anymore. Don't get in your dad's face on my behalf. And don't come around for a little while. It's safer that way."

"You're...sending me away?" I stammered.

"We..." He cursed under his breath. "I'm sorry, Sophie. I shouldn't have started up with you again. We were over the day your brother died. It's not fair to you for me to pretend otherwise."

"*Pretend*," I spat. "You said you'd do anything for me."

"Yeah?" His voice roughened and his eyes got red. "I guess I lied to you. I do that sometimes."

At that, the worst wave of pain I have ever felt sliced through me. It was worse than the awful night three years ago when I didn't know if he was alive or dead. Because then I still had hope.

I jumped up off the edge of the couch as the first sob escaped me. Then I ran out of the room.

In the kitchen, I grabbed my coat and boots. I mumbled some kind of apology to a sympathetic May, and then stumbled out to my car.

I drove home with tears tracking down my face, my inner DJ silent for once. There was no song sad enough for the way it felt to hear him deny me.

Not REM's "Everybody Hurts." Not Pearl Jam's "Black."

Not even the Jeff Buckley version of Leonard Cohen's "Hallelujah."

I was willing to do anything for Jude. And none of it mattered if he wouldn't let me.

Chapter Twenty-Eight

Jude

Cravings Meter: 1 for drugs. 9 for Sophie

I stayed at the Shipleys' only a few more days. A doctor gave me permission to start using my arm and a more versatile cast, so I asked Griff to drop me off at home again.

"You sure, man? You can stay longer. You're not in the way."

That was bullshit, of course. "It will be good to get back in the garage," I told him. And that was almost true. As usual, I needed to keep my hands busy. But this time I needed the busy work to prevent me from thinking about Sophie.

Just getting through the day was a lot of effort. With a bum arm and a sore body, it took me four times as long to do things like eat breakfast or take a shower. I did some hours in the garage, basically keeping the lights on so that people would still come to us with their problem dents and their dings.

Strangely enough my father rose to the occasion. His MO had always been to put in the bare minimum of effort. But with my right arm in a cast, the bare minimum was a little more work than it used to be. I don't know what Father Peters said to him, but every time I knocked on the door for help with a job, he'd turn the TV off and come outside to hold a rod or the lug wrench when I couldn't manage it myself.

"I got an offer," he said one day into the silence between us.

"On what?"

"The property. Guy wants to pay me six hundred grand for the house and the garage together."

"Shit." I fumbled the wrench I was holding and it fell to the concrete floor with a clatter. "That's a lot of money. Who wants to pay that?"

"Fella who owns the doggy daycare in Montpelier. He wants to expand. Apparently people pay a lot for that shit."

I laughed, because it was either that or cry. If he sold the garage, I'd have literally no place to go.

"I won't say yes until you have a plan for yourself."

That startled me into locking eyes with my father for the first time all day. We generally avoided eye contact whenever possible. "It's your property," I said. "You can do what you want with it."

He looked away, uncomfortable. "You keep the place afloat lately, though."

True enough. "Would it be, uh, good for you to be retired?" Six hundred g's would buy a lot of hooch. He might just go on a big bender until it killed him.

"I'll have to think about that," he said quietly. "Seems like I need someplace to go every morning. Maybe I'll get a part-time job somewhere just to get me out of the house."

That sounded like a hell of a plan. I'd get one myself if I thought anyone would have me.

The phone rang then, and I crossed the garage to answer it, because answering phones was a good job for the one-armed repairman. "Nickel Auto Body," I said into the receiver.

Now the place would never be *Nickel and Son*.

* * *

The rest of the week went slowly. It was January and bitter cold. My drafty bedroom over the garage never got warmer than sixty-five degrees, and the garage was even chillier.

To keep myself busy, I sorted through our entire collection of exterior paints, throwing away the ones that were too old to use, and labeling the ones that were still good. A month ago I'd assumed the cleaning jobs I did would contribute to the future marketability of the place. Now nothing mattered, and it was depressing as hell.

Every minute I didn't worry about my future I spent worrying about Sophie. I wondered where she was and what she was doing.

On Wednesday, I went to the NA meeting in the church. The others fussed over my arm and asked me where I'd been. I spared them the tricky details and told them I'd gotten jumped. They made sympathetic noises when I told them all about the unwitting fix they gave me at the hospital and how awful the withdrawal had been.

"And I had seven months clean," I grumbled.

"You still fucking do," the Harley dude argued. "It doesn't count unless you did it to yourself."

"On the bright side," I added, "I'm on Suboxone, and that shit works."

Some of them had taken it before so I got some tips. "And when they start to wean you off it, ask us for help," Harley dude insisted.

"Will do," I said. And I meant it, too. I felt shored up by this group of people, even if I wished I'd lived my whole life without knowing what meetings were like. I both loved and hated meetings, which is funny because I both loved and hated heroin, too. But one of those things wouldn't leave me homeless and toothless within a decade. So I guess meetings were it for me.

When the meeting ended, though, I snuck out of the church and went home alone. Instant buzz kill. I ate some take-out food and listened to the radio just to hear other voices.

And I tried like hell not to wonder what they were serving at the Community Dinner and whether they needed any help. Now that I'd finally done the wise thing and distanced myself from Sophie, I knew I couldn't go there anymore.

Having somewhere to go on Wednesday nights had been good while it lasted.

The next day, May drove all the way to Colebury to pick me up for Thursday Dinner. I didn't want her to go to the trouble, but if I skipped it they'd worry. I brought a big, beautiful cheesecake and did my best to look cheerful and healthy. I let little Maeve Abraham draw on my cast with her crayons.

Friday afternoon I had a doctor's appointment a few miles from home. So I got into the Avenger for the first time in weeks and drove it very carefully to the medical center. Shifting gears with my broken arm was a little clunky, but I got better at it by the time I reached the parking lot.

This clinic was new to me. It was a drug treatment center where they'd prescribe my Suboxone on an ongoing basis. Every two weeks I'd have to submit to a urine test and show up for a counseling session, or they wouldn't give me the next installment of my prescription.

I was happy to pee into a cup if it meant that I could keep feeling mostly normal.

The low-slung building was nothing special. It didn't scream BEWARE OF JUNKIES.

The receptionist handed me a clipboard and directed me toward an empty plastic chair. There were six or eight people in the waiting room. Except for one woman who held a sleeping baby, all the patients were men, most younger than thirty.

People think they know what an addict looks like—they think he's shaking in a gutter somewhere and missing all his teeth. It's possible to end up that way. But the addicts I've met look like the guys in this waiting room—ordinary. You can't tell from their T-shirt choices or their shoes that they have a problem. (Maybe the per-capita tattoo and piercing ratio is a little higher than the general population, because addicts aren't afraid to do shit to their bodies. But that's just a theory I have.)

You can't detect anyone's addiction by looking at the outside. The guy sitting next to me might have done crank or ket or vikes, but it didn't show on his face. Maybe if I got up close and looked into each pair of eyes I'd recognize something familiar. A flicker of shame. The shadow of mistrust. The memory of a loss or a heartbreak that was numbed with chemicals instead of human interaction.

I took the pen and began filling out my details. Name.

Address. Depressingly, the form actually had to ask, "Do you have a permanent address?"

Why yes I do, but maybe not for long.

What followed was an ordinary medical history, including a laundry list of conditions I might have. The only boxes I checked were for drug addiction and family history of alcoholism.

"Nickel?"

Looking up, I found a square-jawed woman with a blue buzz cut scanning the room. When I stood, she beckoned to me. I followed her down a long hallway and into a small room with a table and two chairs.

"Good morning," she said. "I'm your counselor, Delilah. Can we just get one thing out of the way—can I see some ID?"

"Sure." I pulled out my wallet. They'd need to know for sure who they were handing drugs to.

She squinted at my driver's license, writing the number down on a form. "Thank you, Jude. Have a seat."

When she sat down, she explained that Denny had filled her in on my unwitting return to opiates at the hospital. "And I understand that you were prescribed Suboxone, too. Had you ever taken it before?"

I shook my head.

"Are you on any other medication at all?"

"I'm taking Advil while my arm heals, but only when it starts to throb."

"All right." Her brow furrowed. "Please be very accurate when you answer this question, because your health depends on it. Before the hospital gave you opiates during surgery, when was the last time that you used any narcotic?"

"Um..." I paused to get the math just right. "I went to detox when I was released from prison and that was seven months ago."

Her eyes widened slightly. "And..." She cleared her throat. "What substances did you use *after* your stay in detox?"

"Nothing. Well, caffeine and sugar. I have a Pepsi problem."

She drummed her fingernails on the clipboard, and I

noticed that they were navy blue. "But you still had cravings?"

"Every day. The Suboxone I started taking on Christmas Eve really nipped that in the bud, though."

"Okay. And before Suboxone, what did you do about those cravings?" She squinted at me.

Was this a trick question? "I didn't know there was anything *to* do about them. That's why I'm here." Actually, I was no longer sure why I was here.

"You're an interesting patient," she said. "At the initial consultation when I ask how long ago people have used, I usually hear seven hours, not seven months."

"Well, it wasn't a walk in the park." *Am I taking home a trophy or something?* This whole experience was giving me the itch, to be honest. I wanted out from under her stare.

"Very impressive, sir. Now let's go over some details about the drug regimen, because I don't want to assume that the hospital gave you all the right information."

She explained the bi-weekly drug tests and the dosing. "After a couple of months we'll begin to taper your dose down so that someday you won't need it anymore. In the meantime, it's a pretty special drug. It dampens cravings in the majority of people who take it. And those who fall off the wagon and try to use often find that they can no longer get high."

I'd heard all this before, but I nodded politely.

"Did you eat breakfast and lunch today?"

"Sure."

She grinned at me from across the table. "Can you be more specific?"

"Oh, uh, I had bread and jam for breakfast." Ruthie Shipley had sent me home from dinner last night with what she called "leftovers" but that looked suspiciously like a big shopping bag full of food. Her homemade bread was divine. "And egg salad for lunch." I'd put her plastic containers out on my top step to keep them cool. Luckily, no raccoons had found my Shipley stash.

"Good. If you eat regularly—and don't skip meals—it's easier for the Suboxone to work properly. So keep it up. There are a lot of people passing through this office who will tell you that the drug is the only thing that helped them pull their lives back together."

"That's cool," I said. But no drug in the world could undo all the shitty things I'd done. "It's made my cravings all but disappear. I can only feel them now when I'm stressed out."

"Tell me about that. What's stressing you out these past couple of weeks?"

"Well, everything. My broken arm means I can't do my job. My father might sell our shop. And..." How truthful did I want to be? "I broke up with my girlfriend."

"I'm sorry," she said quickly.

"It's for the best."

She seemed to consider that idea. "Well, when you're trying to stay clean, it's important to keep away from the toxic relationships in your life. Does your girlfriend use drugs?"

I laughed out loud. "God, no."

"Oh," she said softly. "Then does she blame you for using? Guilt isn't helpful, either, if you're trying to forgive yourself and move on."

"Uh, no." Sophie was perfect. It was me who was the problem. "We're just not very compatible."

Delilah studied me again, her smile calm. "Breakups are always hard. But they're especially rough on someone who's trying to get a handle on his addiction. Do you feel sad?"

"Of course," I admitted.

"Depressed?"

"I don't know. It hasn't been anything I can't handle, if that's what you're asking."

She pushed a business card toward me on the desk. "Here's our main number, and also our emergency line. If you think you might do something you'd regret, I'd like you to call us first. Can you do that?"

"Sure," I said slowly. But as I pulled the card across the wooden tabletop, something important occurred to me.

I'd removed myself from Sophie's life because I was convinced that I was always one bad day away from falling off the wagon. That I couldn't be trusted. This week had sucked, and I missed her like crazy, but I hadn't been truly tempted to use. Not even once.

And that's the thing—losing Sophie was pretty much the worst thing that could happen to me. Yet I wasn't cruising the streets of Colebury for a hit right now. I was handling my bitterness the same way other people did. By being a grumpy asshole, basically.

"Be kind to yourself, okay?" my counselor said. "Get some exercise and do something that makes you feel good, as long as it doesn't involve chemicals."

"Okay," I agreed.

"I mean, for heartbreak, binge-watching Netflix is a good place to start."

I didn't have Netflix or any way to watch it. But I wasn't looking for pity, so I kept that to myself.

After Delilah asked me a few more questions and made sure I knew about every NA meeting in a twenty-mile radius, it was time to pee in a cup.

She led me to the sample room. There was no sink, and the toilet water was dyed blue, just in case someone was tempted to dilute his sample. I did my thing and turned in the evidence. It's weird to hand a cup of your warm pee to a woman. What's one more slightly humiliating moment in the life of an addict?

Afterward Delilah dispensed two weeks' worth of Suboxone strips with a smile. "You're doing great, Jude. Keep up the good work."

"Thanks." God, it was embarrassing how much I enjoyed hearing that praise. "See you next time," I said.

When I left the clinic it was after five PM. I drove slowly through Montpelier just to amuse myself, and the movie theater came into view. The marquee promised a showing of the latest Marvel superhero movie.

I found myself pulling the Avenger into a parking spot and checking my wallet. Seventeen bucks, plus a credit card.

Be kind to yourself, the counselor had said.

Tonight that meant a mindless action movie and a bucket of popcorn. *Sophie should be here next to you,* my asshole brain suggested as I settled into my seat in the theater. Even if it was true, I needed this. Sophie might not be happy with me right now, but I needed to know if I could trust myself without her.

Tonight, at least, the answer was yes.

Chapter Twenty-Nine

Sophie

Internal DJ soundtrack: "Hallelujah" by Leonard Cohen, the Jeff Buckley version

The first week of January crawled by while I looked for Jude in the grocery store and in line at Crumbs. I watched for him at the gas station and at the bank ATM.

It had been two consecutive Wednesdays now that Jude didn't come to work at the church dinner. Father Peters assured me that Jude was still going to his NA meeting, though. "He'll be okay, Sophie. Give him some space."

The one place I found him was the only one I wouldn't have expected: my email inbox. Jude wasn't an emailer. But one cloudy January afternoon I found a PayPal notification. "Jude Nickel has sent you $2147." There was one line of text to explain. He'd written, "From Porsche parts sold. For your music school fund."

That was it.

I wanted to tip my head back and scream at the heavens, and maybe I would have, except I was at work and still hoping against all logic to get a full-time job at the hospital.

And yet Jude wanted to ship me off to New York. That asshole!

For a few minutes I sat at my desk thinking up angry replies, telling Jude exactly what he could do with his money.

"Sophie?"

I lifted my head quickly to see Denny watching me. "Yes?"

"Your eleven o'clock appointment is here."

I jumped up from behind my desk, finally noticing that my client Mary and her daughter Samantha were standing behind Denny. "Hi!" I said quickly to the mom, adding a wave at her toddler. "Thank you for coming in today."

"Anytime," the young mother said, putting a hand on her daughter's silken head. "She's all healed up from the procedure. It took her only a day to feel better, I swear."

"Children are amazing," I agreed. "Shall we step into the conference room and talk?"

"Sure."

I led the way, feeling gloomy because I'd failed this family. I'd found them some funding for the follow-up care for Samantha's cochlear implant, but not enough. We were still a few thousand dollars short. The only news I had to share with Mary today was yet another entry on another foundation's waiting list. Until something came through, the young mother would face mounting interest payments on her credit cards.

That's when a wonderful idea occurred to me.

I whirled around. "Good news! I've found a private donor to help cover your out-of-pocket costs." From across the room I saw Denny's head pop up in curiosity. But I just ushered Mary and Samantha past him, closing the conference room door. "Let's schedule Samantha's activation date!"

* * *

"Do you want to talk about it?" Denny asked the next evening as he put on his overcoat at the end of the day.

"About what?" I asked, looking up from my computer screen.

He shrugged. "About whatever is causing you to make that kicked-puppy face all the time."

"What face?"

"It's like this." Denny grabbed the lapels of his coat and scrunched his face into a pathetic frown with droopy eyes.

"Ugh. No. I do not look like that."

He smiled. "Okay, not *just* like that. But still..." He cleared his throat. "Want to have crepes for dinner? My treat."

That did sound good. Except I'd bought three chicken breasts to roast at home with baked potatoes. I started to say that I couldn't make it, but somehow I said, "Fuck it," instead. "Sure. Let's go." If my parents hadn't figured out how to feed themselves by the time I got home at seven o'clock, I could still cook for them. They wouldn't starve to death in ninety minutes.

We took Denny's car to The Skinny Pancake, which was a Main Street Montpelier cafe not too far from the hospital. Denny ordered the lumberjack—a ham and cheddar crepe. I got the crepedilla because it was always fun to try to pronounce it.

Right after we sat down, Denny addressed the elephant in the creperie. "I just want you to know that whatever the hospital decides in January, I'm sure we'll both end up with good jobs."

I cringed. "Well, just try to remember the little people when you sit down behind the desk inside your new office."

"Sophie," he warned. "They might not choose me."

"They should," I said, voicing my fears. "You have a masters and more experience. It's okay, though. I'll find something. I kind of thought Norse would have made a decision by now. Why do you think he hasn't?"

He took a sip of coffee. "I think he was trying to put in for more budget. Maybe he thought he could offer us one-and-a-half jobs? It wouldn't be ideal to stay part time, but it looks savvier to hunt for a job when you already have a job."

Ugh. "Which is a kind way of pointing out that I should have already begun my job search."

He grinned over the rim of his mug. "Graduating is a natural breaking point. Nobody would expect you to job hunt while taking finals. Or *me*," he added quickly.

Apparently I wasn't the only one who assumed he was a shoo-in. "Hey Denny—have you ever hired a private investigator?"

He looked a little startled at the sudden change of topic. "I have not. But once in a while the social work office needs to recommend someone, so there's a file at work with names in it. I could find it for you."

"Thanks."

The waitress delivered our food, and Denny tucked in. "Aren't you going to tell me why you need a PI?" He asked between bites.

"I'm not sure I do," I hedged. "But I've been reading the police file from the accident."

"Wait. The one from..." Denny didn't quite finish the sentence.

"Yes, *that* accident. There are some things that seem weird to me about it."

Denny sat back in his chair. "What good does it do to go there?"

That was a perfectly good question, and one that Jude had already asked. Gavin was gone, and Jude had done his time.

But I couldn't shake the idea that everyone was holding out on me, and I couldn't stand it. "I feel disloyal all the time," I admitted. "I still love Jude. And I'm not trying to prove that he's innocent or anything. But I can't figure out why he and Gavin were together that night. My brother was an ass to Jude every chance he got, always trying to put him down..."

I trailed off as I thought about this. You're not supposed to speak ill of the dead. But Gavin had called Jude every kind of name. Depending on his mood, Jude was trailer trash or a loser. Or both. And once he'd called Jude a junkie and I went ballistic. It had been spring break of my freshman year in college, which would have been less than a month before Gavin died.

A chill snaked up my neck just remembering it. At the time I'd been so angry, because I'd suspected Jude took some drugs, but I'd prayed it wasn't a real problem.

Had Gavin *known* about the drugs? How?

"You could just ask Jude what happened," Denny said, taking another bite.

"He won't say much about it. And we're not, uh, exactly on cozy terms right now."

Chewing, Denny raised an eyebrow. I guessed he meant to make some kind of point about Jude's contribution to the shit show that was my life, but I wasn't going to take the bait.

"I just want to *know*, Den. There's a scribble in the file about a tox screen for my brother. But the results don't turn up. Why would there be a tox screen for him? Maybe Jude wasn't the only one with the drug problem. On the other hand, it could just be a typo."

Denny pointed his fork at me. "Now that's simple enough to figure out. If a test was done, the hospital might have a record of it. Looking that up would be a hell of a lot cheaper than hiring an investigator."

I looked across the table at Denny's slim, handsome face and felt a rush of love. "You are a freaking genius."

He smiled. "Keep talking."

"Don't push your luck." I laughed.

"I won't. Learned that lesson already." He looked down at his crepe and sighed. "Just be careful, Sophie."

"Careful of what?"

"What if you learn something you don't want to know?"

"That could happen," I admitted. "Reading the police report has already made me re-think that Officer Friendly bullshit they taught us in elementary school. There are boldfaced lies on the first page."

He grunted.

"My brother was killed in Jude's vintage 1972 Porsche, which is still parked behind his father's garage. I took a quick look at it last month." *Before Jude interrupted me.* "The front of the car was crumpled like a soda can, and the windshield was gone."

Denny looked a little sick. "Damn," he whispered. "I'll bet that used to be an amazing car."

I snorted. Boys and their machines.

"Why were you looking at the car?" Denny asked.

"To try to figure out how the crash happened. The driver's side is still intact. But the passenger door is missing." The first thing I'd seen when I'd lifted the tarp on that side was the textured seat fabric—black and white, with tan strips down either side. I'd always found the design strange. Though the sight of it was so achingly familiar that I'd felt the sting of tears in the back of my throat.

Denny cleared his throat. "And you think that's strange?"

"Yeah, I do. Supposedly they had to cut Jude out of the car. Why remove the passenger door to get the driver out?"

Sarina Bowen

"Maybe because the other door was blocked?"

I shook my head. "The crash was head on, from the looks of it. The driver's door isn't even *scratched*. And they pulled him out of the passenger side just for fun?"

"That is a little weird," Denny admitted. "But there are probably pictures of the crash site."

"They're missing from the police file," I said. "Look, I know I sound like Nancy Drew right now."

He grinned.

"Go ahead and laugh. But if you were me, you'd want to know what happened."

His smile faded. "I'm sure I would."

Thank you. I cut my crepe with a fork and let the mystery do another circuit of my mind. As if I could stop it even if I wanted to.

After dinner, Denny drove me back to my car in the hospital parking lot. "Thanks for dinner!" I told him. "You cheered me up."

"My pleasure." He nodded at my car. "Drive safe."

I could see he was going to wait there while I got in. But I wasn't getting in. "Actually I'm going back to my desk for a minute," I said, trying not to sound shifty. "See you tomorrow."

He narrowed his eyes at me. "Let me guess—you're going to look something up in the patient database?"

"No," I said firmly. "And I wouldn't tell you if I was."

"Ah." His smile was sad. "Be safe, okay?"

"Always." I watched Denny drive away, and then I went into the darkened Office of Social Work and switched on my computer. After it blinked to life, I typed Jude's name into the computer database. There were three entries for him: one for his recent admission and surgery, and one dated June of this year.

That one surprised me, so I opened it. But then it all came clear. *Admitted to Deep Pines Inpatient Drug Treatment Facility*, it read.

Right. And now I felt like a snoop. From the menu I clicked on the third and oldest file, from May of 2012. There it was—his tox screen from the night of the accident. The results were exactly like the police report had said.

For a moment I just sat there staring at it, hearing Denny's question echo in my head. *What if you learn something you don't want to know?*

I realized that I'd been holding out a slim hope that Jude's tox screen wouldn't look like this. My foolish heart had been hoping to exonerate him. But there it was in black and white, blinking on the page. His bloodstream showed Oxycodone, and not a small amount. And another substance, too. I wrote the chemical down in my notebook to look up later.

Then I clicked on the doctor's name. As I'd hoped, a list of the other tests he'd ordered the same day appeared before me. And there it was: *Gavin Haynes, age 24. Dead on arrival.*

One click later I was staring at my brother's autopsy report. Thanks to my hospital job, I'd read these before, and they always gave me the willies. I really didn't need to know how much my brother's brain weighed on the day he died, so I skimmed. My eyes snagged on the words *ineligible for organ donation.* And then I saw why.

Gavin's tox screen revealed Oxycodone, too. And not a small amount. Plus another chemical—the same one in Jude's bloodstream.

Holy...!

I must have sat blinking at that screen for five minutes, wondering if I was crazy.

My brother had been high, too. *Gavin was on drugs.* I tried this idea on in my mind and it didn't fit well. Gavin the athlete. He'd snorted pills?

Not only was this unexpected, but now I had a problem. The tox screen didn't prove anything at all except that my family had withheld information from me. That was mean, but not illegal. So what the heck was I supposed to do with this information?

Instead of printing the file, I took a screenshot because it seemed stealthier. Then I printed that out, tucked it into my backpack and went out in the darkened parking lot to my car.

For a moment I just sat there in my car feeling shaky. It had never occurred to me to wonder if my brother took drugs.

I'd never thought he was the type. Gavin was a sort of my-body-is-my-temple athlete—always drinking imported spring water and making protein shakes at the kitchen counter.

In other words, I'd bought into the same pile of bullshit social profiling that everyone else did. They looked at Jude's tattoos and saw trouble. They'd looked at Gavin's lacrosse stick and saw the great American athlete.

Two tox screens. Both positive for two different drugs. I thought my skull might explode just from trying to wrap my head around it. On the one hand, it cleared up a few things. I'd never believed that Gavin would get into a car with a strung-out Jude behind the wheel. I couldn't picture him getting into a car with Jude *at all*. But if Gavin's judgment had been impaired, it made more sense.

Of course, there was one person who could actually explain what happened that night. And he hadn't yet. I started my car, cursing Jude. I wanted to throw the car into gear and speed over to his place and bang down the door. *What the hell were you thinking?* I wanted to scream.

But, damn it, first I had to wait for the engine to heat up. I counted to sixty, feeling insane. *Fuck you, and the Porsche you rode in on.*

It was snowing as I drove to Jude's neighborhood and parked around the corner from his house, hoping none of my father's policemen would happen by. It was dark out, though, and I didn't see a soul. I got out and scurried down the alleyway running behind the Nickel property.

My plan to storm Jude's room demanding answers remained intact until I skidded to a stop at the bottom of his stairs. The wrecked car was right in front of me. I took a step forward. Then another. I grabbed the tarp and yanked it all the way off.

The fabric crumpled to the ground with a louder thud than I'd been expecting. I braced myself for Jude's door to pop open. But the sound of radio music was just audible in the nighttime air.

Looking at the car was almost as frightening as viewing a corpse. The front had been crumpled like a soda can. The windshield was gone. But the very top of the car's hood still gleamed, the dark purple paint shining like oil in the night.

Just then I had another memory of Gavin and not a comfortable one. My brother had actually tried several times to buy this car from Jude. He'd insult Jude to his face and then offer him money for the Porsche.

Naturally, Jude always turned him down. "Thanks, man," he'd say in a voice that was far more casual than he felt. "I could never sell her. Spent too many hours on this baby."

My brother hadn't ever let it drop, though. I used to get tense whenever he brought it up. I could always hear how badly Jude wanted to tell Gavin just to fuck off. But he never lost his temper somehow.

So much of my life swirled around this ruined hunk of metal. The missing windshield was like an open wound. I took a deep breath and eased around to inspect the side.

The driver's door was just as I'd remembered it—still in perfect shape. The passenger door was entirely missing. Pulling my phone out of my pocket, I took a few pictures, praying that the flash of the camera didn't bring anyone into the alley.

It didn't.

Gingerly, I reached a hand through the gap until my fingers met the old upholstery of the passenger seat. I'd been happy with Jude. Maybe that made me an idiot. He'd had a terrible problem, and I'd ignored it. But I still ached for my own naiveté and for flying down the road on spring days in this car, our windows open to the breeze.

Talk to me, I inwardly begged the car. *What happened here?*

But the alley was silent, except for the persistent bark of a dog in the distance. *Arf-arf-arf!*

I'd come here to rage and threaten. To demand answers. But now all the fight had left me. Lifting my chin, I looked up at Jude's window, where lamplight shone between the blinds. He was right there—so close. My heart spasmed at the image of Jude lying on his bed with a book alone, when he could be with me instead.

I don't see a future for us, he'd said.

The snowflakes fluttered down, sticking to my eyelashes, accumulating on the cuffs of my coat.

I didn't storm up the stairs.

Instead, I grabbed a corner of the tarp off the ground and wrestled it onto the car. It took some work until the thing was covered again.

Then I walked back down the alley again, Jude none the wiser.

I got back into my own car and turned the key. I was counting to sixty when I realized there was someone else who should know what I'd found. I took my phone out again and tapped on a contact's name.

Officer Nelligan answered on the first ring. "Miss Sophie! What are you up to on this fine evening?"

"Thinking deep thoughts about the police file you gave me."

"Uh-oh." He gave a nervous chuckle.

"Uh-oh is right, because I found something weird." I told him about the missing tox screen, and how I'd dug that up at the hospital.

"Oh my," he said afterward. "I'm sorry to hear that about your brother. That should have been in the file. But I can see why your father wouldn't want it publicly known."

Maybe it's not the only thing he didn't want known? The whole thing troubled me. "Can I ask you a question about procedure?"

"Shoot."

"How is a police report filed? What are the steps? Is there a digital copy of the report you showed me? And if it's altered, is there a record of that?"

Silence. And more silence.

"Hello?" I asked. "Did I lose you?"

"I'm here. I'm just thinking. Why are you asking me this instead of your father?"

Right. "Well, Rob, my father lies to me with great frequency. I clean his house, I cook his meals, and he never misses an opportunity to make sure I know that the wrong kid died. And now I know that my brother was mixed up in

264

something nasty. *And* there are some assholes out there beating the crap out of my ex and dropping my name. You can forgive me for having a little curiosity."

"Well, dadgummit," Nelligan muttered. "You make a few good points. But I could lose my job for sticking my nose in this."

"I know it makes you uncomfortable," I admitted. "On the other hand, if there's something shady about this case and your boss is responsible, don't you want to know? Let me just share a weird detail with you. Both of the officers who assisted with Jude's arrest and interrogation moved across the country within three months of the incident. Neither of them had family outside of Vermont. They both lived here their whole lives."

"That doesn't mean they did something wrong," Nelligan argued.

"You're right. And if you pull up this file at your desk and find nothing weird about it, who does that hurt?"

There was a lot more silence. I held my breath, waiting to hear what he'd say.

"What am I looking for exactly?"

"I have a list of inconsistencies. Got a pencil?"

His laugh was rueful. "Why am I not surprised? Let's hear 'em."

Chapter Thirty

Jude

Cravings Meter: 1,
Stupidity Meter: 11

This week I drove myself to Thursday Dinner. I brought two-dozen cupcakes from Crumbs and made it just in time for the meal. "Hey guys!" I said as I slipped into the dining room at 6:29, narrowly avoiding a reprimand by Ruth.

"Hey Jude!" someone yelled.

"*Heyyy Jude*," sang Griff to the Beatles tune.

"I'll bet he's never heard that one before," Audrey said drily. "Sit here, sweetie." She patted the last empty seat, the one next to her.

Grandpa Shipley said grace and then dishes began to circle the table. Tonight Mrs. Shipley had made braised beef short ribs and Audrey had done spicy broccoli rabe and a mushroom risotto that smelled so good it made me want to weep.

An unfamiliar young woman sat across the table from me tonight. She had beautiful dark hair and a round, very pregnant belly.

"Have you met our friend, Zara?" Griffin asked.

"I'm *Audrey's* friend," Zara corrected. "Griffin I could take or leave."

That got her some laughs all around.

"You manage the Mountain Goat," I said, remembering where I'd heard her name before. Zara was Griff's ex, but they were friendly now, even if she liked to tease him. "We haven't met because bars aren't really my thing anymore."

"Well, they seem to run in my family," she said, passing a basket of bread to Grandpa Shipley. "Did you hear? My brother Alec wants to buy that mill the state is auctioning off. The announcement was in the paper every day this month."

"Does he really? It's a cool old structure," Griffin said. "I think it's been empty since the flooding from Hurricane Irene. I would have assumed it was too much of a wreck to save."

"It's not in bad shape," she said. "Here, I'll show you." She dug her phone out of her purse and tapped the screen to pull up some photos she'd taken. "It has a beautiful interior," she said. "The exposed brick walls still look great, and the original floorboards are mostly intact."

"Is your brother really going to buy it?" Audrey wanted to know.

"If he can get it cheaply enough. My uncles are worried that he'll overpay. They keep telling him how hard it is to make money running a bar. But I think they just don't want the competition."

Audrey whistled. "Ouch."

"Right? At least I'm not the one everybody's mad at this month. Becoming an unwed mother is old news now, I guess."

"Does the place need a lot of renovation?" Griff asked.

"Yes and no. Alec has big plans for the building. He wants to make himself a big apartment upstairs. That will take a lot of labor. But apparently just getting the bar up and running won't be such a big deal. They won't serve food, so they don't need a functioning kitchen."

"Just a liquor license and a pool table," May suggested.

"Works for me," Griff agreed. "We'll be his first customers."

"Zara, would you jump ship and work for him?" Audrey asked.

Zara shook her head. "I don't think I could work for Alec. We'd kill each other. The only reason I can manage my uncles' place is that Uncle Bill never shows up. Though he's going to have to in the springtime." She rubbed her belly.

"How've you been feeling?" May asked.

"Can't complain. I've stopped feeling nauseous, which

really helps. The baby is kicking me right now. Want to feel?"

May got up and stood by Zara, putting a hand to her round belly. "Omigod. That's so cool. I think she's doing yoga in there."

"Who says it's a girl?" Griff demanded.

"Who says it's not?" Audrey challenged, giving her man a big, teasing smile.

He gave her a hot look, and I had to look away. Those two had what Sophie and I used to have—love, passion and the promise of more to come.

"So, Jude?" Zachariah said quietly from a couple seats away.

He was a soft-spoken guy, so I had to strain to hear him. "What's up, Zach?"

"I went up to Marker Motors to order some parts last week, and I heard Marker say he was looking for a body guy."

"Did he, now?"

"Yeah. He was grumbling about his guy moving away to get married. Marker's a good dude, too. I like 'im."

"Do you know him well?" I had to ask. "If I just walked in there and filled out an application, I'd never get a call."

"Why not?" asked Dylan Shipley.

"My resume is pretty shaky," I said, which made a few people laugh. "Seriously, though. There's always a box to check that asks if you've been convicted of a crime. You check that box, nobody calls you back. The end."

Griffin refilled his girlfriend's wine glass, a thoughtful expression on his face. "What if we all had to confess the worst thing we'd ever done to the people we meet—the meanest thing you ever said or the most careless you've ever been?" He made a face. "It wouldn't be pretty. Just because someone hasn't broken the law doesn't mean they're a good person."

Zara set her water glass down with a thunk. "I'd never have a job again if confession was a requirement."

"You're not mean!" Audrey cried. "You're the nicest person in Vermont."

Zara shook her head. "Not always. And I was a *horrible* teenager. Really the worst. My mother went entirely gray—

every hair on her head—between my thirteenth and my eighteenth year." She put a hand to her belly. "I hope karma isn't real, or I'm in trouble with this one."

Everyone laughed.

"If we're all going to write down our most embarrassing thing…" Ruth paused to think before she finished her sentence. "We should also be able to write down the *best* thing we've ever done. That counts, too."

There were murmurs of agreement, but I didn't feel soothed. The worst thing I'd done was easy enough to identify. But the best thing I'd ever done? Well, I hadn't done it yet. I hoped.

* * *

"You just missed Sophie," my father said as I entered the garage the next day after going out to buy sandwiches.

Damn it, my heart said even as my asshole brain said, *Good thing*. "What did she want?"

"To give you this." He passed me a sheet of paper folded in two.

I flipped open the note.

Jude—

I found a good use of the money you made off the Porsche parts. I donated it to a great cause, and I really want you to see the results. Meet me at the hospital tomorrow at ten AM in the Neurology Department on the second floor, B-Wing.

—Sophie

"Uh. I guess I have to go somewhere tomorrow morning for a couple hours."

"Okay."

I read the letter three more times, looking for clues. Her instructions didn't leave any room for argument—she just ordered me to show up. That pissed me off for about two seconds, maybe three. Then I spent the next twenty-four hours counting down until I could see Sophie, if only for a few minutes.

The hospital was only a fifteen-minute drive away, but I hadn't accounted for all the snow we'd been getting. The parking lot's snow banks were so high that it took me extra time to find a spot. By the time I made it to the Neurology Department I was about five minutes late. Sophie wasn't in the waiting room.

"Are you Jude?" a woman wearing scrubs asked me.

"Yeah."

"Please come with me. Sophie has already gone into the auditory testing room. You're going to watch from here."

I followed her into a darkened, closet-sized room with a window and two chairs in it. The window was one-way glass, so I could see into an office with a table and chairs and a desk with an unusual computer on it.

There were four people there, but my eyes found Sophie first. She looked ridiculously beautiful in a soft blue sweater and black pants. She bent over a toddler—a little girl who was sitting on her mother's lap. Sophie seemed to be trying to entertain the child while a technician in a lab coat fit something over her ear. A hearing aid, maybe?

The toddler watched Sophie with a rapt expression as Sophie held out a book—the kind with the cardboard pages that babies can't destroy very easily. "What's this?" Sophie asked, opening to a page I couldn't see.

With one hand, the toddler raised her fingers up in the air and made a bouncing motion.

"Bunny!" said her mother behind her. "Good girl."

"Okay, we're all set," the technician said, leaving the hearing aid on the baby and walking around the desk to take a seat in front of the computer monitor. "I'll just need a minute to make some adjustments."

Sophie had told me about her case with the deaf toddler who needed cochlear implants. But she'd never told me how that had turned out. This must be the child?

The baby began to look restless, as if she wouldn't mind climbing down off her mother's lap to go explore some of the machinery in the room. She made an impatient whine.

"Almost there, baby girl," Sophie said.

"Here we go, I'm turning it on," the woman at the terminal said. "Talk to her, Mom."

"Can you hear me?" the young woman asked her child. The

mother could not have been more than twenty.

The baby didn't react to her question. She watched Sophie, waiting for her to turn another page in the book.

"Keep talking," the technician suggested. "I'm going to adjust the volume."

"Hi, baby," the mother said as her daughter continued to look the other way. "Can you hear Mama's voice? Hi, Samantha. How is Samantha today?"

Suddenly, the toddler's whole body jerked with surprise. Her eyes popped wide and her mouth fell open. She made a breathy little gasp and turned her chin toward her mother.

"Hi, Samantha," her mother said, voice shaking now. "Can you hear me, baby girl?"

Samantha gave a loud squeal. She raised both chubby arms in the air and shook them.

"Do you hear your name?" Tears leaked from the mother's eyes.

Samantha squealed again. She lifted one stubby hand up to her mother's mouth and patted her lips.

Her mother laughed and cried at the same time. "She can! She can *hear* me. Finally."

The little girl gave another little shriek, still touching her mom's mouth.

"You want me to sing?" Her mother smiled through her tears. She took a shaky breath and then sang the first line of an old song. "Hush little baby, don't say a word. Mama's gonna buy you a mockingbird..." But then she burst into tears. The toddler began to look worried. Her little chin quivered.

Sophie to the rescue.

My girl scooted her chair closer and took the little girl's hand in hers, getting the baby's attention. Then she sang the next line of the song. "If that mockingbird don't sing, mama's gonna buy you a diamond ring."

It was the first time I'd heard Sophie sing in more than three years. Her perfect voice rose up, clear and shimmering. The baby turned to Sophie with wide-open eyes, her round face rapturous.

"And if that diamond ring don't shine..."

Something wet dripped off my jaw and splashed onto my hand. Startled, I wiped my eyes with both hands. On the other side of the glass, Sophie continued to sing, her gorgeous voice cutting through every one of my defenses. The first time I ever heard her sing we were really just kids. Right away I'd wanted to be a man for her—to take good care of all that beauty.

I'd just had no clue how.

Her sweet voice went on, wrecking me all over again. "...you'll still be the sweetest little baby in town."

Fuck. I shoved my fist against my mouth as Sophie began a new song. "You are my sunshine," she sang.

On the other side of the glass, the young mother wiped her eyes with a succession of tissues, and even the technician looked pretty misty as she made adjustments to her equipment and took notes.

The tears rained down my face and I gave up trying to stop them. It had been a long time since I let myself feel hopeful. That's what Sophie had done to me today—forced my cranky self to be optimistic. She walked into this building every day and helped people find their own miracles.

She'd been trying to help me find mine, too. Like a jackass, I hadn't let her.

Shit.

Bracing my head in my hands, I just let it out. I don't know if it was one minute or ten minutes later when the door clicked open, and Sophie sat down on the chair beside me. I pressed my fingertips to my tear ducts and tried to breathe deeply.

"You paid for that," she whispered.

"But you made it happen. You kill me, baby. Every day."

She took my hand in hers and held it. "But it's the same for me. What if we stopped trying to worry so much about who was responsible for every little thing that happens? Otherwise we'll miss all the good stuff." She nudged me to look through the two-way glass again where the young mother was holding her little girl, telling her how much she loved her.

Maybe Sophie was right.

"I'm sorry," I gasped.

"Why?"

"I didn't think I deserved you. Fuck, I *still* don't. But maybe it isn't about that."

My words didn't make a whole lot of sense out of context, but Sophie and I had always been on the same page. "It *isn't* about that," she agreed, laying a hand on my back and rubbing. "Maybe you also didn't deserve a pack of shitty friends who told you it was a good idea to snort your first pill."

Not a bad point, really.

"I mean it, Jude. Enough worrying about what we deserve. Let's appreciate what we have."

I sat up and pulled Sophie against my chest. I buried my wet face in her hair and wrapped my arms around her. "The only thing I have ever been afraid of is losing you."

Sophie snorted into my shirt. "So why did you say we couldn't be together?" She didn't add "dumbass" to the end of that sentence, but I heard it anyway.

"I didn't want to dread what I thought was inevitable. That's why I used drugs in the first place. Dread."

"Of what?"

This wasn't easy to admit. "I knew you were leaving Vermont, and I wasn't going *anywhere.* You were the best thing that ever happened to me, and I knew I was going to put you on a plane to New York and you'd be gone."

"Jude!"

"I'm not trying to make you feel bad."

"Honey, that was a really grim outlook. Maybe it wouldn't have happened that way."

"I was nineteen, Soph. I thought I knew everything."

She hugged me tighter. "I need you, dumbass."

There it was. I laughed.

"...and you are smart about a lot of things. I think so highly of you. But I need you to give yourself a little more credit."

"I do. I will. If you let me try again, I won't be such an idiot."

"You better mean that," she said, her voice shaky. "Don't run away from me again, Jude Nickel."

"I won't. It doesn't fucking work, either. You own me. You always have."

"Even when you're not perfect, you're still mine."

Shit, I really was. "Okay, baby. Okay. I get it now. I'm truly sorry."

She pressed closer. "I know you are. And we're going to be okay. But you have to believe it or it won't be true."

"I want to believe it. I love you, Sophie. Always have."

"I love you, too."

My eyes leaked again. We sat there for a long time until I got myself under control. "You probably have places you need to be," I said, rubbing her back. I could hold her all day.

"Not for a couple hours," she said. "Let's go sit somewhere and have coffee."

"Where?" Just because I was ready to admit that I wanted to be with Sophie didn't mean we could go public.

"Anywhere. The diner on Main Street."

"But what if...?"

She shook her head. "We're not in Colebury. It will be fine. My dad's spies are at work or sleeping off the night shift. Let's not *worry* so much for once. Come on." She offered me her hand.

I took it.

Chapter Thirty-One

Sophie

Internal DJ tuned to: "You Are My Sunshine"

Sitting there in the booth with Jude, I felt happier than I'd felt in a long time. He watched me with big silver eyes and listened to baby Samantha's story.

"Every month that went by without her hearing could have produced up to a three-month language lag," I told him. "No moment of my work life has ever been as rewarding as watching her hear for the first time."

Jude smiled at me over his coffee cup. "It was so freaking cool, Soph. I can't believe a machine can make a deaf child hear."

"It depends on the cause of deafness. But it works for Samantha. After she gets used to the implant, hopefully she can get another one in the other ear. But insurance doesn't always pay for two. It barely paid for this one. That's why I kicked in that money…"

He put his ridiculously attractive face in one hand and smiled at me again. "Good use for it."

"I'm glad you think so."

The waitress brought us our food—BLTs with extra-crispy bacon. As he took his first bite, Jude's feet captured mine under the table. He and I were due for some peaceful, sunlit moments together. I watched the man I loved eat his sandwich, and my heart swelled a little more.

"What?" he asked, wiping his mouth. "Did I get mayo

somewhere mayo shouldn't be?"

"No," I whispered. "You're just beautiful, that's all."

He rolled his eyes a little, because men don't like to be called "beautiful," even when it's true. "Back atcha, babe."

"I have some things I need to ask you about," I admitted. "But I think I know a way that we can stop rehashing the past. If you'll hear me out."

Jude tucked his napkin into his lap and studied me. "I'll always hear you out. But I do worry about you."

"I know. And it's possible that I've been a tiny little bit obsessive with my curiosity."

"A tiny bit, huh?" He hid his smile behind his coffee mug.

"Okay, a lot obsessive. But I have a plan to settle things once and for all."

"Let's hear it."

I cleared my throat. "You know May is in her second year at the Vermont Law School."

"Right."

"She has a lawyer friend there who looks at criminal appeals on a pro-bono basis. What if we shared with him all the things that I think are strange about the way your case was handled? If he thinks there's something there, you would ask him to pursue it. But if he doesn't think it looks fishy, I'll just drop it. I'll stop asking questions."

Jude set down the mug and looked out the window at the foot traffic on Main Street. Montpelier was a fun little town, with its tiny legislature and ragtag college students. I wondered what he saw when he studied them. "Okay," he said, still gazing out the window.

"Really? You'll do it?"

He turned toward me now. "Sure, Sophie. I'll go to the lawyer with you. If that's what you want to do."

"I do. I just need someone to look at all the things I found and tell me whether I'm crazy."

"You're not crazy, baby," he insisted. "You're the smartest girl I know. But sometimes that's not enough."

True. "I got very mad at you last week."

"I know." He picked up the second half of his sandwich.

"No, I mean I got very mad after I dug through the hospital database and found my brother's blood work from the night he died. Why didn't you tell me that he was high, too?"

Jude's eyes widened. "He...what?"

I groaned. "Don't even tell me you don't know what I'm talking about. I pulled up tox screen results for both of you from the hospital's database. They're almost identical. Oxycodone and another drug."

"Jesus." He put down his sandwich. "Gavin was high? That doesn't sound like him."

"Jude!" I hissed across the table. "How could you not notice that?"

"Gee, Soph." His tone was laced with sarcasm. "Maybe because I was so high I couldn't feel my face. Never said I was intelligent."

Don't yell, I warned myself. *Don't ruin a good day.* But I felt my blood pressure double. "Why were you with Gavin at all? Won't you just tell me?"

"I will, baby." He pushed his plate away, his expression sad. He reached for my hand and gave it a squeeze. "If you're sure you want to know."

I nodded.

"Gavin wanted to sell prescription painkillers to my junkie friends."

"He..." I replayed Jude's words, and they made no sense. "Wh-what?" I stuttered. What a mind fuck. "He wanted to sell them? Like a dealer?"

He nodded slowly. "More or less. He had a friend from the lacrosse team—his roommate I think? The guy's dad was a doctor. They stole a prescription pad and accumulated quite a stash of painkillers. There was some trip they were trying to fund for after graduation."

"Jamaica," I said slowly. Gavin and his pals had wanted to party in the Caribbean.

"Yeah. So your brother decided to go slumming. He asked me to introduce him to some customers."

"So you said, 'Sure, bro! Hop in my car'?"

"No, first I turned him down. But then Gavin offered me

some free samples, and I changed my answer faster than you can say *hooked*." He rubbed my hand. "Remember, I was not in a good place. I would have gotten into that car with Darth Vader, Soph. And I would have driven him anywhere. My body wanted pills. He had pills. The end."

That shut me up. These past two months I'd often begged Jude to be honest with me. And then when he was, I wished I didn't have to imagine him that way.

He stroked my hand patiently. My pain was probably written all over my face. "I wasn't in a good place," he repeated quietly. "I didn't know your brother was using. But if you're telling me he was high, I'd have to guess that it was a brand new hobby for him."

"So you didn't see him take it?"

Jude shrugged. "I don't remember. He had two different drugs on him that night. One of them was unfamiliar to me— some other painkiller. But I did a line anyway, because I'm so smart like that. That might be why I got so fucked up. Or maybe his stash was a lot purer than what I was used to. But that's what happened. That's how I got into the accident on the way back into town."

"On the way...back? From where?"

"I took him to Dex's trailer and I did some lines there. That's the last thing I remember."

"Oh."

There was a dreadful silence while I pictured Jude and my brother snorting lines of drugs into their noses.

Shit.

"I'm sorry, honey," he whispered. "I'm so sorry."

My throat threatened to close up. "I still don't *get* it, Jude." My voice cracked. "Why didn't anyone tell me my brother was trying to sell drugs?"

"Because he's *dead*, Sophie. I tried to tell the cops. They threw a baggie of pills in my face during the interrogation. I said they were Gavin's, then the cop kicked me in the face. So I stopped saying that. Besides, it doesn't matter if the passenger was high, right? It's not illegal to be high in a car unless you're behind the wheel."

My neck did its tingling thing now, because I wasn't sure that anyone sitting at this table actually knew who had been behind that wheel. "Jude, do you remember actually driving away from Dex's trailer?"

"No," he said, his voice flat. "I remember sort of stumbling down off that milk crate Dex had instead of a front stoop. And I remember arguing with your brother about the music." Jude let out an unhappy grunt. "Because that seemed so crucial at the time."

All the hair stood up on my neck. "Say that again?"

"Say...which part?"

"You argued about the music."

"Yeah. He changed my radio. You know how nuts I used to get when somebody fiddled with my car."

"Shit," I whispered.

"What's the matter?"

"He had a thing about the car stereo—that the *driver* picks the tunes. He was really rigid about it."

"Yeah? Well he was also high as a February heating bill according to your tox screen. Maybe he was just in a bossy mood."

Ugh. I was so confused. "I just want to know what happened."

"But you *do*, baby. That's what I keep trying to tell you. Even if I can't remember the way it happened, the outcome stays the same."

"Does it? What if my brother was behind the wheel? What if you aren't even responsible for his death?"

He got very quiet. "You're messing with my head, Sophie."

I really was. "I'm sorry."

"Part of drug treatment is to accept all the shit you can't change. That's how I get through the day."

"Okay," I said, trying to be kind. "I'll save all my conspiracy theories for the lawyer."

Jude stroked my palm with his thumb, a serious expression on his face, his eyes cast down at our joined hands. "I can't plan my life around a miracle." His eyes lifted to meet mine. "So we need to figure out how to be together, anyway. I don't want to be the reason your dad slaps you a second time or gets on your case at home."

"I know we have hurdles. I need to move out of my parents' house sooner rather than later."

"All right." He lifted my hand to kiss my palm. "I've heard worse ideas."

I rubbed the stubble on his chin. He felt so good I wanted to climb over the table and sit in his lap. Somehow I restrained myself. "Everything will become a little clearer next week. The head of my department at work is finally going to let Denny and I know who gets the full-time position."

"You'll get it," Jude said, kissing my palm again. "We can move here to Montpelier."

"Together?" My heart lifted.

He gave me a sexy wink. "I like the idea. But I'll need a job, too."

"This is an excellent little fantasy we're cooking up here. But I probably won't get the hospital job. I'll have to look around. I might end up in Burlington or Waterbury."

He kissed my knuckles. "We'll figure it out. First your job, and then someplace for you to live. Is your mom going to be okay?"

I wish I knew. "I used to think I was helping her by living at home, and now I think I'm just making it worse. If she had to put in more effort, she might be happier."

"My reasons for wanting you to move out are all selfish," he said, turning my hand over in his and stroking it. Under the table, his knees hugged mine.

The waitress put the check down on the table and Jude paid it. We left the restaurant holding hands, and I felt a hundred pounds lighter than I had only yesterday. My car was parked partway down a poorly shoveled side street, so we picked our way between the tall snow banks. The snow was still white and pretty, so the Winter Wonderland look was in full effect.

"You look adorable in that hat," Jude said, giving me a flirty smile. "It's very...kindergarten," he teased.

"Don't mock the dinosaur hat." It was purple with a row of

scales down the center in a Mohawk formation. "A patient's mother made it for me."

"Aw. I won't mock you. But I might do this." He pushed me up against a parked car and kissed me.

"Mmm," I sighed against his lips, my hands jumping to his chest.

The kiss went hot and dirty immediately. His lips scraped hungrily against mine as our tongues waged a war for dominance. "Jesus," he muttered between kisses. "We need a whole weekend in bed just to take the edge off." He wedged his knee between my legs and dipped down for one more scorcher.

We broke apart, panting. "A long weekend," I demanded. "I hope we get one soon."

"I'll wait as long as it takes." He kissed my nose and pulled me into a hug.

That's when I knew for sure we'd be okay.

Chapter Thirty-Two

Sophie

Internal DJ tuned to: "Love Shack" by the B-52s

On the following Wednesday, Jude came back to work at the Community Dinner. My silent *hallelujahs* were not the holy kind. In celebration, I'd worn very naughty panties and a tiny push-up bra under my clothes and couldn't wait to show them off.

Jude didn't have to wear his sling over his cast anymore, so he was able to do prep work even if it was a little slow. I helped him peel potatoes when he fell behind. It was fun to stand there and talk to him, even if Denny studiously avoided looking in my direction the whole time.

"Is it okay with you if I ask May to set up that meeting with the lawyer?" I asked as we finished up the spuds.

"Yeah, baby. Go ahead. I'll be there."

"I know you think it's a little nuts, but…"

"It's okay, Soph. Don't worry." He gave me a sweet little smile. "Now go, because Denny is looking for help setting up the serving table."

We served meatloaf and garlic mashed potatoes for a hundred and fifty people. At some point I brought a plate back to Jude, who leaned his hip against the counter and took a break to eat. His hair was tied into a short ponytail in back tonight, and the way his T-shirt stretched across his chest made me want to rip it off him.

In another hour or so I would get to do that. Jude and I had decided that until I was out of my father's house, our Wednesday hookups were the only face-to-face time we'd take in Colebury. But we made good use of Jude's new phone. Every night this week I'd lain whispering on my bed while we caught up at the end of the day.

It was nice to have my friend back, even if we had to limit our toe-curling sex to once a week for a while.

Cleanup seemed to take forever. Jude left before me, as was our plan. I was almost out the door when Mrs. Walters decided she wanted to ask my opinion of *Fifty Shades of Grey*.

"The, uh, book or movie?" I asked, wondering if I was being punked.

"There's a movie?"

"Yeah." *But the man who's waiting for me is hotter than Jamie Dornan.* "What do you want to know?"

"Is it a good book-club book? Will we have lots to talk about?"

"Um…" That depended. "If you think bondage and a hot dude in a suit makes good conversation, then yeah." I was the wrong person to ask. I thought Ana should have gone for Christian Grey's construction-worker brother. I obviously had a thing for guys who worked with their hands.

"Interesting," she said. "I'll take it under advisement."

And then I was free.

I skipped out the back door of the church and then high-tailed it to Jude's place. He'd asked me to drive instead of walking alone in the dark, but it was only a couple of blocks and I kept my head up.

Good thing, too. Because as I came around the corner of the alleyway toward Jude's room, I caught a flash of light at the top of the stairway.

"Can I come in?" a man asked Jude through the open door.

My heart leapt into my mouth as the man stepped over the

threshold, and lamplight spilled on his face.

It was Officer Rob Nelligan.

I shrank back into the shadows, and Nelligan never turned his head in my direction. When the door shut behind him, I let out a gasp. Curious, I stepped out into the alley and scanned the area for his car. It was at the far end, parked at the curb, hazards flashing.

Maybe he didn't plan to stay long.

Turning back the way I'd come, I took a slow, casual stroll around the block, wondering why Nelligan had gotten in the way of my booty call. By the time I'd made it all the way around, the cruiser's taillights were on. I waited in the shadows until it pulled away from the curb and rolled down the street.

Then I ran the rest of the way to Jude's staircase and sprinted up, two steps at a time.

He opened the door before I could even knock. "Holy shit," he said, a freaked-out smile on his face. "Did you see..."

"I did! He didn't see me, though."

Jude clutched his bare chest as I passed him. He was wearing a towel, his hair damp from the shower. "I was positive you were going to end up knocking on the door when he was standing right here."

"Wouldn't *that* have been awkward?" I asked, grabbing his towel and giving it a tug. The knot undid itself in my hand, and then all of Jude's golden skin was on display. He still had a tan line at his waist from picking apples in the sunshine. I skimmed my fingertips across it.

"I'm still not over the heart attack," he said, stepping in to kiss my forehead. "I opened the door in my fucking towel. It's a miracle I didn't yell something lewd when he knocked."

"What did he want, anyway?" My fingers wandered into the soft, curly hairs at his groin.

I cupped his balls, and he tipped his head back and groaned. "Tell you later?"

"Tell me now, and you'll get a reward."

Laughing, Jude grabbed the back of my head and kissed me once. Then twice more. "He wanted to show me a few mug shots. It took me five seconds to pick out the asshole who put me in the hospital."

"Wow! Are they going to catch him?"

He kissed me again. "Hope so." His fingers unzipped my jacket. "Apparently this guy was already on their radar. But enough about me. Let's see some more of you."

I let him strip off my shirt. At the sight of my slutty little bra, he made an approving nose in the back of his throat. "Someone missed me," he said, dragging the tip of one finger across my breasts where they swelled above the edge of the bra.

"True story," I agreed.

"Damn." He ducked his head to kiss his way across my cleavage. "What else have you got under here?" Eager hands found my zipper and slid it down. Just the sound of the metal teeth unzipping filled me with anticipation. After tugging my jeans over my hips, he groaned at the sight of my panties. As clothing, this pair was pointless. They were nothing but a whisper of black lace. And they were missing one important panel of fabric, though Jude hadn't figured that out yet.

He dropped to his knees to reacquaint himself with my lower belly. He kissed his way down into the wedge below my hip. I threaded my fingers in his deliciously long hair and waited for him to discover my secret. He kissed his way between my thighs and...

"Oh, *fuck*."

I opened my mouth to make a snarky comment, but that's when he pushed his tongue between my legs. So I made a whimpering noise instead.

Jude grabbed my hips and pushed me down on the bed. A second later he'd snatched my jeans away. "Someone's feeling naughty," he whispered.

Was I ever. Tonight wasn't the start of our long weekend in bed. We had an hour together at most. And Jude didn't make me wait. He had a firm grasp on me, his hands on my knees now. He pushed my legs apart, and a bolt of lust shot through my core. "God damn that's hot," he said, his voice strained. He stroked a thumb through my neediness. "You should wear this pair every day."

A moan was my only answer. I loved the way he

manhandled me. Every commanding touch was accompanied by his hungry gaze. That's why I'd never once been afraid of his touch, even when I was a bumbling virgin. He watched me so carefully. He *saw* me.

Right now, he saw how much I wanted him.

My hands reached for him. I wanted to pull him down on my body, but he pushed them away. "Hands over your head," he ordered, just because he could.

I complied in a hurry.

"Good girl," he breathed, leaning down to take my mouth.

He'd said I couldn't use my hands, so I gripped him with my knees. Our kisses were bottomless, but my patience was not. My hips twitched, trying to trap his cock where I wanted it.

"Patience, missy," he breathed. He moved his head, sucking my earlobe into his mouth while I groaned. He licked a wet line down my neck and between my breasts. "Fuck, I missed your tits." He sucked one nipple into his mouth and my whole body quivered with eagerness.

I gave his head a shove, and he bent to my will, kissing down my belly, nosing between my legs. I'd shaved for him, and he made a tender sigh of approval. He began dropping little kisses everywhere he could reach.

"Ohmyfuckinggod you're a tease," I complained in one breath.

He chuckled from between my legs. Then he gave me one good lick and we both moaned.

"Please," I begged.

"You want my cock or my mouth?" he asked. "You can have either one."

Unff! "Both," I whined and he laughed again.

"Can't go slow," he said, his lips grazing my clit. "One of these times I'm going to take my time with you. But tonight is not that night. It's been too long."

Indeed. He began licking and worshipping me, and I whimpered and moaned. "Oh fuck," I panted. *So close.* "Come. Here," I demanded.

"Yeah?" He tongued me sweetly. "It's gonna go fast."

"*Now*," I demanded.

Two seconds later he'd parted my thighs and pushed all the way inside. "Fuck, yeah," he said, his voice strained. He leaned down on his forearms, tattooed biceps flexing, and began to pump his hips.

I wanted to touch him everywhere at once. My hands flailed over his hair and down to his shoulders. My knees clutched his hips. *More more more.* What I needed was just out of my reach until I looked up into Jude's serious, silver gaze. His cheeks were flushed, and his lips parted. But he still saw me. And he liked what he saw. "Love you," he mouthed.

I couldn't even reply, because I was too busy sinking back into his bed, my body quaking with release.

Groaning, Jude chased me to the same sweet finish line, and we shuddered and gasped together until the last panting breath.

He rolled off my body, turning his head to smile at me. "That didn't take long. But I'd say you look properly fucked."

"Cocky," I teased, panting.

"I don't hear any complaints."

A beat later, we rolled toward one another at the same moment, meeting in the middle, my nose at his neck. His arms folded me into his chest. *Love you*, thudded my heart against his.

Likewise, his replied.

We didn't say it, but only because we were still catching our breath. I traced the pattern of roses on his right biceps. The second time we'd ever had sex I'd asked him why he'd chosen those flowers. "My mother liked roses," he'd replied. "Took me a while after I got that tattoo to realize how psycho it was to tattoo her favorite flower on my body. As if I could get her to care about me if I was wearing 'em."

I'd always pitied him a little for his family situation. But now I knew how easy it was to shatter a family. My parents were still married, but they were only faking it. My mother hadn't abandoned me when I was a third grader like Jude's. But she'd abandoned the land of the living when my brother died.

We cuddled and kissed for a little while, but the clock ticked later and later, and I knew I had to leave.

"I can't wait until next Wednesday," I said, trying for a laugh.

He sighed instead. "This is temporary, right?"

"Right."

"Good. Because I'm pretty sick of letting you go."

"I love you so much," I said.

He kissed me once more and then gave me a gentle shove to sit up. "I love you more. Now get out of here already."

Chapter Thirty-Three

Jude

Craving meter: 1

The next morning I realized it had been a full week since Zachariah had given me the tip about Marker Motors. I hadn't called Mr. Marker yet because I dreaded checking the felony-conviction box on the application.

Nothing ventured, nothing gained, though.

So I fetched my father into the shop around ten. "I'm going to stop in at a garage that might have an opening for me," I confessed. "If you sell this place, I'll need to find something else."

His face gave an uncomfortable twitch. "Yeah, okay. Good idea."

I drove over there in my best shirt and clean jeans. At the front desk, I told the cashier that I'd heard there was an opening in body repair.

"Let me grab Mr. Marker," she said immediately.

The shop was awfully classy. There was a clean, quiet waiting room with a flat-screen TV and vending machines. When I peered through the window into the repair bay, I saw a dozen lifts and at least as many mechanics.

Damn.

"You're here about the bodywork job?"

I spun around to greet a tidy man in his sixties dressed in a golf shirt and khakis. He wore an apron, though, and had a little grease on his hands. "Hi. Yeah." I was nervous, which was something that drugs used to cure for me. But now I had to face all these moments stone-cold sober. "My name is Jude Nickel..." I reached forward with my broken arm to shake his hand.

He shook it carefully. "That cast is probably not helping your dexterity." He chuckled.

"That is true, but it comes off in ten days. Simple break, they tell me." I did not elaborate on the cause. A beating by violent drug dealers would not look good on my résumé.

"Good to hear," he said. "Tell me about your experience in the body shop. You're a little young."

"I started early. I was fourteen when I started helping my dad in his shop."

A light dawned in his eyes. "Oh, you're *that* Nickel."

Shit. I felt a familiar jolt of dismay. I was so used to being infamous for killing the police chief's son that it took a moment for me to realize that this man likely only recognized the name of a competing garage. "My father owns Nickel Auto Body."

"Ah. And you don't work there anymore?"

"I do work there. But Dad is thinking of selling the property, so I need a new gig." That was a vast oversimplification of the problem, of course.

"I see. Come have a seat in my office. Let's talk body repair."

We did that, and I told him about my Prius client who couldn't find anyone nearby to help him with a commercial decal. "I think there might be a niche there."

"Fascinating," he said. "I like your idea. So fill out an application for me. I'd like to hire you on a trial basis as soon as that arm is healed."

And here came the awkward part. "I love this plan... But there's something you need to know." I swallowed hard. "Three years ago I was convicted of manslaughter. I was addicted to painkillers when a passenger in my car died. It's the only time

I've ever been arrested. And I've been clean now for a while."

"How long have you been clean, Jude?"

This was exactly why I hadn't looked for a job yet. "Eight months, sir. It doesn't sound like much, but I'm doing really well. I cut out all the toxic people in my life, and I'm part of an active drug-treatment program. I'm tested every two weeks. The clinic will fax you the documentation if I ask them to."

I watched for the grimace, but his expression was thoughtful instead. "Eight months is pretty impressive. My son never made it that far."

That was so not what I'd expected him to say.

"See this?" He tapped the *Marker and Son* logo on his apron. "I thought I'd always have my son working beside me. But I lost him when he OD'd five years ago."

Jesus. "I'm so sorry, sir."

Mr. Marker smiled. "Thank you. It took me a long time to cope with it. This business was a shambles for a while. I was sure his addiction was all my fault."

"I can promise you it wasn't, sir."

"That's what they tell me." His smile was tired. "Listen—if you're working for me, and you get your one year chip from NA, I'll give you a bonus."

"That's, uh, a really generous thing to say. I'm going to make it to one year and then keep on going." I hadn't ever announced that out loud before, but it felt good to hear myself say it.

Some people beat this thing. Why not me, right?

"Let's get you that application."

"Yes, sir."

"How long did you say it would take that cast to come off?"

"Ten days."

"That's good news, Jude. Good news indeed."

* * *

I sat in the Avenger and called Sophie, just to hear her voice.

"Jude?"

The sound of my name on her lips made me close my eyes in gratitude. "Hi, baby. How are you doing?"

"I'm nervous about tomorrow," she confessed. She was having her Come-to-Jesus meeting with the hospital boss. "It's going to stink to hear him tell me I didn't get the job, even if I already understand why."

I wanted to argue with that assumption, because Sophie was everything to me and I couldn't imagine anyone turning her down. "No matter what they say, I'll hold you tight next time I see you."

"Promises, promises. Are you heading to the Shipleys' tonight?"

"Sure am. Sneak out and come with me? Take your mind off your troubles?"

"God, I want to. But I'm making stuffed chicken breasts and trying to get Mom involved. Today I basically told her I was going to move out and probably leave Colebury to find a new job."

"How'd she take it?"

"She was…" Sophie sighed. "Resigned, I guess. But I asked her to cook with me tonight and she said she would. But we'll see."

"Okay. I'll be patient."

"Love you!"

"Back atcha babe. Later."

I hung up without telling her about Mr. Marker's job offer. If Sophie didn't get the job she wanted in Montpelier, I didn't want her to mourn the fact that I'd somehow landed one just on the other end of town.

After a couple hours in the shop I headed over to the Shipleys. In addition to the cake I bought at Crumbs on the way out of town, I bought Zachariah a case of fancy beer. Lawson's Liquids' Sip of Sunshine was one of the craft beers that people drove from out of state to try.

When I went to prison, beer was just beer. When I came out, the whole world had gone crazy for Vermont brews. I didn't really get it.

"Here, man," I said, pressing it into Zach's hands when I found him in Ruth Shipley's kitchen. "This is for finding me a job."

"Finding...really?" he asked.

"Really. Marker will hire me, even with the felony conviction."

"SCORE!" Griff shouted, thumping me on the back, and then all the women piled on to hug me.

Life could really be worse.

"Zach, can I have one of your fancy brews?" Griff asked. "I'll be your best friend."

"Well, in that case," Zach said, tugging one out of its cardboard restraints.

"Do you need a glass?" Ruth asked as Griff popped the top of the can and immediately took a sip.

"No way! Cans are in again, Mom. You're supposed to drink it out of the can so you don't oxidize it with a quick pour."

"Yeah, I just *hate* accidental oxidation!" Audrey teased, removing the can from Griff's big hand.

"Hey! Stop, thief!"

She sipped. "Wow. I'm keeping this."

Without a word, Zach tugged another can out of the case and handed it to Griffin.

"Griffin, give your grandfather the ten-minute warning," Ruth demanded. "And find Daphne so she can set the table."

"I'll set the table," I offered quickly. "My sling is gone. That's my other news. Oh—and Sophie and I patched things up."

"WHAT?" Daphne hollered from the kitchen. "Back up. You're back together with Sophie?"

"Yeah." I pulled open the linens drawer in the dining room hutch. "The green napkins or the white?"

"Green!" Ruth called at the same time as May yelled, "White."

Right. I pulled out the green because Ruth had more clout.

Audrey came through the room again to set a salad on the table. "You are full of good news tonight," she said.

I really was.

Then my phone vibrated in my pocket.

Chapter Thirty-Four

Sophie

Internal DJ set to: "Tradition" from Fiddler on the Roof

At five o'clock I walked into my mother's room and stood bodily between her and her television. "Time to make the chicken," I announced.

It was bossy, but it worked.

With a sigh she clicked off the television and followed me into the kitchen.

"I got six breasts so we could have leftovers. And I already zested the lemon. Now what?" I'd chosen this recipe tonight because it was one of Mom's specialties back in the day, and I told her I had a craving for it. Of course, I really had a craving for her to get her skinny butt into the kitchen and act like her former self.

Though the chicken would be tasty, too.

"We mince the garlic next," she said. Her gaze traveled around the kitchen, looking a little lost. As if, after a twenty-year absence, she'd wandered into a neighborhood she used to know.

"The garlic is right there," I said, pointing to a bulb on the counter. "And I'll grab you a cutting board."

We worked together in relative silence, but it was nice to have some company in the kitchen for once. I sliced open the chicken breasts while she mixed garlic, olive oil, feta cheese and lemon zest.

"This gets a little messy," she admitted as she began to spoon the cheese mixture onto the chicken breast. "Is the oven pre-heated?"

"Whoops. I'll do that now."

Someday I'd make this dish for Jude in *our* kitchen. At the end of a long day we'd cook dinner together and decompress. Jude would tell me stories about the crazy ways people managed to dent their cars, and I'd tell him about the cases on my desk at work.

I'd mince the garlic while he prepped the salad. We'd eat together at our tiny kitchen table, make out on our sofa and then make love in our bed.

These were the happy thoughts that got me through the long days without him. Even if we had the world's smallest apartment somewhere, I couldn't wait to close the door and throw the lock in a home that belonged only to us.

It was totally going to happen.

My phone vibrated in my pocket. Hoping it was Jude, I left my mom washing some spinach and took the call in the living room. "Hello?"

"Sophie?" a male voice whispered. "It's Rob Nelligan."

"Oh, hi Rob!" I said a little louder than necessary. But I didn't want to seem as if I was sneaking off to take a call if no sneaking was required.

"Listen," he said, his voice so low I could barely hear him. "That file you asked me to check out? I found some highly irregular things."

"You...really?"

"Yeah. But now I think the chief knows I was digging. Maybe I'm just being paranoid. But the network shut down right when I was in the middle of reading it."

"Hmm." Now we were *both* paranoid. "What did you find, though?"

"Well, every case file has a digital log cataloguing each time it's edited. Each edit gets a timestamp. It notes every change made to the file and when the pieces were uploaded. Stuff like that. Nobody can alter the log—that's a security feature."

"Okay?"

"The log for this file shows a bunch of crime-scene photos uploaded the day after the accident. But they're all gone now. Someone deleted them a few hours after they were uploaded. And there's no video of the interrogation, which is especially weird."

"Because...interrogations are supposed to be taped?"

"Yeah. And on a sensitive case like this? It's a real red flag if there's no tape."

"Wow. Is that all?"

"No. The text of the report was uploaded twice, which isn't that weird. But the new version doesn't show what was changed, which is also against procedure. Someone just wiped the slate clean about forty-eight hours after the first report was filed."

"So you mean..."

"Oh shit," he swore. "Gotta go."

Click.

I stared at the phone in my hand for a long moment, trying to make sense of what he'd just told me. The file had been doctored. Photos were missing.

This was going to make our visit with May's lawyer friend even more interesting. But where the hell were those photos? If anyone knew, it would be my father. But there was a zero percent chance he'd tell me if I asked.

I couldn't ask. But I could look around.

Leaving the living room, I tiptoed toward the back of the house. My mother had already departed the kitchen, retreating back upstairs. I heard her TV switch on. Otherwise, the house was silent.

Keeping quiet, I made a beeline for my father's den. He had a big oak desk in the corner where he sat to pay bills. I'd never opened the file drawers in here before. But now I tugged the handle for the top drawer, and it rolled open on well-oiled glides.

Not for nothing did my dad spend eight years in the military. Each file folder had a label ("bank statements," "heating oil") typed in black on a shiny white label. I checked the lower drawer, too, finding the same thing.

On every folder but one.

I tugged out the blank file and popped it open in my hands. Glossy photos spilled out immediately, and I scrambled to keep them from cascading to the floor. They were color prints—plain old four-by-six inchers—of Jude's wrecked Porsche. There were no people in the photos. But the passenger's side door had been removed. And the passenger's seatbelt strap dangled uselessly from the ceiling where it had been cut in half.

Cut. As if to extract a passenger who was stuck because of the crash.

My heart thumped wildly as this new information sunk in. Jude *was the passenger*, not the driver. He had to be. My brother had not been wearing his seatbelt at all when he was ejected during the crash. His seatbelt wouldn't have been cut, because he wasn't wearing it in the first place.

A car door slammed outside the house.

Holy shit.

The photo in my hand—with the cut seat belt—I jammed into the back pocket of my jeans. Then I slapped the folder shut and stuffed it into the drawer, near the back. I kicked it closed and bolted out of my father's office. I was too freaked out to face him so I took the stairs two at a time. I sat down on my bed and listened to my heart gallop.

Below me, the kitchen door opened and closed.

I should have walked out the front door when I had the chance. Now I was trapped upstairs.

No, calm down, Sophie. No need to be dramatic. My hands shook, though, as I pulled that photo out of my back pocket. I flipped on my overhead light and propped the picture up on my desk, where I took several shots of it with my phone. It took me a minute to get the angle just right, so there'd be no glare.

Downstairs I heard someone stomping around. Then there was the clink of ice cubes into a glass.

My heart thumped at the base of my throat as I texted the

photo to Jude's new phone. The progress line as it uploaded seemed to creep across the screen in slow motion. But eventually it read "delivered." Then I sent a copy to Nelligan. Just in case.

Jude's reply was almost instantaneous, and it broke our no-texting rule. *WTF? Call me.*

Can't talk, I replied. *Don't call my phone.*

I jammed the phone into my pocket even as it vibrated again. I needed to get out of this house. There was no way I could speak calmly with my father over stuffed chicken breasts tonight.

All I had to do was walk downstairs and outside, right? My father was probably heading into his den. If I were lucky he'd turn on the television.

And was I ever coming back? Now that I could prove my father had squirreled away evidence of Jude's innocence, everything had changed.

I grabbed my book bag off the floor. The police report was still inside. If I left that behind my father would know exactly what I'd been up to. I slid my computer into the bag as well, then opened my dresser drawers and added a couple clean T-shirts and underwear.

That would have to do for now.

My father was still stomping around downstairs. I sat on the bed and worked to keep my breathing calm and regular. Minutes ticked by. It got quieter. Still I waited. The more engrossed he was in his den, the easier this would be.

After I was sure that there had been no footsteps downstairs for several minutes, it was time to go.

I slid my book bag onto my shoulder and took a deep breath. *Look casual, Sophie.* My car was right out in front of the house, the keys in the cupholder, because nobody stole a cop's daughter's car.

Piece of cake, right?

At the top of the stairs I listened again. My mother's TV could be heard behind the closed door to her room. My father was probably in his den. Maybe he was even on the phone.

Thank goodness for the carpet runner my mother had

chosen for our stairs back when she used to care. The soft pile of the rug muted my footsteps. On the bottom stair I hesitated. Front door or back? The kitchen door was closest to me, but the car was in the other direction.

Stillness beckoned me toward the living room, and I followed it, easing past the dining table toward our front hall.

When a hand shot out, locking around my forearm, I opened my mouth to scream. The sound got stuck in my throat as my father whipped me around to face him. I got my first look at his stormy expression as a hand collided with my face, the impact of the slap ringing loudly through the air.

There was no time for outrage. The momentum of his slap knocked me sideways. My hip and then my cheek both collided with the corner of wall. I stumbled and slid down the wall until my ass met the floor.

"Where the *fuck* do you think you're going?" he shouted, his face as red as raw meat. "Was it you in my file drawer?" He kicked me in the thigh. Hard. "Meddling *bitch*."

A whimper escaped me as I grabbed my leg in two hands. I knew I needed to get up off the floor. I was way too vulnerable down here. But panic made me clumsy. "Don't know what you're talking about," I said shakily, pushing myself up off the floor.

As soon as I was vertical, my father shoved me by the shoulders against the wall. "Don't play me, you stupid slut," he spat. "What the fuck do you think you're doing, sticking your nose where it doesn't belong?"

I'd spent my whole childhood trying to please him, or at least appease him. And every year it had gotten harder. Now I just *snapped*. "GET your hands off me!"

"I'll put 'em where I goddamn want 'em!" He wrenched me away from the wall and tossed me toward the piano bench.

I half fell, half sat on the thing, bones jarring from the rough impact.

My father stood over me, staring down, a vein in his forehead standing out. "Cut. The. Bullshit. Did you ask my officer to look at that file?"

"Yes," I said quickly. Dad had a Grade-A bullshit meter, so

it was better to stick as close to the truth as I could.

"Why?" he fired at me.

Time to bring out the social worker's psychobabble. "Because we're all stuck. The only person who's moving on with his life is Jude, Daddy. In this house we just wallow."

The vein in his forehead throbbed. "You seeing him?"

"No," I said vehemently. "But he's out, and I can't believe it's been three years and we're still a wreck in this house. I just wanted to know what happened that night." There was just enough truth in there to make me sound convincing.

His teeth ground together. "What *happened* was you ran around with that junkie like the little whore you are. And your brother wound up dead."

As soon as he called me a whore, an eerie calm settled over me. "That is not how you speak to your daughter," I said, my voice cool. I knew he wouldn't listen, but I needed to say it. The words came out sounding tougher than I really felt.

Or maybe that was exactly how I felt. There was no way for me to fake it anymore. The time had come to an end when I could pretend that things in this house weren't irrevocably broken.

My father continued to stare down at me. Then he did something I hadn't anticipated. He reached down and plucked his Glock 22 from his ankle holster and fingered the safety. "What does Nelligan know?"

The gun was pointed at the floor, but the threat was unmistakable. My gut loosened in my belly, and time slowed way down. "He knows I'm curious," I said slowly. "I asked him to access the file and print a copy for me to read. He asked me why and I said I didn't want you to feel badly seeing it. But I've never read it, and I was curious."

My father chewed his lip, thinking. The gun stayed pointing at the carpet, but I kept sneaking looks at it. My father had done many obnoxious things in our years together, but never once had he *held a gun* while arguing with me. Logically, I knew it was just one of his tricks. The man was a master at interrogation. That's what he'd done during his years in the military—interrogation and intelligence.

Judging from the fact that my knees were currently knocking together in fear, I guessed he'd been pretty good at his job.

"What did Nelligan tell you tonight?"

"Um…" Shit! "He called to say that he couldn't print out the file because the network went down."

My father's lip curled. "What else? Don't you fucking lie."

He stroked the revolver with his thumb and I indulged in a fantasy of cold-cocking him with the damn thing. "He said some kind of log wasn't properly done, but it didn't necessarily mean anything."

"Do you have any idea?" My father's voice was gruff.

"What?" I whispered, unsure what he was asking.

"What it's like to investigate your own child's death?" He was actually sweating now.

"No," I said slowly. "It must be awful."

"Were you in my den today?"

"Uh…" The change of topic threw me. "No." Fear was making me stuttery and stupid.

"So what's in the bag, Sophie?"

"What?" My head spun from the rapid change of subject. "What bag?"

He pointed with his free hand, and that's when I discovered that the bag was still on my shoulder.

"Oh." Oh, shit. Oh. My. God. The police report was in there, and my whole story was about to fall apart. "Books, as usual," I lied.

His eyes narrowed. "Exams are done."

"Yes, and thank you for congratulating me." The taunt was unwise, but the words just slipped out. As Gavin's graduation had approached, my parents were practically preparing a ticker-tape parade. For me? Silence.

With one strong yank, my father ripped the bag off my arm, grabbing it.

"Hey!" I tried to grab it back.

My father held it out of my grasp. He flipped the safety on the gun and switched hands before unzipping the bag and plunging his hand inside.

He must not have been expecting me to fight back, because when I dove for the bag I was able to get a grip on it.

But it wasn't enough.

My father shoved me out of the way. Hard. I went down again, this time hitting my head on the corner of the piano. While I sat there, stunned, my father ripped the bag open and overturned it on the floor. The folder hit the floor with a slap, the words COLEBURY POLICE DEPT. stamped onto its exterior.

"Lying little shit!" The vein throbbed in his forehead as he moved closer to me.

Still moving too slowly, I cowered, pulling my arms over my head.

There was a loud knock on the front door.

"Who the fuck is that?" my father hissed.

Having no idea, I said nothing.

He nudged me with his foot. "Answer me. Who is that?"

I pushed myself up feeling dazed. "No idea."

"Sophie!" a male voice called out. Not Jude's. Not Nelligan's. "Are you ready, Sophie? You said seven o'clock."

Was that Griffin Shipley? His face swam through my terrified brain.

"Sophie, honey! It is Thursday, right?"

Thursday. Jude went to dinner at Griff's house on Thursdays. Jude must have been there when he got my strange texts.

I opened my mouth to yell Griff's name, but my father clapped a hand over it. "*Quiet.* Who is that?" he whispered. He showed me the gun just to make his point.

"My date. Griffin Shipley. From church."

My father gave me a sneer. "I'll get rid of him. Don't you fucking move. We're not done here."

"Sophie!" Griff called again. "Is it open?" I heard the doorknob rattle.

Cursing, my father stuck the gun in the waistband of his pants. "Who's there?" he snarled, making it to the door just as it opened.

"Hi! You must be Sophie's dad." Griff's voice had an odd,

theatrical tone that wasn't helping matters. "She and I are going to miss the movie if she doesn't get downstairs. Hey, Soph!" he yelled.

"Sophie isn't feeling well," my dad tried.

"Oh, no!" he said with a cringe-worthy bellow. "Lemme just say hello to her, and we can plan it for another time."

"No, I don't think so…"

I wobbled to my feet and lurched around the corner so that Griff could see me. "I'm right here!" I croaked.

"Hey there, honey!" Griff took a step into the house, which was really into my father's personal space.

"Step back!" my father said in his cop voice. "Sophie, sit the fuck down."

"I need to talk to her," Griff said stubbornly.

"Get out of my fucking house," my father ordered him.

"No can do!"

Dad turned so quickly I wasn't ready. He grabbed me around the waist with one arm while his free hand closed around my throat. "Get out," he snarled at Griff.

There was a sudden, earsplitting crash. I fell backward, and it was just like in a bad dream. My arms were confined so I couldn't break my fall. I landed on my father, our heads knocking together.

The pistol fired and somebody screamed.

One second after that I was rising through the air again as Griff Shipley lifted me up off the ground, leaving my father on the floor.

Behind him stood my mother, a broken lamp in her hands.

Chapter Thirty-Five

Jude

When I heard the gun go off, I couldn't stay in Griff's truck one second longer. I threw open the door and powered up the walkway to the house. In the open doorway, Griffin sort of passed Sophie to me. The moment my arms closed around her she sagged against my body. "Oh my God," she whispered.

"Shh, it's okay."

And it was. Griff dropped down to the floor and actually sat on the Chief of Police, holding down his arms so he couldn't start swinging.

"Get the fuck off me," the chief complained.

"No can do."

"My weapon discharged. I'm hit."

"You grazed your ass, I think," Griff said. "Your wife is calling 9-1-1."

Mrs. Haines had the phone pressed to her ear. "The chief was involved in a domestic disturbance," she said to the dispatcher. "Send an ambulance and a county sheriff. *Not* one of his police officers. There's a conflict of interest."

"Go, Mom," I whispered into Sophie's ear, and she turned to me wide-eyed.

Sophie had temporarily lost the ability to speak, and she was actually shaking. So I steered her out the door and toward Griff's truck. Lifting her gently, I set her on the passenger seat and then climbed in beside her, pulling her into my arms.

"Dad was... I got caught snooping," she stammered.

"Okay. It's okay now." I rocked her.

"My mother broke a lamp over his head."

"Your mom is a badass."

Sentence fragments were still pouring out of her. "He pulled his gun on me! I just can't even... What an *asshole!*"

"Shh, shh, shh," I said, stroking her arm. "It's over now."

"Griff came to the door? I was so confused."

"I know." I pushed the hair off her forehead. "He wouldn't let me do the knocking."

"Because my father would have *shot you.*"

"No he wouldn't," I tried, just so she could calm down.

"Tonight he would've." She gave a big shudder in my arms.

"Didn't happen, though," I whispered.

We heard a siren, and a few seconds later an ambulance pulled up behind Griff's truck. The driver hopped out and approached us. "What's the scenario inside?"

"The police chief's gun discharged accidentally," I said with a calmer voice than should have been possible. "He's bleeding. But my friend is restraining him because he threatened his daughter with a gun earlier. And then his wife broke a lamp over his head."

The paramedic's eyes widened. "Should I wait for the sheriff?"

But the front door opened and Mrs. Haines waved him in.

I stayed put in the truck, holding Sophie as the other paramedic carried a stretcher inside.

Then the sheriff's car pulled up. Two men got out and approached us. One of them greeted Sophie by name. "Are either of you hurt?" he asked.

"Not at all. Just shaken up," I answered for both of us.

"Don't go anywhere," they told me.

"We'll wait right here."

They went inside, and the sound of Sophie's father shouting emerged from the open door.

Sophie took a deep breath and let it out. "I'll have to talk to the sheriff."

"I know, baby. But there's no rush."

"Did you see the seatbelt in the picture I sent you? Do you know what it means?"

My stomach did a swerve. "I think I do."

The door of Sophie's house opened again, and the EMTs

emerged with their stretcher. The chief was strapped onto it, cursing. When they reached the end of the walkway they turned, and that's when the chief saw me in the truck with Sophie.

"FUCK!" The man actually tried to roll off the stretcher in my direction, and the two EMTs staggered as the balance of gravity shifted. But they kept him on it.

"Calm down, Chief," the sheriff said, laying a hand on his shoulder. "I already read you your rights. If you don't stay put I'm going to add resisting arrest."

"And you're getting your ass sued," Chief Haines hissed. But it's hard to look threatening when you're bleeding from an ass cheek on a stretcher.

One of the deputy sheriffs went with the ambulance, and the other one came to take our statement.

"What happened?" the man asked, his pad and pencil ready.

"It's a long story," Sophie said, sitting up straighter.

"I've got the time. Shall we talk inside the house?"

Sophie turned to take my hand. "He goes where I go."

"That's fine."

We went inside together. Sophie's mom looked shaken, but she didn't freak out about my presence. She just watched me with wide eyes as I took a seat in her living room for the first time ever.

"I need to get something from my father's den," Sophie said. "The reason he freaked out today is because I found some photographs he's been hiding."

"All right," the sheriff agreed. "Let's see them."

* * *

During the next few days, things happened fast for me.

The sheriff's office called in the Vermont Office of Internal Affairs. Those policemen interviewed Officer Nelligan and then Sophie. We learned that Nelligan had been fired by Chief Haines before the chief had his violent outburst at home.

Sophie's father was charged with a long list of things, including tampering with evidence and hampering an investigation. He was deemed a flight risk and denied bail.

The criminal case against me was reopened with the help of May's lawyer friend, though now he had to play catch-up in order to represent me.

Another surprise was that I liked my lawyer immediately. I'd expected a stuffy guy in a blue blazer. But this counselor was not cut from the prepster mold. He had eyebrow piercings and Celtic tats peeking out from his rolled-up shirtsleeves. In addition to the usual diplomas, his office wall was hung with framed photographs of vintage airplanes.

Best of all, he didn't talk to me like I was a loser.

I met him two days after the chief's arrest. He opened with: "So, I really want to throat-punch the public defender who represented you in court."

"Is that so?"

He nodded, his piercings glinting in the light. "I can tell this case had a real stench from the first minute. But he didn't seem to smell it."

"I heard he was disbarred."

My lawyer tapped his pen on the desk. "Maybe they gave you the town clown intentionally. It's something to consider. I'm hiring an investigator so we can look into it."

That sounded expensive. "How can I help?"

"I want to ask you to recount the night's events to the best of your memory."

"My memory is the main problem."

"I understand that. You probably had a concussion that nobody diagnosed. Luckily, your girlfriend did an excellent job finding some holes in the official story, and we're going to do our best to exploit them. So start at the beginning."

I did.

An hour and a half later I'd drunk two bottles of water and recounted every last thing I could remember about the night of the crash. My lawyer burned through half a legal pad taking notes, and he recorded our conversation.

"I'm going to get started right away on your petition," he said. "I want to manage your expectations…"

"I know," I said quickly. "We might get turned down."

He grinned. "We might. But usually I'm starting from

scratch. This time I have Internal Affairs and a prosecutor already looking into the matter. I've never had a case start off like this before. It makes me feel optimistic."

Optimistic. Now there was a word I never used. "How am I going to pay for this?"

"You're not. I'll handle the appeal for nothing. If we're successful, you'll sue the state for wrongful imprisonment, and they'll settle. My office will earn a cut of the settlement, and that money will go back into our pro bono pool."

"That sounds like a better deal than I'd get anywhere else. So I guess we're done here for now?"

He looked amused. "You didn't ask me what a guy gets paid for wrongful imprisonment."

I shrugged. "If it comes to that, I figure you'll let me know. I'm not in this for the money."

"That's a good attitude." The lawyer stood up. "But if we're successful, it could change your life. You could go back to school or buy a house."

A house. I liked the sound of that. "Thank you for helping me." I bussed my empty water bottles into his recycling bin.

"Are you kidding? This is going to be fun." He rubbed his hands together. "When you see May Shipley, tell her she owes me a coffee date."

"I will."

After I left the lawyer's office I called Sophie immediately. "How's my girl today?"

"I'm good. Mom is on the plane to Virginia." She'd gone to stay with her sister. "So if any hot guys wanted to come over for dinner, I'd be available."

To her house? Now there was a first. "I just happen to know a guy who's free for dinner."

"Tell him to get over here, then."

Chapter Thirty-Six

Sophie

Internal DJ playing: Daft Punk's "Get Lucky"

Waking up in my bed with Jude the next morning made me as happy as I'd ever been. We'd waited a long time for this moment of true peace, with the sunrise turning my curtains from pink to orange and then yellow. We lay curled together, his chest against my back, his arm around my waist.

It was perfect. In fact it was so perfect that he decided to shift me onto my back and drop kisses on my bare breasts.

"Good morning," I whispered as he began to suck sweetly on my right nipple.

"Mmm," he agreed.

I moved my hand to his tousled hair and sighed. "We're living out my high school fantasies right now. I always wanted to have you in my bed."

He released me with a wet pop. "It's the best thing ever," he mumbled, turning his attention to my other boob.

"It could only be better if my father knew," I pointed out. "He'd die to know you were naked in my bed."

"Gonna be naked in some other places in a minute," he said as his fingers coasted down my body.

"You're insatiable," I said, though it was a false complaint. I'd never felt so desirable.

"I could blame three years of incarceration," he said, licking my hipbone. "But it's really just you."

Swoon! "Get over here, then."

"When I'm ready," he said in a bossy tone.

But when he glanced up at me, I got a smile—a hundred watts and then some.

* * *

After that first-rate beginning to my morning, it was time to prepare for my big meeting at the hospital. Mr. Norse had been kind enough to push the meeting back three days due to my father's arrest. He pushed back Denny's meeting, too.

Now I'd have to face the music, which intimidated me. So I put on a real suit, a silk blouse and heels.

"*Dayum*," Jude teased me from the kitchen table. "I'd hire you."

"You're biased. And I've dressed this way only because I want to be fired in style."

"That's the spirit."

I flipped him off, but then smiled, ruining the effect. The sight of him shirtless at my kitchen table was pretty uplifting. I hoped my mother stayed in Virginia for a little while so I could see it again. "Let's make coffee."

Jude pointed at the machine. "I started it already."

"I could get used to this."

He grinned.

* * *

At nine sharp I walked into Norse's office and took a seat across from him.

"How are you holding up?" he asked. "I would have given you more time, but..."

"It's fine," I said quickly. "The department can't wait for my family soap opera to play out."

He gave me a sympathetic look. "Then I'll cut right to the chase. You've impressed us, Sophie."

A *but* was coming. I could hear it.

He cleared his throat. "Sophie, there's something I need to ask you, and it's not an easy topic of conversation." He pushed a folder toward me. "I need you to tell me your involvement with a request for a bed in an inpatient drug treatment program our office received in May. Please take a look at this file."

"Okay?" I had no idea what case he might be talking about. So I took the folder and flipped open its cover. On top was a letter—one page—on the letterhead from the state prison.

To the parole board,

I am up for review in ten days. If I'm released, I would like to request a transfer to a drug treatment program. I have been told that requests like mine are rarely granted due to funding and space constraints. In fact, I was discouraged by other prisoners from talking about the fact that heroin is available in prison. But I never tried it before stepping into your prison. It's not a habit I'd like to take with me when I leave. Bottom line—if you release me without drug treatment, I fear I will quickly be back here.

Sincerely,

Jude Nickel

Holy crap. I raised my eyes to Mr. Norse's, trying not to cry. "I've never seen this before."

"Turn the page," he said.

The other sheet of paper in the file was a request form—the kind that was frequently routed through our office. The parole board requested an inpatient drug treatment bed for one Jude Nickel. The request was granted on the same day it arrived at the hospital, with a bed at the Green Hills Center for the following week.

Again I met my boss's gaze. "It was approved awfully quickly. There's usually a long wait."

He nodded slowly.

"The requester got lucky?"

He shook his head slowly.

I studied the paperwork again, this time reading the codes at the bottom. Whoever had approved this request had tagged the patient as a VIP. My whole time at the hospital I'd only seen one patient request tagged VIP, and that was the son of a big donor to the hospital foundation. "Who tagged this?" I asked stupidly.

"That's what I wanted to ask you."

My jaw dropped. "I certainly didn't do it. I never saw this request."

"You know that patient, though?"

"Of course I do. He's my boyfriend. But when this request came through..." I squinted at the date on the page. "I hadn't seen him or spoken to him in almost three years. And I would never redirect public resources as a personal favor. I wouldn't even *touch* this request, honestly. If this came into my hands I'd pass it on immediately. In fact, that's exactly what I did just before Christmas when this same person became a hospital patient."

He tapped his fingers on the desktop absently. "I know you did. But then who gave this file the VIP treatment?"

"I have no idea?" My voice sounded high and panicked. "Which computer login was used?" I asked. "That seems like something you could check."

"That's true," he said carefully. He must have thought of it already. Obviously he wasn't about to reveal to me what he'd learned.

"Mr. Norse, I walked in here today knowing that I might be passed over for the full-time position if you awarded it to someone with more experience. I could live with losing the job that way. But I *can't* live with the idea that you think I used the hospital to grant favors to someone I love."

My boss closed his eyes as if in pain, and then opened them again. "Thank you for making that clear, Sophie. But the matter is obviously not settled yet. I won't be making any decisions about the full-time position today. As soon as I know more, I will contact you."

That was it. He'd just dismissed me from the conversation. He didn't believe me.

And holy crap, my eyes got hot and my throat got tight and I was in danger of crying in my boss's office. "Thank you," I stammered. Then I got up and got the hell out of there.

In the outer office I passed Denny, who was waiting for his own meeting. The moment he got a look at me, his face softened. "Hey, are you..."

I didn't even let him finish the question. I just grabbed my coat off the hook and ran.

A cold January breeze hit me as soon as I stepped out of the hospital doors. I stomped over to my car and got inside, slamming the door. But I didn't drive off, because I was too stunned to decide where to go. A held-back sob wrenched from my chest, and tears of frustration began tracking down my cheeks.

I'd spent a year courting this job. And now they thought I'd broken the rules.

It took a few minutes to calm down. A nagging feeling set in, because I realized how odd the situation really was. Someone *had* given Jude's request the VIP seal of approval. But who?

Politically, drug treatment was a big topic in Vermont right now. The governor had made it a priority. But if Jude was some kind of test case, my boss would know about it. He would have approved it himself.

Jude had no allies in the world except for me. And the Shipleys, of course. But at the time of his appeal, he hadn't even met them yet.

Then who?

I was still sitting there behind the wheel, fuming and confused, when Denny emerged from the building. But there was no happy bounce in his step. I saw him pace slowly toward his car, his gaze cast down, his mouth tight.

Before I could think better of it, I opened my door and got out.

The movement caught Denny's attention. He stopped on the asphalt beside his car, looking torn.

"What?" I barked into the wind, running toward him. "What happened?"

He cast his gaze toward his shoes. "I'm out," he said, his voice rough. "He didn't say it, but I think the job is yours."

"What?" That made no sense.

His brown eyes flipped up to meet mine. "It was me. I moved Jude to the top of the waiting list this past spring. Norse asked, and I confessed." He swallowed hard. "Because I knew he'd think you did it."

"You..." All the air squeezed out of my lungs. "Why?" I gasped. That made no sense at all.

Big brown eyes blinked at me, and there was hurt in them. "He was hooked on *heroin* and headed back to town. I didn't want you to have to deal with that. The waiting lists at those places are as long as a year."

A different version of this year flashed before me—Jude back in Colebury, his body demanding heroin. A Jude who was still thin and unhealthy, hoping to get off a waiting list somewhere before it killed him.

I shivered in the wind. "But Denny, you risked..." Everything. "*Why?*"

He closed his eyes. "If you don't get it by now then I really can't explain it to you." He turned away from me and yanked on the car's door handle. When the door opened, he got inside. A half second later the motor was running. He backed away while I was still standing there trying to make sense of it.

Mind. Blown.

I walked back to my car, freezing now. I started the engine and let it warm up for sixty seconds, just as Jude had always advised me. My phone rang while I waited, and the display showed Norse's office number.

"Hello?"

"Sophie, I'm terribly sorry to doubt you. It was..."

"Denny," I warbled. "I wish he hadn't done that." Tears threatened again.

"I wish he hadn't either. If he'd met with me about it instead, we might have been able to find the patient a treatment program without breaking all the rules."

"Is there anything you can do for him?" I begged. "He'll need a recommendation."

There was a beat of silence on the line. "I'm not sure what I'll be comfortable writing," he said. "I'll speak to Denny again later this week after I've had time to think."

"All right," I said softly.

"The job is yours, Sophie. Come to work for me full time. You'll be terrific at it."

I knew I would, but my eyes leaked nonetheless. "It should

be Denny."

"Not necessarily," he said. "You were always in the running. I won't press you on it today, but call me later in the week so we can go over the job and the benefits, and you can tell me your decision."

"Okay," I said dutifully.

"Talk soon," he said. "And chin up."

Right.

I dialed Jude, who would be waiting for me to tell him what happened. I thought there were two possible outcomes today: success and joy, or rejection and despair. I hadn't seen the third choice coming.

"Hey, babe," he said when he answered. "Tell me everything."

So I did.

Jude exhaled on a sigh. "Shit. I don't know what to say."

"You don't have to say anything."

"I know but...shit! He saved my life, and he gets fired for it."

"Pretty much."

"He did it for you."

"I got that," I snapped. "Sorry. It's just...really stressful. I'm getting his job."

"No," he said softly. "You're getting *a* job. He's going to have to find another one. He can use his college professors as references, Soph. It's not like he worked for your hospital for ten years, and they're the only people he knows."

I hadn't thought of that.

"We didn't make him do that," Jude pointed out. "But I can't say I don't appreciate it. Never thought I'd bumped somebody off the list."

"There are ten people waiting for every drug treatment bed in Vermont. *Everyone* who gets treatment is bumping someone else off the list."

"How fucking sad."

We were both quiet for a moment.

"Sophie?"

"Yeah?"

"Does this mean we're staying in the Montpelier area?"

"I guess it does. Who knew?"

"Are you busy right now?"

"Nope."

"Can you meet me somewhere? I'm in Montpelier—on Bailey Avenue."

"Where?"

"Type it into your phone. I'm just north of Terrace. You can't miss my junker."

"This is very mysterious," I said.

"Not really. I'll explain in a few minutes when you get here."

He wasn't kidding—the street was an eight-minute drive from the hospital even though I hit every red light. Jude's Avenger was parked on a side street in front of a white clapboard house with black shutters and a peaked roof.

Jude jumped out of the car when I drove up. When I got out, he hugged me. "Sorry your day is a stress fest," he said.

"So am I."

"He might land right on his feet, Soph."

"I know. Now show me your thing."

"Really baby? Right here?" He made a show of reaching for his zipper.

"Jude!"

He laughed. "Follow me."

I trailed him up a walkway to the generous front porch of the white house. "Who lives here?"

"Well..." He chuckled. "That's the question." He turned the knob and opened the front door.

"What do you mean?"

"On a lark I was browsing the rental listings."

"This is for rent? A whole house?" I stepped inside. The place was completely empty.

"Yeah. But the owner would prefer to sell. He's an eighty-year-old man, and he's moved into an assisted-living facility. This has been on the market for several months. He lived here for forty years without renovating, so it needs work."

I looked around. The house had to be a hundred years old,

but in a good way. It had gorgeous old wooden floors and a shiny banister over the stairs to the second floor. The plaster ornaments on the ceiling looked original, and there were pretty leaded glass windows everywhere. "It's gorgeous. Can we afford this house?"

"Maybe," he said. "We could rent with an option to own. At the moment we don't have a down payment. But..."

"We both have jobs, and if the State of Vermont pays you for wrongful imprisonment..."

"...we'll have a down payment."

"Exactly."

I turned around slowly. "God, I love it."

"The bathrooms and kitchen are old," Jude warned. "But if we do get to buy something, I want a fixer-upper. I'm not afraid of doing the work myself. You could pick all the colors. I'd do all the plumbing and tile work myself. I'd be slow, but there's two bathrooms, so only one would be out of service at a time."

Joy bubbled up inside my chest. "You'd do that for me? Renovate our house?"

He stood behind me and put his chin on my shoulder. "Nothing would make me happier than to make a home for you."

"Wow. I thought we'd live in a tiny apartment somewhere and save up until we were sure we could buy."

He put his hands on my shoulders and squeezed. "That would be the conservative thing to do. But I feel optimistic, Soph. For once, I feel like we're going to come out on top."

I spun around and checked his face and found something unfamiliar there. *Hope.*

"I love it," I told him truthfully. "I'd love to live here with you. Show me more."

Hand in hand, we walked up the antique staircase together so I could see the bedrooms and the upstairs bathroom.

We spent a good hour exploring the house. The cellar was a little scary, but otherwise it was perfectly livable, if dated. I pictured the rooms freshly painted. I dreamed of colorful throw rugs and Christmas stockings on the mantel.

Reluctantly I followed Jude outside, where he relocked the

door and hid the key under the mat. That's how we do things in Vermont.

"I want to live here with you," I told him. "If you think the rent isn't too much, let's do it."

He walked me to my car and stood there in the street beside the door while I warmed up the engine. I rolled down the window to say goodbye one more time. He leaned in and kissed me. But my sixty seconds weren't up, so I waited some more.

"Something wrong?" he asked.

"No! Just waiting for the engine to warm up. You always said it took sixty seconds."

He grinned.

"What? For three years I thought about you every time I started my car. Even when I didn't want to."

He tipped his head back and roared.

"What's so funny?"

"Oh, you are so fucking cute."

"*Why?*"

"The long warm-up is for a car with a carburetor—like the old Porsche. You need that warm-up time to get the right balance of air and fuel. But your baby has fuel injection."

"Oh," I said, my face coloring. "You should have been more clear."

He smiled. And, damn it! I loved that smile.

"Talk later?" He leaned in for one more kiss. Then he backed away waving.

I blew a last kiss and then pulled away from the curb. I drove away, shaking my head. So many things I thought I knew about my life were wrong.

But that happened sometimes. All we can do is listen harder, hug harder and hope for the best.

Three Months Later

Sophie

Internal DJ turned to: "Memories" from Cats. Unfortunately. Because, ugh, Cats.

"Are you still up for heading to this party later?" I asked Jude as he piloted my car through the streets of Colebury.

"Sure. I'm all dressed up, aren't I?" He was wearing khakis and a button down shirt, which for Jude was all dressed up. "And I want to dance with you in that dress."

"Why? Do I want to know?"

He gave me a quick glance before turning his gaze back to the road. "It hugs you ass, in the best possible way."

"That wasn't my ass you were just checking out."

He grinned at the windshield. "That dress is like Vermont, baby. Great views everywhere."

I gave a very unladylike snort as he pulled into a driveway and shut off the engine.

When I saw where we were, the smile slid off my face. We both looked up at the place where the Nickel Auto Body Shop sign used to be. Now it was just a blank spot on a building that would soon be demolished.

"You might miss the place a little," I said into the silence.

"I don't think I will," he said with a low chuckle. "Our new place is pretty great."

This was true. We'd been slowly furnishing the old house in Montpelier. A few pieces of furniture came to us from my childhood home, which my mother had recently sold. The Virginia condo she'd purchased near her sister's house wasn't

as large, so she gave us the dining set and my bedroom furniture.

Before she moved away, Father Peters and I had emptied Gavin's room together, because my mother still wasn't ready to do it. Though she was doing better in so many other ways. Learning the full extent of my father's treachery had woken her up. There were many tears when she learned how Gavin had really lost his life, but the shock of it seemed to drain the well of self-pity she'd been drowning in. And with my father out of her life now, she'd risen to the challenge of taking better care of herself.

I didn't understand it entirely, but I was pretty excited to see her become more active. When she announced she wanted a change and that her sister had proposed she move down south, I was astonished but supportive.

As for my father, he was currently incarcerated in the very jail where he'd illegally sent Jude. The sentence for framing Jude was just a year and a half. Both deputies who helped him with the cover-up all escaped jail time entirely by testifying against him.

But my father wouldn't be coming out for *three* years, because they also got him on possession of drugs. All this time he'd kept Gavin's big stash of pills locked in his gun safe in our basement. Nobody would have ever known it was there if it hadn't been for the photographs I'd found. They triggered the search warrant. The searchers opened the safe, and the mother lode of pills they found inside sealed Dad's fate.

The night I heard about this, I made Jude sit down to hear about the stash.

His big, gray eyes widened, and his stubbled jaw fell open. "I didn't see that one coming."

None of us did.

Since my father was facing intent-to-distribute charges, he had to tell the prosecutor where he got the drugs. It turned out that Gavin had the entire stash in his duffel bag the night he died. My father had been horrified. He'd blamed Jude rather than let anyone know his own son was a dealer. But he couldn't frame Jude for possessing such a big stash, because it was such

a flashy news story that people would have asked too many questions. So he'd quietly tucked the bulk of the drugs away and let Jude hang for manslaughter instead.

Jude's conviction was officially overturned just two weeks ago. The letter was stuck to our old refrigerator in the kitchen. Jude and I both paused there every time we opened the fridge just to admire it.

And now I realized that both Jude and I were staring up at his father's garage, lost in our own thoughts. Jude's might be awfully sad, too. "I love you," I said quietly.

He reached across the console to take my hand. "Love you so much it hurts. Here comes the old man."

His father pulled up beside us. He'd moved out yesterday to an apartment on the two-lane road between Colebury and Montpelier. He'd taken an hourly job at an auto parts store.

The closing on this place was tomorrow, which meant there was one last thing to take care of.

"Hey," Jude said to his dad, climbing out of the car.

"Hey."

The Nickel men seemed to communicate entirely in one-word sentences.

"You okay?" Jude asked.

His dad actually smiled. "Yeah. The end of an era."

I could almost hear Jude's thoughts. *Not a good one.*

This awkward little discussion was interrupted as a wrecker rolled slowly up the street. Jude jogged over to tell the driver that he was in the wrong spot—he needed to back into the alley behind the building.

We all walked up the drive to wait for him in back. My phone buzzed with a text, and I pulled it out. May Shipley had sent me the address of the venue where tonight's festivities were taking place. *This place is great,* she added.

See you soon! I returned.

When I glanced up at Jude, he was taking something from his father's hand. He shoved it into his pocket awfully quickly. Then he glanced guiltily over his shoulder at me.

That was a little weird, but I decided not to worry about it. If he and his father were suddenly closer, that could only be a good thing.

The driver of the flatbed had positioned his truck right where he needed to be, and now he jogged toward us. "Jude Nickel?"

"That's me."

"This is her, right?" The driver pointed at the Porsche.

"Yessir." Jude leaned forward and tugged off the tarp, exposing the wrecked car in all her ugly glory. Not only was it a wreck, but Jude had stripped it of all its useful parts, including the seats and metalwork. It was nothing but a carcass now.

The driver shook his head. "Can't believe a car like that became scrap metal."

"Take it," Jude said forcefully. He glanced at his father. "The end of an era."

The old man actually chuckled.

"All right," the driver said. "This is for you." He reached into his pocket and drew out an envelope.

Jude held up a hand. "You bought Ryson's Junkyard?"

"Yeah, well, my father-in-law bought it."

"Keep the check," Jude said. "I stole parts off that lot to buy drugs when I was a teenager. Mr. Ryson never knew. He trusted me."

The driver winced. "Awful story, son." He looked Jude up and down. "Looks like you're doing okay now."

"I am, thanks." He reached over to take my hand. The arm he'd broken at Christmas was all healed up now. And the thugs who'd hurt him had been convicted, too.

The driver eyed the check in his hand. "If you're sure…"

"I'm sure." He tipped his chin toward the sky. "I'm sorry, Mr. Ryson," he said, and I recognized it as a twelve-step apology. But the wrecker driver might have thought it was a little weird.

Jude wouldn't care, though. He seemed more at peace with himself now than he'd ever been.

The driver put the check into his pocket again and went to work. We watched while he attached what was left of the Porsche to the tow truck. "Hope the back wheels still roll," I said.

Jude put an arm around me. "I think the rear axle can do a few more country miles."

It was sort of like watching a funeral. The wrecker driver got in and cranked his engine. Then the Porsche, where I'd spent so many hours of my teen years, slowly rolled away.

"Well," he said into the silence. "We have a party to go to."

He shook his father's hand and wished him well. Because apparently the Nickel men never hugged. Then he got into the driver's seat of my car and started her up.

The first part of our drive out of town was silent. "Are you sure you're in the mood for a party?"

"You're still wearing that dress," he said. "So yes."

"It's at a bar." That's why I kept asking. We were headed to the grand opening of Zara's brother's bar.

"I know. That's fine."

"I don't want you to be uncomfortable."

He gave me an amused look. "Baby, if I say it's fine, it's fine."

"Sorry," I said quickly. I wasn't usually so protective of him, and he appreciated that. But tonight everything seemed more laden with emotion, and I didn't want him to be dragged to a party if he didn't want to go to one.

"Some time soon you should come to a meeting with me," he said suddenly.

"Yeah?"

"Yeah. I want you to see what it's like. Some of these guys? They have wives who love to party. They get drunk and do drugs and ask these recovering addicts why they're not fun anymore."

"Jesus. That's horrible." Jude and I were still in the early stages of navigating his recovery. But I knew I was a thousand times more supportive than what he'd just described.

"It is horrible. But you need to trust me if I say I can go somewhere or do something. And with you for company, there aren't many places I can't go." He gave me a quick smile. "You're not much of a drinker, and the Shipleys don't really go out to get wasted. So the fact that I'll be standing in a place where they sell a lot of alcohol isn't really a big deal for me. It's all about the company I keep. Not the venue."

"Okay. But Griff said you never went to the Goat with them last summer."

"Ah. I was just getting my legs under me. I'm good. I promise."

"Just love you," I said, touching his arm. "I never want you to be uncomfortable."

"Everybody is sometimes uncomfortable," he said, accelerating onto the highway entrance ramp. "It's what you do about it that defines you."

He was right, of course. So I relaxed, sitting back in my seat and stealing occasional glances at his handsome profile all the way to the brand new bar.

Jude

Zara's brother Alec was going to do well for himself.

I pulled up in front of a gorgeous old brick building with wooden shutters. THE GIN MILL was lit up in neon over the entrance.

Inside were many, many bodies in a groovy space. There was good lighting and the dark orange hue of bricks and old wood. A gleaming copper bar stretched across one end of the room, where several people worked furiously to serve customers.

On the other end were a few booths and a DJ that I doubted would be there every night. But the opening of The Gin Mill was rocking, and people were dancing already.

"Wow," Sophie yelled into my ear.

"Right?"

"I think I see Griff." She pointed.

Joining hands, we wove through the crowd toward the wall. Griff, Audrey, May, Kyle and Zach were clustered together, cocktails in hand.

"Hey!" Griff said, raising his hand for a high-five. "You made it. Kind of crazy here."

"Isn't it?"

"What are you drinking?" Griff asked my girl. "Alec makes

his own tonic water and it is tasty. And he's pouring a Vermont-made gin with honey as its base."

Suddenly I could taste the bitter sweetness of gin and tonic on my tongue. But that didn't mean I had to have one. "Maybe I'll get just a tonic water and lime." Close enough.

"I got it," Sophie said, slipping away from us all and heading toward the bar before I could stop her.

Griff took a sip of his. "This place is going to do well."

"I was just thinking the same thing."

"Alec looks happy." He jutted his chin toward the bar, where Zara's dark-haired brother was working hard to serve drinks.

"I thought you and Zara's brothers weren't close," I said.

Griff leaned in to speak privately. "He likes me more now that I'm not banging his sister."

"Ah," I said, while Zach blushed profusely beside us.

God, I loved these guys. It had taken me a long time to feel part of their circle, but I did now. I wasn't just some guy they'd paid hourly wages to over the summer. Griff and his family were my friends, and I wasn't ever giving them up. Sophie and I went to Thursday Dinner as religiously as we went to Community Dinner on Wednesdays. This summer, on my days off, I planned to help out Griff with the renovation of the little house he shared with Audrey.

By some miracle I'd populated my life with good people. So sign me up for a lifetime of helping them wherever I could.

"What are you dudes gossiping about?" Zara asked, appearing in front of us. "Were you discussing the ridiculous shape of this belly?" She put a hand on what was, indeed, an incredibly large baby bump. It wasn't even a bump. It was a *blimp*.

"How long will it be?" I asked.

"Any minute now! I can only thank her for waiting until the opening. It's been a crazy week." She rubbed her giant belly.

"You did a lot of work on this place?" Griff asked.

"Yeah, I couldn't stand to watch my big brother fuck everything up. He had no idea how to do a liquor inventory. He's a rookie who thinks he knows what he's doing. It's the worst."

"Hey—everybody's a rookie sometimes," Audrey insisted, appearing beside Griff. "I'm, like, a permanent rookie in life. I have empathy for poor Alec."

"But see—you *admit* when you don't know something," Zara argued. "Nobody in my family is *ever* wrong." She rolled her eyes.

Sophie returned a minute later with two glasses, handing me one. "What did you get?" I asked.

"Same as you!" She touched her glass to mine.

"You didn't have to do that." She could have a few drinks if she wanted to.

She stood on her toes and kissed me. "I know. But why not? Gin makes me sleepy."

I kissed her again, putting my free hand to the silky fabric of her dress. How was this my life? I had everything I'd ever wanted right here.

"Break it up you two!" Zara complained. "I want to show you guys the patio, because it's less loud and less crowded. Follow me."

We all trailed after her, and it was totally worth it. The patio stretched the length of the rear of the mill, overlooking the Winooski River. There were strings of lights on the banister and candle sconces on the wall. It was a surprisingly warm April evening for Vermont, and the nighttime air promised that spring was really coming.

"Wow!" May said, and I could hear her because it was quieter out here. "Pretty."

"What a spread!" Audrey crowed. "They could rent this space for private parties."

"Like, *weddings*," Griff's cousin Kyle said. "Maybe if Griff ever gets around to proposing, you guys could have the reception here."

Griff gave his cousin an evil glare. "I'll take it under advisement."

"What?" Kyle said. "Just a suggestion."

"You can't throw a man under the bus like that," May argued. "These things happen on their own time."

Kyle grinned. "Just hangin' it out there. All men are a little squeamish at the mention of weddings. It's a guy thing."

"Nobody's squeamish," Griff argued. "Some people have to do some home renovation before they plan a wedding."

"Is that so? I thought maybe you were chicken."

Audrey rolled her eyes. "You're an ass, Kyle."

"I'm perceptive, that's all."

Sophie tugged my hand, and I followed her to the railing away from the group. "The moon is shining in the river," she said. "Look."

"Beautiful," I said, finding the moon on the surface of the water. But the real beauty was her.

"Is it true?" she asked, pinching me playfully on the ass. "Do men get all clenched up when someone brings up weddings?"

I gave her what I hoped wasn't too awkward of a smile. "I wouldn't say that." My heart began to beat a little wildly in my chest, though. And not because weddings scared me.

Quite the opposite.

She lifted her chin to kiss my jaw. "This is an awfully nice spot in the world. Maybe the nicest spot anywhere. I predict there will be lots of romantic moments happening out here."

"Yeah?" I asked, stealing a kiss. "Should we test that theory out?" My pulse accelerated again, because I was about to do something a little reckless.

"Sure." Her smile was playful. "Kiss me, then."

I pulled her into me, skimming my lips over hers. The last couple of months had been a dream come true. My job was going well and every night I came home to someone I loved. There was nothing like walking into the house we shared to hear her call out, "In here!" from our kitchen. I always kissed her hello, then ran off to take the fastest shower ever so I could go back and help with dinner and hear about her day.

And the nights? Heaven. Holding her in my arms every night was all I ever wanted.

I took a sweet sip of her mouth now, and she gripped my biceps and sighed. It took all my willpower to break the kiss and step back. I jammed my hand into my pocket and closed it around something my father had given me earlier.

That's when I got down on one knee.

My girlfriend tilted her pretty face to the side, as if waiting for the punchline of a joke.

"Sophie, I've waited a long time to be able to ask you this. There were years I didn't think it could ever happen. Will you be my wife?"

Her eyes widened in shock. "Are you teasing me right now?"

"Not at all." I opened the top of the little box my father had given me earlier, revealing my grandmother's antique wedding ring.

She put her hands to her mouth.

"Holy shit!" Griffin crowed. "What the hell is happening here?"

Sophie grabbed me around the neck and pushed her face against my cheek. "Of course I will."

I stood up and lifted her off her feet, while Audrey whooped and May shrieked.

"Holy shit," Griffin said again. ""You're making the rest of the men look like assholes now."

"Oh, shut it," Zara complained. "The word you're looking for is *congratulations*."

Their voices barely registered with me, though. I held my girl tightly and fought off misty eyes and a scratchy throat. "I will do everything in my power to be good for you," I promised.

"I know," she said, kissing my cheek. "We'll help each other."

"You make me feel so lucky," I told her. It was the truest thing I'd ever said.

"We're *both* lucky," she insisted. "Let's plan to stay that way."

"It's a deal."

THE END

Also by Sarina Bowen

COMING SOON
Rookie Move
Hard Hitter

TRUE NORTH
Bittersweet (True North #1)
Steadfast (True North #2)
Keepsake (True North #3)

THE IVY YEARS
The Year We Fell Down #1
The Year We Hid Away #2
Blonde Date #2.5
The Understatement of the Year #3
The Shameless Hour #4
The Fifteenth Minute #5

GRAVITY
Coming In From the Cold #1
Falling From the Sky #2
Shooting for the Stars #3

AND
HIM by Sarina Bowen and Elle Kennedy
US by Sarina Bowen and Elle Kennedy

97494973R00185

Made in the USA
Columbia, SC
11 June 2018